BARRINGTON

BARRINGTON

by
John Rowan Wilson

Doubleday & Company, Inc., Garden City, New York
1971

*All of the characters in this book
are fictitious, and any resemblance
to actual persons, living or dead,
is purely coincidental.*

For Pauline and Campbell

CONTENTS

PART ONE

Laidlaw

I went to Sotheby's the other day. It is not a place I often visit, but on this occasion there were a number of items in which I had a personal interest. "Lots 17–240. Letters and papers of Edward Barrington. Original manuscripts. Collection of books. African sculpture and ritual masks. By order of the Barrington Trust." It might have added that the Trust itself had been up for auction and found no bidders. The lease had run out not only on its handsome building in Portland Place, but on the personal mythology of the man who had created it. Only a few mementoes remained to be disposed of.

One could present it as a nostalgic occasion, and perhaps it was to some of those present. But to me it only put a final period to something which had really ended seven years ago, at the time of Barrington's death. To a man in my profession, the forced disposal of property is too much a matter of routine to be an occasion for sentiment. It is all part of the continuity between one generation and another which it is our job to arrange; a process of tidying-up. That is what lawyers are for.

I went there, not to buy anything, but to assure myself that the ceremony was carried out in as seemly and dignified a manner as Barrington deserved. I would not have liked to see the treasures of his life knocked down casually for a trivial sum before a small and indifferent audience. I need not have worried. Sotheby's have a sense of style. The collection was well displayed and the auctioneer obviously understood the significance of what he was selling. The room was full of people. Barrington had the capacity to draw an audience, even to the end.

Most of those present, I suppose, were dealers. I did not envy them their task. They must have been hard put to it to make an estimate of the value of some of the exhibits, since their worth was essentially dependent on what one thought of Barrington

himself and his possible importance to posterity. It is difficult
enough to assess the significance of a name in the present, without
having to make a guess as to its fate over the next twenty years.
In the event, the bids were rather higher than I had expected,
though inevitably lower than they would have been when Barrington was at the height of his fame. On the whole, it seemed to be
a reasonably successful auction.

I stayed at the back of the room and left before the end.
I was not particularly anxious to speak to any of Barrington's
friends and relatives who were present. I did not know what
they thought of me, but it was at least possible that some of them
might blame me, however unreasonably, for what had happened.
Nor had I anything very much to say to them. The affair was
over, so far as I was concerned. They were no more to me than
names in a report, the characters in a story that had preoccupied
me for six months of my life, but was now closed and filed away.

I glanced round the room. I could see most of them. Crane,
tall and white-haired, occupying as always a place of privilege
at the front of the audience. Mrs. Barrington, still austerely
elegant though nowadays needing a pair of glasses to read her
catalogue. Rosamond, sitting nervously at the end of a row. Even
Werner was there. Was it possible that he had come specially
from New York just for the sale?

Only Laidlaw was absent. I scanned all the rows, but there
was no sign of him—and he was certainly not the kind of man
one would miss. It seemed strange to me that he could have lost
interest so completely. And then, just before I left, I saw a young
man sitting on the end of the last row of seats. He was smartly
but discreetly dressed and he was watching the scene intently,
as if memorizing it. He took no part in the bidding. He looked
like a man who had been sent with instructions to observe and
make a detailed report. I felt an instant certainty as to who he
had been sent by. Right from the beginning, there was always
somebody watching for Laidlaw.

*

I had first met Laidlaw just over a year ago, when he made an
appointment to see me at my office. I had heard of him before
that; most people had. He had recently had a good deal of

coverage in the press as an example of the new kind of businessman who was going to put Britain on the map again after the
doldrums of the years following the war. He was pictured as
a lively, informal, and relatively youthful tycoon, full of ideas
and vitality, with an easy, no-nonsense approach. If there was
such a thing as a swinging, trendy financier, Laidlaw was it.

According to the newspapers he was just over forty years old
and had been born in Northern Rhodesia. His main field of
business activity was in Africa, particularly in the newly independent countries on the eastern side of the continent. It seemed
that he had been particularly successful in taking over some rather
ossified companies of the colonial era, and transforming them
into more flexible entities which could be adapted to a changed
situation. He had a reputation for good labor relations and for
appointing Africans to his staff whenever possible. As a result,
he had formed a relationship with the new African leaders which
was unique in the business world. It had borne fruit in a variety
of ways—concessions, trading agreements, and special arrangements about currency. He was now well known to be a very rich
man.

What was less clear was why he was coming to see me. Men
like Laidlaw are customarily surrounded by batteries of lawyers
to take care of their ordinary daily needs. On any matter of routine
business, it was unlikely that he would feel the need to move
outside his own circle of advisers. I tried to make a guess as
to what his problem might be. Some family feud that he wished
to keep as quiet as possible? A settlement on a discarded mistress?
An action for slander? A divorce?

I rose to meet him as he came in. I had been prepared, as so
often with men in the public eye, to be slightly disappointed on
meeting him in the flesh, but, physically at least, he was impressive. He was tall and fair-haired, with a pleasant if rather
pugnacious face, and he looked younger than his years. As I
assessed him I could see him weighing me up at the same time,
trying to form some impression as to whether I knew my job
and was likely to justify the recommendation which had brought
him to me.

He came to business quickly. "Mr. Perrin," he said, "I'd like to have your advice on a delicate and confidential matter." He paused. "I'm thinking of setting up a Foundation."

I inclined my head with appropriate reverence. It is always a solemn moment when a businessman first announces that he is about to give birth to a Foundation. I had been present on these occasions before and I knew only too well the mixed emotions which animate the central figure in such a momentous event. Underneath the peculiar radiance and self-satisfaction conferred by the pregnancy itself, there are a multitude of unspoken anxieties. What are the dangers involved, the risks of abortion or, even worse, of creating some embarrassing monster which may escape from parental control? It is a situation which calls not only for expert advice but also for reassurance, and a touch of the bedside manner. The patient should be encouraged to talk. This, in my experience, they are usually only too ready to do.

Laidlaw was no exception. He started by giving me a fairly lengthy description of his firm's activities in Africa. It was mainly mining, I gathered. But when I referred to it as such, he looked wounded. "That's a very narrow way of looking at it," he said, "we think of our task as something more than just buying and selling or digging ore out of the ground. We feel we have an important part to play in the progress and the development of the emerging nations."

He paused as if waiting for a reaction. I gave him an encouraging smile.

"That is our genuine belief," he said earnestly, as if defying me to contradict him. "We in the company know it, and our investors know it. The constant problem is to convince the Africans themselves that everything we are doing there is in their interests. Many of them are suspicious of white men. They soon get the idea that if we are making money we are taking it from them."

"It's a common misconception," I said.

"It's to try to counter this, that we're setting up the Foundation. Our plan is to set aside a large sum of money each year to be used entirely on philanthropic work in Africa. It will be a unique service to the area and it's intended to demonstrate our involvement on every kind of level—not only commercial but social, medical, and cultural. You see what I mean?"

"Yes indeed." It seemed quite straightforward. Thus far, Laidlaw was acting in a fairly standard way for the prospective parent of a Foundation. A certain amount of genuine idealism, with a dash of calculation and an undercurrent of tax avoidance. I felt I could confidently predict the future course of our interview. I waited for him to give me a lecture on all the good he intended to do, and then we could get down to discussing loan stock and debentures. Instead of which, he surprised me. Without any warning of the change of subject, he asked, "Tell me, what's your view about Edward Barrington?"

It was not an easy question to answer. It was rather like being asked to state an opinion about Gandhi, or Churchill, or Jack Kennedy. There are certain individuals in our society who have been so immersed in the whirlpool of public discussion that it becomes difficult to know where the facts about them have been merged into mythology. In a curious way, one has the sensation of knowing these people better than one's intimate friends, and yet at the same time less well than the most casual acquaintance. Not only Barrington's work, but also considerable information about his private life, were public property. Several books and innumerable newspaper and magazine articles had been written about him. He had also written, with impressive style and fluency, about himself. The spectacular sacrifice of his life and career and the tragic details of his death had already taken on the dimensions of a twentieth-century folk tale. He was, by any standards, a phenomenon. How far the phenomenon was genuine, and how far it was a creation of public relations, was something beyond my personal knowledge.

I explained this to Laidlaw. He frowned at my last remark. "I've always been brought up to understand that Barrington was a great man. I mean, this hospital he ran at—what do you call it?"

"Kalundani."

"Yes, that's right. Well, people used to go from all over the world to see it. Almost like a pilgrimage. In fact, I've intended to go there myself but things kept coming up and then—well, it was too late. The Trust seems respectable enough. I spoke to the president, Lord Crane—you know him?"

"Slightly."

Crane was, as a matter of fact, a client of ours. I hadn't

realized that he was the president of the Barrington Trust, but when I heard it I was not surprised. Crane was a great man for being president of things. Also, something stirred in my memory, some connection between him and Barrington, but I could not for the moment pin it down.

"Well, I must say I was very impressed by him. Not only a brilliant man and a distinguished scientist, I'm told, but business-like into the bargain. I told him what I had in mind. The way I looked at it was this. We were setting up this fund, we had this money we wanted to do some good with, but it wasn't our business to know the best way to spend it. We'd have to set up a special organization and still we'd probably make mistakes. Now, as you know, the Barrington Trust has been in existence for about fifteen years. It operated during Barrington's lifetime and since his death it's contributed to all kinds of valuable work in Africa, in memory of him. In fact, it's doing just the kind of thing we want to do. But, of course, all these charitable outfits have difficulties nowadays. It's a tough business collecting money. There are a lot of agencies competing for what's going and the smaller ones tend to go to the wall. We would be in a position to guarantee a solid income to any group we went in with. My idea was that we should set up a joint organization with the Barrington people. We could call it the Laidlaw-Barrington Fund. Something like that. You see the idea?"

I saw it very well. I began to realize how Laidlaw had managed to come so far so fast. If you set up a Foundation on ordinary lines it takes time for people to get to hear about your benevolence. Years go by while donations are processed and research projects are developed, and it is only gradually that the public at large realizes what wonderful work you are doing. Laidlaw wasn't prepared to wait that long. The association with one of the most famous and revered names in Africa would put him on the map immediately. Respectability, like so much else nowadays, could be made instant.

It was amusing to see the way his mind worked. Most successful men, in my experience, have achieved their position by the skillful use of one particular technique. They stick to what they know. Laidlaw, as I had learned from study of his commercial growth, had never started any business from scratch. His trick was the takeover. He used the money generated by his own self-confidence to buy up the people whose self-confidence had waned. He was obviously reluctant, perhaps even a little frightened, of striking out into the field of philanthropy on his own.

"What was Crane's reaction?" I asked.

"Oh, very good. You see, they haven't found it easy this last year or two. Frankly, I don't think they've been too enterprising. Crane's got a retired naval man there, a Commander Willis—you know him?"

"No."

"Pretty much of a deadbeat, I'd say. You know how it is in this country. There's an idea that retired officers can turn their hand to anything. Frankly he wouldn't be a lot of use to me, but we could sort that out somehow or other." He spoke with the assurance of a man who had disposed of a lot of dead wood in his time. "The point is that with the backing of my Foundation they'd have a sure financial basis and it would be possible to plan ahead on a much more ambitious level."

"I can see that." It was a perfect situation. The distinguished, creaking, slightly apathetic Board of Governors, the retired officer, the stodgy appeals pulling in less and less money every year. To sell off the goodwill of the Barrington name for an assured income would seem an attractive proposition. As for Laidlaw, it wasn't costing him a thing, really. He'd have the gallant sailor out in a matter of months and one of his bright young men in his place. Before the Board knew it, he'd be controlling the whole works. He would, in effect, have stuck the Barrington name and the Barrington reputation on to his own Foundation, for no expenditure at all.

"And what would you like me to do?" I asked. "Draw up an agreement for you?"

"Not quite that simple, I'm afraid," said Laidlaw. "You see, my idea of going into this thing was founded on a certain view about Barrington. I suppose it goes right back to my mother, who used to say he was the greatest man in Africa since Livingstone. I read all the stuff about him and I believed it. It seemed to me that it would be a great privilege for us to be associated with him. Then somebody in the office showed me this."

He opened his wallet and took out a folded newspaper cutting.

He handed it to me across the desk. It was an article from a
New York paper and it took up practically a full page. It was
headed BARRINGTON—MAN OR MYTH? and was by some-
body called Carlos Markham. I said, "Do you mind if I read it?"

"Go ahead."

He lit a cigarette and stared out of the window while I skimmed
through the article. Carlos Markham, of whom I hadn't previously
heard, was evidently a special correspondent with a rather loose
assignment, at present traveling through the African continent.
In the course of his wanderings he claimed to have unearthed
some remarkable facts about Barrington. According to Markham,
his journey had started out as something in the nature of a
pilgrimage. Like most of the rest of the world, he had thought
of Barrington as a kind of secular saint, a twentieth-century
amalgam of Pasteur, Tolstoy, and Francis of Assisi. But the more
he investigated him, the more he began to be assailed by doubts.
Ultimately his faith capsized under the weight of evidence, to
be succeeded by a sense of outrage. He laid into Barrington with
all the righteous malice of the disenchanted. He ended with a
savage peroration.

"Nobody likes to destroy an image which has acted as an
inspiration to millions of honest and devout people. But it cannot
be right for devotion to be built on a lie. The unhappy truth is that
every aspect of the Barrington myth is, on close examination,
contradicted by the facts of his life. He is known as a man of
great kindness and compassion; yet in his private life he was selfish,
ruthless, and arrogant. He was married twice, in each case unhappily. He drove his first wife to her death and quarreled
irremediably with his second. He has been painted as a model of
probity, yet his career was advanced by dubious financial deals
with reactionary politicians. At one time he was not only bankrupt
but on the verge of being indicted for fraud. The medicine he
practiced in Africa and the whole atmosphere of his settlement
and hospital was paternalistic and old-fashioned. Behind his
vaunted austerity there was a love of power, of good living, and
the admiration of women. Behind his compassion for the Africans
was an attitude of mind closely approaching contempt. Like so
much of the British record in this unhappy continent, the story

of Barrington is the story of ruthless personal advancement mas-
querading as Christian charity."

"Well," said Laidlaw, "what do you think of it?"

"Strong stuff." I glanced down the page again. "Of course, he's
very careful not to mention any living individuals. There's nothing
obviously actionable."

"Hell, I'm not interested in that," he said. "What I want to
know is—how true is it?" He leaned forward. "You've got to
understand my position. I'm thinking of putting up half a million
on the strength of Barrington's reputation. I don't want to buy
myself into a scandal."

I could see his point. A name is like any other commodity—
when a man buys it he wants to know what he is buying. Laidlaw's
own reputation might not be anything special, but it was better
than the one Carlos Markham had given Barrington. On the
other hand, I thought he was perhaps making too much of a
newspaper story.

"This kind of thing happens pretty often," I said. "The bigger
the man's reputation, the greater the temptation for somebody
to debunk it. If Christ were crucified today, there'd be plenty
of psychiatrists ready to say he was just a paranoid schizophrenic."

"I know all that. Just the same, I can't let it go. I've got to get
the story straight before I commit myself." He paused and I
waited. I knew we were getting to the real meat of the situation
at last. "I'll be quite frank with you. I went to Crane and told
him what I've told you. I suggested that I put one of my own
men on to sorting this matter out and asked for his co-operation.
I'm sorry to say he flatly refused. He also said that if I went
ahead without his agreement the deal was off anyway. We very
nearly parted company there and then. But in the end he came
up with a compromise suggestion."

I had the script now. "Me?" I said.

"That's right. He knows you and he trusts you. Evidently
you're a man with a great reputation for discretion. From all
I hear, you'd give us an honest analysis of the position, which
is all I want. The Foundation would pay your fees and all
necessary expenses. Crane would give you access to the files of
the Barrington Trust and any introductions you wanted. I don't
know whether the proposition would interest you?"

"Well," I said, "it's a little outside our usual line of practice . . ."

One grows conservative as a lawyer. It is very easy to become trapped inside the tedium of the job. I found in myself a reflex action that prompted me to refuse, to stay in my office with my files and books. Here in Lincoln's Inn I was safe, I was detached, I was always at an advantage. Who could tell what awkward situations, what personal confrontations and embarrassments I might encounter if I put my nose outside my shell? On the other hand, most legal work is very dull, and the most lucrative aspects of practice are the dullest of all. I felt that I had done more than my share of this recently—no doubt my junior partner was impatient to get his teeth into some of the trust work and conveyancing. As I thought it over, I knew that I would almost certainly agree.

Nevertheless, long-established habit prevented me from committing myself immediately. "Perhaps," I said, "it would be a good idea for me to have a preliminary chat with Lord Crane."

2

A few days later I telephoned Crane. He greeted me cordially and sounded pleased that I was considering acceptance of Laidlaw's offer. He suggested that I should come round to the offices of the Trust one morning the following week. Commander Willis would show me round and describe the work they were doing. He himself would come in later and take me out to lunch.

The offices were in a large terrace house in Portland Place. There was an imposing portico, with BARRINGTON TRUST in discreet letters just above the doorbell. A commissionaire who looked as if he might easily have been in the Navy with Commander Willis let me in. The entrance hall was large and bare, with a tiled floor. It was dominated by a huge photograph of Barrington, full length and considerably larger than life. He was walking along a footpath in a driving, purposeful way. His face

was leathery in texture; his fine eyes were surrounded by tiny
wrinkles and overhung by bushy white eyebrows. His hair, worn
rather long, curled up under the rim of a battered sunhat. He
was wearing a kind of Russian peasant's smock over crumpled
drill trousers and he carried a heavy knotted walking stick in
his right hand. His left hand was partially concealed by his sleeve,
but what one could see of it was twisted and deformed. It was an
injury of which he had always refused to speak. The popular
story was that he had been savaged by a lion while treating the
victim of a hunting accident.

I had seen the photograph before, but never in such magni-
fication. At this size, and in this place, there was something
almost overpowering about it. It was as if Barrington were still
alive, daring me to take any view of him but the one he wished
to impose. I turned away. I was not prepared to be ravished
quite so early as this.

Willis lived in an office at the back of the building on the
second floor. He was a square, short man with a pink face and
wispy hair. He wore a double-breasted suit of old-fashioned cut,
in the kind of thick, durable worsted which isn't used much
nowadays. His collar was stiff and snowy white, his tie black,
the expression on his face serious and intent. On the bookcase
behind him was another photograph of Barrington, of a rather
less dramatic nature, showing him talking jovially to a group of
small black children. There was an inscription on it, *to my
good friend and faithful ally, Dick Willis. Edward Barrington.*
The handwriting was curiously sprawling, almost childish.

I glanced at the books in the shelves. I suppose men who
read do this automatically, as a way of gauging the tastes and
attitudes of new acquaintances. The top shelf was taken up with
copies of Barrington's own books and the various publications of
the Trust. Below this I was just able to discern some more personal
literature—*The Imitation of Christ,* a biography of Billy Graham,
Honest to God, and a paperback of *H.M.S. Ulysses.*

Willis rose from his desk and shook me firmly by the hand.
"I'm very glad to welcome you, Mr. Perrin," he said, so earnestly
that I assumed he probably wasn't. Perhaps, as a religious man,
he thought he ought to be glad to see me. "I told Lord Crane
from the beginning that we ought to consult our legal advisers

about that American article." He had a copy of it on the desk. He picked it up as if it were contaminated with typhoid fever. "A filthy, disgusting thing." The edges of his mouth quivered with emotion. "I knew him, Mr. Perrin. I know what sort of man he was. This is a wicked libel."

I nodded sympathetically. "Unfortunately most of the people concerned are dead. Apart from Mrs. Barrington. She might have a case."

"Somebody told me that she was thinking of taking action. It implies in one part that—" He hesitated, then said primly— "that they might have lived together before they were married."

"You think she'll go through with it?"

"I couldn't tell you. Personally I shouldn't welcome being dragged through the courts on such a matter, but—" He made a gesture that seemed to imply that he wouldn't put anything past the second Mrs. Barrington. Then he sighed heavily. "You see, the fact is, Mr. Perrin, that in later life Barrington had to contend with a number of—unfortunate influences. He became famous and people flocked round him. Often these were people who were a little unstable or who had personal problems of their own that they thought he could solve. It wasn't that he was taken in by them exactly. He saw through them but he was too kind to send them away. He felt they needed him, just as the Africans needed him, but in a different way." He brooded for a moment. It was obviously a very sore point. "But when a man becomes a world figure in the way he was, his life, in a sense, becomes public property. It's easy for his actions to become misunderstood. I tried to explain this but I couldn't get through to him. He was a curiously simple man in some ways, Mr. Perrin. Perhaps that was part of his greatness."

He went on to tell me about the beauty and dedication of Barrington's character in a way which reminded me of some of the Trust's promotional literature. Perhaps Willis wrote it himself. After a while he looked at his watch and realized he was running late. "I'd better take you over to the Institute now. There isn't a great deal to see but you'll want to be able to find your way around. I'd like to say that anything we have in the way of information is entirely at your disposal. Our files are open to you and our librarian has instructions to help you in every way she can." He gave me a frosty little smile. "We have nothing to hide."

There was indeed nothing much to see in the building, but it was surprisingly large for its purpose. There was an office section at the back where the appeals and the distribution of money were handled, a very large and very empty conference room, another handsome room for social functions, and the library, which was completely deserted apart from a lonely looking female librarian. Willis was a great man for visual aids. One wall of the library was covered with a map of Africa with pegs on it to mark areas where the Trust was supporting research. He explained this to me in considerable detail. He was obviously extremely proud of it.

After we had left the library he said, "Well, that's it. As you see, it's not very pretentious, but it fulfills its function."

Personally I had thought it was rather pretentious, considering what Laidlaw had told me about the financial condition of the Trust. It certainly represented a considerable capital investment. But this part of London was a leasehold area. I asked, "How long has the lease to run?"

"Five years." A harassed expression appeared on his face. "Goodness knows where we shall ever find the money to renew it. Still"—he cheered up a little—"Barrington was in much worse difficulty than this, many a time. He didn't despair, and we mustn't. No doubt God will provide, somehow or other."

Or Laidlaw, I thought. It was an unconventional shape for Divine intervention to take, but then God was well known to work in mysterious ways. I wondered if Willis would have been quite so complacent if he had realized that he himself was cast in the role of sacrificial lamb, to appease Laidlaw's thirst for dynamism and efficiency. I began to feel sorry for the little man. He was probably completely useless but he was a true believer— Barrington really meant something to him. There was no golden handshake in existence that could compensate him for the loss of what he had here.

When the tour was over he took me along to see Crane. Crane looked what he was—a distinguished, intelligent, and aristocratic Englishman, handsome and well preserved at the age of seventy. He was also a living answer to the traditional criticism that great scientists tend to be lacking in breadth of vision. Ever since I could remember he had been deeply involved in all kinds of humane and forward-looking activity. There was hardly a liberal cause that he had not espoused at one time or another. He was a vocal opponent of book and stage censorship and of capital punishment. He was prominent in the United Nations Association and the Anti-Apartheid League. He wrote letters to *The Times* calling attention to the sufferings of political prisoners.

Of recent years I had noticed that his activities had become a little muted. Perhaps age was taking its toll. Perhaps disillusion had crept in. So many of the things he had fought for had come to pass—socialism, colonial independence, mass education, economic planning, the conquest of poverty—yet the world was still in a sorry mess, when you came down to it. It was enough to take the heart out of anybody. Whatever the reason, Crane had become gradually transformed from a tempestuous intellectual radical into an elder statesman. He had accepted a life peerage from the Labour Government, but nowadays he took part only rarely in political controversy. On the other hand, he spoke a good deal on science, particularly its wider aspects. He had delivered a notable series of Reith lectures on the philosophy of research. He sat on numerous Royal Commissions.

He dismissed Willis and took me downstairs, where his chauffeur was waiting. "I thought we'd go to Bennett's," said Crane. He added, rather unnecessarily, "If that's agreeable to you." I imagine he would have been taken aback if I had said it wasn't. Bennett's is an elegant club. Its atmosphere is one of stylish Whiggism, of earnest progressivism tempered by respect for the values of the past. The building is a splendid example of Georgian town architecture, and the furnishings and original decorations have been lovingly preserved. The food is good and the service attentive. In Bennett's it has been found possible to preserve the illusion that high thinking need not necessarily mean low living and that a belief in the Welfare State can be satisfactorily combined with a taste for château-bottled claret.

Crane was, one might say, the archetypal Bennett's man. Never, surely, had there been a more aristocratic radical, a more fastidious supporter of proletarian advancement. He nodded gravely to a couple of Cabinet Ministers as we made our way across the dining room and exchanged a quick word of greeting with a bishop. When we had settled down at a table and ordered our lunch, he said, "I hope Willis told you all you wanted to know."

"Yes. He was most helpful."

"He's a good fellow. Tremendously loyal. Perhaps a little bit old-fashioned in some ways." He paused momentarily. "The trouble is, everything changes so fast nowadays. You see, when your main concern is raising money, you have to take into account the kind of people who've got it. At one time it was the middle classes, but that's not so any longer. Now it's the business people and the teenagers. Some of these relatively new charities like Oxfam have done very well by appealing to the young. A sort of contemporary image, you know. Students going around with guitars and so on. But that's hardly Willis's style."

Nor his, really, I could tell. Crane gave the impression that while in principle he was prepared to endorse the changing society, he would have been better pleased if the process had moved a little more slowly. And unlike most aging men, he couldn't even relieve his feelings by huffing and puffing about it. I said, "I gather there's some difficulty about the leasehold."

"Yes." It was plainly a sore point. "Frankly, that was a bad mistake of Barrington's. He was determined to have a big impressive place. It was quite unnecessary, as I told him at the time. Somewhere much smaller would have done. We could have bought a freehold or a long lease with the same money and we would never have had all this trouble."

"You weren't able to influence him?"

Crane said, "You'll find out, as you go into this question, what sort of a man he was. If he set his mind on something, it was impossible to do anything with him. The smallest issue was treated as a vote of confidence. If you wouldn't fall in with what he wanted, he was prepared to pull everything down round your head rather than give in. The result was, he tended to get his way. And now, of course, here we are. We're stuck with it." He sounded irritated that Barrington had tricked him by dying before the lease expired. "Let's face it—that's one of the reasons why we need Laidlaw. If he came in with us—"

I could see he had a picture of all his problems being resolved by a miraculous transfusion of money and commercial expertise.

But I had a suspicion that he would find Laidlaw brought in other problems of his own. "What about Willis?" I asked. "Would he have to go?"

"Oh, I don't think so," said Crane. "Why should he?"

"Laidlaw seemed to imply—"

"He would find he wouldn't get all his own way," said Crane.

I wondered how confident he really was. "Is this the kind of arrangement you would have chosen if the money position had been different?" I asked.

"Perhaps not. One would always prefer not to be dependent on people. But there it is. A scientist has to be a beggar nowadays, you know. There's no alternative."

He smiled in a melancholy, self-deprecating way. Actually, as I knew, Crane himself was a wealthy man. Our previous dealings had been concerned with the disposal of £150,000 in a complicated system of discretionary trusts, designed to frustrate the Commissioners of Inland Revenue. But in the law one grows used to these contradictions. I smiled back, accepting the fiction.

"You see," Crane went on, "there are a number of factors to consider. I'm not getting any younger and I shan't really be able to carry the responsibility of the Foundation much longer. There's a lot to be said for a younger man, with some reliable financial backing. Old fuddy-duddies like me are all very well, you know. But one has to move with the times."

In other words, he was looking forward to backing out. He had had enough. Ever since I had entered the offices of the Trust that morning, I had caught the authentic flavor of a dying organism. It was there in the grandiose, echoing building, the dusty offices working at half pressure, in Willis with his Bible-slapping imperialism and his antiquated loyalties. And here it was in Crane too. The fact was that he was bored. The Trust no longer held relevance or reality for him. Perhaps, for all his criticism of Barrington's personality and behavior, it was his vitality that had been necessary to keep it alive. Now that he was dead it had become a mausoleum, a shrine at which fewer and fewer people worshiped every year.

Crane said, "I'm very glad that you're considering taking on this commission. For some time I have been thinking we ought

to be collecting more information about Barrington. He was a
very unusual man, you know."

"So I imagine."

"He had his faults, of course. It would be absurd to pretend
otherwise. He was no plaster saint. But he had something—a
quality quite different from anyone else I ever met. In part, it
was a quality of total concentration on what he wanted or felt
should be done at any particular time. You felt he was in the
grip of a compulsion. He believed absolutely in what he was
doing. In defining his ends he really took no account of anyone
else at all. Yet combined with that was a curious element of
calculation in the means he used. The combination of the two
was at times very disconcerting."

"Was he aware of the calculations or were they unconscious?"

"Very hard to know. You've read his books?"

"Yes."

"What do you think of them?"

I thought for a moment. It was not easy to answer. It is very
difficult for a man to avoid revealing his personality in a book,
yet there was an elusive quality about the work which had made
Barrington so famous. *Sunrise at Kalundani* had appeared in the
early 1930s. It was the kind of odd, unusual book that publishers
are wary of. It fitted into no category. It was a collection of pen
portraits, sketches and poems, all centered in some way round his
experiences at the Kalundani Medical Center. There were descriptions of the people, of the animals and the austere African
scenery, the dramatic dusks and dawns, rains and droughts of a
remote bush station. It was unashamedly romantic. It was in fact
the account of a love affair between Barrington and the life he
had chosen to lead. It was powerful and evocative. The poem about
his wife's death was particularly moving and was commented on
by most of the reviewers.

The book was rapturously received. It was praised, not only
by the critics, but even by other poets. As for the general public,
in both England and America, they found it almost too good to
be true. This was not only authentic art, vouched for by acknowl-
edged masters, but it was actually pleasurable to read as well.
It was comprehensible, touching, and in places even amusing.

There was an added attraction in Barrington's own life. It

is always a help for a poet to be a romantic figure, even if this only involves quarreling with his mistresses or getting drunk on public occasions. Barrington was presented by his publishers as a remote, brooding, austere recluse, so isolated in his remote corner of Africa that he was hardly aware of the fuss being made about him. What began as a best-seller became extended into a cult.

Perhaps the cult began to put the critics off a bit. The more generally popular Barrington became, the more they began to express reservations. His second book, *The Flowering Desert,* had a cooler reception. The lyricism was condemned as facile sentimentality and it was pointed out that there was a regrettable lack of political consciousness. By this time, however, public interest in Barrington had rendered him more or less independent of critical support. The cult had taken over.

It is now generally accepted that Barrington was overpraised as purely literary talent. Yet if the literary gift lies in the capacity to transmit emotion, he had succeeded, at least as far as I was concerned. He brought to me, in my sedate office in Lincoln's Inn, a feeling of the vast emptiness of the African bush, the smell of woodsmoke hanging in the still heavy air, the hum of insects and the river flowing endlessly through the parched ocher-colored earth. I could feel the boredom of his isolated life, the blackness of the night, and the incessant temptation to despair.

Yet somehow, after reading the books, one was still left with a mystery about Barrington himself. Somewhere, between the intensity of the emotion and the conscious artistry of the form, the man escaped. One felt at times that Barrington was deliberately withholding some aspect of himself from the reader. I asked Crane if he agreed.

"Possibly," he said. "But it's equally likely that he just wasn't aware of any contradictions. He wasn't very analytical about himself, you know. And he didn't talk about his writing much. He wasn't an artist, in the true sense of the word—what he wrote was always subsidiary to his own life. He valued it chiefly because it brought him out of obscurity. It gave him the chance to do what he wanted to do. Before that he was just one of a thousand people doing similar work in Africa. Afterward you'd have thought, to talk to people over here, that he was the only doctor in the entire continent."

As before, I detected a slightly waspish note in Crane's remarks. One had the feeling that he was trying hard to be fair to Barrington but had never really liked him. I tried to draw him out further, but he became evasive, as if he felt he had already said too much. Eventually he said, "Have you decided definitely whether you'll be prepared to do this?"

"Yes. Of course, I can't tell you how long it will take—"

"That isn't important. The main thing is that you get all the facts. I'll help you in any way I can. We have a lot of letters in the library you may find useful. And there are a few people you really ought to see. There's Barrington's daughter by his first wife. Then Brian Adams, who worked with him at Kalundani. Horace Werner of the Mallory Foundation had a lot to do with keeping him afloat when Kalundani ran into difficulties. And then, of course"—he spoke with slight distaste—"there's the second Mrs. Barrington. I suppose you ought to talk to her."

"Are they all in this country?"

"No. Werner's in New York, of course, and Adams is still out in Africa. I'm not sure about Mrs. Barrington. I'll find out for you. I think I should start with the daughter. She lives in Dulwich. She's my goddaughter, by the way, I don't know whether you knew that." I shook my head. "Yes. She lived with us for some years after her mother died." He paused. "The first Mrs. Barrington was my wife's cousin."

This surprised me. I had somehow thought of Crane as somebody who had been brought into Barrington's affairs in later years. "So you knew them both right from the beginning?"

"Oh yes. Yes. Very well indeed."

He answered my unspoken question. "But I think it's best that you speak to the others first. You'll find out why as you go along."

3

Rosamond Nicol lived in a large rambling house in East Dulwich. It was ugly in an assertive, grandiose fashion, like the Victorian spinsters who had no doubt once inhabited it. The garden had now gone to seed and the gates of the drive had long since disappeared. There was an empty wooden garage by the side of the house that looked as if it had been bought in sections through a mail order advertisement in the back of the *Radio Times*.

It was the kind of house, once thought to be completely impractical and fitted only for demolition, which had become increasingly fashionable over recent years among academic intellectuals with large families. A sacrifice of external tidiness was made voluntarily and indeed ostentatiously, in favor of interior space and some degree of style. It was the expression of a revolt against neatness, convenience, and uniformity in suburban living.

It said something about the Nicols which fitted into the brief picture Crane had outlined for me at the end of our luncheon. Nicol was a Senior Lecturer in Biochemistry in the University of London. He was able, and had done some useful research on steroid hormones, but somehow he had never been lucky. His experimental work had turned out, through no fault of his own, to be a blind alley. He was a good teacher and a competent administrator, but he was outspoken and had made powerful enemies. He had been in line for a chair but had been passed over. Largely, I gathered, on representation from Crane, he had been offered a professorship at a provincial university but had refused. He was now almost forty and was in danger of becoming one of those people, common enough in academic departments, who are growing too senior for the jobs they hold and yet are impossible to promote.

Rosamond Barrington had married him when they were both students at Cambridge. She was, according to Crane, a quiet,

serious girl. She was very shy and rather secretive. In the years
she had lived with them, neither Crane nor his wife had ever
felt they understood her and were at the end unsure whether
she even liked them very much. After marrying Nicol she had
seemed happy to let go her connections with them. Nowadays
they were on friendly terms but hardly ever saw her.

I parked my car in the drive and rang the doorbell. Rosamond
herself let me in. It occurred to me as I looked at her that this
was my first confrontation, however indirect, with Barrington
himself. But I could see little physical resemblance. She was pale
and fair and almost good looking. But somehow not quite. Her
features were small and her expression lacked animation. Her
hair was cut short, following a contemporary fashion, and she
wore a dress made of striking material but of somewhat amateurish
cut, as if she had run it up herself on a sewing machine. She
wore no stockings and a pair of sandals on her feet which flapped
a little as she moved across the bare tiled floor of the hall.

She greeted me without smiling and led me into the main
living room. It was a very large, lofty double room with folding
doors separating the two halves. It was plainly a room in which
everything occurred. The walls were lined with bookshelves. In
one corner was a deal table, obviously homemade, loaded with
papers, books, a dictating machine, and a portable typewriter.
There was an aged upright piano and shelves stacked with music.
The mantelpiece was covered with photographs of children.

Altogether it was a delightful room in a pleasantly improvised
way. When I told Rosamond so, she smiled for the first time,
rather thinly. "It needs a lot doing to it," she said. "Now that
the children are away I'm hoping to make a new set of curtains.
One really can't afford to buy them nowadays." She motioned
me toward the sofa. We sat down awkwardly, looking at each
other. She was not going to be an easy conversationalist. "I'm
sorry Bernard isn't here," she said. "He has a string quartet on
Thursdays. They're just amateurs, of course, but he couldn't let
the others down."

I was pleased on the whole. It would give me a chance to
talk to her alone. "It was very kind of you to invite me," I said.
She did not reply, but looked at me as if waiting for me to take

the initiative. "I suppose Lord Crane explained what I'm hoping
to do?"

"Oh yes. Uncle Alan said—" She stopped. "Of course, he's
not really my uncle, you know. I just call him that because he
brought me up. He said you want to know something about
my father."

"Yes."

"I did tell him—" She was obviously defensive. "I said I wasn't
really sure I could be of very much use to you. You see, I didn't
see much of them. My mother died when I was very young
and my father wasn't able to look after me. I was brought
up in England. I only went back to Kalundani on two or three
occasions."

"You saw your father when he came to England?"

"Oh yes. But not for very long. He was always busy. There
was a lot for him to do. Money to raise, committees, lectures,
personal appearances—that kind of thing. It was all pretty remote as far as I was concerned."

She talked about him completely without animation, as if he
were some distant relative she had encountered only occasionally.
"You were fond of your father?" I asked.

"Naturally." There was a note of resentment in her voice.
Perhaps she regarded the question as impertinent. "But you know
how it is when you're young. You care most about the people
who are around you at the time. I really looked on the Cranes
as my parents."

I had the feeling that she was deliberately drawing away from
even thinking about her father. I asked, "Have you read this
recent article about him?"

"Yes." She frowned. "I really don't understand it all. This
thing about my father has always bothered me. Everything about
him seems to be so absurdly exaggerated. I suppose some people
might enjoy the attention it brings but I honestly don't. I find
it tiresome and embarrassing." It seemed to occur to her that
she was being less than fully co-operative. "I'm sorry if I don't
sound too forthcoming, but you've no idea what it's like to have
people coming up to you all the time and saying in an awestruck
voice, 'Tell me—what was he *really* like?' Especially when I can't

give them much of an answer, when you come down to it. So I try to keep the relationship as quiet as possible."

She spoke in a plaintive, slightly aggrieved voice, and her glum egoism was unattractive. Yet I could sympathize with her to some extent. I had known the same kind of withdrawal in children of theatrical parents, as if they were making a desperate attempt to hang on to some kind of identity of their own. But it was obviously not going to make things any easier for me. I moved the conversation temporarily away from Barrington and began to ask her questions about her own life.

At last she began to talk to me easily and with something approaching animation. She was plainly wrapped up in her husband and children. She spoke expertly of O levels and A levels, of scholarships and the politics of academic preferment. She was also well informed on the latest artistic and literary fashions. She believed that a woman with a family shouldn't allow herself to vegetate. She worked for charity and went to evening classes in arts and crafts. Every year they went abroad for a holiday. When the children were young they had taken a Land-Rover and a tent, but now that the family was growing up they hoped to go on their own and stay at a small pension kept by some friends of theirs in the Dordogne . . .

I asked, had she never wanted to go back to Africa?

"No." She spoke with a touch of defiance. "I've made my life here. Kalundani was my father's place, not mine. I didn't have any real feeling for it." She paused and added, "But I don't want you to get the idea that I'm irresponsible about African problems. I do half a day a week for Oxfam."

*

Nicol came home soon after that. He was a tall, lanky man in his late thirties, with longish hair and a slightly exaggerated, histrionic manner. He apologized for being late. As it happened, he would have been better off staying at home. The quartet had been a disaster—the new cellist couldn't play a note. Personally he needed a drink.

He went into the kitchen and came back with three glasses and a large carafe of vin rosé. He told me with some pride that he bought it in bulk from a firm in the city and that it worked

out at no more than eight shillings a bottle. He thought there
was a lot of pretentious nonsense talked about wine. Didn't I
agree?

He was obviously not planning to offer an alternative. I sipped
at it warily. Nicol said, "I gather you're collecting information
about Barrington." I nodded. He stretched his legs and took a
long draft of wine. "He's not the sort of chap I go for myself,
but there's no doubt that he was an enormously symbolic figure."

"Symbolic of what?"

"Of his time. The nineteen-thirties. Dying imperialism. It was
a time when white self-confidence was just beginning to crack.
There was an uneasy feeling around that perhaps this white-man's-
burden stuff might after all be just a cover up for exploitation.
And then Barrington came along. He represented the European
conscience: he was there to expiate the collective guilt of his class.
While he was out there in the bush, sweating and suffering and
writing his head off about it, they felt better. They could fool
themselves that perhaps the Empire was a piece of sweet benev-
olent paternalism after all."

"Kalundani wasn't in the Empire," I protested.

He was not put off. "Not officially, perhaps. But there was
British influence there. Anyway," he went on cheerfully, pouring
himself a second glass of wine, "what I'm talking about isn't
geography, it's an attitude of mind. Barrington wasn't just a
man. He was a sacrificial figure to exorcise a sense of collective
guilt. Naturally, of course, this wasn't apparent to them at the
time. But we can see now—"

He carried on in this vein. It was plain that Nicol was a
member of that happy breed of men who are convinced that all
wisdom and virtue lies in the present and that, with the exception of the poor and downtrodden, all previous generations were
composed of rapacious and hypocritical scoundrels. It had been
left to Nicol and his friends, fortified by the latest fashion in
contemporary thought, to clear up the mess of centuries and introduce a fresh breeze of altruism into the world. His complacency
was a little irritating but I couldn't help envying his assurance.
If one was going to have a delusion, it was a comforting one to
have.

"The ironical thing is," he said, "that in spite of everything

Barrington did for the Africans, he was still, by modern standards, a racialist."

Even after reading Mr. Markham, I found this a little startling.
"You really think so?"

"Of course. You've read those books of his?" I said I had.
"They're full of implicit racialism. He writes about the Africans
quite differently from the way he writes about Europeans."

"Hard to avoid, surely. After all, they *were* quite different."

"Read them again," said Nicol confidently. "You'll see exactly
what I mean. There's a patronizing tone, like a man writing
about children. That fellow he wrote the famous poem about.
What was his name?"

"You mean Toffee?"

"That's right." He spoke as if he had already proved something. "Hell, it's there even in the name, isn't it?"

At this point Rosamond broke in. I had almost forgotten she
was there. "It was just short for Christopher," she said. "Africans
tend to put ee on the end of things. It's the way they talk."

"Look, I don't care how it arose. You wouldn't call an Englishman that, would you? I mean, it's the sort of name you'd give
to a dog or something. And the poem itself—real Uncle Tom
stuff." He grinned sardonically. " 'Some of my best friends are
natives.' "

I had the impression that she didn't often stand up to him
and didn't feel any special loyalty to Barrington. She just objected
to what she regarded as a perversion of her own experience. "It
wasn't like that," she said. "Father loved him. He really did."

He was patient with her. "Roz, you have to try to see this
from an outside point of view. It's no use being sentimental
about it. One has to start off by accepting the fact that people
like your father are by definition pretty complicated psychologi-
cally. That's what gives them the drive to do extraordinary
things. Under the simple hero-pattern that people like to read
about, there's a person with great internal problems to resolve.
We know now that Joan of Arc wasn't just a simple little peasant
girl who saw visions, and there's more to T. E. Lawrence than
a clean-limbed lad who loved his motor bicycle. If Mr. Perrin's
going to understand your father, he's got to get under the surface
and not be scared of facing anything unpleasant that turns up."

Nicol wasn't like Carlos Markham, who just wanted to pick up material for an article by digging out a little dirt. He believed that the dirt was really the story itself. The springs of action were bound, in the last analysis, to lie in some form of character distortion. I did not know, at this early stage, whether he was right or not. But one thing was certain. If I did not find out that Barrington had been a homosexual or a masochist or a secret drunkard, there would be one person who would think I had scamped my job.

Dinner was served on a pine table in the other half of the big living room. The rosé, I found to my disappointment, was still with us—Nicol produced another decanter from his seemingly inexhaustible supply. The main dish was a casserole from a recipe Rosamond had found in the *Observer* color supplement. It was accompanied by savory rice with pimentos, which had no doubt looked wonderful on the color plate. Afterward there was a Yugoslav cheese which Nicol claimed to be indistinguishable from Reblochon.

At the end of the meal I felt I had made little real progress. Rosamond, who presumably had at least some of the information I had come for, had hardly opened her mouth. Nicol talked almost continuously, but it turned out on tactful questioning that he had only met Barrington briefly on two occasions and had very little to say about them—like many talkative men with ideas, he was evidently unobservant. However, the attention I gave to his theories paid off surprisingly well in the end. When I hinted that to study them further I should need more information, he turned to Rosamond.

"Roz," he said, "you really ought to let him see it."

She frowned. I had the feeling that he was taking up some discussion which had occurred before my arrival. When she did not reply, he went on aggressively. "It's no use keeping it locked up forever. If you won't let him see it, who will you show it to? You can't have it buried under your tombstone."

She seemed to weaken a little. She nibbled her lower lip indecisively. "I don't know. I've always felt—"

"Roz, stop fighting yourself."

She looked at him, then at me, bit her lip again and finally got up from the table and went upstairs. Nicol, for once, remained silent. It was as if he felt that the slightest thing, even something that happened when she wasn't there, would induce her to change her mind. When she returned she was carrying a large buff envelope. She handed it to me. "This is a journal my mother wrote," she said in her abrupt, sulky fashion. "She kept it almost until the day of her death. It was sent to me by an American priest who was with her when she died. She'd said she wanted me to have it. I don't think my father ever saw it."

I took the manuscript out of the envelope. The ink had faded on some of the earlier sheets and the paper had a brittle feel to it. It gave me an extraordinary feeling of excitement. Nicol saw the light in my eyes. "This should be pretty valuable to you," he said.

"It seems like it. Of course, until I've read it—"

"I've read it," he said. "You needn't worry. It's the stuff you want."

I was eager to get home and start reading it, but I had to preserve the social decencies. We talked for a little while and then I got up to go. I thanked them for their help and promised to take good care of the manuscript and return it to them as soon as I had finished with it. Rosamond said good-bye at the door but Nicol said he would show me to my car.

When we got out into the drive he said, "My wife has always been a bit difficult about that manuscript." I didn't say anything. "It's ridiculous to keep it to herself. After all, it's an important document." He paused. "And probably quite valuable, wouldn't you say?"

"Very probably."

"It might even be worth publishing on its own. I've tried to persuade her to take it to a publisher and see what he thinks about its possibilities. Or perhaps she could sell it to the Trust. I don't know. I'm not a businessman."

"Nor am I."

"But you know about these things. You could advise us." He implied that it was a small enough return for being allowed to see the manuscript, as indeed it was. I could see now why he had been so eager to help me. No doubt the unexploited possibilities of the manuscript had been a thorn in his side for years. "Perhaps we could have a talk about it after you've read it."

*

When I reached my home in Chelsea it was almost midnight, but I was too curious about my discovery to leave it until the morning. I made myself a cup of coffee and settled down with the manuscript in my study.

As I began to read, it became apparent that Joan Barrington's journal was not a diary in the conventional form. It consisted of a series of entries of differing length, separated by irregular periods of time. The entries varied from mere catalogues of events to long and intimate outpourings of violent emotion. Sometimes they followed each other at intervals of a few days and at other times there would be a gap of several months. Every now and then she would become discouraged and speak of abandoning the journal altogether. But always she came back to it in the end. The final entry was dated only a few days before her death.

It was the kind of journal that I suppose a lot of young people keep, when they have a desire to write but no real confidence in their own creative ability. It was obviously not written for publication, but more with the object of trying to make some meaningful pattern of all her hopes and fears and doubts about herself. At the beginning my reaction was one of disappointment; the style was elaborate and oversensitive. The earliest section, covering her experiences as an undergraduate, made rather dull reading. But when she met Barrington the journal changed. It became simpler and more urgent. She finally forgot about literature and the narrative came to life.

PART TWO

Joan

I

She first met Barrington at a party given by Crane. She was just down from Cambridge with a First in Modern French Literature and casting around for something to do. Her cousin Olwen, who was married to Crane, had suggested that she might care to come round one Sunday evening and meet some people who might be useful to her.

At the age of thirty-two, Alan Crane was already a famous man within a restricted but highly important circle. His scientific record was spectacular. He had made a significant discovery about the structure of chromosomes while still working for his PhD and had subsequently expanded it in a series of simple but classical experiments. He had been elected to the Royal Society before he was thirty, and had only recently been appointed Director of the Sutherland Laboratory in the University of London. In addition to this, he had made a name for himself as a political and philosophical essayist. He was already a prominent figure in the intellectual wing of the Labour Party.

He had private means and lived in some style in a rambling old Georgian house in Hampstead. Olwen herself was a promising sculptress, and between the two of them they knew almost everyone who counted in the high intellectual circle of their time. They prided themselves on their interest in young people, and had a pleasant custom of keeping open house on Sunday evenings, when their younger friends could come and argue with each other over drinks or coffee. Usually there were at least one or two celebrities present, who would be introduced by Crane to the more favored members of the group.

Olwen dutifully introduced Joan to a Governor of the BBC and the editor of a weekly review. Joan did her best with both of them but she had a feeling, which was common with her, that they would forget about her the moment she turned her back. When the editor moved off to speak to somebody else, Olwen noticed her standing alone. She came across to her and said, "There's someone over there you might find interesting." Joan followed her without any great anticipation. This phrase usually meant that Olwen had some wallflower she felt responsible for; as a member of the inner circle, Joan was expected to help out.

Olwen led her to a young man standing on his own in a corner of the room. He was large and slightly ungainly in appearance, with thick dark hair and a heavy jaw. He was wearing a crumpled gray tweed suit; it looked as if he had put on weight since he had bought it.

"His name's Edward Barrington," said Olwen, as they moved toward him. "They tell me he's had one or two poems published in the *New Statesman.*"

She introduced them and left them immediately. Joan set out to do her duty and put him at ease. This usually presented few problems with the men you met at the Cranes. Most of them were interested in the same kind of thing. The fashionable topics of the moment were Mr. T. S. Eliot's latest book of poetry and the outrageous activities of the newly installed Italian dictator, Benito Mussolini. She tried him on both of these, but without great success. He seemed vague and abstracted. When she asked him about his own writing he was not very much more helpful.

He seemed to realize her bewilderment. "I'm sorry," he said. His voice was deep, with a dry northern intonation. "I'm afraid you must find me a bit of a fraud. I'm not really a writer at all. Those poems were just a bit of fun, really. I was surprised the editor published them."

"Then what do you do?"

"I'm a doctor. I work on Machin's unit at the Metropolitan Hospital."

Machin was a friend of Crane and a colleague of his son on a number of political and scientific committees. As for the Metropolitan, it was still in the early stages of its existence as a postgraduate institution. It had been recently started by a group of doctors who were interested more in research than money and repelled by the commercialism of Harley Street. There was great competition to work there, in spite of the poor financial rewards.

It tended to attract a particular type of dedicated, hard-working, and rather self-satisfied young man.

They began to talk about his work. Now at last he spoke fluently, not simply about medicine but about himself. In background at least, he was a typical Metropolitan man. He had no money or influence. He had come from a northern university with a good degree and an Honors B.Sc. in physiology, together with a letter from his professor of medicine saying that he would be better suited to the laboratory than to clinical practice. It was easy to understand the professor's viewpoint. On the most cursory acquaintance it was clear that he had no bedside manner whatsoever.

He made no pretense of having much general education. "I'm just another dumb doctor, really," he said. "I was always too preoccupied with getting myself out of my provincial rut to learn anything much about art or music or painting. I suppose I'm what is called a late developer."

He smiled at her, and she had the feeling of having at last made some kind of contact. They began to talk more generally and she was interested to find that his narrowness of interest was at least in part a defensive pose; he was a good deal better informed than he pretended. There was also something warm and spontaneous about his manner that she found attractive. She was just beginning to think, rather regretfully, that she ought to move on and talk to someone else, when he said abruptly, "I don't suppose you'd care to come to a concert with me next week, would you?"

She was slightly taken aback. "What concert?"

"Oh, anything you like. There must be something on. I'll get some seats."

She could not help saying, "But I thought you said you didn't care for music?"

"I don't. I just thought it might induce you to come out with me."

He was smiling and she smiled back. It was rather flattering to think that he was prepared to put up with an evening of boredom just to see her again. "All right," she said. "But don't imagine you'll be able to get out of the concert. I shall make you sit through it."

He took her to Bertorelli's for dinner beforehand. Away from Crane's household he was much more at his ease. He was obviously an habitué of that highly individual restaurant. He cracked jokes with the proprietor, threw his coat over the hatstand, and flirted absentmindedly with the black-eyed little waitress who brought the menu. Joan found herself slightly disconcerted by his assurance. She realized that she had visualized herself as doing a favor to this awkward north country lad by agreeing to go out with him, but evidently he did not regard it as a favor at all. He ordered a great mound of spaghetti for them both, and when she played delicately with it he accused her of picking at her food—obviously a serious fault in the circles in which he had been brought up. He also polished off most of the carafe of Orvieto which came with it. "Do you know," he said, "I never tasted wine until I was twenty-three? Where I came from it was always draft bitter or Tizer or something like that. Whisky if I could afford it, which I usually couldn't. Then somebody took me here when I came up for my finals and they gave me a glass of Chianti. I've been trying to make up for lost time ever since."

He would have to be careful, she thought unkindly. He was a big man, over six feet tall, but he had the heavy physique of someone who might easily run to fat. Yet she could not help being impressed by his vitality. It reminded her vaguely of one of D. H. Lawrence's rough Midland heroes, who were all the rage at that time. She had actually met Lawrence at one of Crane's Sunday evenings and had been extremely disappointed in him—she had a memory of a weedy, excitable man with a small pointed beard. Barrington, she felt, was the kind of man Lawrence should have been.

He was egotistical but by no means without humor, and he had an engaging insight into his own deficiencies. One of his more attractive characteristics was his lack of self-doubt. Joan was accustomed to talking with sensitive young men who spent most of their time lamenting the future of society and agonizing about their own efforts to influence it. Barrington seemed to have little contact with these fashionable preoccupations. Even his poetry, which she had taken the trouble to read before meeting him, was some distance off the fashionable track—it was unideological and concerned mainly with exploring the inner recesses of working-

class life in the northeast. Joan suspected that the editors who
published him had read a social criticism into the poems which
did not really exist.

His freedom from the agonized confusion which beset most
of her friends at that time was based on a deep belief in the
value of the work which he was doing. He felt delighted and
privileged to be a doctor and to be accepted at the Metropolitan.
The ordinary small change of bourgeois life, which she took completely for granted, was a source of endless pleasure to him.

At the end of the evening she found that she had enjoyed
herself more than she would have believed possible. When he
asked her to meet him again the following week she agreed
readily. This time he did not offer to take her to a concert. He
had been quite genuine in saying that he had no ear for music.
However it turned out that they had a mutual passion for the
theater. He was the first person she had met who enjoyed Shake-
speare as pure entertainment, without literary associations, as an
Elizabethan might have done. They sat entranced in the upper
circle throughout the season at the Old Vic.

But most of all he loved the music hall. For all the formative
years of his life, it had been the only gaiety, the only magic, that
he knew. It was something outside her experience, and at first
she found it hard to share his enthusiasm. But after a while she
was surprised to find herself seduced by its surging energy and
honest vulgarity. She began to laugh at the jokes and enjoy the
uninhibited response of the audience. It was a delight to her to
watch Barrington throw off the north country constraint of his
manner and bellow out the choruses with the rest.

She waited nervously for him to make love to her. She pictured something crude, rough, and masterful. In the event she
was surprised. He showed no awkwardness or diffidence at all; he
was totally at ease. She was reminded of the kind of athlete who
shambles clumsily up to the pavilion in a shiny ill-fitting suit and
then later emerges with total confidence and grace on the field
or the track. Sex, it was plain, was a field in which Barrington
had an easy natural skill of which he was fully aware and enjoyed
using.

They saw each other a great deal. To Joan, brought up in a
tight, self-sufficient academic world, there was something exotic

about him. Almost everything he did surprised her, and she was fascinated to listen to him talking about his youth. He was the son of a small, not very prosperous butcher in Sunderland who had died when he was sixteen, leaving very little money. His mother had gone to live with her married sister and Edward had worked his way through Manchester University on a series of scholarships. He was egotistical in an overt unself-conscious way that disarmed criticism. He took it for granted that he would have to fend for himself throughout life, as easily and naturally as the people she had been brought up with assumed that there would always be somebody around to help them.

He did not criticize the values and attitudes of her friends and her parents. He simply saw them as totally irrelevant to himself and his own problems. All the members of the Cranes' set were politically involved. They were very concerned about the rise of fascism and the grievances of Germany and looked forward to the imminent disintegration of the capitalist system. They took part in marches and rallies and discussed well into the night the rights and wrongs of making a Popular Front with the Communists. Joan was upset to find that she could not interest Edward in any of these issues. "But you're working class," she protested. "You should be more involved than anyone."

He hated to argue. Dialectics bored him. One of his favorite ways of avoiding discussion was to embark on an anecdote marginally related to what was being said.

"You remind me of a story my father used to tell," he said. "About when he was called up for the Army in the last war. He had a wife and kid, so of course he kept out as long as he could. When they finally got him to the recruiting board he said he was deaf. They were convinced he was having them on but they couldn't prove it, try as they would. Finally the officer gave up. He told him he was graded unfit for service. Then, when my father walked out of the door, the officer yelled after him, 'And close that door behind you!'" Barrington grinned reminiscently. "My father used to say, 'Even if I'd heard him I wouldn't have taken any notice. Let them close their own bloody doors.'"

He saw the puzzled look on her face and explained. "That's the working-class outlook, you see. My father wasn't ashamed of what he did. If they had been smart enough to get him into the Army, he'd have fought and fought well. But he didn't feel any obligation to fight. As he saw it, his first duty wasn't to the State or to a collection of foreigners who were always quarreling with each other for some reason or other. It was to look after his wife and children. When you live the way we did, you don't have anything to spare for big causes." He smiled at her. "That's the difference between your people and mine. You've been educated to feel you have a responsibility to the whole world. We've always had enough to do, taking care of our own."

2

They were married six months later. It was a quiet, registry office wedding, and the few people present were mostly Joan's friends and relatives. They went for a short honeymoon to Brittany and then settled down in a small semidetached house in Ealing.

She didn't much care for Ealing, but it was convenient for the Metropolitan and she was deeply in love. They had very little money. All Edward's savings had gone on a deposit for the house and they had to buy their furniture on installments. The Metropolitan paid very badly, but it never occurred to either of them that he should leave his job to make more money in private practice. It was taken for granted that his reward would come later. His research was going well and Arthur Machin, the head of his department, was known to think very highly of him. He had confided to Crane that Edward Barrington was a certainty for a chair somewhere or other within the next ten years.

Barrington worked very hard. He seemed to have limitless reserves of energy, and when he was interested in a project he would work seven days a week at the hospital, sometimes not getting home until nine or ten o'clock at night. On the other hand, on matters where his interests were not engaged, it was almost impossible to get him to do anything at all. He left the routine decisions of their normal life entirely to Joan. He was generous, and indeed rather careless with money, but parsimonious with his time. He flatly refused to give his mind to the domestic accounts, or to do odd jobs around the house. He wore the same suit every day until she nagged him to change it.

After a few early quarrels, they were happy. She became used to his moods, his egoism and his occasional outbursts of temper. She admired him for his intelligence, and loved him for his warmheartedness and lack of affectation. She was sometimes lonely, and missed her friends in Kensington and Hampstead, but she consoled herself with the thought that her exile would not be for long. Edward's success was so inevitable that they would certainly be moving back to civilization within a few years.

After they had been married for about twelve months, Rosamond was born. Edward was an affectionate but absentminded parent. He seemed to have no idea that the state of fatherhood imposed any special obligations on him. She was prepared to tolerate his detachment up to a point, but the extra work of bringing up a small baby made her weary and irritable. Then, as a final straw, Edward fell into a remote, melancholy mood that she had never experienced before. For two weeks it was as if neither she nor the baby existed for him at all. She felt sure something was troubling him but he evaded all efforts to get him to confide in her. Finally she lost her patience. She attacked him one evening after dinner.

"It's simply not good enough," she said. "You treat this house as a hotel. Sometimes I think I might as well not have a husband, for all the interest you take."

He made the answer she had expected. It was impossible, he said in an aggrieved voice, for him to give his mind to everything at once. He had enough to cope with at the hospital. His work . . .

For once she dared to stand up to him. "I sometimes think you make too much of that," she said.

He frowned at her. "What do you mean?"

"Well, I know it's terribly important to you, but you don't have to absorb yourself in it totally, to the exclusion of all else. It's bad for your health, for one thing. These last few weeks you've been impossible. You're living on your nerves."

"You don't understand," he said impatiently. "You have no idea—"

"It's unnecessary," she said stubbornly. "You don't have to take it so much to heart. Alan's a scientist too. He's one of the best in the country, everyone says. You don't imagine he carries on like this?"

"No," he said. "I don't suppose he does." He paused, as if wondering whether to tell her something, and then decided against it. He stood up, with the air of a man determined to end a conversation, and put his arm gently around her shoulders. "I love you," he said, "and I don't want to argue with you. Let's go to bed."

She let it go at that. She knew it was no use pressing him, and she hoped that what she had said might have taken some effect, even if he was not prepared to accept it at the time. He slept badly that night, and she could feel him tossing and turning in the narrow double bed. At breakfast he was heavy-eyed and uncommunicative. In this mood there was something oppressive about his presence. She was relieved when he finally left for the hospital.

That night he came home earlier than usual. The moment he entered the door it was obvious to her that something appalling had happened. His face was gray and his hands were trembling. When he took off his overcoat he fumbled clumsily with the buttons. As she took the coat from him she smelled the sweat on his body; his shirt clung to him in damp folds. "What is it?" she said. "What's wrong?"

Without answering, he walked into the living room and sat down. He ran his hands through his hair and then looked up at her. The expression on his face was baffling to her—it was agonized and desperate, and yet at the same time there was something triumphant about it. It was the expression of a man who had just taken some catastrophic yet decisive action. He said, "I've finished at the Metropolitan."

There was a perceptible note of relief in his voice, as if he had finally taken a decision that he had been considering for some time. She was maddened by the thought that he might have destroyed their whole future without even discussing it with her beforehand. "What are you talking about? What have you done?"

"I've destroyed some valuable property."

"What kind of property?"

He paused, as if reluctant to embark on the story. Then he shrugged his shoulders, as if deciding that she would have to know some time. "It was a dog."

She looked at him in perplexity. "A dog?"

"Yes. A beagle, actually."

"What on earth—"

He became suddenly irritable. "For God's sake, girl, don't interrupt me. I'm trying to tell you." His irritation subsided and he went on in a normal voice. "Machin sometimes uses beagles for animal experimentation. They're docile and, like all hounds, they're not very bright. They don't eat you out of house and home but they're big enough to be convenient to operate on. They're particularly useful for certain biochemical experiments."

He spoke in a deliberately dispassionate way. It occurred to her that he had never before spoken to her of the animals he used for research; he had mentioned the work often enough, he had described the results and the problems at great and often tedious length, but he had never before spoken of the animals themselves.

Haltingly, and with considerable pauses, he went on with the story. It seemed that Machin was interested in working out the precise mechanism of liver failure. He had done some work on white rats which had turned out to be inconclusive. He thought they might do better with a larger animal. He had acquired two pure-bred beagles and set up a fairly elaborate experiment. The animals were kept for several months in controlled conditions. They were given special food and detailed examinations were made of their blood and urine. When they had been exhaustively investigated, it was planned to tie off one of the arteries supplying blood to the liver and see what happened.

Machin asked Edward to operate on the first of the two beagles. He had carried out the operation a few weeks before. Despite his big hands and apparent clumsiness in ordinary affairs, he was a good experimental surgeon. He exposed the vessels and bile ducts under the liver, gently isolated the artery leading to the left lobe of the liver, and divided it between ligatures. Then he sewed up. It was a quick, neat operation. The dog slept peacefully under the anesthetic. At the end of the operation it was in excellent condition.

The next day Edward went to see it, just as you would go to see a patient in a ward. The beagle was lying in its box in a cage in the animal house, looking a little sorry for itself. It had made no fuss at all, said the animal house attendant. It had always been a docile, well-behaved dog. They had the usual problem, of course, that it tried to lick the strapping off the wound.

Edward went into the cage. The beagle rolled over on to its back, as if eager to show him the operation area. The fur had been shaved away over the whole abdomen and the skin, so silky elsewhere, showed up livid and unnatural. Edward touched the area around the wound to make sure there was no inflammation. The dog whined gently. As he took his fingers away it leaned forward and licked his hand. He turned away abruptly. "That's all right," he said. "No temperature?" The attendant shook his head.

Edward came back to the animal each day, to inspect the wound, to take blood pressure measurements, and blood and urine specimens. The beagle began to get used to him. It barked joyfully when he came in through the door and rolled over to be petted when he came near it. "He's taken a real fancy to you," said the attendant.

"It's just a reflex," said Edward irritably as he took out the syringe and felt for the vein in the beagle's leg. "They make a fuss of anyone who pays attention to them."

The attendant shook his head. "I feed him every day and he doesn't give a damn for me. It's funny how they know who's the boss."

The beagle was well and happy for about a week. Then it began to scratch. Within twenty-four hours it had taken off an area of fur several inches square from its left shoulder. It had lost some of its liveliness. When Edward looked at its eyes they had a faint yellow tinge. The urine had darkened and the blood test showed an early stage of liver failure. It seemed to Edward that the dog was beginning to look at him in a plaintive, puzzled way. It refused to eat and its fur was becoming matted and luster-less. Yet it was still pleased to see him. It barked a greeting and licked his hand as he touched it. It whined when he went away.

As the animal grew weaker and more miserable, Edward became increasingly distressed. He slept badly and sometimes, when he did finally go to sleep, he would find himself dreaming of the operation he had performed. He saw the pink, healthy tissues of abdomen, with the blood pulsating through them, flawless and vibrant with life. Then he saw his own hands in the rubber gloves gently isolating the artery, hooking the aneurysm needle around it, inserting the silk thread, and without any hesitation tying the knot which would turn the living flesh to corruption; dealing out death as surely as if he had cut the animal's throat or smashed its brains in with a hammer.

One day he said to Machin, "I think we ought to sacrifice that beagle, sir."

Machin looked at him in surprise. "I thought you were still getting some interesting readings."

"I don't think we shall get much more. It's very weak." When Machin seemed unconvinced, he added, "I think it's suffering."

Machin frowned. It was as if he had been confronted with a new aspect of Barrington's character, one he was not sure he liked. "All right," he said, "let's go and have a look at it."

When they went into the animal house the beagle raised its head, but for the first time it seemed too tired to bark. Its eyelids fell shut. It snored a little, and one of its back legs twitched as if in a dream.

"I think it's all right to carry on," said Machin. "They become gradually comatose, you know. And the terminal readings are an important part of the picture. It would be a pity to spoil the whole experiment by cutting it short." He added sententiously, "If we take the lives of the lower animals—as after all we must sometimes—we owe it to them not to sacrifice them in vain."

The beagle survived three more days. As Machin had predicted, it spent most of its last hours in coma. It recognized Barrington only intermittently. When it died he carried out the post-mortem. The liver was swollen and gangrenous, the abdomen was full of fluid, and the organs were stained with yellow. The two ends of the severed artery were just as he had left them, constricted with their tiny knots of white silk thread. The beagle's eyes were glazed and its jaws lay open. It looked like any other dead animal. It was hard to remember that it had once listened for his footsteps and licked his hand when he bent down to caress it.

Barrington wrote up his report, and then went into the library, where he could be alone. He could not bring himself to return to his work. He had operated on other animals and it had not affected him very much. A guinea pig or a white rat is a passive thing; it does not recognize the experimenter and insist on building up with him a relationship of affection and trust. Barrington could not get it out of his mind that all the time he had been in the process of destroying the beagle it had loved him and looked to him for protection. His act, no matter how much he might justify it on other grounds, was a betrayal of innocence.

The library was closed at six o'clock and he had to leave. He wandered aimlessly about the corridors of the hospital for some time, and then finally made his way back to the laboratory. He was not sure why; there was some vague idea in his head of talking to Machin and explaining his worries, perhaps of asking him to think again about proceeding with the experiment. But when he reached the laboratory, only the animal house attendant was there. He walked past the empty cage where the dog had lived. In the cage next to it he saw the other beagle. It did not jump up to the bars of the cage as he had expected, but lay on its bed of straw, breathing stertorously. He shouted to the attendant. "Clark!" he called. "What's happened to the dog?"

The attendant came up. "Nothing, sir. It's all right. Dr. Machin thought it was time to do the second control. He operated on it this afternoon."

Barrington looked at the beagle with horror. There passed through his mind a picture of the animal on which he had done the post-mortem a few hours ago. He thought of its weeks of misery, the vomiting, the uncontrollable itching, the gradual lapse into coma. He remembered the obscenely swollen state of its abdominal organs and the yellow traces of poison in all the tissues of its body.

Without saying anything further to the attendant he went into the laboratory and closed the door behind him. He carefully filled a syringe with a lethal dose of morphine and came back to the animal house. When he entered the dog's cage it lifted its head and looked at him with sleepy curiosity. It was still not completely around from the anesthetic. He gently lifted one of its paws and found the vein running underneath the skin. As he made the injection the animal gave a tiny shudder. Then its eyes closed and its head fell back on to the straw.

*

When he had finished the story they sat in silence for several minutes. Finally Joan said, "And what did you do then?"

"I went and told Machin."

"And what did he say?"

"Well, you can imagine. He was very angry. It wasn't just the dog. It was three months' work gone for nothing. I tried to explain what I felt, but—" He shrugged his shoulders. "It was hopeless, I could see. He just thought I must have gone mad. After a while we both lost our tempers. He ended up by saying that if I was capable of doing things like that he hadn't any further use for me."

It was as bad as her worst imaginings. It was not simply Machin. The academic world was small and closed—once it became known what he had done, his chances of advancement were finished. She could already see the longed-for professorship receding into the distance. "I can't understand it," she said. "How could you do such a thing? Surely you could have spoken to Machin beforehand—or something—"

"I don't want to argue about it," he said. "Either you can see what it meant to me or you can't. And it's done now anyway. It's no use hashing it over." He saw the distress on her face and his voice softened. "I'm sorry," he said. "I'm sorry to have brought this on you."

"Have you thought about what to do now?"

"No, I haven't. I haven't had time. I'm too tired tonight—"

She thought for a moment. She could not bear to accept the complete abandonment of all their hopes. "I'll have to talk to Alan," she said. "He may be able to help us."

3

She made an appointment to see Crane in his office at the
Sutherland. It was in a large modern block in Bloomsbury, just
behind London University. Crane's office was austere yet tasteful,
with white bookshelves around the walls and a bowl of fresh
roses on a side table. Above the desk was a recent work by Ben
Nicholson.

Crane kissed her on the cheek and showed her to a chair. He
arranged for his secretary to fetch her a cup of coffee. There
was something in his manner which made her sure that he
knew what she had come for. When the girl had closed the door
behind her, Joan said, "You've heard about Edward?"

"Yes. Machin telephoned me last night. He was in a great
state about it all." He smiled. "He's always been rather an excitable
fellow."

Hope began to flood back into her under the influence of
Crane's easy, reassuring manner. He did not seem to be very
concerned about the matter at all. Perhaps Edward had got the
whole incident out of proportion. She said, "Do you think there's
any possibility—I mean, for instance, supposing Edward were to
apologize—"

"Perhaps," said Crane. "The best thing would be for you to
tell me his side of it. Then we can talk."

She gave him an account of her conversation with Edward
the evening before. At the end, Crane said amiably, "As a director
of a research unit myself, I have to say that my sympathies are
with Machin. Plainly science would come to a standstill if we
allowed people to go around murdering our experimental animals.
On the other hand—" He paused. "You say Edward's been working very hard for some time?"

"Far too hard. It's been wearing him out. Only a few days ago
I was telling him he couldn't go on like this indefinitely."

"Yes," he said, "that's it, of course." He spoke as if his own suspicions had been confirmed. "Machin was carrying on, saying that Edward had become unhinged and I don't know what else. You wouldn't agree with that, would you?"

"Good heavens, no."

"I'm sure you're right. The fact is that he's been overdoing it for months and cracked up. It could happen to any one of us. I told Machin that."

"What did he say?"

"He wasn't best pleased, but he'll come round. He's always thought very highly of Edward. My guess is that he doesn't really want to lose him. On the other hand he keeps saying there's a matter of principle involved." He smiled again. "My experience is that people usually say that when they suspect they've made asses of themselves."

"Then what do you think we should do?"

"Does Edward really want to go back?"

"I'm sure he does. He lives for the Metropolitan. He hasn't another interest in the world."

"Good. Well, if you'll leave it to me, I think the best thing is to arrange a meeting. We'll do it one evening at my house. I'll give Machin a good dinner and soften him up a little."

He rose from his seat and she knew it was time for her to go. As she left she looked at him gratefully and said, "You're so good to me, Alan. How can I ever thank you?"

He patted her gently on the arm and led her to the door. "I'm very fond of you both," he said. It was hard sometimes to realize that he was still quite young. He already had the easy paternalism of a great man, conscious of his uniqueness, yet careful not to flaunt it before others. Already he was in the position of one who gives favors rather than asking them. Characteristically he had studied his role and played it to perfection. There were few people more adept than he at the art of accepting thanks gracefully.

*

The meeting with Machin was arranged for the following Friday, and the Barringtons were told to arrive at half-past nine, when dinner would be over. Edward was nervous and taciturn on the way to Hampstead. The atmosphere at Crane's house always intimidated him, and he was not looking forward to the encounter with Machin. Joan herself became increasingly anxious as they chugged up the hill in the little Morris. It seemed likely that Edward would not show up at his best. He had an unfortunate tendency to be aggressive when he was ill at ease.

The housemaid took their coats and showed them into the drawing room where the others were sitting over coffee and brandy. Machin was a lanky, restless man. He was very short-sighted and behind his heavy glasses his eyes looked larger than life-size, like those of a nocturnal animal. He was of a similar age to Crane but considerably junior to him in the scientific hierarchy.

Joan noticed the slightly cornered look on his face and she could imagine the way that dinner had gone. She had seen the Cranes in action before when they wanted to pressure some-body. They were gentle but remorseless, and they worked beauti-fully together. They were rich and they spent money as lavishly as charm in the achievement of their ends. If they took up a cause, they were prepared to use any method available to enforce their will.

Olwen would have flattered and charmed Machin, while Crane threw out hardly perceptible hints about the things he might be able to do for his future career. Wealth and influence are just as impressive in their way to men of science as they are to those engaged on more prosaic occupations. One day, Crane and Machin were both agreed, a better society would be forged in which everything was decided on merit. In the meantime there were matters in which an influential sponsor made all the dif-ference. Election to the Royal Society, the raising of finance, Government support for research—Crane sat on committees where he could do Machin either a great deal of good or a great deal of harm. And Machin was well aware of the fact.

Barrington nodded curtly to Machin, refused a brandy and asked for whisky and soda. An awkward silence fell. The rest of them tried to talk about general matters in the pretense that this was an ordinary social evening, but the attempt was a failure. Finally Crane decided to delay no longer. He turned to Barrington.

"You know why I invited you here tonight, Edward," he said. "Arthur and I have been talking over dinner about that un-fortunate incident at the Metropolitan." He gave Barrington one of his sweetest, most reasonable smiles. "I like to feel we're all friends here. I'm sure there's nothing that can't be mended. Do you agree, Arthur?"

He spoke with confidence, and it was plain that he had secured Machin's vote in advance over dinner. Machin pushed his glasses up on to his forehead and rubbed his eyes. "Yes, I suppose I do. I'm prepared to admit that in the heat of the moment I may have been a little offensive. But you must admit I was provoked."

He was really doing very well, thought Joan. He had right on his side, he had seen three months' hard work destroyed at a stroke. There was no call for him to make the first overture. She waited anxiously for Edward to respond. There was a rather alarming silence before he replied.

"That's very generous of you," he said finally. "I can see how the incident must have looked from your point of view. In conventional scientific terms it was quite inexcusable."

Machin was plainly relieved at the prospect of an easy way out of the situation. "Ah, well, never mind," he said. "We're all overworked. The life gets on top of us now and then—"

Joan had a wild hope that the crisis might be smoothed over there and then. But Edward interrupted him, not rudely but with a kind of desperation, as if terrified that reconciliation might proceed at such a pace that he might never be given the chance to explain himself at all. "Unfortunately it's not quite as simple as that. I wish it was. I think in fairness I must try to explain my feelings about this."

She saw Crane frown and raise his hand as if to stop him, but it was too late. Edward was not looking at Crane, nor indeed at any of them. As always when preoccupied he spoke, not to an audience, but almost as if he was trying to explain something to himself. Slowly and with many hesitations, he spoke of his problems of conscience about the animal in the same way as he had spoken to Joan. As she listened, she was dismayed to find that he told the story less convincingly than he had done when the two of them were alone. It was as if, after a while, he sensed a lack of sympathy in his audience and it led him into a disastrously stubborn, almost aggressive posture. He was a man who could talk fluently, and with great warmth and persuasiveness, to those who were in sympathy with him. But when his audience was unresponsive, he seemed to feel the necessity to bluster. His voice became harsher and less fluent, his northern accent was accentuated.

At the end he stopped abruptly and said, "Well, there it is. I had to tell you, otherwise you wouldn't be able to make sense out of the affair. I don't expect you to feel much sympathy with my point of view."

Machin rubbed his eyes again in a baffled way. He seemed to be having some difficulty in grasping the essential issues that were worrying Barrington. "There are one or two things I still don't quite understand. I accept the fact that you are in"—he found it impossible to keep the distaste out of his voice—"some kind of a moral turmoil. But why didn't you tell me about it? Why did you have to take matters into your own hands?"

"I don't know," admitted Edward. "It was an impulse, I suppose."

"I see." Machin pondered again. "Now we come to the more important issue. Are you saying that the work I'm doing—that we're all doing—is unjustifiable on ethical grounds?"

"I was afraid you'd look at it that way," said Barrington gloomily.

"Good God!" said Machin, his equanimity shattered at last. "How do you expect me to look at it? What other way is there?"

"It's not simple," said Barrington. "We can't understand it if we talk about it as if it were. I know it's the convention among people like us to pretend that it's all quite straightforward and that anyone who disagrees with us is a crank—"

"I don't know what to say to you," said Machin. "I really don't. That beagle made a reflex movement of allegiance which is built into its biological nature as a pack-hunting animal. You did experimental work on smaller mammals and never lost a wink of sleep over them. But because a dog goes through certain rituals which flatter your vanity, suddenly your conscience is aroused."

He became angry and contemptuous. There was more emotion in his manner than he had shown all evening. It occurred to Joan that his anger was excessive for a man who was entirely sure of himself. Perhaps in his heart he too was not entirely at ease about some of the things that were done.

"An animal is an animal," he said dogmatically. "We take it that man, as the highest evolutionary form, has a right to sacrifice the lower forms for his own benefit. If we don't make that assumption we can't swat a fly or kill a mosquito, we can't exterminate vermin, we can't eat meat. If we do, we have just as much right to carry out an experiment on a dog to advance the cause of medicine as we have to kill a lamb to make chops out of it. I shouldn't have to tell a person in your position elementary things like that. I shouldn't have to remind you that without animal experiments we wouldn't have vaccines or insulin, we shouldn't be able to do toxicity tests on drugs. If you don't believe in vivisection, you don't believe in medicine. You have to go back to poultices and herbs and half a teaspoonful of whisky to bring down the temperature. That's the choice. You say it's not simple. It is. It's as simple as that."

"Yes, I know. I know," said Barrington. It was an argument he had heard often before, ever since his student days. He had no answer to it. He sat there hunched in his chair, helpless to defend himself.

There was an embarrassed silence. Crane said sympathetically, "We all recognize your dilemma, Edward. I think any biological scientist with any sensitivity has been through this phase to some extent or other. All of us are very conscious of the issues that are worrying you—"

In his voice and manner there was a complete confidence in his own probity and pureness of motives. Crane always gave the impression that there was no issue which he had not considered, both intellectually and with a deep moral sense. It was impossible not to be impressed by it.

Barrington seized gratefully on this crumb of sympathy. He said, "The last thing I want to do is to pretend to be better than anybody else. One of the worst things about feeling the way I do at the moment is that you're bound to sound self-righteous and critical of other people. That's one of the reasons why I kept quiet for as long as I did. This is my problem, not anybody else's." Suddenly he seemed very young and bewildered. He paused and added unhappily, "Perhaps I'm just not cut out for this kind of work."

Machin was not appeased. "Then what do you want to do?"
he demanded. "Go to work for Mark Linley—or Charteris?"
These were two ancient enemies of his on the Harley Street circuit.
"Buy yourself a black suit with pin-stripe trousers?" He shrugged
disgustedly. "I suppose they'd have you if you swore you were a
reformed character."

Barrington ignored the gibe. It was an indication of how serious
the matter was for him that he was prepared to allow himself to
be attacked without hitting back. "I honestly don't know what I
should do," he said seriously.

Machin stood up. "Well, that leaves nothing more for me to
say," he said curtly. "It's up to you now, Edward. Think about
it and make up your mind. I'm not going to try to talk you into
anything. I think you could do some good work with us—but not
if you have any doubts about what we're doing. If you have, it's no
good. We don't want you back."

He nodded to the rest of the company and Crane took him
into the hall and showed him out. When Crane came back into
the drawing room he said, "I really thought Arthur behaved
rather well."

"Extremely well, considering everything," said Olwen. "He's
not usually the most tactful of men. And you didn't make it too
easy for him, Edward."

Barrington shifted uncomfortably in his chair. "I know what
you're all thinking. You've done the best you can to help me.
And God knows it's true. You've all been very sympathetic.
You practically persuaded Arthur to apologize when he wasn't
even in the wrong. All I have to do in return is to forget the
whole thing and go back to work. It seems little enough, doesn't it?
And you can't imagine how tempted I am to repay you by doing
exactly that."

"That wouldn't do any good," said Crane with authority. "And
not just from a moral point of view—"

"Yes, you're quite right," said Barrington, with a faint smile.
"He'd know, wouldn't he? When you work together on a project,
you have to agree on certain basic principles or it doesn't work.
If I went back to Arthur with any reservations, he'd find out and
have me thrown out within six months. And he'd be right to do so."

"Can I ask you one thing?" said Crane. "Are you absolutely sure of yourself? After all, you have to admit that Arthur was logically in the right. Can you be certain that this isn't just a transient excess of—well, I won't say sentimentality." He searched for a more neutral word. "Emotion perhaps."

Barrington shook his head. "No, I can't say that at all. If I could it would be easy, wouldn't it? And it's not easy."

Joan was consumed with anxiety for fear Crane should finally lose his patience and wash his hands of the whole business. After all, he had long since done far more than could be reasonably expected of him. Edward's conscience was becoming an intolerable burden to them all. It was like having an extra person in the room—and rather a stuffy and unlikable person at that. She felt embarrassed that they should be causing everyone so much trouble.

Yet she was afraid to speak. She feared that if she proposed to go home and end the whole business, it would be eagerly accepted, and Edward's only hope of support would be lost. While Crane was fighting for them, she still had hope. But fortunately he did not seem to be as irritated by the situation as she would have expected him to be. It was as if the philosophical nature of Edward's dilemma was intellectually fascinating to him. She had the feeling that as a matter of personal interest he was reluctant to let go of it.

He wandered round the room with a decanter, filling up glasses. "You know, Edward," he said thoughtfully, "what I think you really need is time to make up your mind. It's obviously not at all clear in your head at the moment." He paused and sipped his brandy. "I'm going to make a suggestion to you. I have to go on a lecture tour of East Africa in just over a week's time. I could do with somebody to help me. Preparing notes, writing reports, things like that. I'm quite sure I could persuade the Metropolitan to give you time off to come with me. Would you like to do that?"

Barrington's gratitude was almost touching. "Well, of course—" he said eagerly. Then his face clouded. "But I couldn't afford—"

Crane brushed him aside. "That's not a problem," he said. "We have a special grant at the Sutherland for that kind of thing. The Travel and Research Fund. We can fix your expenses out of that."

Barrington accepted eagerly. Joan felt that she had at least a reprieve. In fact, as she found out later, the Travel and Research Fund was largely a myth. It was a device that Crane used to enable him to help people without putting them under an obligation.

4

Edward was gone for two months. They had not been separated before, and the small house seemed dreary and empty. Fortunately she had the baby. Rosamond was a placid, affectionate child and Joan found a constant delight in her. Yet even the joy in her child was muted by her feeling of loneliness. She was alarmed to discover how much she needed him.

Edward wrote regularly. He sounded cheerful and healthy, and he was obviously enjoying the experience. He had never been out of England before and everything was delightfully new to him—the sun, the sea voyage, the teeming life of the ports at which they called, and the mountains shimmering in the desert heat on the banks of the Red Sea. When they reached Africa his letters became ecstatic. The country and the people seemed to have bewitched him. He filled pages with descriptions of the native markets and the wild game wandering unharmed by the side of the railway line which led up from the coast. He never mentioned his work or his troubles at the Metropolitan. One would have imagined that he had forgotten them completely.

His last letter reached her a few days before he was due to return. In this, for the first time, he mentioned his future.

"We have been wonderfully entertained here. Of course, Alan is a great man, and it is a feather in their cap that he has agreed to come out and lecture in such a relatively remote area. The result is that we are feted and made a great fuss of. I am not used to such grand treatment myself, but Alan takes it easily, as a matter of course. He has the natural instincts of royalty, and behaves always in an extremely gracious and dignified fashion.

"We have been taken everywhere and given a unique picture of African life, not only in the big towns but in the remote country as well. We have met some fascinating people. And at last I feel I am beginning to get a clearer picture of the problems which troubled me so much before I left. I won't go into this in a letter, but I think I can say to you now—don't worry. Things will be all right. We can talk about it all when we meet . . ."

She was relieved. She pictured him coming gradually out of his depression under the influence of travel and new experiences; she saw him talking to Crane in the long still evenings and seeing his affairs in a new perspective. Alan had been right, she told herself. All that was needed was a rest and a change of scene to regain his sense of proportion.

When she met Edward at Victoria Station she was surprised and pleased at his appearance. He was leaner and the pudginess of his face had vanished—with this and the deep tan he had acquired he was almost handsome, in a gangling way. There was something subtly different about his manner too. It was easier and more poised. The trip seemed to have given him a new confidence in himself.

In the taxi they spoke mainly of trivialities. He described the later part of their travels, after he had sent the last letter to her. He kept emphasizing how kind Crane had been to him, but she had the feeling that toward the end the two men had had enough of each other. Edward admitted he had begun to find Crane a little pompous and self-important, and she could imagine the things about Edward which Crane would find irritating. Fortunately they had managed to last out the eight weeks without any real friction.

She waited for him to mention the question of his future. She had resolved not to be the first to talk about it, but she became increasingly impatient as time went by. It was not until they were at home that he finally broached the subject.

Still talking of Africa, he said, "It was the greatest experience of my life. Nothing I ever saw before can compare with it." He paused and then said gravely, "I want to go back."

He had probably no idea, she thought, of how much the trip had cost. A holiday on that scale was quite beyond their means.

But she did not wish to discourage him. "Perhaps, if we saved up . . ."

"I don't mean for a visit," he said. "I mean to work."

"To work?" She was surprised. "Why? Did somebody offer you a job?"

"Yes."

"I didn't know they had research out there."

"They haven't. I've finished with research." Seeing the look of astonishment on her face, he went on, "That was one of the things that became clear to me as I was traveling. I never want to go back to a laboratory again." He said reflectively, "I was never right for it really, you know. I just drifted into it because I was clever and I wasn't smooth enough to be an ordinary clinician. It wasn't really my sort of thing."

"But you cared for it so much. You worked day and night. You thought of nothing else—"

"That was because I believed in it. But I could never do that again. The very idea of it disgusts me. Do you know—I still dream about that dog?"

"Then what are you saying? What *do* you want to do?"

"I want to do medicine," he said simply. "The thing I was trained for. And I want to do it in Africa, where it's needed."

"You mean the Colonial Medical Service?"

"No. I don't see myself as a Civil Servant." He sat down close to her, and said, in a reminiscent voice, "I was taken to the most wonderful place. It's remote but incredibly beautiful. A little bush hospital in a village called Manusha. You approach it by boat along an enormous river, and then you walk for a few miles through the bush and there it is in front of you, with great blue mountains rising up behind it. It's high up, so it's not too hot and there isn't any sleeping sickness. It has the most magnificent birds I've ever seen in my life—"

She was bewildered. He was going too fast for her. And she found his enthusiasm alarming rather than reassuring. "Wait a moment. I don't understand this. Are you saying you want to go and work in this place?"

"Yes."

"Well, first show me where it is. On the map."

He took out an atlas and turned to the page on Central

Africa. After some trouble he finally pointed to one area with a pencil. "It's somewhere around there."

"But—I've never even heard of it. It's not even a British colony."

"It is in all but name. They have a king but he's pretty firmly under British influence. There's no need to worry about being eaten by cannibals or anything."

"But I still don't understand. Who owns the hospital? Who would you be working for?"

He showed his first sign of embarrassment. "Well, I should be completely my own boss, of course. I shouldn't be responsible to anybody." Aware that this did not answer the question, he added, "The actual owner of the property is the Church. Technically, it's a medical mission."

"A medical missionary? You?" This idea was so ludicrous that she could not help laughing. "But you're not even a Christian."

"I don't know what I am," he said. As usual, he shied away from logical definition. "In any case, that's not important. It's a question of doing something worth while—something I want to do. Not like that stuff I was doing at the Metropolitan." He was very serious. "If I don't go, these people will have nobody. They'll be completely alone."

"Is there nobody there now?"

"There's an English doctor called Ferguson. But he's only temporary. He's ill. He'll have to leave fairly soon."

She shook her head. She could not accept it. She wanted to believe that it was simply a quixotic idea he had got into his head. He had been captivated by the country and this picturesque little place. No doubt somebody had talked him into it. After a few days back in England he would realize how absurd it all was. "It's quite impossible," she said plaintively. "You must see that."

"Why?"

"Because—oh, surely it's obvious. We're not that sort of person. I'm sure they're very wonderful people and all that—" She found it difficult to explain it to him. If he had only been brought up under the same social conventions as herself, it would not have been necessary. Religion itself was outdated enough, but medical missionaries, sitting out in the bush in solar topees dishing out quinine pills, were really too nineteenth-century for words. It was not only an uncomfortable, dangerous life, it was something even worse. It was a joke.

"Edward, I can't do this," she said. She found she was pleading with him. "I really can't. Please say you don't mean it."

She looked eagerly for some sign that he might give way to her, but there was none. In the same even-tempered yet relentless tone he said, "I've got to do it."

His obstinacy maddened her. "And what about me? Don't you care about me?"

"You know I do. But this is my career. I have a right to make a choice. Do you want me to spend my life doing something I despise?"

"And Rosamond? Have you thought about her?"

"We can make some arrangement." Seeing the expression of outrage on her face, he went on, "This is nothing new, you know. It's been done a thousand times before. I can see the idea comes as rather a surprise to you—"

"A surprise!" In her frustration she felt like striking him. There was no way of concealing it from herself any longer: he was in earnest. He meant to do this absurd, hateful thing. And from her experience of him, she knew how impossible it was to argue with him once he got an idea into his head. Often he was not very clear himself why he wanted to do things. He followed his emotions. But this vagueness about his motives did not signify any lack of determination; quite the reverse. Once he had decided on a course of action, only the most violent means could divert him from it. In desperation she cried, "Supposing I refuse to come with you?"

He considered for a moment. "I don't think you will," he said finally, "when you've thought about it."

It was a gentle, reasonable statement, yet it struck terror into her. She knew in that moment that he was determined to go at all costs, and that if necessary he would leave her, and Rosamond too, in order to do what he felt he must. Helplessly she looked around the living room. She had thought it ugly and second rate. Now it seemed like a haven, from which she would soon be torn to face a terrifying new world. The future appeared before her as something hostile and menacing; she had no faith in her capacity to cope with it. She would go with him in the end, she knew, because he was more determined than she, and because in the last resort he needed her less than she needed him. He would give her many things—love and loyalty and the companionship of a man unique in breadth and greatness of spirit. But she would pay a heavy price for them. Safety and peace of mind would always be denied to her.

5

They came up from the coast by train. At first it was stifling in the compartment. They traveled across a small plain covered with plantations of millet and cassava. In the villages black children played between the houses of straw and baked mud. Barrington viewed the landscape with delight. "It hasn't changed in thousands of years," he said. "They were making huts exactly like that when Julius Caesar invaded Britain. Look at the colors and the proportions."

She nodded, doing her best to respond to his enthusiasm. From a purely aesthetic point of view, the primitive buildings had indeed a genuine architectural quality of their own; they had the inherent symmetry arising from their natural geometrical pattern, and the pale brown walls were the color of the sunburned stucco one saw on elegant villas in Italy. She tried to induce in herself a state of proper appreciation, and to forget the heat and the humidity and her increasing travel weariness. But it was not easy.

It was two weeks now since they had left England. It had been a dreadful time. The sale of the house and furniture had been depressing enough. Then there was the advice from the Mission headquarters in London that she would be wise to leave Rosamond in England until they were properly settled in at the hospital. The Cranes had been wonderful and had been glad to take her, but it was nevertheless an appalling wrench to leave her behind.

They had traveled tourist class on the boat to save money, and the crowded discomfort had aggravated her natural homesickness. Now, as a final straw, she seemed to have eaten something which disagreed with her. She felt the sweat break out on her forehead as she was struck by a sudden wave of nausea.

"Are you all right?" said Barrington.

"Yes, I'm all right. How far is it?"

"Another five hours or so. But of course they don't always keep to schedule," he said tolerantly. He seemed to find the unreliability of African life attractive rather than otherwise. "Sometimes they stop and you find it's to pick up a friend or buy a basket of pineapples. There's no use bothering about it. That's the way it is out here."

She powdered her face to give an illusion of coolness, then took out a book and tried to read. It was a currently successful novel about the beautiful, primitive sexuality of the Mexican Indians. It described the tropics as a lush, green, mysterious place, peopled by bizarre animals, handsome, lustful men, and compliant, fertile women. There was nothing in it about prickly heat and bad food and intestinal colic and ancient smelly trains. At one time it would have held and moved her, but now she found it impossible to develop any sympathy with it. The engine rattled on over the steaming coastal plain.

Eventually it slowed a little and then it began to climb. The vegetation became thinner and the railway line cut its way through rocky ravines and toiled up mountain passes. It was lunchtime and Barrington suggested having something to eat, but she shook her head. She had hopes that if she stayed in the same place and exerted the maximum willpower she could just manage to prevent herself being sick. Together they nibbled fruit out of a paper bag.

After lunch she slept fitfully, her head bouncing uncomfortably against the corner of the carriage. The journey seemed interminable and the queasiness in her stomach like an affliction she would carry with her to the grave. She could not restrain a feeling of resentment. She had wanted to love this life for Edward's sake, she had entered the country determined to see it in its most attractive and favorable light. It was as if, at the moment of introduction, it had driven a great, black, ruthless fist into the pit of her stomach.

The railway line had crossed the mountains which sealed off the central part of the continent from the sea. Now it moved on to the flat land of the plateau. The country on each side was no longer tropical swamp and forest, but arid bush. There were few houses and no farms. Many of the squat trees were stripped of their bark, and once, over in the distance, she saw a group of gray-brown dots which Barrington said were a herd of elephants. Then, quite unexpectedly, the railway line moved on to an embankment which overlooked the river. After the desert through which they had passed, it was a breathtaking sight. At first it was hardly like a river at all. It was more like a lake, dotted with tree-covered islands. The banks and the islands were astonishingly fertile, and African villages were spread along them. They traveled like this for perhaps fifteen miles, and then the river changed. It became narrower. There were small falls and foaming rapids. After a few miles it spread out again. She watched it, hypnotized by its resourcefulness and its variety. She visualized it winding its way through Central Africa, cutting through plains and lakes and mountain sides, descending into a vast swamp, and then passing northward through the desert to its mouth two thousand miles away in another continent.

At the railhead they picked up the launch which would take them to Manusha. It was a squat, battered craft powered by a laboring diesel engine, which had been brought up by a firm of mining engineers on a geological survey and abandoned when the survey had proved disappointing. The owner was an anxious-looking Indian who was also the proprietor of several shops and a restaurant in the shantytown at the end of the railway.

The boat fought its protesting way against the current throughout the sultry afternoon. Hippos basked in the shallows and crocodiles lay immobile, like dead logs, on the banks. Unfamiliar birds streaked over the water searching for fish. Her stomach improved a little, away from the stale air of the railway carriage. Edward was happy and at ease. He pointed out the animals as they passed and tried to identify the birds with a book he had bought in Nairobi.

In the late afternoon they rounded a bend in the river and he pointed to an area of bush which seemed to her almost indistinguishable from any other. "It's over there," he said. "You can't see it because there's a small hill hiding it, and anyway it's three miles from the river. The landing dock is just around the next bend."

"How do we get to it?"

"There's a bush path. It's quite a pleasant walk. I expect Ferguson will be there to meet us."

But there was no sign of Ferguson at the landing dock. Instead there was a party of half a dozen porters, led by a tall, handsome African in khaki slacks and a bush shirt. As they stepped off the boat he greeted them with great solemnity, taking their hands in his and bowing his head.

"Welcome," he said. "Welcome to Manusha." It was obviously a set speech. He said to Joan, "I am Christoph Manongo. Dispenser, medical assistant."

Barrington said, "But everyone calls him Toffee. Isn't that right?"

Toffee nodded his head and smiled. It was a dignified smile, that of a man prepared to be friendly on level terms. He said, "We get your baggage now."

When he turned to the porters the dignity remained on his face, but the smile left it. He rapped out a series of commands. Sleepily they began to load Barrington's baggage on to their heads. Toffee turned back to Barrington and said, "Dr. Ferguson sorry. Too much work at hospital."

"That's all right," said Barrington. He turned to Joan and said encouragingly, "Not far to go now."

It was a monotonous walk. The elephant grass rose on either side of the narrow path, effectively blocking their view of the surrounding country. The afternoon was still hot, and large flies buzzed around them as they trudged along. Every now and then they would encounter a cobweb several feet across, white and opaque, with a huge green spider poised expectantly in the center of it.

Toffee took the lead. He carried a stick with which he pushed aside the cobwebs and probed in suspicious areas for snakes. Edward strode behind him and Joan followed, just in front of the porters. When the path widened, Edward would come up alongside

Toffee and engage him in conversation. Toffee answered questions slowly and deliberately, in slightly ponderous English. It was plain that he was a man of responsibility. He had received a mission education and then a training as a dispenser in a hospital in the south. He had come to Manusha when it had first started. He had been there ten years, first with Dr. Stanton, then with Dr. McBride, now with Dr. Ferguson.

When Barrington asked him if he was a native of the area he shook his head quickly, almost as if shocked by the suggestion. The people of the area were Sosima, he explained, pointing with something like contempt at the porters behind them. He himself was Luako.

Barrington explained to Joan the significance of what he had said. The Luako were the rulers of the country. For centuries they had dominated the more submissive tribes like the Sosima. The king and all the high officials were Luako also. Barrington turned back to Toffee. "Round here is all Sosima country?" he asked.

"All—all Sosima."

"And where are you from?"

Toffee pointed to the West. "Far. Far. Maybe hundred miles over mountains. That is Luako country. We call it the land of the kings."

Like a man making a religious observance he stopped and gazed to the west. They looked after him but there was nothing to see. Even the mountains were hidden by the thorn scrub and the elephant grass. The little caravan came to a halt while he gazed reverently in the direction of the country of his birth. After a while he moved off again and they all followed him.

The sun was setting as they emerged from the bush path and saw the hospital. The bush had been cleared over an area of several acres. The main building was a T-shaped central block from which a path ran down, marked with white stones. The T-shaped building, Toffee explained, contained the out-patient department, the dispensary, and the stores. Behind it were two long buildings, containing wards for men and women. Smaller buildings served various special purposes such as an operating theater and a carpenter's shop. They were all built in traditional style with a framework of wooden poles packed with mud and thatched with straw. At the rear of the hospital, Toffee pointed out a larger house distinguished from the others by the fact that it was built in brick and had windows. "Doctor's house," he said.

As they approached, Ferguson came out of the door of the outpatient building. He was a tall, stooping man with a dusty complexion, wearing a faded khaki shirt and long baggy shorts like those of a scoutmaster. He held out a bony hand in greeting.

"I'm sorry I wasn't at the landing dock," he said, in a harassed voice. "I was snowed under, as usual. The trouble is you have to do everything yourself. You can't leave them for a minute. I was just getting ready to come and meet you when I found they'd all gone off."

"Who had?" said Barrington.

"The workmen." Ferguson acted as if everyone should have known it was the workmen. "They promised faithfully to have the P.K. finished for this afternoon—"

"The what?" said Joan.

Ferguson looked at her and gave an embarrassed wriggle of his bony shoulders. "It's a local term—for the—er—"

"He means the lavatory," said Barrington cheerfully. "I'll show you it later. Most interesting. They dig a damn great pit, seventeen feet deep, and then put planks and a mud floor over it with a hole in the middle. Isn't that right?" he said to Ferguson.

"More or less," said Ferguson primly.

"It's fascinating. Applied bacteriology. They find they don't need disinfectants or anything. It's a combination of bacterial action and insects. You'd think it would breed flies but it doesn't." He said to Ferguson, "Decent of you to build a special one for us."

"I'm afraid it's far from completed," said Ferguson glumly. "It's always the same thing. They start off with enormous enthusiasm. Singing and laughing and really working very hard. Then one day they just disappear. Impossible to find out where they've gone." He noticed Toffee walking across to the dispensary and rushed to intercept him. There was a short, excited conversation. Then he came back. "This time it's the maize," he said with disgust. "They've all had to go off to plant the maize. Or so they say."

"You don't believe them?"

"Impossible to know. If it isn't the sowing it's the harvest and if it isn't the maize it's the millet or the cassava. Or there's a wounded buffalo and they all want to go out and try to kill it. You'll find they come back in due course. The maddening thing is that they get very hurt if you reproach them." He shrugged his shoulders irritably. "Anyway, least said soonest mended. Perhaps you'd like to see the house."

The house consisted of two main rooms, a bedroom and a sitting room, and a corridor leading back into the kitchen quarters. Ferguson had vacated the bedroom and moved into a small guest hut about twenty yards away. The rooms were lit by paraffin lamps. An extra bed had been moved into the bedroom and both beds were covered with vast pyramids of mosquito netting, suspended from hooks in the ceiling.

Apart from the extra bed it was still a bachelor's room. There was only one dressing table and a single large Victorian wardrobe. There was a washstand with a bowl and jug in blue and white enamel. They washed and went into the other room where Ferguson was waiting for them. It was larger than the bedroom. There was a cheap dining-room suite at one end, and at the other several battered leather armchairs. The bookcases lining the walls contained a few aged devotional volumes and a great number of tattered paperbacks, most detective stories. On the table next to the wall were two stuffed birds.

There was a smell of cooking from the corridor. Ferguson said, "Dinner will be ready in a moment. We eat early here." He seemed ill at ease, as if he were unused to entertaining visitors. "Would you like a drink?" He looked vaguely around the room. "I think there's some sherry somewhere."

"No thanks."

Ferguson accepted the refusal thankfully. "I don't drink myself. In a place like this—it's a very lonely life, you understand. One feels the necessity for self-discipline."

It was one of those casual remarks which open a window on to a man's life. Joan pictured him sitting alone in this room night after night, reading the same paperbacks over and over again and playing patience with a tattered pack of cards, depressed by the work and the climate and the fact that the Africans had all disappeared into the bush for no apparent reason. Drink-

ing was not an activity to be undertaken lightly in these circumstances. "Do you find much to do in the evenings?" she asked.

"I have my hobby," he said. "It's very important to have a
hobby." He walked over to the stuffed birds. One of them was
a magnificent creature, a kind of heron. "I do these myself," he
said. "I'm just an amateur, of course."

"It looks very professional to me," she said politely. In fact it
didn't. The mounting was crude and the bird seemed lopsided.
But in the circumstances it was certainly a creditable achievement.

"I have a little hut at the back of the carpenter's shop. I'll
show it to you tomorrow. Most of my specimens are packed up
now. But I thought I'd leave these two for you if you wanted
them."

"Are you sure you can spare them?"

"Oh yes, I have a great many more." He looked at the heron
with something like fondness. "You'll find there are very beautiful
birds around here. When the Africans heard I was interested, they
started bringing them to me." He noticed the frown on her
face and said, "Yes, I'm afraid they trap them. But then if I
didn't buy them, they'd eat them. And even in the wild, few
birds die natural deaths, you know. They starve, or they are
taken by hawks—" He wriggled his shoulders unhappily. "Nevertheless, I agree. It's a moral dilemma."

There was an embarrassed silence, which was broken by the
entry of the servant with the supper. There was a bowl of stew
with boiled potatoes and tinned peas, followed by peaches in
syrup and Carnation cream.

"We have to live very simply here," said Ferguson apologetically
to Joan. "It's difficult to get fresh fruit or vegetables. My cook
isn't bad, as Africans go. I work very hard at teaching him
hygiene, but I would advise you to keep an eye on him just
the same." He said to Barrington, "He has a full medical
examination every few months. He's clean now but they pick up
things in no time."

Joan had managed to forget the nausea which had troubled
her through the earlier part of the day. Now it returned. She
regarded the stewed beef without enthusiasm. "I hope you'll find
the quarters adequate," said Ferguson.

"Excellent," said Barrington. He helped himself to more potatoes. "You've done wonders for us."

"It's not luxurious, I'm afraid. You'll find this is rather a Cinderella among missions. I've explained often enough the need for better facilities. But there it is. This will never be a rich hospital. Even by African standards the Sosima are very poor."

Barrington looked at him in surprise. "You make them pay?"

"Yes, of course. All the missions do. We have to support the hospital somehow. The donations aren't enough. We don't charge them much. Sixpence a visit, and we let them off that if they can't afford it." He said defensively. "They really prefer it, you know."

"Prefer it?" Joan could not conceal her disbelief.

"Yes. They don't think the medicine is any good unless it costs them something." He shook his head gloomily. "I'm afraid they're not a very idealistic people, and they don't understand idealism in others. You won't find it very easy to get the Christian ethic over to them."

"That's not what I'm here for," said Barrington. "I'm a doctor, not an evangelist."

"Yes, of course, the bishop told me. Well, you'll certainly find enough medicine to occupy you. They've got just about everything here. Malaria, worms, anemia, bilharzia from the river— don't go bathing there, by the way. Quite a lot of leprosy. The usual thing is that they go to the witch doctor first and if he can't help them, they come along to us."

He paused to ladle some tinned fruit on to Joan's plate. "Incidentally, they're not fools, the witch doctors. They're pretty shrewd at guessing when somebody's going to die. What they like to do is to send the incurables to us so that we get the blame for killing them. If you're absolutely certain they're going to die, the best thing is not give any treatment at all. Otherwise the relatives will think you've poisoned them."

He picked listlessly at the food in front of him. Joan had a picture of him picking at his life in the same helpless way. Cynicism was perhaps forgivable if expressed with style, but not in this dingy, defeated form. Ferguson did not seem to have even the energy to be bitter. She tried to stop herself despising him, to tell herself that he was a sick man who had lived too long in isolation.

"How long have you been out here?" she asked.

"Five years in Manusha. It hasn't been easy, I can tell you. We've been perpetually short of money. Compared to the Catholics at Kivu, we're just paupers."

"How far away is that?" said Barrington.

"About five miles, on the other side of the mountain. They're American. Valenti and O'Dwyer. Valenti is a doctor as well as a priest. They're Holy Ghost fathers, or some such. They get a lot of donations from places like Boston and Chicago—so, of course, they have much better facilities than we do. Also they have the nuns to help them. It's quite impossible for a single-handed mission like this to compete with them." He brooded for a moment on the unfairness of the situation. "But I think I can claim to have held my own."

"Do you see much of them?" Barrington asked.

"Not a lot. You'll find it's better to keep them at arm's length." Seeing the startled expression on Barrington's face he went on quickly, "I know it's a temptation to pal up with them when there are so few white people around, but it's a mistake. However friendly they seem, you'll find they're playing for their side, just the same." He hesitated and then said, "Also, these things get back, you know."

"To whom?"

"Oh," said Ferguson vaguely, "I don't know really. Africa's a great place for gossip, you'll find. Everybody knows everybody's business."

For the first time an acid note came into Barrington's voice. "These things don't concern me. If I can co-operate with the fathers, I shall be happy to do so."

Ferguson shrugged the question away. "Well, no doubt you'll manage things your own way. I can only give you the benefit of my experience." He seemed offended at the rejection of his advice. "Anyway, I think you'll find yourself with very little time for social life."

"I suppose so."

The servant came in and began to clear the table. Ferguson waited until he had finished before speaking again. "I can promise you one thing, you'll find yourself fully stretched here. Not only as a doctor but as a human being. There's a constant struggle with the country and the climate. And sickness of course. As you know, I've been far from well . . ." He explained to Joan, "I have this chronic—er—intestinal complaint, as your husband probably told you. I'm going home to England to have it investigated."

"When will you come back to Africa?"

"There's a possibility of an administrative job in Nairobi. The bishop is being very helpful to me. I think he understands that my health won't really stand any more work in the bush."

The servant brought in coffee and they moved away from the dinner table. A large beetle scuttled across the floor and Ferguson put his foot on it absentmindedly as it passed. It made an unpleasant crunching sound. Within seconds a colony of black ants had appeared from nowhere to feast off the corpse. "Yes," said Ferguson in his melancholy voice, "life in the bush is a hard taskmaster. You'll find you need God's help twenty-four hours a day."

*

As soon as she could, Joan excused herself and went into the bedroom to unpack. Soon the lack of drawer and cupboard space brought her to a halt; she had to leave most of her clothes and all Edward's suits in the cases. There were only four coat-hangers for the pair of them.

Tomorrow she would get something done about it, she thought. In the meantime she must not give way. She must show Edward that she could be a tough, resourceful missionary wife. She had agreed to come out here and she must make the best of it. She took out her book and sat in the chair beside the bed. By the flickering light of the paraffin lamp, she did her best to read.

It seemed a very long time before Barrington came in. She was surprised, looking at her watch, to find that it was only half-past nine.

"Hallo," he said, "I thought you were unpacking."

"I ran into a snag. There's nowhere to put anything."

He looked around the room. "I suppose there isn't. We'll have to get the carpenter on to it. Ferguson tells me he's quite good in a rough sort of way. Have you been outside?"

"No."

"You should. It's a remarkable sight. The stars are so near you feel you could touch them. The sky's never like that in England. And so warm—not a breath of wind." He took off his jacket and opened his shirt. "It's something I've always dreamed of when I was a kid. In those cold dark streets in Sunderland, with the wind whistling down them turning your guts to ice. It's funny—in some way I longed for this even before I knew it existed."

He was like a boy on his first visit to the seaside. You could see that he felt nothing of the depression which she was trying so hard to fight. The isolation attracted him, and he found the inconveniences of the life colorful and amusing.

She tried, without destroying his mood, to give some intimation of her own anxiety. "It gets dark very early, doesn't it?" she said.

"About six o'clock. It's the same all the year round, of course, being so near the equator. Everyone goes to bed early and gets up at dawn. Ferguson tells me the dawn here is really magnificent."

"Does he?" She could restrain herself no longer. She said acidly, "He seemed in a great hurry to leave it just the same."

Barrington frowned. "Oh, I don't know. I think that's a bit unfair. He's a sick man, you know."

"He doesn't seem so ill now as you described him."

He thought it over. "It's true, he does seem to have picked up a bit. These things come and go, you know." Seeing the look of disbelief on her face, he said defensively, "Oh, come, you don't suggest he was putting it on, do you? Good heavens, a chap like that—"

"Like what? I don't know him. All I know is that he seems to dislike the Africans and distrust the Catholics and thinks it wise to keep on the right side of the bishop."

Barrington's face was troubled. "He's been alone for five years, remember. We all have small, mean, petty thoughts inside us. In ordinary European society we learn how to keep them secret and avoid giving ourselves away. A man on his own tends to say what comes into his head."

She was infuriated by his credulity. For a man of his intelligence he was extraordinarily easily deceived. He believed what he wanted to believe. If it concerned something he wanted to do, or some decision he had already taken, he was prepared to turn his back on any fact, no matter how obvious, that did not suit him. In his world everything was black or white; men were either saints or knaves, they were either condemned out of hand or forgiven unreservedly.

"That may be true," she said impatiently. "But the fact is that he wanted you here so that he could get away to a desk job in Nairobi."

He nodded his head tolerantly. "Yes, I know that. I'm not so stupid as you think. He's had enough, hasn't he? You can feel it in everything he says, in every movement he makes. He's beaten. He wants to give up. But that doesn't mean he made me come here. You know me better than that. I came because I wanted to."

He was right, of course. He had used Ferguson just as Ferguson had used him. Each man had seen in the other the satisfaction of his own need. If it had not been Manusha it would have been somewhere else.

She wanted to cry out: But what about me? Don't I also have needs and desires? You are in a conspiracy, the two of you, against me, you are cheating me out of my life . . . But it was no use. She did not want to fight him, she needed his comfort and reassurance. She said, "I'm afraid, Edward. Don't laugh at me, be kind to me. I'm afraid."

He look at her in astonishment. "Of what? There's nothing to be afraid of."

"It beat him. You said it did. Five years and—well, look at him. How shall we be in five years?"

He smiled reassuringly and put his arm around her. There was something comforting in his great physical bulk. He had no doubts and no fears.

"I'm not Ferguson," he said confidently. "And anyway he was alone. There are two of us. That makes all the difference."

6

She was awakened by the sun striking through the thin net curtains which covered the single window. A cock was crowing and she could smell woodsmoke. The little room, which had seemed frightening in the shadows cast by the paraffin lamps the previous night, now appeared simple and clean and cheerful, like the bedroom of a doll's house.

It occurred to her that she had slept surprisingly well. She had been prepared for sleepless and terrifying nights. After Edward had turned out the light she had crouched under the unfamiliar folds of the mosquito netting, listening to the sounds of the bush around her—chatterings, rustlings, and an occasional cough which Edward said was a baboon but she knew in her heart was a lion. The thatch above her creaked intermittently. From temperature changes, as Edward asserted? Or inhabitants of one kind or another? The bed was hard and the pillows like stones. She lay rigid, telling herself that she would never get a good night's sleep in this place, so long as she lived. Then, suddenly, it was dawn. And, greatest blessing of all, the nausea in the pit of her stomach had disappeared.

Edward's bed was empty. She got up and went along the corridor to the bathroom. The bath was an old zinc tub and there were several jugs of hot water beside it. The P.K., with which she had had a first nightmare encounter the previous evening, turned out in the daylight to be not so much intimidating as inconvenient and rather comical. As she went back to the bedroom to dress, the smell of frying bacon came to her from the kitchen. She remembered that she had eaten hardly anything for the last twenty-four hours.

The men were waiting for her in the living room. Edward was obviously in great spirits, and even Ferguson seemed more cheerful than he had been on the previous evening. Perhaps, she thought, the prospect of his imminent departure was beginning to brighten him up. After breakfast he offered to show them around the hospital. "There isn't a lot to see," he said. "I'll take you around the buildings and we can go through a morning's work together. That should give you an idea of the way we do things." He smiled sourly. "You'll find it a little different from the Metropolitan."

At least the mission hospital had one advantage over the Metropolitan. It was not offensive to the eye. In its simple way it had architectural style. Around the hospital building proper were the huts of the Africans. Dotted about on the periphery of the compound, they made up a pattern of a small village. Poultry scuttled in and out of the huts and small naked children played on the mud paths between them. The women sat around winnowing their corn into shallow wooden bowls. The sky was clear blue and the sun still low.

They visited the carpenter's hut and discussed furniture, then saw the primitive baking oven and the operating theater. The two wards were in the charge of African male nurses. Each contained twenty-five beds. Joan had expected to find them full of patients, but to her astonishment they were half empty. Afterward they went to the outpatient department for Ferguson's morning clinic. There were only about a dozen patients waiting.

Ferguson sat down at his desk in the outpatient clinic. "If you'd like to watch—" he said. He indicated two chairs. "It's not nearly so busy as usual at the moment. I expect it's got around that I'm leaving. They're very conservative, timid people. You mustn't be surprised if it takes them a little while to develop confidence in you."

He worked his way through the line of patients, speaking to them through an interpreter. A few brief questions and a cursory examination were all they received. Then he scribbled orders for treatment on a piece of paper which was sent through to Toffee in the next room. The last patient was a woman with a swollen, infected leg. There were tiny red lines running up the leg and her face was heavy with fever. Ferguson prescribed some ointment. As she was about to leave, Barrington said, "Oughtn't we to take off her clothes?"

Ferguson shook his head. "There are great modesty taboos here," he said. "You have to be very careful. I don't do a complete physical examination unless it's absolutely necessary." Conscious of Barrington's disapproval, he added, "Of course it will be easier for you. Having Mrs. Barrington here." He said to Joan, "As a nurse, you'll obviously be able to help—"

She broke in. "I'm not a nurse."

"No? Somehow I'd taken it for granted. Most of the mission doctors marry nurses, you know. Naturally it's a great help."

His voice was almost reproachful, as if she had failed in the qualifications expected of her. She said defiantly, "Well I'm afraid I'm not." In a rather obscure attempt to show him that she was not completely useless, she added, "My subject is French Literature."

"Indeed," said Ferguson. He made no attempt to conceal his contempt for French Literature as a training for equatorial medicine. He turned to Barrington. "Perhaps in the circumstances you should have put pressure on the Church Missionary Society to find you a nursing sister. Not that you'd have found it easy. I used to have one, but she left after six months."

"Why?"

"I don't know really," said Ferguson vaguely. "She was never entirely satisfactory. Since then I've had to make do with native orderlies." His lips tightened in a way that she had noticed before when he spoke of the Africans. "I've done my best to teach them, but they're fundamentally unreliable. You find they all go off duty together without telling you. You can never find out the reason. Toffee's much better than the rest. As a Luako he has more sense of responsibility. On the other hand the Luako have their disadvantages too." When Barrington looked at him questioningly he went on, "They're very temperamental. They're great babies in some ways. They easily take offense and turn awkward. You've always got to be watching what you say to them. And even then the interpreter can get it wrong. One thing about Toffee—he speaks quite tolerable English."

He took them into a small room off the dispensary. "This is where we store the drugs. We have to be very careful to keep it locked. Toffee has one key and I have another. I'm afraid we're very short of modern medicines." He locked the door behind them as they went out and handed Barrington the key. "You might as well take this key now. I hope you don't mind my leaving tomorrow but I have to get to the coast in time to catch the mail boat. It's probably best anyway to jump straight in and get your feet wet, don't you think?" He gave Barrington a thin smile. "I'm sure you'll soon find your own way of doing things."

*

They saw him off the next afternoon. As he walked down the bush path toward the river, with the porters behind him carrying his battered suitcases, she was able for the first time to see him as pathetic—a sad, defeated man, poor in spirit as well as earthly possessions. And yet it was impossible to suppress a feeling of relief. The air seemed to lighten with his departure.

"Well, that's something," she said. "If he'd stayed much longer, I was going to shoot myself."

Barrington laughed. "He wasn't the most encouraging introduction perhaps. But we're on our own now." He looked up at the vast African sky, with the fleecy clouds running before the wind and the mountains shining blue in the distance. He turned back and gazed at the brown huts and the Africans squatting in front of them. "This is our place now," he said with great satisfaction. "These people are ours, they depend on us. We have a chance to do something really important for them. Don't you find that exciting?"

His enthusiasm was infectious, but she could not quite suppress a nagging doubt at the back of her mind. There was something about the strangeness of the Africans which unnerved her. "I don't know," she said. "When you look at them, they seem so blank, somehow. So completely shut away. What do they really think of us? Do you think they really want us here?"

"We'll make them want us," said Barrington. "It's our job to make them understand what we have to give."

"Doesn't it worry you that we might be just interfering? And they might prefer the life they have?"

"No." Barrington spoke with complete certainty. "These people aren't happy, laughing, carefree primitives, you know. They're sick and lethargic. Rousseau's noble savage has a spleen full of malarial parasites and a chest rotten with tubercle bacilli. He's anemic and badly nourished and the reason he's still in the Stone Age is that he hasn't the energy to drag himself out of it. His average length of life is about thirty years. People who sit in Hampstead drawing rooms and rhapsodize about the simple values of primitive life ought to look down a microscope at a few samples of intestinal worms. That might bring them back to reality." The contempt he had always shown for intellectual pretension was even more overt than usual. He spoke like a man on home ground. "When I think of the Metropolitan—those caged animals, the dog lying on the table, gasping from the tube in its throat—and I see this, I know what I was born for. There's nothing we shall do here that we shall ever need to feel ashamed of."

7

When Ferguson left, it was as if he took with him their last connection with European life. The cord was cut. The rest of the world ceased to exist for her, and London was a city on another planet. Her physical horizon was bounded by the river and the mountains; her days were measured by the sun, the weeks and months by the waxing and waning of the moon.

A change came in the entries in her journal. They lost the tense, querulous note which had run through her descriptions of the voyage out. She realized now that the fear which had paralyzed her at first was not a fear of the experience but of her own weakness. She had been afraid that the isolation, the work, and the discomfort would be too much for her and that she would give way under the strain of an unfamiliar experience. But in fact it was easier than she thought. While she missed Rosamond and her friends in London, the very remoteness of her situation seemed to diminish their reality, and it became almost hard to believe that they had ever existed. They were like something she had dreamed long ago.

Her days were so full that she found herself without the time to worry over minor discomforts. The sunset came as a surprise, always before she was ready for it. And when the sun went down, the day was finished. Then they sat on the simple veranda in front of the hospital, smoking cigarettes, exchanging news, and watching the mountains change color in the rays of the vanishing sun. At seven o'clock there would be dinner, and then when the meal was over, they would read or listen to music. Fortunately they had brought several cases of books, together with a gramophone and records, from England.

Often she would find herself nodding off halfway through a symphony. The hard work and the tropical sun tired out them both. They were usually in bed by ten o'clock. They slept heavily until the dawn broke through the curtains.

There was a great deal to do, but both of them were surprised to find how little of it was connected with the actual treatment of patients. The outpatient attendance remained low. Ferguson's explanation that the Africans were devoted to him personally and were suspicious of a new doctor had never seemed entirely convincing to Joan. Eventually she asked Toffee if there were always so few patients. He looked embarrassed. "Sometimes many patients—many. Sometimes few."

"But why? Why so few now?"

"Maybe they go plant corn. This season is the time for planting."

"You mean, if they're ill, they wait for treatment until the weather changes?"

"Yes—sometimes."

He said it without conviction. It seemed to Joan that he should surely know the answer, one way or the other. "You really think that's the reason?"

"Yes," he said, after a pause, as if he had decided on reflection that this was the answer she really wanted.

*

This was a pattern she became accustomed to in conversation with Africans. Replies to questions were usually given in vague unformulated hints, as if they hesitated to commit themselves without some contribution from her. Then, when she lost patience and tried to express one of the hints in more precise form, they seized on this delightedly, as if her expression of it had made it in some way more real, and more likely of acceptance. And once agreed, no matter how absurd it might eventually turn out to be, there was no possibility of getting them to budge from it.

She gradually began to accept the fact that it was impossible to know exactly what went on, or what the real reason was for many of the small events which took place in the hospital's daily life. Stores would disappear (often articles of no obvious value to anybody), a routine job would fail to be done, a pleasant, happy workman would turn unco-operative and surly. She would ask for an explanation, and sometimes Toffee would give her one quite clearly. At other times, a curtain of mystification would descend. She had to accept the fact that she would only learn those things that they thought it suitable for her to know.

Though the lightness of the medical work was rather baffling to both of them, it was certainly welcome at the beginning. The administration alone was sufficient to take up a large part of their day. The hospital, which looked picturesque on superficial examination, turned out on closer inspection to be in a bad state of repair. The walls in the male ward were almost on the point of collapse. Barrington not only supervised the reconstruction himself, but also took part in the laboring work, learning how to strengthen the beams and pack the mud and repair the thatch. The carpenter, it turned out, was willing but limited. He could cope with only the crudest kind of shelving. Even the simplest job took an amazing length of time. Yet if they expressed impatience the work became even slower or was abandoned altogether. It was only by constant and repeated efforts that they could adjust themselves to the tempo of African life.

She soon found that there was no possibility of shutting herself off from any part of the life of the hospital. It was useless to tell the orderlies that she was not a qualified nurse—the fact that she was a white woman and the wife of the doctor gave her automatic responsibility over a bewildering variety of areas, from the counting of bed linen to the complications of female circumcision. She had to learn, roughly and by improvisation, from instructions given by Edward or by Toffee, how to be a nurse, a housekeeper, and a diplomat—how to interrogate through an interpreter, and how to exercise discipline without giving offense.

She learned early to dress wounds and to deliver babies. Edward operated on two mornings a week and he taught her to boil up the instruments in the primitive sterilizer and to assist him at the operations. She learned how to give a simple anesthetic by pouring ether on lint and holding it over the face of the terrified patient. She was surprised at the number of things she was able to do without fear or disgust. Within a few weeks she developed a doctor's acceptance of natural processes and was no longer repelled by dirt or disease. Sheer familiarity developed in her a feeling of immunity toward infection.

The routine of the days was almost hypnotic. Each morning there was the same dramatic sunrise, the same stir within the compound, the cocks, the voices, and the woodsmoke. She would walk from the house and see a watchman sitting outside his hut, toasting his feet before the remains of his fire. At his side would lie the ancient rusty rifle with which, he claimed repeatedly, and without any real expectation of being believed, he had once killed a man-eating lion.

After breakfast the same routine would possess her, varying only in detail and in the character of the current domestic cries which added a touch of variety to the day. She determined that she would not be like Ferguson and keep herself aloof from the Africans. She tried to involve herself as much as possible in their lives. It was not easy. The language was difficult. She was able to pick up some basic words, but the complexities of its grammar eluded her. She found the children cheerful, engaging, and uninhibited, but after puberty a change came over them. They became shy and withdrawn. The charm was still there and they laughed easily, but they began to inhabit a world of their own where it seemed that she was unwelcome to follow them.

The adults listened patiently to her advice about food and hygiene. They were always polite and even seemed grateful, but she found afterward that the advice was usually forgotten and seldom followed. They loved and spoiled their children, yet more often than not they starved them because they would not take the trouble to prepare their maize flour in a way that a child could assimilate. Their attitude to sickness was maddening in its inconsistency. They would put up with the most dreadful deformities and injuries with cheerful stoicism. Yet at other times very minor discomforts would turn them into whining hypochondriacs.

They had little concept of money and seemed to care nothing

about improving their own poverty. They worked only for immediate subsistence, to obtain food or drink or some childish luxury which took their fancy. Some of their traditional crafts had a great intrinsic beauty, and she tried hard to encourage them, but without success. On one occasion some itinerant basket makers came to the hospital. They made baskets for a week, asking for only a trivial payment. She tried to induce them to stay. She had visions of sending the baskets to the capital and building up a small center for native arts and crafts. She explained, repeatedly and at length, through Toffee, how they could earn money and become prosperous. At first they giggled and answered evasively, but after an hour or two the leader of the group seemed to understand what she was offering them. He thanked her gravely and agreed. She went to bed that night with a feeling of accomplishment. The next morning the basket makers were gone. They had left, she was told, at first light, without any explanation. They never returned.

Edward was constantly preoccupied with the larger problems of the hospital, and she found herself dependent on Toffee for help and advice. She wondered sometimes how she would have managed at all if he had not been there. He was quiet, dignified, reliable, and always available. He seemed to have no interests outside his work. He was constantly on duty. The dispensary was always neat and tidy, the drugs were accurately recorded. He spoke with touching reverence of the work of the hospital. With the other Africans he was friendly but aloof and a little pompous, like an English butler in an aristocratic household.

In conversation he was slow and repetitive, with certain favorite turns of phrase. He knew all the gossip of the village, and liked to tell stories of the mission school and his training as a dispenser.

About his own family life he was less communicative. He had a wife and children and a patch of land somewhere in the west, but it was never possible to find out where. "Far—far—" he would say, with a vague wave of the hand. Did he plan to go to see them? "Soon—soon—" he would reply indifferently. The subject plainly bored him. He would return to an account of some baboons which had been eating the maize crop, or of the drunken, shiftless ways of the Sosima.

After they had been there three months, Olwen came out to

visit them with Rosamond. They met in the capital, where they engaged an Indian nurse who was recommended by the bishop's wife. They bought some cheap furniture, all the books they could find, and a pair of black Labrador puppies. As the large party traveled back along the river, it seemed to Joan that she was happier than she had ever been in her life.

8

From time to time she heard stories of the Holy Ghost fathers on the other side of the mountain. Among the Protestants in the capital it was said that they were typical Americans—brash and self-confident and purse-proud. Instead of walking or going on mule-back like the other missionaries, they had insisted on importing a Model-T Ford truck, which was always going wrong and caused great amusement among the Africans. They had no understanding of the country and were perpetually trying to introduce fancy modern ideas that might be all very well in Europe or America but were quite unsuitable for the bush.

One morning she was left on her own in the hospital while Edward and Toffee went off to see a man in a nearby village who had been badly mauled by a hyena. She was speaking to one of the medical orderlies when he lifted his head and turned away to look in the direction of the mountains. A moment later she heard a faint throbbing noise which was unfamiliar to her, and saw a moving cloud of dust in the hot still air. The throbbing grew in volume. Soon it was unmistakably the sound of a motor engine.

Shortly afterward the Model-T emerged from the bush path leading from the mountain, shaking and grinding as it negotiated the bumps in the track. It was being driven with more dash than delicacy, and steam spouted out of its radiator like water from a surfacing whale. The Africans came out from their huts and watched it with something approaching awe. Each moment it appeared as if the engine would stall or the springs smash in two, and the truck would come to a stop forever. It labored on, coming to a final halt in front of the dispensary. With a convulsive heave the engine subsided. Only the hissing of steam from the radiator broke the silence.

Two very dusty young men jumped out of the cab. They were dressed in check shirts and jeans and looked rather like engineers from an oil rig or loggers from a lumber camp. One of them was short and square and red-faced; the other thin, aquiline, olive skinned, and very handsome. The thin one gave the impression of being the senior of the two. He walked up to Joan and held out a hand.

"Mrs. Barrington?"

"Yes."

"I'm Father Valenti." He turned to his companion. "This is Father O'Dwyer."

"Hi," said Father O'Dwyer, rather awkwardly. He gripped her hand in an enormous hairy fist. The other hand held a large black, half-smoked cigar.

"I hope you don't mind us calling on you," said Valenti. "We were over this way and thought we'd drop in."

"Yes, yes, of course. I'm afraid my husband's out in one of the villages but he'll be back soon." She felt a little flustered. It was quite an event to have unexpected callers. "Come up to the house. I'm sure you'd like a wash."

"If we could possibly have some water for the truck—"

"Naturally. Anything you want."

Valenti gave instructions to the orderly and then they walked up to the house. While the men were washing, she prepared some coffee and a jug of lemon squash. When they came back into the living room, Valenti said, "You're really making this place nice."

She found herself blushing with pleasure. It was absurd. Loneliness did strange things to you even when you were not conscious of it. She had thought she was quite happy in her isolation, but now she was greedy for conversation and terrified that they might go. "You'll stay to lunch, won't you? Edward will be back quite soon."

"Thanks a lot."

"I was hoping we might see you. We've heard so much about

your hospital over the mountain. I'm told it's much more palatial than ours."

"It's not exactly Johns Hopkins," said Valenti, "and it's certainly not so pretty as yours. It may be a little bigger, but of course we've been around longer. You must come and have a look at it."

"I'd love to."

"Just fix a day. I'll send the truck over for you."

He began to talk about the hospital. A matter of months ago this conversation would not have interested her in the least. Now she was avid for information about sterilizers and sanitation, supplies of dressings and methods of organizing outpatients. She listened enviously to his description of a new diesel pump which he had installed for the well behind the hospital and his plan (when he could raise the money) to buy a small generator for electric light. He was a charming, likable man but she could not repress a twinge of envy at the thought of the small luxuries he could afford which were denied to them.

"How many beds have you altogether?" she asked.

"A hundred and twelve. Four wards of twenty-eight—two male and two female."

"And just the two of you?"

"We have four sisters. I'm the only doctor. I look after the medical side, Kevin handles their social problems—of which, believe me, they have plenty."

"When did you come here?"

"Seven years ago. Before that I was in Rhodesia. You been there?"

"No."

"It's a great country. There are quite a few of us Holy Ghosters down there. Not so many up here in the north."

She looked at him in fascination. She had never met a monk before in her life. She had had a vague picture of them as cowled figures flapping in sandals along cloistered corridors and taking part in superstitious rituals. Monks, in her imagination, were always Italians or Spaniards. They spoke ponderously; they were bigoted and limited and knew nothing of the world. They did not lounge about in dirty jeans speaking American slang and smoking cigars. Confirmed agnostic though she was, she could not help feeling slightly shocked by it all.

She saw Valenti regarding her with a crooked smile on his raffish Mediterranean face. His next remark showed that he had read her thoughts. "We don't wear the full habit in these parts," he said. "It gets kind of inconvenient." He added, teasing her, "I guess you expected us to be dressed up like Arabs." He pronounced it Ay-rabs.

She was confused at first, and then smiled. "It's your own fault. If your Church will make you wear funny clothes—"

The two men laughed. They were suddenly at ease with her and she with them. She felt able to ask the question that had been in her mind since they had first arrived. She wanted to get it in before Edward came. "Tell me," she said. "Are you very busy? Do you have a lot of patients?"

"Oh sure," said Valenti. "Usual thing, you know. One on the floor for every one on the bed. We try to keep them off the verandas but it isn't easy. I mean, what can you do? If they're really sick . . ."

She said abruptly, "We aren't very busy here."

It was like a confession of failure, almost of guilt. What interested her was that Valenti seemed more embarrassed than surprised. "No? Well, I guess—"

She interrupted him. "I asked Dr. Ferguson about it. He said they didn't like coming to a strange doctor."

"Maybe." He spoke without conviction. "They're certainly an odd people."

"Our dispenser says they're busy planting the maize."

O'Dwyer shifted in his seat. He looked at Valenti. Then he spoke for the first time. "Peter, I think you ought to say something." Valenti waved a hand to tell him to be silent. Joan looked from one to the other.

"What is it?" she said. They remained awkwardly silent. "You don't believe it, do you? You think there's some other reason?"

O'Dwyer scratched his left shoulder. He was obviously suffering from prickly heat. "Mrs. Barrington, let me put it to you this way—"

He was interrupted by an uproar outside. The dogs began barking and there was the sound of African voices raised in greeting. Over them rose Barrington's booming cheerful tones.

Valenti stood up, terminating the conversation with obvious relief. He said, "I guess that's your husband."

They all went out to meet Barrington. He was in great spirits. The man who had been mauled by the hyena was still alive. He had lost a great deal of blood and there was an enormous laceration on one side of his face and neck, but he was a strong young man and his general condition was astonishingly good. A temporary dressing had been put on his wound and he had been brought back to the hospital on a stretcher.

The Africans crowded round the stretcher, exchanging excited greetings with the man's relatives. The story was being passed around to the accompaniment of cries of delight. Plainly, within a matter of a few hours, the episode would become a part of the folklore of the little community. The children stood sucking their thumbs and gazing awestruck at the stretcher, the excited people, and the big white doctor giving orders. Toffee went off to prepare the theater for an operation.

Joan introduced Edward to the two priests. He greeted them effusively. They couldn't have come at a better time. He badly needed both an assistant and an anesthetist. Could they possibly spare the time to help him?

When he did the operation it was almost like being back at the Metropolitan. Valenti gave the anesthetic, O'Dwyer assisted, Toffee acted as theater nurse, and Joan prepared the instruments and looked after the swabs. Barrington had always been a swift and competent surgeon, and he was at his best in front of an audience. The operation was an awkward one. The flap of skin which had been torn away was badly bruised. When he had excised the edges he was left with a gap which could only be closed by rotating skin from the neck and covering the raw area with a split skin graft from the thigh. It was work which would have taxed the skill of a specialist plastic surgeon, but he tackled it decisively, neatly, and without hesitation. It was two hours before he put in the last stitch. When he had bound on the dressings, he took off his cap and mask and wiped his sweating face with a towel.

"Thanks very much, everybody," he said. "God knows how I should ever have managed to handle that one on my own." He turned to Valenti. "That was a lovely anesthetic, Father. It's not easy to keep them as light as that with open ether."

"It was a pretty smart piece of surgery," said Valenti. "Is that your speciality?"

"I've done a bit of plastic work in my time. Not much. If you want my opinion, they make too much fuss about it. It's just dressmaking really." Barrington unfastened the tapes of his gown and dropped it in a heap on the floor. He felt the patient's pulse. "Just over a hundred. Not bad in the circumstances. Let's go and have some lunch."

He led them to the house, talking as he went. She was slightly apprehensive at his mood. He was a man who hardly ever got drunk on wine but was easily intoxicated by a sense of occasion. With the sensitiveness of a wife to the most delicate nuances of her husband's behavior, she could tell that the unexpected visitors after such a long isolation, together with his success in the operating theater, had gone to his head.

The trouble was, as she knew from experience, that in this frame of mind he did not show at his best. He became arrogant and overconfident. He had a tendency to show off. He reverted to the kind of rough banter which was the normal conversational currency in the industrial town where he had been brought up, but which grated on her more sensitive ear. It became obvious to everybody on these occasions that he was no gentleman. And though in theory she derided the whole concept of gentlemanly behavior, in practice she could not help but be embarrassed.

Over lunch, Edward talked a great deal and listened very little. He ate voraciously, and with a rather absentminded intensity which was typical of him in these phases. It was in curious contrast to other moods of his, in which he hardly seemed conscious of food at all. If Valenti or O'Dwyer tried to speak, he talked them down. He chaffed them about America and the Catholic Church. He bragged about his successes at the Metropolitan and left them in no doubt that he considered himself a cut above the average mission doctor.

Miserably, she watched the atmosphere of comradeship and shared experience ebb away as the lunch went on. If only, she thought, she could take the two priests aside and explain to them that he was not really like this; that when they were alone he was not gross and overbearing, but a kind, sensitive, and in some ways very vulnerable man. She wanted to explain that much

of his bad behavior came from excess of vitality and that his
egoism was merely the outward show of his determination to excel,
combined with the incessant torment of self-doubt. But she could
only sit in silence, hoping that they might have the perception to
understand.

She had a feeling that Valenti at least was able to see through
the braggadocio to the qualities that lay beneath. His smile was
tolerant, he disagreed gently and submitted to being interrupted
without apparent resentment. O'Dwyer was a simpler man. His
broad Irish face flushed when Barrington poked fun at his country
or his church. Sometimes he opened his mouth as if to retort and
then closed it sharply. He would look up to the ceiling as if calling
on God to help him to keep his temper in the face of provocation.

After lunch Barrington offered to show them the hospital. He
was particularly anxious to demonstrate the new labor ward he
was building. It was now almost finished. The wooden framework
and the roof were up, and the men were busy packing the mud
around the walls.

"We really need this," said Barrington. "It's hopeless at the
moment. We just have the one theater where all the septic work
goes on, and we have to take the women there for labor. It's
dangerous as well as inconvenient. When this place is finished
we shall have a small labor ward and a delivery room off it."

He looked at the priests for approval. Valenti was regarding
the building with a troubled expression. O'Dwyer walked off to
one side and climbed a bank just behind the building.

"It's simple, of course," said Barrington, "but I think it will
work, don't you?"

"Yes—it's great, great," said Valenti. He sounded abstracted.
O'Dwyer jumped off the bank and came back to the group,
brushing the dust off his hands.

"Dr. Barrington," he said rather formally. "I wonder if you'd
mind if I gave you some advice." He spoke stiffly, in the way of
a man preparing to give bad news. The cheerful confidence left
Barrington's face. "Of course not," he said. "Why should I?"

O'Dwyer looked uncertainly at Valenti. Receiving no definite
assistance, he plunged on. "Well, it's not easy," he said. "As you
know, there's always been this problem between the different
confessions. Believe me, I'm not saying the faults are all on one

side—some of our people are just about as bigoted as they come. But I'd like you to take what I'm going to say straight—man to man, one guy to another. You know?"

"Of course," said Barrington impatiently. "What is it?"

O'Dwyer waved his hand toward the hospital compound. "This is a nice little place right now. Much prettier than ours. That's for sure. But in a month you're going to get the rain. And then it's different." He pointed to the land on the other side of the bank. "Back there you have a dried-up water course that floods one year in three. Even when it doesn't flood, there's seepage which gets down into the lower ground here. I'm sorry to say this, but you've built your new labor ward on a potential swamp."

Barrington was silent. His gaiety and self-confidence had been suddenly and completely destroyed. Instead, a sulky, resentful expression came on his face. Valenti saw the change and cut in smoothly. "I know how you must feel about this, but it's really better that you should know. Father O'Dwyer is fairly experienced on matters of construction and drainage . . ."

"Oh I'm sure," said Barrington. "He has that Yankee know-how that we hear so much about." He swung round savagely on O'Dwyer. "Is there anything else you feel you ought to tell me?"

"If you want to know the worst," said O'Dwyer slowly, "you can have it. This is a bad location all ends up. It's inconvenient to get to and it has a bad reputation for disease in the wet season. Sometimes it gets cut off when the floods come. The tribes on the other side of the river don't come because it's Sosima country and they don't like the Sosima. The Sosima themselves mostly find it more convenient to come to us. The reason you don't get many patients is because there never were many here. Whatever Ferguson may have told you, neither he nor any of the others could make a go of it, no matter how hard they tried."

Joan turned her head away. It was dreadful to see the pain on Edward's face. After a long silence he said, "I don't believe you. I don't believe a word of it."

Valenti's voice was gentle. "It's true, I'm afraid. Believe me, it's dreadful for us to have to tell you. You're a man of great ability. I could tell that by the work you did today. I couldn't bear the thought of you carrying on wasting yourself—over something that's impossible—"

"You just want me out of here," said Barrington. He said it with utter certainty. It was as if his mind had closed like a trap, shutting out any other possibility. And with this certainty came bitterness. "I'd never have believed it," he said. "Ferguson tried to warn me. He told me what you were. I thought he was imagining things. But he knew. He knew how it was."

He was not talking to them. He had retreated into some corner of himself, some citadel where no doubts could reach him, where everything was seen simply in terms of a vicious and brutal fight between Barrington and the hostile world. She knew that it would be hours before she could communicate with him, and probably days before he could speak of the matter without passion.

Valenti turned a troubled, apologetic face to her. "Maybe we shouldn't have spoken," he said. "I guess we'd better be going."

He looked at Barrington as if wondering whether to offer his hand. He decided against it. "Thanks a lot," he said. "It was a real privilege to help you on that case."

The attempt at an olive branch was lost, perhaps never even heard. Barrington's expression did not change. Valenti and O'Dwyer turned and walked toward the truck. Joan went with them, leaving Barrington where he stood. O'Dwyer said, "I'm sorry, Mrs. Barrington. I didn't want it to be like this."

"Never mind." She wanted to say that Barrington would come round in time, but she doubted whether it was true. Together with her anger at Barrington's behavior and her pity for his disappointment, was a realization of what she herself had lost. These were the only people within forty miles that she could talk to, and now she might never see them again. She remembered how delighted she had been when they came, and her hope that at last they had made some friends and were not entirely alone. "I hope we shall see you again," she said rather helplessly.

"Sure," said Valenti. "We'll be around." They both shook hands with her and climbed into the Ford. Before Valenti started the engine he said, "Believe me, I understand how he feels. If you want any help when the rains come, you know where we are."

9

The first sign of change appeared on the mountains. The fleecy cumulus clouds which hung eternally over the highest part of the range began to thicken and turn darker—some of the peaks disappeared altogether behind a blanket of mist. Each day the heaviness in the sky moved a little nearer, and then one morning Joan woke up to hear a sound which she had almost forgotten over the long months of drought; the singing of wind among the thorn trees and the patter of rain against the thatch.

By the time they had dressed and finished breakfast the rain had stopped. But the traces of it lay everywhere in pools of water on the paths between the hospital buildings. Already, as the Africans passed to and fro upon their daily duties, they were beginning to churn the puddles into mud. The whole atmosphere of the place seemed strange and unnatural to her. This gray dampness did not form part of her picture of life in the tropics. It was the kind of weather she would have hardly noticed if it had occurred in London. But here, after the months of sunshine, it was unfamiliar and depressing.

The rain was a reminder, too, of the relatively primitive construction of the hospital. In the dry weather, the mud of the paths and walls had seemed as hard and durable as asphalt; but one heavy shower of rain had revealed its inherent vulnerability. What had been for months a group of solid buildings was now revealed as little more than a camp.

As she picked her way across the puddles to the outpatient department the rain started again. The Africans crouched beneath the eaves of the buildings, huddled miserably in blankets. The day's work proceeded slowly and lifelessly. The Africans lacked their usual gaiety and even Edward seemed downcast. Toffee told her that the rains were likely to last at least two or three months.

In the first week, the showers were intermittent. Vicious squalls would be followed by an hour or two of sunshine before the clouds returned again. Gradually the intervals grew shorter and disappeared almost completely. The puddles and the mud became a permanent feature of their life. The days were still relatively warm, but at night they had to use blankets on their beds.

The damp was everywhere. It lay on every surface, every wall, every article of furniture. Mold spread over their clothes in the cupboards, and one day she opened a linen drawer and found it infested with silverfish. Now the night rustlings in the thatch never ceased, as the insects and small mammals buried themselves in it to escape the rain. She had endless inconclusive battles with flies and cockroaches in the kitchen.

There was a change in the pattern of work in the hospital. There were far more patients now, and for the first time both the male and female wards were full. She found to her surprise that the commonest illnesses were the ordinary British winter ailments, such as colds, bronchitis, and pneumonia. The native huts, so picturesque in design, were ill-designed to cope with the wet or the cold. The children and the old people, always malnourished and without proper covering against the weather, suffered dreadfully. The increase in flies brought dysentery, not only to the patients but to the staff of the hospital. First Edward, then she herself were affected. The P.K. ceased to be a joke and became a place of sickness and pain.

An epidemic of measles swept through the small community, and Rosamond, who played all day with the African children, soon became infected. She was fractious and miserable, and lay awake at night whining and crying. Joan began to think wistfully of England, where there was fresh fruit and milk, and clean white children to play with. And looming above her always was the problem of the child's education. In a few years she would have to leave them again and go home to school. Were they really being very fair to her?

She found herself, to her shame, becoming daily less tolerant of the Africans. While in some ways she admired their casual, improvident attitude toward life and believed that they retained certain basic virtues that had been lost in modern urbanized civilization, they were nevertheless exasperating when one wanted

to get something done. Even more than the Europeans, they
were dependent for their good spirits on the sun. In the bad
weather their gaiety left them and they became glum and sulky.
She found that beneath their apparent acceptance of the missionaries, there lay a residue of cynicism and suspicion which revealed
itself in moments of tension. She was shocked to discover their
ineradicable belief that the missionaries were in Africa to make
their fortune out of the natives. The tiny contributions which
they were asked to make toward the upkeep of the hospital
represented to them considerable wealth, and they imagined that
every time a doctor left Manusha he went home to live in
style in his own country.

It was impossible to counter these absurd myths, since the
Africans would never in any circumstances engage in argument.
They merely agreed politely and went on thinking as before. To
one who had been born and bred in an atmosphere of analysis
and intellectual discussion, this amiable obscurantism was maddening. But when she mentioned it to Barrington, he merely laughed.
So far as she could see, it did not worry him in the least.

Indeed, it seemed to Joan sometimes that the greatest barrier
between her and Edward was the difference in their emotional
reactions to the Africans. She herself found dealing with primitive
people a constant and uphill effort. It was distressing to her that
this should be so. She was an idealistic girl, and she had been
brought up from her earliest childhood to believe in the equality
of man. She had no religious faith, but believed implicitly in the
moral values of the British liberal tradition. She detested colonial-
ism and looked forward to the political liberation of all subject
peoples. When she was in London she had gone out of her way
to entertain Indian and African students. She had always felt
at ease with them and often said she found them so much less
inhibited and more entertaining than Europeans.

Yet somehow at Manusha it was different. She tried hard to
love and understand the Africans, but her success was only intermittent. For the greatest part of the time she found them
mysterious and exasperating.

Edward, by contrast, was totally at his ease. He behaved toward
them in a casual, unself-conscious way which was in curious
contrast to his awkwardness in London society. His irritations

with them were transient. He cursed them and laughed with them, and they had great jokes together over his early stumbling attempts to speak their language. He treated them as wayward and attractive children. He loved them, with a deep, unaffected, paternal love. And they loved him in return.

Joan was maddened by the unfairness of it. She knew that in almost every respect he was less intellectually tolerant than she was. But he had an exuberant natural vitality which simply swept aside most of the squalid details that she found so difficult to bear. He did not seem to notice when the men blew their noses with their fingers or the children piddled over the floor of the clinic. He admired their gaiety and warmheartedness: he shrugged off their obstinacy, their tendency to deceit, and their callous indifference to anyone but the members of their own tribe.

It seemed to her sometimes that his very tolerance contained an element of patronage, as if he regarded the Africans as too far from his own level to be taken seriously as individuals. One evening she taxed him with this.

"No," he said. "It's not that. It's just that these people live on an emotional plane, and that's where you've got to make contact with them." He grinned. "Of course, I can see it's difficult for you, with your academic upbringing. It's easier for a working-class chap like me."

It was his favorite method of teasing her, to paint a picture of her as a solemn, high-minded intellectual, married to a rough country boy. This time she was too disturbed to be amused by it. "You once told me," she said, with an edge to her voice, "that the working classes looked after their own."

"So they do."

"Sometimes I wonder who you regard as your own. Myself and Rosamond . . . ?" She looked out of the window of the house at a group of Africans sitting on their heels before the fire that burned outside the outpatient hut. "Or them?"

He regarded her in astonishment. "Great Scott, I do believe you're jealous! Oh no, really—!"

He obviously regarded it as a great joke. But she could not laugh. There was just enough truth in it to hurt. She resolved to punish him by being cold and withdrawn, but soon she realized

that even that weapon was denied to her. She was lonelier than
he was. She could not punish him without hurting herself far more.

Eventually even Toffee began to get on her nerves. Though
both his English and his intellectual grasp were quite remarkable
considering his circumstances, his conversation nevertheless became
tedious after a time. He was vain of his vocabulary and he liked
to use it. He talked a great deal and there was nobody to whom
he could talk in English except herself and Edward. He spoke
very slowly and ponderously and he repeated himself a lot.

Habits which had seemed engaging when she had first met
him now began to exasperate her. Like many of his country-
men he had a tendency to transpose r's and l's and to add a
final ee to the end of nouns, so that elephant became erephantee
and Barrington's own name Daktaree Ballington. He liked to
repeat adjectives for emphasis and to connect together episodes
in the same story with a solemn and repeated "therefore" before
continuing his narrative.

One of the problems was that Edward had formed a habit of
asking him to the house every Sunday evening after dinner. This
seemed a harmless enough practice at first and a suitable way of
recognizing Toffee's special position in the hospital. But after a
few months, the evenings began to drag. For all his intelligence
and charm, Toffee's field of experience was necessarily limited.
European ideas and concepts were remote to him, and what he
liked to do best was to tell anecdotes of bush life between long
sensual inhalations of Barrington's cigarettes. He had only a
limited repertoire, and repeated it all too often.

His favorite story was of a leopard which his brother-in-law
had killed with his bare hands, using a special technique by
which he grabbed hold of the animal's tail and twisted it violently.
This, according to Toffee, confused the leopard so much that it
lay dazed on the ground while his brother-in-law took out a
knife and cut its throat. He told the story with much detail
and a wealth of gesture. It was repeated like a theatrical performance, always in the present tense and in an identical form.
Joan began to wait with her nerves on edge, maddened by the
repetition of the dramatic effects, the mime of his brother-in-
law stalking through the bush, the surprise confrontation "and

what do he see—reppard!" Then the eager, eye-glinting grin as he mimed the cutting of the throat.

One Sunday they sat down after dinner as usual. It had been a terrible day. The rain had been almost incessant. They had found termites in a case of cough syrup and had had to turn out the entire dispensary. Joan was sure she had a cold coming on. Toffee drew on his cigarette and began to speak. Before he had completed two sentences she knew he was going to tell the leopard story. It was more than she could stand.

She interrupted him. "You mean the leopard, do you? The one your brother-in-law killed by twisting its tail?"

Toffee paused for a moment and regarded her gravely. "He kill it with knife," he corrected her. "But first I tell you—"

"You've told us before," she said firmly. She felt badly about it, but it had to be done some time. Otherwise she had a picture of herself twenty years hence, sitting gloomily over her coffee, and still listening to the same story, too apathetic to resist. She deliberately refused to meet his eye. "It's an interesting story," she added in an attempt to soften the blow, "but you've told it to us before."

Toffee sucked meditatively at his cigarette. He seemed to be quietly evaluating the significance of what she had said. As if determined to get the whole thing straight in his mind, he said, "You not like hear story about reppard?"

"No, it's not that. It's just that we know it, you see—"

Plainly this argument meant nothing to Toffee. In his world, a story was thought to gain by constant repetition. In an African village, if people refused to hear stories that they had heard before, all conversation would come to an end. He gave a tiny, perplexed shake of his head. It was impossible to know whether he was offended or simply baffled at being confronted by a situation that was totally outside his previous experience. After a long and embarrassing silence, he stood up abruptly and said, "I better go see to dispensary."

"No. Don't go," said Barrington. "Please sit down. There are things I'd like to ask you—"

But Toffee was firm. "Maybe nothertime." His tone precluded further argument. He bid them both a respectful good night and left.

When he was gone, Edward turned on her. "I suppose you realize what you've done?"

"I'm sorry if I've hurt his feelings. But we have some rights too, you know. I just couldn't face listening to that story once a month for the rest of my life."

"His whole life centers around the hospital. "He's a loyal, sensitive chap—"

"If he's so damned sensitive, why doesn't he realize that we don't want to hear the same thing over and over again?"

"God, don't you understand these people at all? This isn't just an anecdote such as you might tell in Hampstead. It's a tradition, a piece of tribal ritual. It's their substitute for poetry. You might as well say that you don't want to see *Hamlet* because you know the plot."

"All right, it's their poetry. But it's not mine," she said. "And I'm not going to be such a humbug as to pretend it is. I like Toffee, but I don't see any reason to indulge him as if he were a precocious child. I paid him the compliment of treating him as an adult human being."

"So it was a compliment?" said Edward sourly. "Perhaps you ought to explain that to him. I rather think the subtlety of it escaped him."

She struggled with the impulse to carry on the quarrel and to pour out all the bitterness she felt at this miserable life and his total lack of sympathy with what she had to suffer. She stood up abruptly and went to the drawer in which she kept the loose-leaf exercise book in which she wrote her journal. She set it down on the end of the dining-room table, and sat down to work on it, deliberately ignoring his presence. Her hand shook as the pen scratched across the page. She wrote in her journal, as if to an unseen audience, of her misery and frustration. In that moment she hated him. It was intolerable that he should ask her to make such sacrifices. She had given up her friends, her home, and her career for him. She had abandoned the kind of work for which she was trained and turned her hand to menial tasks for which she was hopelessly unsuited. But to him it meant nothing. He simply assumed that she should fit in with his own desires and criticized her when she showed the slightest tendency to independence.

As she listed her grievances, her resentment fed upon itself. She began to think she must have been mad to have given away so much and demanded so little. However, it was still not too late for things to change. From now on she would be hard, she would demand her rights, she would insist . . . She was not too clear about what she would insist on, but insist she would. He must be forced to see her point of view. She would not give in again.

She heard him rise from his seat. She did not look up. A moment later he pulled out a chair and sat down opposite to her. After a while his silent presence made it impossible for her to concentrate and her writing gradually slowed down. When he saw that she had finally ceased writing he said, "It's this bloody rain."

He waited for her to reply. When she said nothing he went on. "I never used to mind it at home. In Sunderland it rained practically every day and I never noticed." He waited again. Then he put out his hand and laid it tentatively on hers. "We mustn't quarrel," he said. He spoke very gently. "We're alone here. We have nobody but each other."

"Do you think I need to be told that? God knows there isn't a day—"

"This is a bad time. I know it's hard for you. I know what you sacrificed to come here with me."

He was a man who varied between obtuseness and great sensitivity. Characteristically, when it mattered to him he could always read her mood. It was only when he was preoccupied with his own affairs that he was clumsy and insensitive. She gave way a little. "It's all very fine to say that," she said, still resentfully, "but what does it amount to? The fact is that you don't really care. You say these things when you have to."

"We've been married three years. It's not what we say that counts. You know how much I care for you."

"As much as you can, you mean? As much as you have left over?" It was an old, very deep cause of bitterness between them.

He did not deny it. "You knew the sort of person I was when you first met me. My work comes first because my work is what I am. Without it I'd turn into somebody different—somebody you wouldn't have wanted."

"And *my* work? Supposing I said that should come first too?"

"It wouldn't be true. In that case we wouldn't have married. Women like that recognize my sort of man straight away."

"So what it adds up to is that I ought to do whatever you want if you say it's necessary for your work."

"No, it isn't that. You know it isn't. But this is the life we have. I know you didn't choose it, but you agreed to share it with me. So we might as well do it as well as we can. We knew things were bound to go wrong sometimes but we've got to stand up to them. If we lose our heads when we're confronted with difficulties—"

The solemnity of his manner infuriated her. "Oh for Heaven's sake," she said impatiently. "Do you have to be so pompous about it? Supposing I *did* offend Toffee—"

He stood up and walked away from her. "It's more than that, I'm afraid." He seemed almost afraid to meet her eyes. "I'm afraid the rain's beating us. We shall have to abandon the labor ward."

"Why?"

"The water's pushing up under the floor. One of the walls started to collapse this afternoon. Toffee tells me that once that happens there's nothing much to be done."

Her anger was lost in pity for him. The incident itself was not so terrible as all that, it was the blow to his pride that was hurting him. Yet even so he must be made to face the truth. "So the priests were right?"

"In that respect, yes."

She persisted. "And what about the other things they said— that this whole place is just a dreadful mistake—supposing they're right about that, too?" He remained obstinately silent. "Aren't you prepared to consider it?" When he still did not reply, she became exasperated. "I thought you were a scientist—prepared to examine any possibility?"

"They want us to leave," he said. His face was set. "Whatever happens, I'm not leaving. I don't know how much truth there is in what they said. Nobody can know. But even if they were genuine, it's only their opinion. I'm not Ferguson. Whatever it is that I'm up against here, I'll beat it."

"And what about me? You haven't asked me how I feel."

"Are you saying you want to give up?"

She did not really know what she was saying. At the moment she hated Manusha. She was weary of it. The thought of a return to London was seductive beyond words. But she knew him well enough now to be sure he would never leave. He would never return as a failure to his old life. He would sooner die here, fighting the rain and the drought and the mosquitoes, the ingratitude and the indifference. If she said she was determined to go home he would let her go and stay here on his own. She would never see him again.

And she knew in her heart that she loved and needed him. She could never be happy anywhere without him. It was an unfair struggle. Sooner than exhaust herself and lose in the end, she might as well give way now.

"I'll do whatever you want," she said wearily. If there was to be capitulation, it might as well be complete. "And I'm sorry about Toffee. I'll apologize to him tomorrow."

The next morning she went up to Toffee at the dispensary and apologized. The gentleness and dignity with which he accepted the apology made her ashamed of her own rudeness. She asked him, as a personal favor to her, to keep on coming to the house on Sunday evenings. The first Sunday he was a little stiff, but on the following week his embarrassment had passed and he seemed to have forgotten the incident altogether.

On the third Sunday, he told the story about the leopard.

10

At this point the records in her journal underwent a subtle change in quality. It became gradually plain that life at Manusha had irreparably changed for both of them. It ceased to be a new experience and became a bitter test of survival. Always before, Joan had held at the back of her mind an unspoken feeling that if things went badly they might at least return to

England. But now Edward had made it plain that there was no turning back. Their life, their relationship, and their marriage would be decided in Manusha for good and all.

She had tacitly accepted that, and she must live with it cheerfully. But the sense of adventure had gone from her and she found it impossible to conceal the fact. Even for Barrington, the old cheerful optimism had been lost. Now he saw Manusha not as a triumphal progress but as a rearguard action, a struggle against odds. He was determined to win because he must win and because he could not accept the possibility of losing. But it was a hard, anxious time.

They evacuated the labor ward as best they could, and soon afterward two of the walls collapsed under the pressure of the water seeping from the stream, which now ran continuously behind the hospital. After a month or so the rains began to taper off. The showers became more intermittent and eventually stopped altogether. The level of the river fell and the stream began to dry up.

"Thank God that's over," said Barrington, looking at the high white clouds moving rapidly across the sky. "Now we can start again."

"What are you going to do?"

"I'm going to build a dam." He spoke with great decision. He had obviously been mulling the matter over for some time but it gave him pleasure to announce the plan in this rather theatrical way. "I've studied the ground. There's a place upstream where the water course flows between two walls of rock. It's quite a wide bed and the stream only occupies a part of it. If we can block up the end of the little valley, we can flood it and make a sort of reservoir." She could see the plan fascinated him. He saw himself for the moment as a hydraulic engineer, taming the desert and the bush. "This means we can control the flow when the heavy rains come, and it won't inundate the compound. What's more, the Africans will be able to use the water. You know how it is at the moment—it's either flood or drought. In the rains, the water's no use to them—it's just lost in the river. This way we can save it and lead it off to their maize patches."

Like so many of his plans, it sounded magnificent as he explained it. But experience had made her cautious. "Are you sure it'll work?"

"Why shouldn't it?"

"Do you know how to build a dam?"

"I can find out. The basic principle is quite simple. It's just a question of working out the details."

"You don't think you ought to ask an engineer?"

He became impatient. "We can't afford it. This is just a tiny project. There's really nothing to it. You just dam back the water into a small lake and control the flow. I've read books about it. Engineers are like everyone else. They make a great fuss about what they do, but it's really mostly common sense."

It was difficult to argue with him. He always ended up by laughing at her timidity and her fear of moving at all unless she was absolutely certain of the safety of what she was doing. He was in the habit of reminding her on these occasions that without his determination and his readiness to take risks they would never have accomplished anything. There was something in what he said, she realized, and yet she was still afraid—as much for him as for herself. She dreaded the effect on him of another failure.

A few days later he went to the capital and came back laden with books. He read them voraciously and took delight in explaining to her the details of construction. There was something boyish and engaging in his enthusiasm. He had a quite remarkable skill for picking up the essentials of a subject, generalizing about it, and explaining it in lucid terms. When he spoke about it, it really did seem as if it were nothing more than applied common sense. When he had absorbed all the information and explained it to her, he collected the Africans together and began to give them lectures on the advantages which would accrue to them from the dam. Using Toffee as an interpreter, he painted a dramatic picture of the new fertility which he would bring to their land.

When the rains were over, he recruited laborers and set to work. It sometimes seemed to Joan, as she watched him urging on the workers, shouting and joking with them, and occasionally picking up a spade himself, that he was happier in tasks like this than in medicine itself. They represented something new, a problem to be solved, a hurdle to be surmounted. The Africans set to and worked with far more than their usual energy—they too liked

excitement and novelty, though they lacked his tenacity in carrying it through.

He built a coffer dam of mud, and a real dam lower down of
bricks and cement. He soon discovered that the men would not
work well for long unsupervised, and often he would leave the
medical work to Toffee while he worked alongside them, digging
and cracking stones or showing them how to lay the bricks.

In December the short rains came, light showers that lasted
only a few weeks. The dam worked perfectly. The lake built up
behind the brick barrier, and the canals led the water to the
maize patches. The maize crop was much greater than usual and
the Africans were delighted. They ate hugely and brewed beer
and feasted for night after night. The one thing he found it impossible to do was to get them to increase their acreage and
grow corn to sell, or to store for the dry season. They were
grateful to the dam for making their work lighter. But to go out
of their way to increase their output seemed to them an absurdity.

Once the dam was finished, life reverted to its former pattern.
She found herself almost hypnotized by the routine of the hospital,
the unchanging weather, and the eternal, dreamlike quality of
the African landscape. Each day was long and yet time in bulk
seemed to pass at frightening speed, so that she would look back
and realize that three months had gone by since some incident
that she thought of as happening only a week ago. Relatively small
events became absurdly important, if only because for a moment
they broke the monotony. When Rosamond cut a tooth or Toffee
at last paid a short visit to his family away in the west, it was quite
an event.

The greatest event of all was a visit from the Cranes. Alan had
been asked to deliver a lecture in Johannesburg and they made
a diversion on their way to stay a week in Manusha. The visit
was only moderately successful. Joan was surprised to find how
quickly she had grown away from Olwen. She had been looking
forward to hearing the latest gossip from London and had visualized
long talks about literature and music and politics. But when the
time came she found she could not whip up any real interest
in a new edition of *Ulysses* or the scandalous behavior of Mr.
Ramsay McDonald. She had grown away from her own life in
London and it no longer seemed to concern her. When Olwen

told her of the fight that was being waged against censorship in the theater, she found herself thinking of Mrs. Acholi in the woman's ward, groaning in obstructed labor, or Mr. Dombiako who was dying slowly from a spreading tumor of his jaw.

As for Crane and Barrington, they tolerated each other, but there was no true sympathy between them. It was as if each of them found in the other's life an implied criticism of his own. Though nothing was actually said, Crane knew that Barrington despised his fashionable success, and Barrington knew that Crane thought his own actions were those of an unbalanced crank. It became difficult to think of subjects to talk about which would not cause friction. It was a relief to Joan when they finally left.

And yet when they had left she missed them. She found difficulty in settling down again to the routine. It was as if she had been turned into a hybrid, no longer fitted for London but not really happy in Manusha either.

Living in such close contact, it was inevitable that she and Edward should get on each other's nerves. He himself was totally absorbed in his present life. He hardly ever spoke or thought of Europe. He worked intensely and never tired. He was endlessly patient and understanding with the Africans, and tolerant of the limitations that circumstances put on his work. He did not seem to mind the inadequate equipment or the poor quality of their assistants. He did not understand that Joan should have any less enthusiasm or patience than he had.

She could see that he was becoming impatient with her. He accused her of being apathetic and unadaptable. Frequently she forgot to do things he had asked her to do, or failed to follow through projects she had started. She was wounded by his criticism, the more so since she knew that it had some basis. Her defense was that the projects were never her own—indeed, her life was not her own. It was his, all his. It was all very well for him to make a virtue of shouldering the details of a job, but it was his job; he had chosen it. She had had a life foisted on her, and a life for which she felt she had no natural talent. The talents she had were useless and unappreciated, and they were going to waste. Even her character was being distorted. Because of this unnatural existence she had been forced into, she was being made to seem lazy and querulous.

Like most married couples they found themselves constantly in the same recurring arguments. In the end Edward always won. He would say "What do you want? Tell me." And she could not, because she did not know. She wanted him, and she wanted to leave Manusha. Yet he and Manusha were one now. She could see no way of escape.

*

The following July the big rains returned. The dam filled. The prestige of Manusha had increased among the Africans and more maize patches had been set up within reach of Barrington's irrigation ditches. The hospital was busier than it had ever been. The labor ward had been reconstructed and was in full operation.

It seemed to Joan that the rain was heavier and more continuous than usual. When she pointed this out to Edward he agreed. "They get a heavier year once in a while," he said. "It's the greatest of good luck that we fixed the dam in time. Otherwise we should have had even more seepage than last year."

Sometimes they went to look at the dam. The water was growing gradually higher, but it was still nowhere near the top. "Even if it gets higher," said Barrington one evening as they stood by it, "we can always increase the flow through the irrigation ditches. We have plenty of time."

They went to bed. In the middle of the night they were awakened by roaring sounds and the high-pitched shrieking of women. Joan knew in an instant what had happened. It was as if in a subconscious way she had been expecting it. She put on her raincoat and rushed out. Edward, who always slept more lightly than she, was already outside.

Through the heavy scudding clouds the moon cast a melancholy light over the hospital. It shone on a river of water several feet deep which was flowing through the most low-lying part of the compound. The labor ward had been almost completely swept away. The mud walls had gone, the poles were bent, and the thatched roof tilted drunkenly. The patients were standing forlornly on the banks of the swirling torrent, moaning gently and clutching one another for comfort.

Joan went to look at the ordinary wards. They were all, including the operating theater, several inches deep in water and mud. When she came out of the wards she stood watching the river tearing through the compound. There was a horrible fascination in the sight of so much destruction.

Something hit her ankle and she bent down to pick it up. It was a small piece of the concrete parapet of the dam. Part of it crumbled away in her hand as she held it. She threw it back into the water.

*

It took several weeks, working in the pouring rain, to clean out the wards, dry the stores, and rehouse the patients. Once the water from the dam had run away, the river returned to its original bed and they were back as before, apart from the tons of mud which had swept into the compound and had to be laboriously carted away. Barrington worked all day and into the night, in bitter silence. At last things were back to something approaching normal.

When the rains slackened a little, he made a trip to the capital. He came back with a fair, middle-aged man with prematurely gray hair. "This is Frank Mortimer," he said. "He's a surveyor."

Mortimer looked at her speculatively. He had the appearance, hard to define exactly, of an old Africa hand. It was something in the texture of his skin, the way he wore his clothes, and his air of being in no hurry and not easily surprised. She could feel him wondering what the situation was and what exactly the pair of them were doing here. After an exchange of polite conversation he went off with Edward to examine the site of the dam.

They came back to the house an hour later. Barrington put Mortimer in a chair and gave him a glass of whisky and soda.

"Well," she said. "What's the verdict?"

Mortimer took a pull at his drink and set it down on the table beside him. "Not so good, I'm afraid. You see, Mrs. Barrington, this is one hell of a country. It's difficult for a person recently arrived from England to understand. You're used to the idea that nature is fundamentally reasonable. If it isn't actually on your side, it's tame, it's docile, you can handle it. Here, you'll find, it's not only stronger than you are, it's also against you."

He nodded respectfully to Barrington and went on, "Your husband did a remarkable job back there, for an amateur. He's a very able and intelligent man. He learned how to construct the thing properly, he calculated the stresses and everything. He gave himself a margin of strength that in any sane environment would have been perfectly adequate. In England the flow of water wouldn't be likely to increase more than two- or three-fold, even in a really bad year. But here—" He shrugged his shoulders.,

Hope appeared momentarily in Barrington's eyes. "So it's just not strong enough. If we built it again—"

Mortimer shook his head. "No good. It's not just the bricks and the concrete. The site's unsatisfactory. The shoulders wouldn't hold it."

The muscles round Barrington's jaw tightened. "You're saying it's totally impossible?" he said incredulously.

"It's not quite as clear as that," said Mortimer. "Theoretically it could be done. But the job would be so expensive as to put it completely out of the question. It would be much cheaper to rebuild the entire hospital in a more favorable site."

There was an easy authority in his voice. Barrington was too much of an expert in his own field to mistake the manner of an expert in another. His resentment turned elsewhere. "Why in God's name didn't they go into all this before they chose this place in the beginning?"

"Search me. Perhaps they had a rotten surveyor. Perhaps they thought they could manage without one." Mortimer said philosophically, "Anything's possible in this cockeyed country."

"So there's nothing we can do," said Barrington. "We shall be flooded every time we have the heavy rains?"

"Afraid so." There was a gloomy silence. Joan took Mortimer's glass and refilled it. He said, "I must say I think it was a bit unfair of the bishop. Getting somebody straight from abroad, I mean. It doesn't seem quite cricket, somehow."

Barrington said, "You mean everyone out here knows what the place is like?"

"Well, you know how it is." Mortimer was apologetic. "This is a small society. News gets around very quickly."

"And I suppose everyone was watching us—laughing at us?"

"I wouldn't say that. They were sorry for you."

She could see that this was almost more than Edward could bear. "Sorry for us!" he said. "Damn their impudence!"

"I think it's the bishop you should be angry with. Frankly, Manusha's been a pain in the neck to him for years. He talked Ferguson into it with the promise of an admin job in Nairobi . . ."

Barrington interrupted. "Why on earth did they set up a hospital here in the first place?"

"Because the Catholics were here, mainly. Showing the flag, you know." Seeing the incredulity on Barrington's face, he said, "I know it sounds absurd, but that's the way it's been."

"Absurd? It's infantile!"

"Of course it is. And you're not the only one who thinks so. There's a lot of resentment about it." He paused and then said significantly, "In very important quarters too."

Mortimer looked down at his glass and shook the whisky around in it, with a curious, knowing expression on his face. Plainly he had some piece of information that he wished to be teased into bringing out. Barrington waited for a moment and then gave way to his impatience. "What exactly do you mean?"

Mortimer smiled. "Have you ever met His Majesty?"

He delivered the last two words with conscious irony, mocking the very idea of kingship in this insignificant African country. Yet at the same time, behind the mockery was pride—a king was a king, however comic-opera, and it was rather pleasant to be able to claim intimacy with him. It occurred to Joan that while they knew theoretically that the king was the ruler of the country in which they lived, they had never for a moment regarded him as a factor of importance in their lives. All the Europeans took it for granted that he was largely a colorful puppet, financed by British money and controlled in any major aspects of policy from the British Embassy. Every so often he was invited for a state visit to Buckingham Palace and was treated with great solemnity. Rather more frequently he indulged in baroque ceremonies of his own, riding out of the gates of his rococo palace in a carriage preceded by a platoon of lancers. But beneath the

trappings and the regalia he was still an African. It never entered
anybody's head that he might consider he had a right to interfere
with the medical services provided by the Europeans for his people.

Mortimer went on, "I know the old man reasonably well. I've
done quite a bit of work for him at one time or another. He
went to Eton and Oxford and he's a cultivated and intelligent
man. He appreciates the work the missions are doing, but frankly
he's getting a bit fed up with them in some ways. Particularly
over the location of hospitals. It's only natural in the circumstances."

"What circumstances?" said Barrington.

"Well, as you know, he's a Luako. The Luako run this country,
they always have. Yet practically all the mission hospitals are here
in the east, in Sosima territory. It's more accessible and the Sosima
are more easy to deal with. The Luako are top dog and yet they
get nothing. They're very sore about it." He paused. "If you
thought of leaving here and setting up a hospital in the west, you
might get a lot of support."

Barrington said nothing. But Joan could see that the idea was
attractive to him. To get away from this hopeless place, to put
failure behind him, and have the excitement of starting something
new . . . It called to everything that was reckless and adventurous
in him. Yet he was no fool, and he could feel, as she could,
that there was something sly and calculating about Mortimer.
It was plain that he had come with this very proposition in mind.
It had been planned and authorized in advance—by whom? A
moment later her question was answered.

Mortimer said, "Have you heard of a chap called Bemba?"

"No."

"He's the king's chief adviser. He's a shrewd chap in his way
and very influential. He's a Luako too, and he's very keen to
build up services in that part of the country. If you're interested,
I could get you an introduction to him."

Barrington thought it over. He deliberately refrained from looking at her, as if even a glance between them might imply that
he was dependent on her opinion. She knew this frame of mind
only too well, when he was determined not to be distracted
by any opinions contrary to his own. After a few moments of
thought, he looked directly at Mortimer. "When?" he said.

II

When Mortimer had gone she said, "I think you ought to be careful of him."

He was instantly defensive. "Cautious as ever?"

"Did you take to him? I didn't. He seemed like a second-rate person to me."

"I suppose he wouldn't be here otherwise. But that's not really the point, is it?" He pondered for a moment. "He said one thing to me just before he left. He said, 'You know, you can't beat Africa—nobody's strong enough for that. You have to come half-way to meet it.' I think he was right."

"You could have a talk to the bishop. See if he could arrange a transfer."

"No." He was decided. "I'm tired of the bishop. He didn't play square with me. And I'm tired of the whole fake of being locked in with a religious organization which I don't really belong to. This place is hopeless, we know that now. We can't stay here indefinitely. It's a question of either moving somewhere else or going back to England."

Then why—she wanted to say—why not go back to England? It wasn't too late, they could start again, the Metropolitan might take him back, and Alan would surely help them to get started again . . . But she knew it was hopeless. If she suggested it there would be a quarrel. He would accuse her of faintheartedness and of letting him down. In the end it would change nothing because if he was determined to stay, he would stay no matter what happened. "Are you going to see Bemba then?" she asked.

"Yes. Mortimer is going to arrange an appointment for me in a fortnight's time."

*

He spent three days in the capital, and when he came back all his natural optimism had returned. He and Bemba had taken to each other immediately. "He's a raffish sort of fellow," he said. "Enormous eater and drinker, and the rumor is that he's killed several people in his time. But you can't judge him by British standards. He's the African equivalent of a medieval baron. Looked at in that light, he's an attractive old rascal. And, unlike most people in this country, he knows how to get things done."

He had had several meetings with Bemba, usually followed by gargantuan banquets, at which he had met other members of the king's entourage. He had even had a short audience with the king himself, a small, dignified, remote man who had spoken to him mainly about the problems of breeding pedigree horses. Barrington had formed the impression that Bemba was allowed to manage the affairs of the government pretty well as he pleased.

"He's offered to take me on a safari to the Luako country. There's a place he thinks I might be interested in up there. It's said to be the origin of the Luako people, before they moved east and conquered the rest of the country. It's very wild and beautiful, he says. It's called Kalundani."

*

He left again a few days later. He was to meet Bemba in the capital and they would travel, first by river, then on mule-back, to the Luako country. He was gone for just over a week, while she and Toffee ran the hospital as best they could. He returned late one afternoon, accompanied by two large Africans armed with repeating rifles. They greeted Toffee gravely in his own language.

"My bodyguard," explained Barrington with a slightly embarrassed smile. "Bemba insisted. They'll stay here overnight and go back tomorrow." As he and Joan walked up to the house, he said, "I'm sorry to have been so long."

"Never mind. We've managed. No real crises."

"That's a relief. I visualized you doing amputations with Toffee reading out from the book of instructions. Unfortunately there was no way of getting back earlier."

In the living room he sank back into an easy chair. "God, it's good to sit down on something soft again." He had the contentment of a man weary from hard physical activity. His face was burned brick red and he had lost weight, but happiness radiated from him, the spontaneous, boyish happiness that had always touched her.

"How did it go?" she said.

"Wonderful. Really wonderful." His eyes were dreamy at the memory of it. "It was a hard, long journey. Farther than I thought. We went over the mountains by mule. It's a great country, very wild. The people are wild too, much more primitive than here. They're very tall and dignified. As we went by, they stopped on the side of the road and raised their right hands, in a kind of salute. They never bow, the Luako. But they acknowledge Bemba as their chief." He said affectionately, "He's a magnificent, tough old rogue. I think he loved it too. He's no courtier at heart. We were riding all day and he was grinning at the end, all over that great big face of his. The chaps who went with us were all relatives of his, by one or other of his wives—he has dozens of them. A remarkable bunch."

"What about the hospital?"

"We found a possible place. Mortimer was with us and he did a rough survey of it. It's on a very gentle slope on one of the foothills of the big range. There's an enormous rock face rising up behind it. It's beautiful beyond words and very sheltered. No torrents or dried water courses. No marshes. We'd have to make sure of water supply but Mortimer says wells are no problem in that area. There's a sizable population within easy reach and no other hospital for a hundred miles." He glanced distastefully out of the window. "Not at all like here. There's one thing about Manusha. It taught me the things to avoid when picking a suitable site for a hospital."

Like so many of his ideas, it sounded perfect as he described it. But the thought of building up a new hospital in a remote part of the country intimidated her. She felt helplessly that she was not made for such heroic endeavors. She had neither the iron will nor the physical vitality which were needed to follow him in the way he was determined to go. She felt something approaching despair at the prospect he opened up in front of her. It seemed to her at that moment that he was determined to destroy her.

Nor could she bring herself nowadays to feel total confidence in his judgment. She had become suspicious of these enthusiasms of his. She plucked up her courage and forced herself to cross him. It was not easy when he was in the full flood of a new project, but she steeled herself to his disapproval. "Are you absolutely sure about all this?" Before he could answer, she added, "After all, it's only a year or two since you were talking to me in the same way about Manusha."

As she had anticipated, he was outraged at this criticism of his judgment. "Really, that's ridiculous. This isn't in the least like Manusha. I've told you—" He obviously regarded it as highly unfair to bring up his previous mistake, which he had by this time managed to suppress from his own mind. "I knew nothing about the country in those days. I was deceived. I naturally believed Ferguson and the bishop—"

"And this time you're believing Mortimer and this fellow Bemba. Are you sure they're so much more trustworthy?"

"What reason would they have for deceiving me?"

"I don't know. I don't know either of them." She appealed to him. "Surely you must see I can't just say I think it's a wonderful idea, on the basis of what you said. It's an enormous step you're proposing. You'll be cutting yourself off completely, putting yourself in the hands of some local African politician. Whatever you think about the bishop, at least he represents the sort of people we know, that we understand and are used to dealing with—"

He cut in quickly on her. "You amuse me sometimes. You always say the Europeans here patronize the Africans. Your line is that they're exactly the same as us and should be treated as equals. Yet when I propose to do that, you talk as if they were savages, and I shouldn't trust them."

"You said yourself Bemba was a rogue," she retorted.

The argument lashed to and fro. Like all squabbles in married life, it soon fell into an old and recurring pattern. Points were scored, inconsistencies were exposed. Previous attitudes and failures were dragged up and used as evidence. But to what end, she wondered wearily, as the dispute wore its way along well-trodden paths toward the inevitable point when one or other of them would give up out of sheer boredom. In the final instance, argument achieved nothing. The issue would be decided, like all issues, in terms of power: whose determination was greater, whose need for love was strongest. In the end she could never win. The most she could gain was a compromise.

Eventually she said, "All right, it may be everything you say. But you must see it concerns me as much as you. I'd like to look at it before I commit myself."

"Of course." He saw her demand for what it was, a move toward capitulation. He moved quickly to make it easier for her. "Everything's at a terribly early stage. Nothing's decided. We'll take a trip up there together and look at it. And before that, you must meet Bemba and talk to him. There's the king, too. I gather he wants to be kept in touch. Before I left Bemba he said he was going to arrange for us to spend a few days at the palace."

"The palace?" Two years ago she would have treated such an invitation as a matter of no significance, but this remote life had changed her. It had made her shy and nervous of social functions. She said, "But what will I wear?"

"Don't worry about that. It's not Buck House, you know. And nobody expects medical missionaries to be smart. You'll be a pleasant surprise to them."

Her mind turned over the complications involved in leaving the hospital for a few days. "But what about the patients?"

"Toffee can manage. It's only for a short time. And Nurse can look after Rosamond. She's very responsible."

"When will it be?"

"In a few weeks. He'll let us know well in advance." He added thoughtfully, "We can call in on the bishop on the way. It's about time I had a few words with him."

12

The palace was on a small plateau, several thousand feet high, just to the west of the capital. One of the king's fleet of open Rolls-Royces met them at the railway station. As soon as they were out of the suburbs of the town the road began to climb, making its way up the side of the mountain through forests of fir and tamarisk. Among the trees they could see the minor palaces of the king's innumerable relatives and of influential Europeans. One particularly magnificent building carried the flag of the British Ambassador.

The royal palace itself was on the west side of the plateau, facing out on to a vast expanse of open plain. It had been built by a British architect in the days when nobody was self-conscious about grandeur. The white, Colonial-style building was poised on the edge of the plateau as if suspended in space. Down from it stretched terraced lawns broken up with poinsettias and jacarandas. Far below, the great river wound its way across the plain.

Servants in the king's livery of tunic and jodhpurs took them up to their room. When they returned downstairs, Bemba met them at the bottom of the main staircase. He was a large, heavy man with a squashed, cheerful face, like a good light-heavyweight gone to seed in middle age. The flesh of his shoulders and thighs bulged the material of his dark tussore suit. He smiled at Joan and extended an enormous hand.

"So glad to meet you at last, Mrs. Barrington," he said. It was standard public school English, but with African overtones.

She took his hand and smiled back politely. Yet there was something in the physical size of the man and his almost oppressive self-confidence which repelled her. "My husband has told me a lot about you. I gather you were very good to him on his recent trip to Kalundani."

"We did our best. Hospitality is a tradition among Luako."

"Among all Africans, surely?"

"More among Luako," he said. There was a firmness in his voice that precluded further argument. "We should go out on to the terrace now. His Majesty will join us shortly."

They sat on the terrace for perhaps a quarter of an hour, making stilted conversation. She felt an expectant tension in herself for which there was no rational explanation. It was all, she reminded herself, a ridiculous pantomime. As a progressive socialist, she regarded any kind of monarchy as an absurd irrelevance. As for the king of a primitive African state like this, with no more than a few million subjects, a bankrupt client of the British

Government, he was little more than a curio. To a girl who had once been introduced to Einstein, this was hardly an occasion for awe.

And yet when the king appeared she found herself rising from her seat and naturally performing the half-curtsy that custom required. He was a small man with thin, ascetic features and enormous dark brown eyes. He greeted them all gravely and sat down in the chair that the butler placed for him. Almost immediately, servants appeared with silver trays bearing afternoon tea.

They were served with China tea from a vast ornate Victorian tea service. There were cucumber sandwiches, bread with strawberry jam, and fruit cake. The king himself ate nothing. He sat, with great dignity, speaking very little, while the servants moved about among his guests and the sun sank rapidly down behind the mountain at their backs. Enormous shadows began to sweep their way across the plain. She sat there sleepily, listening to Bemba talking incessantly and occasionally breaking out into laughter at some remark of his own or Edward's. The hills in the distance turned dark blue. Somewhere beyond them lay Manusha, a tiny clearing in the vast expanse of bush. In this luxurious world of the plateau, it was hard to believe in its existence.

The lights went on in the room behind them and she looked at her watch. It was almost six o'clock. She excused herself and went back to the bedroom, leaving Edward talking with Bemba and the king. There was a particular experience she had been looking forward to since Edward had first told her of the invitation and she did not want to rush it.

The bathroom was large and old-fashioned. She stripped off her clothes, ran herself a hot bath and lay in it, the water lapping against her chin. Her eyes were half-closed and she almost fell asleep from the comfort of it. When the water began to cool, she let some out and refilled it from the hot tap. Her body relaxed, her mind was suspended in a blissful, sensuous vacuum. She was only vaguely aware of the passage of time. She was topping up the hot water for the third time when she heard Edward come into the bedroom. He walked into the bathroom and sat down in a cane chair opposite to her.

"Well, that was hard going," he said. "The king isn't the

chattiest man in the world. He has this way of inclining his head and looking at you with those great liquid eyes, without any real expression in his face at all. Fortunately Bemba stepped into the breach. He's quite a diplomat in his way."

She forced herself to concentrate on what he was saying, but he seemed to be speaking from a long way away. She felt as if she was coming round from an anaesthetic. "Yes, so I noticed."

"I didn't think you took to him very much. He's not everyone's cup of tea, I'll admit. Rather pleased with himself. But the main thing is that they really want a hospital at Kalundani. Both of them, I'm sure of that. They think the Luako up there have had a raw deal. And they're fed up with the mission bosses in the capital. They pretty well promised to put some pressure on the bishop."

"Did they?"

"Not in so many words, of course. Nobody ever says anything straight out here. But Bemba seemed to be pretty confident I wouldn't have to worry. So I shall just have to leave it to them." He yawned, stretched out his legs and put his hands behind his head. The cane chair creaked under his weight. "I feel we're really on the right road now. I'm not a religious man. I'm a doctor. I only got in with those damned clerics because they have a monopoly of medical treatment here. But when all's said and done, they're outsiders. They're Europeans. It's the local people one should be working with." He sat up. "I say, are you asleep or something?"

"No."

"You don't seem to be paying much attention."

"I'm having a bath," she said. There was an edge to her voice. "It's my first real bath for over a year. I'm enjoying it. Is that all right?"

"Yes, of course."

She had a sudden feeling of grievance. "I listen to you all the time. About your hospital and your career and your troubles with the bishop and your intrigues with Bemba. I hear them quite often. I expect I shall be hearing them all my life. I don't mind. I like it, ordinarily. But this bath's something special." Almost pleading, she said, "Do you think you could just allow me to enjoy it?"

He looked at her in puzzlement and then his face broke into a grin. He walked over and kissed her. "You're quite right. I won't interrupt you any more."

After the bath she revelled in the luxury of dressing. Her face was sunburned and her nose was peeling a little, but she was able to cover most of its imperfections with make-up. Her hair, fortunately, never required a great deal of attention. The evening dress was one she had bought the Christmas before she had left London. It had always suited her and she knew she looked well in it. If it was a few years out of date, that would probably pass unnoticed here.

She felt an access of confidence. She felt clean and well-groomed for the first time in years. When she had finished dressing she joined Edward on the balcony. He was in his best dark blue suit. It was shiny and ready-made and rather creased from having been packed away so long, yet somehow he carried with him an air of distinction. She was suddenly very proud of him. She saw him in that moment as a unique man, unconcerned with appearances or the opinions of others, unimpressed by luxury or grandeur. He would go down to dinner in his shabby suit and he would still be the most important person present, because he was the only one who had total faith in himself and what he was doing. She compared him with the uncertain, shy young man whom she had first met at Crane's party, the restless neurotic of the first years of their marriage. Success in London had enfeebled and almost destroyed him, while among the hardships of Africa he had grown and flourished. It was little wonder that he was reluctant to go home.

They went down and drank cocktails on the terrace. The British Ambassador and his wife had been invited for dinner. He was a portly man with large dewlaps and shrewd button eyes. The king and he discussed farming and the breeding of cattle. Edward was trapped in conversation with the ambassador's wife and Joan found herself for a few minutes alone. She moved out to the edge of the terrace, savoring the cool night air. It was never quite like this at Manusha. There, the setting of the sun gave little relief; it was usually a signal for a wild resurgence of insect life.

Behind her the lights of the palace were cheerful and inviting.

At the mission the sunset was a time of sadness; the hurricane lamps were yellow and flickering, the forest was all around and she could hear baboons chattering and the occasional cough of a leopard. Once she had heard a wild cry of animal terror and in the morning Edward's favorite Labrador had been missing from its kennel. At the mission the evenings dragged on interminably. One could not read for more than an hour or two, especially by the kind of light they had. There was nothing to do and Edward went to bed at ten o'clock so that he could get up at five in the morning.

In the palace it was like being back in the real world again. She remembered how she had loved to stay up late when they were in London. A servant came up and offered her another dry martini. It was strong and ice-cold and she sipped it luxuriously. Through a window she could see other servants preparing the dinner table—there were at least two of them to every guest. She tried to remind herself that this comfort and luxury was a sign of degeneracy; it was built up on the sufferings of the people. Yet somehow the right thoughts would not take root in her mind. It occurred to her that it might be possible to loathe something intellectually, yet be drawn to it by an irresistible sensual passion.

At dinner the ambassador was on her right and a silent, non-English-speaking relative of the king's on her left. The food and wine were European. The king apologized for not serving local wine to his guests. "We make a small amount on the high slopes of the mountain but it is all exported to the French"—a faint smile crossed his thin, ascetic face—"who label it Beaujolais, I believe."

The ambassador spoke to her with heavy politeness about the mission. She could see that he had a stock of remarks for use at dinner parties. The platitudes rolled out like the phrases in a handbook of foreign conversation. He had obviously sat next to the wives of missionaries before. As the butler refilled Joan's wineglass, it occurred to her that she was slightly drunk. The two large martinis, after a long period of abstinence, had exerted a definite effect.

"Very wonderful work," the ambassador was saying. "You don't know how much we admire the sacrifices—the spirit of dedication you've shown. Like a great number of people I envy you your sense of vocation—the spiritual values . . ."

He looked like an old bloodhound, she thought. One past its best and not even good at following a scent any more. She had an irresistible desire to prick the bubble of his complacence. "Why do you say things like that?" she asked. "You know you don't mean them."

He frowned for a moment. His puzzlement was comic. For a moment he seemed to wonder if he was at the wrong dinner party.

"Yes, indeed. I assure you—"

"What everyone really thinks," she said, "is that we're fools, that we're wasting our lives." She was alarmed at the sudden change that had entered her mood. It had been a mistake even to allow herself to think of Manusha. The alcohol seemed to have destroyed her control over her emotions. A moment ago she had been muzzily content, bathing herself in this unaccustomed luxury. Now, without warning, bitterness had taken over. "Practicing medicine in this country is like pouring a bucket of water on one of those lawns out there. The sun dries it up in an hour. And disease spreads three times as fast as we can cure it. Surely you know that?"

The ambassador had not spent thirty years in the Diplomatic Service for nothing. "Believe me," he said, "I do understand the difficulties you have to face. And I can see it's sometimes discouraging—"

"Discouraging!" Her anger left her as quickly as it had arrived, leaving her with a feeling of helpless sadness. "You'll never know."

"But surely—" He was more human, almost gentle. It occurred to her that under the diplomatic façade he was probably a kind, affectionate old man. He gave the impression of genuinely trying to understand. "Surely you must be fortified by the feeling that it's all worth while. Otherwise how would you carry on?"

"Yes. Yes, I know. I tell myself that. And sometimes it works, At others—" He was looking at her with an expression of concern on his lined old face. The sympathy almost unmanned her. Yet she had to tell somebody. "At others I hate it," she said. "I feel I shall go crazy. Does that shock you?"

It obviously did. The ambassador, like a great many prosperous,

comfortable men, preferred to believe that people who did unpleasant jobs found in them some secret fulfillment which com-
pensated for all the dangers and the discomfort. She could see
that she had gone too far. Sympathetic he might be, but the
introduction of naked emotion into the conversation was embarrassing and un-British. He was no doubt already reminding himself that missionaries were notoriously unstable individuals. She
took pity on him and changed the subject.

*

Soon after dinner she pleaded fatigue from the journey and
went upstairs to bed. She fell asleep almost immediately and
did not hear Edward when he came up to join her. The next
morning she awoke to find the sun flooding the room and Edward
cheerfully regarding her from the bottom of the bed. He was
obviously in great spirits.

"If you sleep much longer it's going to be time for lunch," he
said. She looked at her watch and saw that it was after ten
o'clock. She had not slept so late since she left England. She
put on a dressing gown and went out, yawning, on to the balcony.
Breakfast had already been set. The butler, uncertain whether
they wanted a British or a Continental breakfast, had sent both;
bacon and eggs, toast and marmalade, croissants with strawberry
confiture, and both tea and coffee. She looked over the balcony.
On the lawns below, half a dozen of the king's innumerable out-
door servants were lazily searching for weeds and tidying the
flower beds. "I could do with more of this," she said.

He laughed. "You certainly slept well."

"What a bed!" She hugged herself at the memory of it. "Where
do you suppose they got it from?"

"Harrods," he said. "Specially reserved for royalty." He sat down
at the table. "But I'm glad to see they can't fry eggs as well as I
can."

When they had both finished breakfast, he lit a cigarette and
said, "I had another conversation with the king last night after
you left us."

The feeling of sleepy relaxation left her. She looked at him
resentfully. If only he would leave her alone, just for a day or
two! Surely she was entitled to this tiny interval of luxury, after

the years of discomfort at the hospital? She did not want to be tormented with anxieties and the necessity for making impossible decisions. She did not know which distressed her more—the thought of spending the rest of her life at Manusha or the prospect of beginning again somewhere else. Her mind recoiled from the whole situation. But she had put him off the previous evening; she could not go on doing so. The issue must be faced sooner or later.

"How did it go?" she said.

"Very well. Almost too well, really." He ran his hand reflectively over the side of his cheek. "You know how it is when you want something from somebody. You start off by selling the idea to them. Then, if they get too keen, it almost frightens you. Last night I got the feeling that the whole project was running away with itself."

"In what way?"

"They want me to start straight away. Leave Manusha and start building over in the west. They'll supply the labor and the materials, they say. I said that it was very generous of them but it wasn't quite so easy as all that. After all, I have an agreement with the bishop to give at least six months' notice. Whatever I think of him personally, I have to honor that. And one couldn't just leave the patients to fend for themselves."

"What did they say to that?"

He frowned. "It's not entirely easy to talk to them. Even the king, charming and civilized though he is . . . Things like contracts and promises don't mean a great deal to them, I'm afraid. As for the patients—well, they're Sosima, you see. The Luako simply don't think them worth bothering about."

"So how did it come out?"

"I told them I'd move in six months, but not before. They didn't like that much—the king's obviously used to getting his own way. But when he saw I wasn't going to budge, he took it very well. He even asked me to extend our stay. Rather awkward in a way."

"Why?"

"Well, it seems that it's something in the nature of a royal command. When I said I was sorry I couldn't they all seemed a bit put out. Bemba took me aside afterward and tried to get me to change my mind. I explained to him that I was very grateful but it was impossible." He frowned. "By the way, what on earth did you say to the ambassador at dinner?"

"Nothing very much. Why?"

"Bemba kept repeating that the old boy had told him you needed a rest. Most extraordinary." He leaned forward and peered over the balcony. "Look, he's got a tame cheetah. There's a man wallking it on a lead."

She did not even glance at the cheetah. Resentment had been rising in her all through his account of his conversation with the king. She looked at him, large, cheerful, complacent, and obviously happy to be leaving the palace and going back to his tiny empire in the bush. For a moment she saw him not as a husband but as a rough, domineering stranger, a man who treated her as his property and was only half conscious of her presence. She said, "I suppose it didn't occur to you to ask me?"

"About what?" He was still looking over the balcony.

"Whether I'd like to stay another few days."

He turned his head and regarded her in astonishment. "You don't mean to say you'd have liked it? Stuck in this ghastly old pagoda for a whole week? I mean, he's a character and all that and obviously one has to play up to him a bit, but there's a limit. Last night I thought I was going to fall asleep over the dinner table. Anyway, I couldn't afford another day away from the hospital."

"That wasn't the question I asked."

"What do you mean?"

"You've told me why *you* didn't want to stay. What I asked you was why I shouldn't accept. Me. I'm an individual person. I think you forget that sometimes. You forget that I could have desires which aren't exactly the same as yours all the time."

"But I thought you'd want to get back. I mean, what about Rosie?"

"Oh, I know that. And you know I want to see her. But surely— oh, you must see that's not the point."

She was almost in tears. He regarded her with concern. "But what is the point? Just that I didn't ask you?"

"Oh, how *can* you be so insensitive! It's the whole bloody thing, don't you see? You promised you wouldn't make any decision about this new hospital without consulting me and you've completely forgotten. You didn't even think it was worth remembering. You sat there after I went to bed and decided everything—from the day we'd finish our stay here to the way we'd spend the rest of our lives! Ever since we got married you've done exactly as you liked in everything that mattered without considering Rosamond or me for a moment. I came out here, I left my friends and my country and changed my whole life, because it was what you wanted. I'm not asking for gratitude—I did it willingly because I loved you. All I hoped for was a little consideration—a little recognition of what it meant to me—"

She could not go on. Now the tears were streaming down her cheeks. He looked at her in consternation, appalled at the torrent of emotion he had released. Then he took her in his arms, stroking her hair, kissing her cheeks and mouth. "Darling—my poor darling—I didn't mean it—I never knew—"

She tried to push him away at first, and then, in her unhappiness gave way and allowed him to comfort her. "You've said that before," she said through her tears.

"I couldn't do without you. You know that. I'd be lost here on my own. We need each other. We're partners." His voice was gentle and infinitely persuasive. "If I took you for granted, I'm sorry. I only did it because—well, I always just assume that we're together in everything. In the future it's going to be different. I promise. I won't do anything until you're absolutely sure you want to." He stood away from her and watched her as she dried her eyes. "Will that do?"

With an effort she smiled. "Yes, I suppose so." Looking at him she could not doubt that he was completely sincere. Perhaps at last their marriage had grown up and become a real partnership. Perhaps things would be different from now on. She took his hand affectionately. "Be kind to me, Edward. Be kind to me. I have nobody but you."

*

Throughout the rest of the day he was kind and considerate in a way that reminded her of the almost-forgotten time of their courtship. It was as if their short quarrel had shocked both of

them into realizing how near they had become to losing everything they had hoped for in those early days. He spent no longer
talking to Bemba and the king than was demanded by politeness to his hosts, and soon after dinner they retired to bed on
the grounds of having to make an early start in the morning.
They lay happily in each other's arms in the huge bed, talking
sleepily and making love, savoring their last taste of luxury before
returning to the austerity of the mission station.

The next day they left for Manusha. They rose at five o'clock
and the same Rolls-Royce trundled them through the early
dawn toward the railway station. They had a long and tedious
journey in front of them—five hours on the train, a wait at the
railhead, and then a four-hour haul by launch up the river.
Yet she felt strangely lighthearted. They were going home. Whatever the worries and discomforts of Manusha, it was their place,
and there were people there who loved them. She pictured
Rosamond and Toffee waiting for them at the landing dock,
Rosamond hopping up and down with delight and impatience
as the boat moved slowly toward the bank.

And, most important, she and Edward were together now.
Whatever happened, no matter where they went, whether it was
to Manusha or Kalundani or anywhere else on the surface of
the globe, it would always be home; it would be a safe, warm,
sustaining place because he loved her and had promised to take
care of her. She felt that at last she had truly cut the cord that
bound her to her old life in England. She had accepted Africa
in the moment that Edward had accepted his need of her. And
perhaps one day she would learn to love it as he did.

The journey seemed surprisingly short. They chatted throughout
it with an ease that they had not known since the earliest days
of their marriage. When they picked up the launch at the railhead
they felt they were already almost home. As they thrashed against
the current along the now familiar river, Joan sat in the stern and
took out her writing pad. She began to write in her journal. As
she did so she looked up and saw Edward watching her.

She bent her head down to the paper. In all the years they
had been together he had never asked to see what she wrote and
she had never had any inclination to show it to him. Now, in

their newfound trust and confidence, she felt a desire to abandon all reticence and offer him the key to her most intimate thoughts, even those concerning himself. There was an excitement in the idea, like the excitement of the time when she first prepared to give herself to him physically. And, as at that time, it was combined with a certain apprehension. Would the offering please him? Or would he perhaps find it banal and disappointing?

She knew now that, one day at any rate, she would take the risk. And, with the acceptance of this, her style began to change a little. There was less spontaneity and more conscious artistry. For the first time since the earliest entries in the journal, she was visualizing the words as they would be read by another person.

She wrote: "In the river there is the whole truth about Africa. It changes all the time. Sometimes wide and placid and so vast in extent that you can hardly see across it. Sometimes narrow and violent and cruel. Always it is mysterious. It rises and falls for reasons unknown. It brings life and fertility—and sometimes it destroys. It is beautiful beyond belief—and yet so diseased that man has only to wade in it for a few minutes to condemn himself to a life of torment. Along its banks men live and die, races rise and are obliterated, leaving only the shadow of their bones as fossils in the gorges. Only the river remains, as splendid and ruthless and uncaring as time itself.

"Beside the river are the shallows and the swamps. And then the bush. Brown and parched, at the end of the dry season, the trees stunted and stark, their bark rubbed off by herds of elephants. The high grass stretches away for miles toward the mountains in the west. The thunderclouds are gathering over the mountains—the rain is very near. One can see flashes of distant lightning and the air is very still. The sun is setting and the colors are fantastic. They change from gold to green and then to a deep, threatening orange-red . . ."

The color changes hypnotized her as she sat there, alternately watching them and searching for the words to describe them. They were close to Manusha now and would be home soon after dark. She would be glad to get back to the hospital—she was always a little frightened of the bush after sunset.

The red in the sky was now the dominant color. As she watched it, it seemed to flicker in an unusual way. She wondered if it was some kind of optical illusion. Then the wind changed slightly and she smelled the smoke.

13

Here the journal came to an end. But attached by a clip inside the back of the folder which held the manuscript was a letter. It was dated 1964, the year after Barrington's death, and was from Father Peter Valenti.

The address was a seminary in Boston, Massachusetts.

"My dear Rosamond,

"It was great to hear from you after all these years and to know that you are now happily settled down in Britain and are free from the shadow of the tragic happenings of the past. I, as you see, have been finally translated to a desk job in Boston. Your letter, after some delay, was forwarded to me from our African mission headquarters.

"You ask me to tell you what I can of the catastrophe at Manusha and of your mother's death. I was not, of course, present until the fire had almost burned itself out, but I heard a full account of it from your father afterward. It seems they were traveling up the river in the gathering dusk when they first saw a glow against the heavy clouds which were moving down from the mountainside. At first they thought it was the sunset—one gets some very dramatic and unreal effects of that kind in Africa—but it seemed to persist and increase. And then the wind changed and they realized what it was.

"They couldn't be certain that it was Manusha, but it seemed more than possible from the direction. There was a lot of lightning about and they imagined it must be a bush fire. From experience I can tell you that there are few things more terrifying. They shouted at the boatmen and helped with the oars but it was still very slow going against the current. The foremost thought in their mind, of course, was that you were in Manusha. Your mother kept crying and blaming herself for leaving you behind.

"They finally got to the landing dock and started the long walk to the hospital. As they scrambled along the bush path in the dark the smell of burning grew nearer. They were both scratched and bleeding by the time they had covered the three miles to the hospital.

"It was an appalling sight. Those thatched grass roofs are beautiful to look at but they go up like tinder at the slightest spark. It had not rained for six months and everything was bone dry. The dispensary and outpatients were a mass of flames and one of the wards had just caught alight. Fortunately all the patients seemed to have been got out. They and the villagers were standing around watching the destruction, chattering and crying to each other. To their intense relief they saw you and the nurse among them. You were holding the nurse's hand and beaming with delight. I suppose, to your mind, it looked like a particularly impressive bonfire.

"Toffee was trying to organize some fire-fighting but was apparently having little success. Your father and mother rounded up all the able-bodied people and made a human chain to pass buckets from the well. It was a hopeless task. The fire spread much more quickly than it could be controlled. It demolished one of the wards and then spread across the bush to the house. The Africans dropped their buckets and began to clear their few pitiful belongings out of their huts. Eventually your father and mother were left helplessly watching their home, their possessions, all the hard-won achievements of four years, go up in flames.

"While they had been fighting the fire, the clouds had been moving down from the mountain into the valley. The first they knew of it was a few heavy drops of rain on their faces. Then there was a clap of thunder and the storm began. Even now you will probably remember what those storms were like. No ordinary fire-fighting mechanism could produce such volumes of water. The rain hissed and steamed as it hit the flames. Clouds of smoke billowed up from the buildings, timbers exploded, and damp ash was thrown out into the silent people, standing there in the soaking rain. Within a matter of a quarter of an hour the fire was under control.

"It was soon after this that Father O'Dwyer and I arrived. We had been brought word of the fire and started immediately. Unfortunately the rains had started earlier on our side of the mountain and we had had to dig the truck out of the mud twice on the way over. We found your father standing dazed in the pouring rain looking helplessly at the horror all around him. Occasionally he would pick up some burned sodden piece of wreckage which had been a chair or an article of medical equipment and drop it helplessly on the ground. Your mother and the nurse were trying to keep you dry under the remains of the roof of one of the native huts. It was the only bit of cover left, but the rain was driving in from all sides. As so often in these great storms, it had turned suddenly cold. The heat in front of the fire must have been almost unbearable. Now everyone was soaked to the skin and shivering.

"We had blankets and waterproofs in the truck and we did everything we could, as you can imagine. Quite a lot of the Africans had disappeared into the bush. We managed to pack everyone who was left into the truck and made our way slowly back. It was a terrible journey. I can't tell you how many times we had to dig ourselves out. I do know that it took us two hours to travel ten miles. One of the African patients died on the way.

"When we got back to the Mission we managed to find beds and blankets for everyone. It was obvious that your mother was badly shocked. The next day her temperature was high and I could see that she was developing pneumonia. Unfortunately this was before the days of penicillin. We gave her what treatment we had, but I think her resistance must have been very low. The drugs did nothing for her. In spite of everything we could do, she died two days later.

"She was a kind, gallant, and loyal woman, who sacrificed her life for the sick and the unfortunate. We all loved her. God rest her sweet soul.

"Your father bore this dreadful loss as bravely as he could, but it was a terrible blow to him. He sat by her bedside all the

time she was ill, holding her hand to support and comfort her.
When she finally died he locked himself away in his room and
spoke to nobody for twenty-four hours. I honestly believe that
his life was changed from that moment. They had striven and
suffered together for so long and now he was alone. It is common knowledge that his character changed from that time. He
became to some extent secret and withdrawn. The determination which was so great a part of him was still there. Indeed it
was if anything increased. But it was no longer the expansive
enthusiasm of youth. It was, to my mind, a somber, obsessive
thing. It made him into a great man, in the world's eyes. But he
was never again the man we knew at Manusha.

"The question naturally arose as to how the fire had started.
I fear this will always remain a mystery. The official explanation
given was that presumably some part of the buildings were struck
by lightning. Perhaps. But the lightning, by all accounts was not
at that time directly overhead. There was talk among the Africans
of strangers seen in the district, Luako men whom nobody knew
and whom nobody saw again. Of course, the Sosima tend to blame
everything that happens on the Luako, but the accounts were fairly
circumstantial.

"Perhaps the most curious factor is the behavior of Toffee
both during and after the fire. For a man normally so resourceful
and clear-thinking, he seems, apart from clearing the people
out of the buildings, to have done less than one would expect to
control the spread of the fire. Afterward he was unusually vague
about the beginnings of it, and seemed to revert to that baffling
unapproachability which is such a frustrating feature of the primitive African. In this connection, one has to remember that for all
his great loyalty to your father, he was still a Luako. One can never
be sure how far the tribal bonds continue to hold a man. They
certainly go very deep.

"We know that Bemba was very anxious for your father to
leave Manusha and set up the new hospital at Kalundani, and
that he tried very hard to persuade your father and mother to
stay another day at the palace. Whether, as has been sometimes
suggested, he was in any way responsible for what happened, we
shall never know. He was certainly capable of it.

"When your father went to Kalundani he moved out of my

orbit and I saw very little of him. I went over once when he was building up the settlement. It was a vast job and he worked day and night. He was quite alone. In the evening he would set aside two hours when nobody might disturb him and it was then that he wrote that very wonderful book which was the beginning of his fame.

"Though he treated me with his habitual courtesy, I had the feeling that my visit was unwelcome to him and I never went again. Perhaps I brought back too many painful memories. Or perhaps he felt I had reservations about the whole Kalundani project—which was true. Looking back, it seems to me that the disastrous end to the project was partly the consequence of the way it was begun. But it is easy to be wise after the event. The conventional rules are good enough for ordinary people like ourselves, but your father was not an ordinary man. He could not fit into them. The result was that both his successes and failures were outside the ordinary run. I would not presume to judge him. But at least I can understand better than most people the temptations to which he was subjected."

*

When I had finished reading it, I folded the letter carefully into its envelope and clipped it back into the folder. Then I sat for a while, thinking over what I had read and wondering what to do next. Finally, I packed up the manuscript and sent it by registered post to Crane.

I heard nothing for several days. Then he telephoned me and asked me to come and visit him at his Eaton Square flat. When I arrived there his manservant showed me into a large living room and offered me a drink. The manuscript was lying on a Hepplewhite table just beside his chair. He picked it up and held it for a moment, as if testing the weight of it. Then he handed it back to me. It was impossible to guess from his face what he thought of it.

"Strange," he said, "that Rosamond should have kept it to herself for so long."

"She wasn't very keen to show it to me," I said. "Her husband persuaded her. I think he hoped there might be money in it somewhere or other."

He gave a nod of understanding. "It was good of you to let me read it. Naturally I found it of absorbing interest."

"I thought it was important to have your views on it."

He shrugged his shoulders. "What can I say? It's quite accurate, so far as it goes. And it explains a lot of things one wondered about at the time. Joan was a very loyal person, you know. We suspected that she often found her life out there extremely difficult, but she never confided in anybody. It's only now that one realizes what she went through." He paused. "So far as my part in the story is concerned—well, I wouldn't have described it in exactly that way. But perhaps I was a little pompous and self-satisfied in those days. Early success isn't the easiest kind of experience to handle."

He spoke simply and without affectation. It was in moments of insight such as these that he was at his most attractive. They did not change his general behavior—he was still Lord Crane, with all that it implied in the way of power and prestige and the consciousness of position. The self-doubt that showed occasionally above the surface was not so great as to make him approachable. But at least it made him human. I said tentatively, "Reading this— I have the impression that you always had some reservations about Barrington."

I was afraid that he might recoil from committing himself, but he made no attempt to evade the question. "Yes," he admitted. "I suppose that's a fair conclusion. What I found most difficult to forgive him was his ruthlessness. He was prepared to subordinate anybody to his purpose—not only his wife, but his only child, too. After his wife died, Rosamond came to England to live with us and he hardly ever saw her. I often wondered how much he thought about her. He was totally preoccupied with building up this new place of his. I found that hard to understand." He shook his head gently, as if still perplexed by it. "If he had been a very religious man it would have been more comprehensible. But he had no conventional faith— just some vague notions about the mystical importance of life and his mission to preserve it. He was in love with everything that was simple and primitive and, as he conceived it, innocent. He felt that they were his people and his first duty was toward them. And, for their sake, he sacrificed the people who cared for him most."

"Father Valenti said in his letter that he changed after his wife died. Do you think that was true?"

"He changed," said Crane. "That much is certain." I could see the scientist in him rejecting the simple, one-cause explanation. "But then a lot of things happened at around that time. The move to Kalundani, the publication of his book . . . he became a famous figure and that always changes a man." He seemed suddenly to feel he had said enough—perhaps more than enough. The caution that I had expected earlier was now heavily apparent in his manner. "But really I didn't see much of him in those days. The man you should talk to now is Adams, who worked for some years as his assistant at Kalundani." He gave me one of his thin, autumnal smiles. "I'm afraid that means you'll have to start on your travels."

PART THREE

Adams

Strangely enough, I knew the country where Adams now resided. I had visited it once before, many years ago during the war. At that time one had to approach it by ship. I remembered a steamy, sandy little port on the Red Sea, with a row of palm trees along the waterfront, a hotel with a wooden veranda and fans eternally turning in the public rooms. The sweat trickled down your back as you sat in the dining room, confronted with a plate piled high with tough roast beef and sauté potatoes. The following day you would take the train to the interior. With each mile you would climb a little higher and it seemed as if you were moving out from under a thick suffocating blanket. Finally, you would emerge into the cool air and the sparkling sunlight of the capital, seven thousand feet above sea level.

Air travel had changed all that. Now the 707 took me from Cairo in a matter of hours, and deposited me at a small airfield a few miles away from the capital. Here I was met by one of Laidlaw's innumerable young men. He introduced himself as Leonard Parkinson, and told me with some pride that he was the head of the local selling agency of the company. He was only twenty-seven and had joined Laidlaw as a management trainee direct from Cambridge. He spoke with enthusiasm of the organization and its policy of advancing young men. He regarded Laidlaw with a reverence that was almost touching.

"He's a tremendous fellow. Really knows what it's all about. He has great vision, don't you think?"

I knew that was Laidlaw's picture of himself. Evidently he was capable of transmitting it to this young man. Like so many successful men, Laidlaw had many faces. To me he had appeared as a limited man, a successful financial manipulator perhaps, but of no great magic or personality. I made a noncommittal noise. But Parkinson was not in any case interested in my opinion.

He went on to tell me about the arrangements he had made. I was to stay at the Imperial Hotel overnight, and then he had a car with a driver to take me to the leper hospital at Dirat. It was a journey of about a hundred and fifty miles, mostly on dirt roads.

"Beautiful scenery," he said. "Especially when you go down the mountainside into the gorge. But you can keep Dirat as far as I'm concerned. The mosquitoes down there are something to remember. That's real black Africa." He laughed. "A man can get up a fever down there."

"Do you know Adams?"

"Not personally. I've heard a lot about him, of course. He's a fairly well-known character, partly because of his association with Barrington. It doesn't take too much to make a man into a celebrity in a place like this." He drove in silence for a little while. Then, as if determined to give Adams his due, he said, "I suppose he does a lot of good."

"You sound doubtful."

"I'm not really. I don't want to denigrate his efforts. I don't suppose many of us would like to end our days looking after a leper hospital. But when you go around a country like this, you see how little individual effort means. Frankly, the place is a hopeless mess, all ready to blow up any minute. There's nothing we can do about it one way or another."

"Don't you think we ought to try?"

"No." He turned his pink, boy's face toward me. "Does that shock you? Your generation was brought up to think Africa belonged to you. You feel obligations toward it. But so far as I'm concerned, that's all over. We're back where we were before the whole imperial thing began—foreigners, traders. That's the reality of it. You know who my biggest competitors are? The Japanese. They're not here treating lepers or distributing dried milk or teaching kids the Sermon on the Mount. And they're just as welcome as we are."

I said nothing. There was nothing to say. Strangely enough, he had something in common with Nicol, Rosamond's husband. They were both in revolt against a past that they believed had let them down. As Nicol condemned it on the grounds of morality, Parkinson rejected it on the grounds of expediency. But the real trouble, as far as both of them were concerned, was that it had failed. They had no wish to inherit failure.

He advised me to make an early start in the morning—it tended to get hot later in the day, down in the valley where I was going. "Adams will put you and your driver up overnight," he said, "then you can come back tomorrow morning." He looked at me with a faint smile. "My guess is that one night will be enough."

The driver called for me at seven o'clock, in a tough-looking new Peugeot 404. He drove fairly sedately through the town and then began to pick up speed as we left the houses behind and entered the vast central plain bounded by the mountains of the plateau. Soon the metaled surface gave way to dust and stones, but he seemed to regard this as a cue to increase rather than slacken speed. We tore along, shaking wildly, with a cloud of dust coloring the barren landscape behind us. Now and then, we passed groups of horsemen, herding their large-horned cattle across the plain.

After an hour or so we began to descend. The air, which had been chill and brittle in the early morning, grew gradually warmer. The savanna turned to scrub and the scrub to forest. My shirt felt damp against my back. There was an itching on my chest and when I opened my shirt I found several angry blotches on it. It looked as if I had picked up a flea at the Imperial Hotel.

The leper hospital lay along a rough track over a mile off the main road. It consisted of about a dozen concrete huts with corrugated iron roofs, scattered through a clearing in the forest. The ground between them was rutted by the rains. The Peugeot jolted to a halt and I got out. It was midday, the sun lay directly overhead, and the heat was appalling.

Adams walked out of one of the larger huts and came across to the car. He was a trim, white-haired man with smiling blue eyes and a brown face covered with wrinkles. He wore a bush shirt and a pair of frayed khaki trousers. When he shook hands with me his hand was dry and leathery. He said, "You must be hot and dusty. Come up to the house and have a wash. There's some lunch waiting for you."

The house was a characterless rectangular structure built of brick, with the inevitable corrugated iron roof. The guest room was a square, whitewashed cell, with an iron bedstead and a table carrying an old-fashioned washbasin and jug. I washed in the basin and went into the living room.

A plain deal table in the middle of the room was laid for lunch. Adams bowed his head and said a short grace before eating. The food was served by a silent barefooted African dressed in shorts and an old khaki shirt. He walked with a slight limp and when I looked down I saw that most of the toes were missing from his left foot. Adams said reassuringly, "It's all right, there's no need to worry. He's been burned out for years." He pushed a dish of beans across to me and told me to help myself. "Almost all the people who work here are cured lepers. The nurses, the field staff who go around the villages giving out drugs, and the cleaners. It's a way of getting ourselves staffed relatively cheaply—and of giving them employment. So many of the people we cure find that the only career open to them afterward is begging."

"Is it a common disease here?" I asked.

"Pretty common. It's a disease of poverty, you know. They pass it around the family. I suppose if we could ever get a situation where the parents slept in a different room from the children we might stamp it out. But as it is—"

"You're not managing to control it?"

"Good Heavens, no." He seemed strangely philosophical about it. His attitude surprised me. I could just visualize a man spending his life in an appalling corner of the world like this, completely surrounded by sufferers from one of the most depressing diseases known to man, if he felt he was making some impact on the problem. But without even having that degree of consolation, it was hard to understand how he remained so cheerful.

"Do you have any other Europeans here?" I asked.

"No. I have had, at one time or another, but they tend to leave after a while." He grinned. "They say the climate gets them down."

"How long will you stay?"

"As long as they'll have me, I suppose."

"Did you always want to treat lepers?"

"No," he said, "I got into it by accident. After I left Kalundani, I asked the British Overseas Mission to send me where I could do the most good. So they sent me here. I'd treated leprosy at Kalundani, of course, but I never intended to make a life's work of it. That's one of the attractions of the foreign missions in a way. You never know how your life's going to turn out. You just do what has to be done."

"And when you leave? What will happen then? Will they send out somebody else?"

"I don't know." For the first time there was a flatness in his voice which might have been despondency. "People like me are a dying breed, you know. We're like the mountain gorillas and the white rhinos—evolution is catching up with us. This"—he waved a hand around the austere living room, the ramshackle hospital buildings—"is the end of an era. For good or ill, we shan't be here much longer."

"But surely they need you?"

He threw up his hands. "If you start thinking what they need . . . They need everything. But that's not the point. People aren't always logical." He paused for a moment and then said meditatively, "I've lived in Africa all my working life. Just now I feel it's like a car going downhill out of control. The man at the steering wheel gives a touch here and there but it doesn't make a lot of difference. Do you know that over half the population of this country is under fourteen years of age?"

After lunch he took me round the hospital. "Was Kalundani anything like this?" I asked.

"Oh no," he said. He pointed at the characterless huts. "This is just somewhere they come to be treated. In due course they leave us—or they die. Kalundani was a *place*. That was how it had to be for Barrington. He was always trying to build up some kind of society. I never thought that was our job. To me, leprosy's a disease like any other. I don't believe in segregation. We only take people into hospital when there's no alternative."

He took me into his office. The wall was covered with maps. Here and there were small blue pegs to show the location of his medical assistants. They were ex-lepers whom he had trained himself to diagnose and treat the disease, to hand out drugs and follow up defaulters. "That's the really important part of the operation," he said. "These men live out in the villages. They cover their areas by mule or on bicycles. Sometimes they have to swim across the rivers. Sometimes the rain washes the road away. I visit them every now and then when I can get away. When they run out of drugs they travel to the nearest telephone and let me know. Sometimes it takes them a couple of days. As for me, I'm just an administrator, really. I do a bit of surgery now and then. Come on and I'll show you my operating theater. It'll surprise you."

The operating theater was in another of the huts. The flies battered themselves against the gauze screens over the windows—a few accompanied us as we entered. Everywhere there was a curious, sweet smell, like flowers rotting in a vase. The operating table was of wood—Adams told me he had made it himself—and the theater was lit by a flyblown reflector lamp with four bulbs in it. The theater assistant was sitting in a corner, rolling plaster of Paris bandages. "We do what we can," said Adams. "God knows it isn't much. We transplant tendons, tidy up stumps, do amputations and so on. Frankly the results are disappointing. Not, curiously enough, because they get infected. You'd think they would, working in a septic dump like this, wouldn't you? But they don't. The real trouble is getting them to move their limbs afterward. You just can't get them interested," he said hopelessly. "Sometimes I think they actually prefer to have a deformity."

He turned his back on the theater and stumped out as if suddenly overcome with disgust at the impossibility of the situation. "Why should I bother you with all this?" he said. He seemed to be angry with himself. I told him that I was interested but he shook his head. "You came here to hear about Barrington," he said. He led the way back toward the house. "My assistant can carry on by himself for once. I don't often get a visitor here."

It was cooler in the house. He produced a jug of lemonade and two glasses. He seemed to calm down a little.

"I'm sorry for that outburst," he said. "Just every now and then . . . Well, I suppose you probably understand. The fact is, we all get attacks of depression sometimes. It's not just the hard work and the isolation. It's the knowledge that most of our work will go for nothing. It's a tiny drop of water in a vast desert of human suffering. It's often misunderstood and not appreciated. Yet in my saner moments I know that I couldn't do anything

else. I was really very lucky to be drawn toward this work. If
the results are less than I had hoped for, it's still worth while.
Even if there were *no* results . . ." He looked at me almost shyly.
"As you probably know already, I'm a religious man. I don't see
how I could keep going if I wasn't. And I think one of the
things God asks of us is acceptance. Acceptance of hardship
and disappointment, of failure even. Of course, it isn't always
easy."

It was almost as if he were talking to himself, in a way I suppose he must have talked to himself innumerable times in the
long, hot nights when he was tempted to despair. "One of the
problems is that when you first come out here, you're really
hoping for gratitude. You don't like to admit it to yourself but
it's a fact. You think you're a wonderful fellow and the Africans
will regard you as a kind of savior. But you soon find out that
gratitude's a rather complicated emotion and simple people don't
feel it very much. They're egotistical in a completely innocent
way, just as children are. They take what you have to give them.
They're often spontaneous and warmhearted but it comes out
of *them,* if you see what I mean. It doesn't relate very much
to what you've done for them. So you tend to feel disillusioned
if you're not careful. You feel there's something missing. You
feel a need to make some more complex kind of contact with
them." He thought for a moment. "That was why Toffee was so
important to us. You've read about him, I suppose?"

"Yes. About half the world has."

"Yes. I imagine so. Barrington made him into a famous man.
People used to come to Kalundani especially to see him. He
loved it. Indeed, in the end he got into the way of hamming it
up, putting on a show for them, just like Barrington himself.
But he always had his tongue in his cheek."

"You liked him?"

"You couldn't help liking him. Of course, he was maddening
in a variety of ways. Rather pompous and repetitive—a little
boring sometimes if the truth be known. But you had to remember how far he'd come, what an enormous achievement it was
for him to be what he was. And he meant something very special
to us. With him, at least, we felt we had some contact on something resembling a European level. He was the only bridge we had

with the African mind. He couldn't tell us all we wanted to know, of course, because his education was limited, but he tried. How he tried. You could see him wrinkling his brows and straining to understand and to express himself. Often he appeared not to listen and that was maddening. But one learned that that was because he had become exhausted by the effort of understanding. Sometimes, too, he would revert and become stupid and primitive. Especially if he was ill or upset. He was touchy. But very loyal and affectionate. We all felt he loved us and valued us. As for us, we not only loved him in return. He was, I suppose, our hope for the future. We saw all our hopes for Africa in him, kind and laughing and eager to learn. Sentimental in a way, I suppose. But try doing a job like this without a hope of that kind."

He was silent again. I was tempted to ask him about Barrington but I had an instinct that it was the wrong thing to do. We had, after all, the evening in front of us, and it was plain to me that a lifetime of solitude had built a different tempo into Adam's thoughts from the one we were accustomed to in Europe. Long silences did not embarrass him. The night fell quickly as we sat there. I could hear a diesel generator throbbing somewhere across the compound. Adams walked to the door and switched on the light.

"We had a lot of trouble getting electricity at Kalundani," he said. "That was one of the things Barrington and I disagreed about." He paused and smiled reminiscently. "One of the many things."

"How did you disagree?"

"He didn't want it. He wanted it to stay the way it was. We could have afforded a generator but he wouldn't buy one. He liked the paraffin lamps. They gave a poor light and they smelled. Also they were dangerous. After all, his first place was burned down, as you know. All that thatch—it was like tinder. But there was no talking to him. He was very dictatorial, very passionate. If you crossed him about anything he flew into a rage. He could be contemptuous and insulting. It was particularly disturbing to me since I started off with a kind of hero-worship for him." He shrugged his shoulders. "Of course, you'll say, quite rightly, that that was rather immature. After all a Christian shouldn't have heroes, should he? Christ should be enough." I had to admire the casual, unaffected way in which he introduced Christ into the conversation, rather in the same respectful but familiar way that Crane talked about Rutherford or Niels Bohr. "I suppose I was rather a naïve young man in those early days."

He went on, "I might as well admit that for some years after I left Barrington I found it very difficult to think of him in a balanced way. I almost hated him. I felt that he had destroyed something very important to me. Then gradually, as I worked here alone, my bitterness against him left me. This wasn't because of any action of my own. Indeed, at first I actually tried to hold on to my grievances, but I found I couldn't. Hatred slipped away from me—it crumbled into dust and ran through my hands. And I ended up by loving him and pitying him. Does that seem strange to you?"

"No, not really." I added, conscious of the inadequacy of the remark, "He was obviously a man who aroused strong emotions."

"Oh yes, he did that all right. You were either with him or against him right from the start. It was true of everyone who met him."

"And even some who didn't," I said. I mentioned Carlos Markham's article and asked if he had read it. Yes, he had, he said. It was very hurtful and unfair. It had caused him great pain at the time. "But of course," he said, determined to be fair even to a man who obviously repelled him, "one has to admit that some of the things he said were based on truth." He frowned, as if remembering something deeply distasteful to him. "That story about Barrington being mauled by a lion for instance. Markham was quite right in saying that it was a fabrication."

I was surprised. This had always seemed to me one of the least likely accusations in the article. "But surely, there was the paralysis of his hand? And that scar on his arm. Plenty of people saw it. How did he get that?"

Adams smiled wryly. He paused for a moment and then said, "I did it." Amused at the astonishment on my face, he went on, "Perhaps I'd better tell you the whole story from the beginning. Then you'll understand how it happened."

2

At the time when he first met Barrington, Adams was a shy, earnest young man, only two years qualified as a doctor from Birmingham University. He had been working for the last year as a resident medical officer at a busy general hospital in the Black Country. He came of a respectable lower middle-class family with strong Wesleyan convictions, and his father had a considerable reputation as a lay preacher. He was intelligent and reliable, and was very well thought of at his hospital. He was generally popular, but had been too studious throughout his career, and too busy since he qualified, to have made many friends. For the last six months, what little time off he had had been spent in pursuing a rather pedestrian love affair with a staff nurse in one of his wards. He had vague ambitions to work for his M.R.C.P., but he had not had the money to take time off to study for the examination and there was no time to do it while he was working. Recently he had begun to accept the fact that he would probably end up by marrying and settling down in general practice somewhere in the area.

Yet beneath his sensible acceptance of the inevitable, there lay a core of rebellion. As he lay at night in his narrow iron bedstead, in the cold, cell-like room which the hospital provided for its residents, he read biographies of Ross and Livingstone and secretly dreamed of adventure, of putting his medical knowledge to use in strange and exotic places. Yet it all seemed too difficult in practice. The days of the explorers were over. The Colonial Service was a bureaucracy in Ross's day, and it would certainly be worse now. When he mentioned his dreams to Doreen, he could see that she did not take him seriously. He doubted even whether he took them seriously himself. It seemed to him that they were bound to become eventually submerged, like so many young men's dreams, in the prosaic routine of a job and a sensible marriage and the necessity for making money.

There is little doubt that he would have accepted his fate, and lived out a fairly contented life as a G.P. in the Midlands, if it had not been for a quite fortuitous incident. He was idly leafing through the papers one Sunday morning when his eye was caught by a startling picture. It was a photograph of Barrington, reproduced full-length and covering half a newspaper page. He was wearing the belted bush shirt and slacks which were later to become associated with him and to register itself in the public mind almost like a kind of trademark. His hair was long and fell in a broad untidy lock over the right side of his forehead. His skin was deeply tanned, his figure tall and spare. He was bending down and speaking to a small Negro child, and on his face was an expression of remote, impersonal tenderness. The child was looking up at him with puzzlement and a kind of adoration. The caption beneath it read *"Spirit of Livingstone lives again in Africa."*

There was not much text around the photograph. It gave a brief account of Barrington's career, including the disaster at Manusha, the death of his wife, and his efforts to start again at Kalundani. Adams also learned that Barrington was in England at the moment, raising money for his hospital and celebrating the publication of his book *Sunrise at Kalundani,* which already promised to be a runaway success.

The next morning Adams went to the nearest bookshop and bought a copy of the book. As soon as his work was over he shut himself in his room and settled down to read.

It was not a long book and he finished it at a sitting. Afterward he sat in the gathering dusk, overcome by a sense of awe at the realization of the new and incalculable factor that had come into his life. It was as if the book had been written for him alone. What it said, quite simply and directly, was that his dreams were not the mere youthful fantasy which any sensible young man should put aside and forget. They could be translated into reality, if he really believed in them.

Adams realized now how near he had come to accepting a totally unnecessary defeat. All through his life, in his home, in his education, in his medical training, the pressure had been toward acceptance. He had seen his father scraping through a life of respectability, a life so lacking in incident that it seemed to have gone almost as soon as it had begun. He had come to visualize for himself an existence as a general practitioner which would carry little more in the way of variety or excitement. Sometimes, when he was out in the evening with Doreen, he had been overcome by a feeling of resignation almost approaching despair, as he foresaw the inevitability of his future.

What *Sunrise at Kalundani* said to him was that this need not be. One of the things about the book that excited him most was the realization that Barrington had been a young man with a background not dissimilar to his own. He too had been a scholarship boy with poor parents and no form of influence or family advantage. He too had pursued a conventional medical career for several years after qualifying.

Then, fearlessly, heroically, he had broken away and had followed the dictates of his own spirit. Adams felt a sense of liberation akin to that of a man who has been able to discard a primitive and terrifying superstition. Yet with his liberation came fear and self-doubt. While he had believed that he was incapable of doing anything great or unusual, he had been able to keep to the beaten path and retain his pride. But from now on he would have no such consolation. If he stayed in England, he would know it was because he had not had the courage to break away.

That night he wrote a letter to Barrington. He had no idea where Barrington was, and he addressed the letter to his publishers for forwarding. In composing the letter he made the kind of approach which he thought would be most likely to attract Barrington's interest. He praised the book with a youthful lack of inhibition. He described his situation and compared it with Barrington's own position at his age. He opened his heart about his restlessness and his craving for a fuller life. Money was unimportant to him and he could stand discomfort. He was not afraid of disease. Was it possible that Barrington could find a use for him?

He waited in great anxiety for a reply. When there was some delay, he began to fear that either Barrington had not received his letter or had simply thrown it away without answering it. He wondered (he was still very young and inexperienced) whether Barrington might be repelled by the flattery in the first few paragraphs.

When the reply came it was short. Barrington, as he later discovered, was an eccentric correspondent and all his letters were either very short or immoderately long. They were also always completely taken up with whatever problem was dominating his mind at that time, whether it concerned the reader or not.

Dear Dr. Adams,
I am not so good as all that, as you will find out in time. But thank you. Sunrise at Kalundani is, thank God, a success. My publishers insist that I exhibit myself in the cause of publicity. Also later in America. It must be done, since we are heavily in debt and need every penny.
Come and see me here if you wish.

Edward Barrington.

The address on the notepaper was the Camrose Hotel in Knightsbridge.

It was an exciting letter, but left a lot of prosaic questions unanswered. Barrington had given no indication about the prospects of employment or how long he was staying in London. However, he sounded friendly enough. Adams asked the hospital for a few days' leave to travel to London on the following Monday. Then there came the question as to what he should say to Doreen about it. He had not mentioned the letter, but a three days' absence was another matter. He hesitated. He ought to tell her. She was always saying what a wonderful thing it was that they had no secrets from each other.

On the other hand his instincts told him that her reaction would be unsympathetic. His feelings about Barrington were still very delicate and vulnerable and he suspected that she might consider it her duty to shatter them. He was in no mood for hardheaded and fundamentally hostile questions about what he was really proposing to do. In the end he solved the problem by telling her nothing and leaving a note behind to say that he had been called away urgently to see a friend.

*

The Camrose was a fairly small, unobtrusive building in a turning off Sloane Street. When he got inside, Adams was surprised to find that it was smartly furnished and obviously expensive. He had somehow visualized Barrington as living in modest if not actually straitened circumstances. When he asked to see Barrington, the receptionist made a phone call and asked him to wait. A few minutes later a pretty fair-haired girl stepped out of the lift and came up to him.

"I'm sorry," she said, "but I'm afraid we can't give you a special interview. The press conference finished half an hour ago and Dr. Barrington has all kinds of engagements. It was on the invitation—"

"I'm not a reporter," said Adams. "I'm a doctor." He was nervous and uncertain of himself and it made him testy. "Dr. Barrington asked me to come and see him."

"When?"

"He didn't say."

When she still looked doubtful, he produced Barrington's letter. She read it and said, "Really, he's too impossible. He tells me nothing. You'd better come up."

They went up in the lift to the fourth floor. Along the corridor one of the doors was open. A loud voice was saying, "Well, he'll bloody well have to get it ready, won't he? I mean, if I can get all the way from Africa on time, I can't see the difficulty in getting a load of assorted junk from Thames Ditton—"

The secretary showed him through the door. It was the sitting room of a large and fairly luxuriously appointed suite, and had obviously recently been the site of a press conference. There were bottles on a side table and glasses on every flat surface round the room. Barrington was on the telephone. He looked very much like his photographs, except that he was wearing a dark gray suit over his bush shirt. He still wore no tie. In an armchair nearby there was a plump man with rimless spectacles sipping a glass of gin and tonic. Making ineffectual attempts to tidy up the room was an angular woman of about thirty-five.

Barrington said into the telephone, "Well, tell him I don't care how he does it or how much it costs—" At the mention of cost, the angular woman stopped in the middle of emptying an ashtray and winced visibly. "Just do it, that's all." Then, in a more amiable voice, "Yes, old fellow, I knew you would. I know I can rely on you." He put down the telephone. "Idiot." He saw Adams for the first time. "You're too late, I'm afraid—"

The secretary cut in. "This is Dr. Adams," she said quickly. "You wrote to him. Don't you remember?"

Barrington clapped his hand dramatically to his forehead. He seemed to go into a momentary trance to rearrange his thoughts. Then he walked up to Adams and clasped him by the hand. "My dear chap, of course I remember. I thought you'd be here last week. I'd given you up."

"I'm sorry. I had to arrange time off."

"Naturally. Of course. I know how it is." He swung round to introduce the others. "Now you must meet everyone. This is Clare Wishart, who works for my publishers. And Sam Hargreaves. He's from a firm called Harcourt Samuel who are organizing the publicity. Miss Baxter you've met." He fixed Adams with an intense, hypnotic gaze and asked urgently, "Do you drink?"

Adams was taken aback for a moment. He had not been anticipating an interrogation on his personal habits at this early stage. "No. Hardly at all."

"Pity," said Barrington. "There's lots left. I don't like it myself, but I don't like to think of it going to waste."

"We really ought to send it back," said Miss Wishart. "I'm sure they'll give us a credit on it—"

"No, don't do that," said Barrington. "People will be coming in and out. We need to have something to give them."

"It's just that I have to account for things," she said plaintively. "I'm afraid we've been a little extravagant."

"Don't worry," said Barrington. He put his arm around her shoulders. "Believe me, Miss Wishart, you're not going to regret publishing this book."

"Oh I know. It's just that—you see, I have a budget—"

He smiled. "You can't tell me anything about budgets. You ought to come out to Kalundani. You'd really see what economy is." He said to Adams, "I was up at the Metropolitan yesterday.

They were holding a symposium on hospital construction. There was a big argument about the best material for operating theater floors—you know, rubber, terrazzo, what have you. Somebody asked me what I used at Kalundani. 'Cow dung,' I told him." He guffawed. "You can't tell me anything about budgets."

Hargreaves took his nose out of his glass. "The press would have liked that one," he said regretfully.

"I thought I'd save it for Frank Soper," said Barrington. "After all, if he's giving us a full page we ought to make it worth his while."

"Yes, you're right." Hargreaves looked at Barrington with respect.

"Fine. Well, that's it, I think." Barrington glanced at his watch. "Dr.—er—"

"Adams."

"Dr. Adams. Of course. I think you and I ought to have a bite of lunch together if you can spare the time." He turned to the others. His manner was dismissive. "We shall all be meeting again at the Wigmore Hall at half-past five. Miss Baxter, will you call into the dining room on your way down and ask them to send us lunch for two. Nothing elaborate. Just chicken or something."

When they had gone he threw off his jacket and slumped into an armchair. "What a circus!" he said. "What a load of mummery it all is. But one has to do it. The first law of the jungle is survival. And survival, as far as we're concerned, means money. This book has quite literally saved my life, Adams."

"It should save a lot of lives," said Adams. "It's a great book."

"Nice of you to say so. If you want the truth, the reason I started writing it was to prevent myself going out of my mind. After my wife died I was quite alone, trying to build a new hospital. It was terrible. Dreadful setbacks and nobody to talk to, nobody to share the worry with. I used to work all day, building, laboring, shifting dirt, and doing as much medicine as I could find time for. Then in the evening I was so depressed I wanted to kill myself. So I began to write. I thought, 'I'll finish the book first. Then, if everything's still as terrible, I'll kill myself then.' When I finished it, I didn't know whether it was good or just awful. But I couldn't resist the temptation to wait and find out."

He smiled the happy smile of a man who has had such a success that he has not yet been able to measure the bounds of it. Then he began to talk about himself. He spoke of his life at Manusha, his break with the missionary organization, the burning down of the hospital, and his wife's death. Then of the struggle to build up Kalundani. He had thought that Manusha had taught him everything that could go wrong, but he soon found that running even the most decrepit existing hospital was nothing compared to the task of building a new one.

Kalundani was remote even by African standards. They had to make do with local materials, and built mainly, as at Manusha, with logs and packed mud, and bricks which they made themselves. Only in one respect did Barrington insist on imported materials. After the fire at Manusha, he was in terror of thatch. He bought corrugated iron at the coast and had it shipped across the country at an exorbitant rate.

One of the greatest of his problems had been the nature of the Luako themselves. They were dignified and attractive, but atrociously idle. The men considered any kind of manual work beneath their dignity. Since the women were usually occupied cooking and tilling the fields, laborers were hard to find. There were no shops and they had little use for money. As for working for the future benefit of the community, such concepts were completely alien to them. Work proceeded with appalling slowness. Barrington was reduced to using hired labor from the Sosima country, men who had bankrupted themselves in lawsuits or were working to pay off arrears on the purchase of wives. The small group, himself included, toiled miserably in the heat and the damp. The Luako, for whose benefit the work was being done, leaned elegantly on their spears and watched them, making no effort to conceal their contempt.

It was a dreadful time. At times he really hated the Luako as he had never hated a group of people in his life. Their arrogance was outrageous. They cared for nobody, they respected nobody but themselves. They asked for nothing and gave nothing. They were dreadfully diseased. The incidence of leprosy was higher than anywhere in Africa. They were rotten with tuberculosis and venereal disease and their infant mortality was astronomical. But they seemed quite indifferent to suffering. Even death held no terror for them. They never cried or complained. They would accept treatment in an offhand manner, smiling sometimes in the remote way of a dowager accepting a cup of tea from a parlormaid. Then they went away without comment. Sometimes they were seen again, sometimes they disappeared for good.

If he grew angry with them, as he often did at first, they never responded; they simply ignored him. They made him feel coarse and vulgar. If he had been an African, they would not have argued either—they would simply have killed him. As a white man and one under the protection of their chief and their king, he was inviolate.

But as time went by, Barrington found it impossible to sustain his anger. One might as well feel angry with a leopard for killing a sheep or his tame buck for slipping into the kitchen garden and nipping the tops off his precious stock of green vegetables. The Luako were as spontaneous, as beautiful and as amoral as the animals among which they spent their lives. As with the animals, there was something breathtaking in their unself-conscious beauty. And something tragic too. For it was a beauty, as Barrington knew, that was doomed to die very shortly, to be washed away by the greed and mediocrity of the modern world.

Gradually he developed with the Luako a kind of relationship far removed from the semi paternal affection he had felt for the easy going, irresponsible people he had known at Manusha. In it there was trust and mutual respect, pity without patronage, and love without possession. But no intimacy or true confidence. Or at least not yet. "One mustn't be in a hurry with people like that," said Barrington. "That's one of the first things to learn when you have to deal with them. Wait, be patient. Let them come to you, let them choose their time. It must be their decision, always. It's my greatest ambition that one day, before I die, they'll decide to accept me as one of them."

3

They talked throughout the afternoon. Barrington had no inhibitions about holding the center of the stage and no false
modesty about his achievements. He spoke of himself and his
work in the complete assurance that his audience had no greater
pleasure in life than to listen to him, and in this case at least
he was right. Before an hour had gone by, Adams was already
in love with Kalundani. To his ardent, idealistic nature, the
isolation and the hardships were in no way intimidating. They
were an inseparable part of the sacrifice that he longed to make.
He listened with cheerful interest to the stories of epidemics and
natural disasters, of the danger from poisonous insects and wild
beasts. He would have been positively disappointed if Barrington
had told him that it was possible to live and work in relative
comfort.

At five o'clock Barrington's retinue returned. Hargreaves looked
at Adams irritably. He said to Barrington, "I told you to rest
this afternoon. You'll need all your voice for the Wigmore Hall."

"Don't worry, Sam." He grinned at Miss Wishart. "He worries
too much, doesn't he, Clare?"

It seemed to Adams that whatever Hargreaves was worrying
about, it was trivial compared with the constant sense of anxiety
which emanated from Miss Wishart. Indeed, everyone seemed to
be worrying except Barrington himself.

They went down to the hotel lobby and piled into a taxi.
Barrington talked cheerfully all the way to the hall, while the
others sat in strained silence. A middle-aged woman was waiting
for them on the pavement outside. "Remember, Edward," said
Hargreaves in a final urgent whisper, "these people are a lot of
Holy Joes—they haven't much sense of humor. No cracks about
Christianity."

It was explained to Adams that the meeting had been arranged by the Federation of Religious Organizations. There was a fairly large committee on the platform. Adams sat in a reserved row at the front with Hargreaves, Clare and Miss Baxter. The hall was almost full. A clergyman with snow-white hair and an exquisite voice delivered a short introductory speech.

Then Barrington stood up. He spoke slowly at first. He managed to give the impression of a simple man, diffident in the face of a large and distinguished audience. He seemed to be picking his words laboriously as he went along. Adams was surprised and a little disappointed. From the fluency of Barrington's private conversation, he had expected something better than this awkward, halting performance. But as Barrington went on, he noticed an atmosphere of sympathy developing in the audience, which seemed to be related to the very amateurishness of his approach. From the occasional burst of applause and murmur of approval it became apparent that they had warmed to this massive, sincere, unsophisticated man, telling in his shambling way a story of high idealism and romance. Gradually, as he sensed the sympathy of the hall, Barrington became more fluent. He described, movingly yet with an occasional touch of humor, the development of the hospital and the details of their day-to-day life. Imperceptibly the awkwardness of his introduction had disappeared into the narrative skill of the born storyteller. He spoke for almost an hour. He never once mentioned his book, and it was only at the end of the speech that he referred to the purpose of the meeting.

"I've often been asked," he said, "why I went to Africa. Was it from a genuine desire to do good, or simply to seek adventure? My answer is that to do good in the world *is* an adventure. The life of a doctor in a remote bush hospital is a hard one—make no mistake about that. Yet we at Kalundani have no complaints. We have found there an excitement and stimulation which compensates us for anything we might have to endure.

"As you have already been told, I am not attached to any particular religious creed. My views on religion are personal and private. While no doubt they are important in governing my own life and comfort, they are not directly related to my work. I would not claim to have been drawn to Africa by a religious vocation.

"Why then did I go? In the first place, before I ever set foot in

Africa, I was deeply dissatisfied with all that I saw around me in European life. We were the leaders of the world. We spread our teaching everywhere. The poorer races imitated all we did. Yet many of us knew in our hearts that our civilization was cheap and vulgar and corrupt. We were without warmth or dignity. We had no true compassion.

"I think in my heart I had always known that my future was not here in Europe. But it was not until I visited Africa that I knew without doubt what I had to do. In Africa I saw my duty laid down for me with great simplicity. Every sight, every experience everything I read about it had a message for me. This was the medicine I had wanted to practice during all those years when I had been training as a doctor. It was there that I could see the greatest need for the skills I had to offer.

"My first hospital was a mission hospital. When it was burned down I resolved to build another on completely new lines. It would be dependent on no individual sect or denomination. Our aim would be medicine, and medicine alone. I was supported by my African friends to the best of their ability. They had little money, but at least they had land, and this they gave me.

"With this we were able to begin. But for our continued existence we must depend on money from Europe and America. What we can achieve depends on the help you can give us. I can assure you that anything you give will be used economically. Over the years we have had great experience in making a little go a long way.

"Kalundani is something different from any other hospital. It has no great organization behind it. It lives from year to year, far away from civilization. It is the only center for treatment in an area the size of an English county. For its continued existence it depends not only on our work, but on your generosity and compassion."

He finished to a storm of applause. Afterward there was a vote of thanks, and then the audience began to file out. Barrington left the platform and went backstage. Adams went with Hargreaves and the others to join him. He was in a small dressing room behind the stage. Hargreaves said to him, "You were great. Great. A natural."

"You think it went over all right?" Like all men who have

given a successful performance, Barrington was eager for acknowledgment of his triumph.

"You know it did. You had it just right, with that slow start. I'll be honest with you, I was afraid you might be too slick. But I needn't have worried.

"You've got all the arrangements fixed up?"

"Yes. There are tables at all exits, with copies of your book and donation forms. I shall be surprised if we don't get a good response. I've some experience of this kind of meeting—" The door opened and two men came into the room. One was handsome and pink faced, with a flower in his buttonhole. He was followed by a silent, melancholy man carrying a camera. Hargreaves said, "Ah hello, Frank. Nice to see you. Come and meet Dr. Barrington. Edward, this is Frank Soper from the *New Daily*."

Soper put out a manicured hand and smiled coyly. "I loved your talk. So moving and sincere." His eyes twinkled a little. It was hard to know whether he was speaking seriously. "Such strength. And compassion too. I can't wait to have a talk to you about it all." He glanced at a delicate gold watch on his wrist. "I'm sure you need to unwind a little now. Why don't we all go along for a quiet drink to the Carlton Grill?"

They filed out of the stage door. Soper had two taxis waiting at a back entrance. From that moment things began to move quickly and rather noisily, and so far as Adams was concerned the rest of the evening was little more than a jumble of impressions. He remembered an attempt by Hargreaves to squeeze him out of the party, which was effectively countered when Barrington took him by the arm and pushed him into a taxi. There were drinks in the corner of a pink, dimly lighted bar and earnest conversations between Soper and Barrington, which seemed to be less concerned with Kalundani than with Barrington's first wife's death, his daughter, and the possibility of his marrying again.

When they moved from the bar into the restaurant there was a small but disturbing incident. The headwaiter stopped Barrington at the door and refused to allow him to enter, on the grounds that he was not wearing a tie. Soper was indignant. In a loud voice he berated the headwaiter and the policy of the hotel. He reminded them who he was and who Barrington was. A small crowd collected. Finally the situation was resolved by a stranger who was just leaving the restaurant. The man gracefully took off his black dress tie and handed it to Barrington. Barrington, who had stayed silent throughout the incident, thanked the man with a faint smile on his face and knotted the tie loosely around his neck. Adams heard a faint pop and the flash of a bulb. Then the headwaiter bowed and they were shown to their table.

They ate a large meal of heavy and tasteless food and drank a good deal of wine. Adams was placed at the end of the table away from Barrington, between Clare Wishart and the photographer. He found nothing very much to talk about with either of them. Barrington seemed to have forgotten him completely in his absorption with Soper. By the time the dinner was over, he felt sleepy and depressed. As they stood outside waiting for taxis he said, "My hotel's quite near. I think I'll walk."

In fact he had no idea where his hotel was, but his frugal soul revolted against paying for taxis and he had in any case no idea how much to tip the doorman. "Good night," he said to Barrington. "And thank you very much. It's been a wonderful day for me."

Barrington looked at him as if at last remembering his existence after having forgotten him for most of the evening. He touched him on the shoulder and regarded him with great warmth and affection. "I'm glad you came at last," he said. "Let's talk again tomorrow morning. Come around and have breakfast with me."

Suddenly Adams's tiredness and depression vanished. Barrington had blown it away with a smile and a touch of the hand. He set off happily on his long walk back to his temperance hotel in Southampton Row.

*

The next morning he arrived at Barrington's suite at nine o'clock, which he had decided after much deliberation was a reasonable time for a breakfast invitation. He was relieved to find that his guess had been correct. Barrington was up and dressed. "Order some breakfast for us, will you?" he said. "I've got to make a phone call."

He went into the bedroom and closed the door. After Adams had ordered the breakfast he looked through a pile of the day's newspapers which lay on a chair in the sitting room. He was rather disappointed by the coverage of the Wigmore Hall meeting; there were only a few small news items tucked away in some of the newspapers. But in the *New Daily*, on the page that carried Soper's column, there was a full page feature, highlighted by a flashlight picture of Barrington being handed the black tie outside the grill room of the Carlton. The caption read, "Best-selling missionary author Edward Barrington was barred last night from a fashionable restaurant for being improperly dressed. Barrington's tieless bush shirt shocked headwaiter Charles Romero. 'The Carlton has its standards,' he said. Fortunately "Pat" Drummond, polo player and friend of the Prince of Wales, rose to the situation. What might have been an embarrassing moment . . ."

Barrington came in from the bedroom and saw the paper in his hand. "Very unfortunate, that," he said. "It was Sam's fault really. He told me I should be all right. I wouldn't have put it past him to have fixed the whole thing."

He sounded a little shamefaced about the incident. Yet Adams could not forget the placid, undisturbed expression on his face at the time. If he had not anticipated what was going to happen, he had certainly accepted it with remarkable aplomb.

Fortunately, before they could discuss the matter further, the breakfast arrived. Throughout the meal they talked of the meeting at the Wigmore Hall and its results. There had evidently been a satisfactory response to the appeal. "But the real money isn't here," said Barrington. "Not nowadays. It's in America. That's where I shall have to go. I'm leaving in a week's time on the *Queen Mary*." He poured himself a second cup of coffee. "So there isn't much time and we'd better decide things now. Are you really sure you want to come to Kalundani?"

"Yes. Yes, I'm sure."

"For life?"

"If you'll have me," said Adams. He added awkwardly, "I'm nothing very special, you know. I mean, I'm just—"

"Oh, I know what you are. I've looked up your record in the Medical Directory. I've talked to you. You're a provincial lad like myself. You're shy and inexperienced, but you're not soft. The main thing is—why do you want to do this?"

Adams felt the temptation, so common in ambitious young men, to try to project into Barrington's mind and give him the answer he wanted—to talk himself into the job. Then he realized

how ridiculously frivolous this would be. After all, he was deciding
his whole life at this moment. "Frankly," he said slowly, "I'm
not too sure. But when I listened to what you said last night—
about why you went to Africa—it seemed to say something very
important to me." He paused. Barrington waited patiently for
him to arrange his thoughts. "I think what I mean is—well,
what I see here just isn't good enough for me—not for the only
existence I have. I don't know if that sounds arrogant, but it's
what I feel. I'm prepared to gamble my life on the hope of doing
something better."

"You might lose, you know," said Barrington.

"Yes. I know that. But it's a chance I want to take."

Barrington nodded. He seemed satisfied. Adams wondered
whether what he had said had really made very much difference.
He suspected that Barrington was the kind of man who made
his choices on an instinctive rather than a logical basis. He felt
that he had been accepted, and he was almost shocked at the
casual way in which Barrington was obviously prepared to make
such a momentous decision. He felt he wanted to warn Barrington
to be more cautious, to get to know him better before placing
so much confidence in him.

"Are you married?" asked Barrington.

"No." Then he qualified it. "Well, not exactly."

"You're planning to marry?"

"Yes." He supposed he was. Certainly Doreen thought he was.
But put in these blunt terms, it frightened him a little. He had
been visualizing it as something which could be put off for some
years. Safe behind the barrier of his poverty, he had felt confident
in his ability to delay any serious commitment.

"That's important, you know," said Barrington. "You shouldn't
take a woman out to a place like Kalundani unless she's absolutely
convinced that she wants to go."

"I suppose not."

"In the bush, a wife can be either a tremendous help to a man
—or an absolute disaster." He paused. "When I first went out
there, I was lucky enough to have a wife who was utterly
devoted to the work. She was like a rock. She was afraid of
nothing. Sometimes I felt like giving up, but she never did." His
eyes misted over. He was obviously deeply moved. "Eventually,

of course, as you know she gave her life. But she never complained and I don't believe she had a single regret. Even at the end, when we seemed to have lost everything, she never gave up hope."

Adams had a picture of Mrs. Barrington as a tall, fair-haired Diana, smiling and serene, resourceful, tender, uncomplaining. He compared this magnificent, invulnerable woman with the Doreen he knew so well. He loved and admired Doreen, of course; that went without saying. She was loyal and sensible and devoted to him. And yet . . . Somehow it was difficult to see her in this particular role. "I'll speak to her," he said. "She'll have to make up her own mind what she does."

*

As he traveled home in the train, he felt he knew what she would say. The more he thought of it, the less likely it seemed that she would be attracted by the thought of spending the rest of her life in Central Africa. She was a neat, conventional girl, fond of children and deeply (indeed, he sometimes thought pathologically) attached to her mother. She liked cleanliness, tidiness, and plain food. She thought foreigners dirty and unreliable. She was looking forward to the life of a respectable G.P. in Edgbaston. Somehow he could not see the idea of Kalundani appealing to her.

It was a tragic dilemma, he thought. He knew he should feel very concerned about it and he tried to direct his mind to the problem it presented. But he had had an exhausting two days and there was something hypnotic about the regular, rhythmic noise of the train as it clattered its way through the Home Counties toward the industrial Midlands. Very soon he was asleep, dreaming of Africa.

4

In the end it was six months before Adams was able to leave
for Kalundani. He had to work out his contract at the hospital,
buy clothes and other necessities of tropical life, and take his
leave of his parents. As he had predicted, Doreen refused to go
with him. There were tearful scenes as she tried to dissuade
him, and a final parting marked more by embarrassment than
depth of emotion. He missed her for a fortnight and then forgot her almost completely in the rush and bustle of departure.

While he waited, he followed Barrington's progress in the newspapers. If the British appearances had been a success, his progress
on the other side of the Atlantic could only be described as a
triumph. The American critics, less disturbed than the British
by the exhibition of naked emotion, had no inhibitions in categoriz-
ing *Sunrise at Kalundani* as a work of genius. Barrington himself
was lionized by society and worshiped by the newspaper-reading
public. His flamboyant presence captivated the matrons of Mid-
west towns as he covered the continent on a lecture tour. He read
extracts from his book to hushed audiences in university lecture
halls, delivered graphic accounts of the splendors and miseries of
life in the bush, and made eloquent appeals for money. He was
photographed with society ladies in New York, political hostesses
in Washington, and film stars in Hollywood. It was said that the
film rights of the book had been sold for an immense sum, and
that Ronald Colman was being approached to play the leading
part. It was rumored that Barrington had already received millions
of dollars of financial support, not to mention several hundred
offers of marriage.

The magnitude of the publicity began to alarm Adams. He
was pleased about Barrington's success, but could not help feeling
that perhaps Barrington might now have grown beyond needing
his help. He thought several times of writing to offer Barrington

a release from his promise. But in the end he was relieved to receive a typically laconic note, written from a hotel in San Diego, California.

Dear Brian,

Nearing the end of all this, thank God. One more week and then back to sanity. Don't believe a tenth of the rubbish you read about me in the papers. I look forward to seeing you as soon as you can get to Kalundani. Let's get to work and forget all this nonsense.

Yours E.B.

P.S. One good thing is that I can now afford to pay your fare. I have told my British publishers to fix everything.

*

He covered the same laborious route as Barrington and Joan had taken when they first went out to Manusha. But now the railway had been extended farther into the interior, and a bridge had been built over the great river. The new railhead was eighty miles from Kalundani. The train, to nobody's apparent surprise, arrived two hours late. He found a white woman waiting on the platform to greet him. She was plain and fair, rather dumpy in figure and aged between forty and fifty. She wore a khaki dress, flat-heeled shoes, and the kind of white linen hat which seems to be confined to district nurses and croquet internationals. "Dr. Adams?" she said, more as a statement than a question. She spoke in a sharp, no-nonsense voice, with a perceptible Scots accent. "I'm Jane Nairn. I run the nursing side of Kalundani. I imagine that Dr. Barrington has told you about me."

"Yes, of course." In fact Barrington had hardly spoken of her at all. He had mentioned, in his vague way, "a sister qualified in Edinburgh—tremendous hard worker," and then passed on to other matters he obviously found more interesting. "He said you were a tower of strength," said Adams diplomatically.

His diplomacy was wasted. "And so he should," she said in a testy voice. "It's lucky there's somebody there to put a bit of order into the place. Where's your luggage?" When he pointed to a pair of battered fiber suitcases standing on the platform, she said, "Get the porter to bring them out to the car. And don't give him more than sixpence. They don't expect it."

The car was a sturdy little Morris Oxford tourer. The porter heaved the suitcases into the back, where they were presently joined by a collection of miscellaneous stores and equipment which had arrived by the same train. When the car was fully loaded Adams got into the passenger seat beside Miss Nairn. She started the engine and they chugged off down the street of the little town, scattering a sow and a brood of black piglets that were scavenging in the gutter. "It's a good little bus," said Miss Nairn. "Fairly new, too. One of the first things he bought with the advance from his book. But how long it's going to last on these roads, only the good Lord knows."

They rattled along at a speed of about twenty miles an hour on the crude dirt road. After a while it began to rain and she put up the hood. "I hope you know what you've let yourself in for," she said.

There was no satisfactory answer to this, so he said nothing. He was not too disturbed by her abruptness and her lack of grace. He had worked for five years in hospital, three as a student and two as a doctor, and he had some knowledge of hospital sisters. If he had to choose between competence and charm he preferred competence. He still knew nothing about her qualities as a nurse, but he was at least impressed by her businesslike handling of the car.

"It's not exactly as romantic as he makes out in his book, you know."

"I suppose not."

"No suppose about it. It's grinding hard work, twelve hours a day, seven days a week. No pretty girls and picture shows. Nothing but blacks, and very primitive ones at that. Do you really think you can stick it?"

"If you can stick it," said Adams, slightly stung, "I don't see why I shouldn't."

"I don't claim any credit for myself," she said. "It's the Lord that helps me. I hope for your sake you have a faith to sustain you."

"I think I have."

"What are you, then. Church or Chapel?"

"My family are Methodists."

"Well at least you'll be able to sing hymns," she said grudgingly. "I'm from the Free Church of Scotland myself. But Jesus Christ watches over us all."

"What about Barrington?"

"He says he doesn't hold with organized religion. But I know he believes in his heart. He's a very obstinate willful man, you know." She blew the horn irascibly as a pair of African children ran screaming across the path of the car. In the tone of one remembering an old grievance, she said, "He never forgave me for setting up the chapel."

"Why not?"

"Because I was too much for him, that's why. And he doesn't like that. You'll find out in due time." She set her jaw and twisted the wheel violently to negotiate some deep ruts. "I pestered him to set up a place of worship and he wouldn't. In the end he said 'All right, you can do it if you can get the natives to build it for you.' Never thinking they would, you see. They're all as idle as dirt. But I got round the headman and they built it for me in the end. Now it's there and he can't do anything about it." She paused, brooding grimly over her triumph. "But he can be spiteful when he's that way out. You know he never mentioned me in that book of his?"

"No?"

"No. Not that I care. It's nothing to me to be mentioned in a book. But it was petty, I thought." The rain was coming down fast now. She turned on the wipers. "And all that stuff about Toffee. He's a good fellow, for a native. But that's no reason to give him a swollen head."

"He sounded very attractive from Dr. Barrington's account."

She shrugged irritably. "He's a good enough lad. You just have to remember to show him who's the doctor. If you don't run him, he'll run you." They came to an incline with a morass of clay interspersed with puddles at the bottom. She changed into low gear and took a run at it. They crashed up the slope, spraying mud out behind them. "The one thing I will say—he comes to my Sunday hymn singing, punctual as a clock. I hope I can persuade you to come too."

Adams smiled noncommittally. He had no desire to commit

himself at this stage to any particular course of action, certainly not one that might annoy Barrington. The picture she painted of the hospital was all too plausible to one accustomed to living, as he had, in enclosed communities. This was another side to Kalundani; while lacking the romance of Barrington's book, it had nevertheless an awful ring of truth. It occurred to him that in his mental preparation for mission life he had perhaps concentrated too much on facing up to the larger and more spectacular crosses he would have to bear—isolation, danger, and disease. He had neglected the smaller, but over a long period perhaps equally exhausting minor irritations inseparable from an institutional life.

They arrived at Kalundani in the late afternoon. The rain had stopped now. They drove across a flat plain with elephant grass high on either side of the road, blocking their view. Over to the west, growing gradually nearer, were the foothills of the vast range of mountains which split the continent in two and acted as a watershed for the great lake and river system which drained the central plateau. Every now and then the high grass would give way, for no apparent reason, to a stretch of barren and sandy scrub. Then the country would open up for a short time in front of them. On one of these occasions Miss Nairn pointed over to the northwest. "There it is. Do you see it? The rock."

In the distance Adams saw a colossal mass of stone, standing like a sentry guarding the entrance to the foothills of the range. Lying beneath its shadow were a few tiny white buildings. He caught the flash of sunlight reflected from a metal roof. "That's the place," she said. "That's Kalundani."

There were still several miles to go across the plain. Eventually she turned the car off the main road into a side turning that was little better than a mule track. She stopped and engaged low gear. "Hold on to your hat now," she said.

For two miles they shook and rattled along the rocky surface, through the puddles and ruts. Then they emerged from the scrub and the full beauty of the place broke upon them.

The rock face was sheer and vertical, rearing several hundred feet into the air. Here and there, shrubs and tiny trees had taken root in cracks in the stone, and near the foot a small underground stream gushed out to form a waterfall which poured into the meadow at the side of the hospital. The hospital itself was in shadow now. The sun had set behind the rock, though the valley below was still bathed in light. The hospital buildings were long and low, and arranged one below the other on the hillside in terraced rows. They were of simple construction, with corrugated iron roofs, but the roofs had been extended forward over the front of the buildings to form shady awnings which were supported every fifteen feet or so by wooden poles. There were houses dotted about around the main buildings, and the whole effect was that of a small, neat village rather than a hospital. Adams had seen photographs of it, but they had not done justice to the magnificence of the site or the quiet distinction of the architectural concept.

"It's beautiful," he said, as the car stopped in front of the main buildings. "Magnificent." All his youthful reverence for Barrington came back in a flood of emotion. "And to think he did it all himself—"

"He and a few others," said Miss Nairn dryly. "Oh, it's a fine place. I'm not denying that. But wait a wee while until you've worked in it. You'll find there's a lot still needs doing." She looked up the path leading to a house that stood slightly apart from the other buildings. "Ah, here comes the man himself."

Barrington strode down the path toward them. He was a little leaner and more sunburned than he had been in London. He came up to Adams and shook him by the hand. "Welcome to Kalundani," he said. "It's good to see you." He turned to Miss Nairn and said, in a more prosaic tone, "I was wondering what had happened to you."

"The train was late, as usual," she said.

"I hoped that was all it was." He said to Adams, "I live in fear of that car breaking down."

It occurred to Adams that without knowing it he might already have been in danger. If the car had failed, he and Miss Nairn might have been stranded out there in the open empty valley, with darkness falling, no food and water, and surrounded by hyenas and leopards. Barrington, who knew the country, had been more anxious than he had. "We'd have managed somehow," he said heroically.

"I wasn't thinking of you," said Barrington. "I was thinking of the car. It's my only means of bringing in supplies." His first formal greeting over, his manner was almost offhand. "Well, how are you? Fit? All ready to work?" When Adams nodded, he said, "Fine. Well, perhaps you'd better start the way you'll have to go on, and carry some of these stores in. I've got to go and mend the water pump."

He turned his back and loped off up the path. Adams felt a little deflated. This abruptness was all rather different from London. He had been unconsciously visualizing an affecting scene of reunion, with the two of them sitting in armchairs and discussing in a leisurely fashion their future plans for the hospital. He saw Miss Nairn's eyes on him, as if she were only too well aware of his discomfiture. "Don't take any notice of that," she said reassuringly. "I'll get one of the boys to hump this stuff in a minute. Come along and I'll show you your room."

She took him to the European living quarters on the north side of the compound. These consisted of four houses, of more or less equal size. One belonged to Barrington, one was occupied by Sister Nairn and her assistant. Nurse Macready. The third contained a communal dining room and sitting room, and the fourth was the one where Adams himself was to live.

"You'll have to share it with poor old Carl," said Miss Nairn. "I hope you won't mind too much."

"Carl?" said Adams, rather taken aback. "Barrington never said anything—"

"He hasn't been here long. He's an inoffensive wee fellow. A Swede or one of those things. A bit odd, but harmless with it. He turned up one day out of the blue and said he wanted to find his soul. The doctor was too softhearted to turn him away. He does a bit of work in return for his keep. You'll find he doesn't get in your way much."

The house contained two bare but reasonably spacious bed-sitting rooms. The one he was to occupy was cheaply and simply furnished, but no more so than the rooms in most British hospital residences. It at least had the merit of a magnificent view through the window, which faced north down the valley. Looking out he could see the great rock towering over him to the west of the hospital.

Miss Nairn showed him the bathroom, an ancient tub with a jug beside it which was filled with hot water each morning by one of the hospital servants—and the earth closet outside the back door of the little house. Then she left him. He washed in a china basin in the bedroom and then began to unpack his suitcases. He did not have many possessions, and most of what he did have had not seemed worth while carrying all the way to Central Africa. The contents of the suitcases were mostly clothes, with a few keepsakes and some photographs of his parents and Doreen.

He took out the clothes and stacked them neatly in the chest of drawers and the wardrobe. He had taken advice from one of the missionary organizations as to what he ought to bring with him. Now that he had arrived, the linen jacket and gray flannels that he had worn for the journey seemed somehow inappropriate. He decided to change before meeting the others for dinner. He put on a pair of drill trousers and a bush shirt and looked at himself in the mirror. Now at last he felt that he was really entering into his new life. His face was tanned from the voyage and he did not look too inappropriate in the garb of a bush doctor. There was only one thing that slightly disturbed him— with his collar buttoned up to the neck, he looked a little too much like a pocket version of Barrington. After some consideration, he decided to leave his collar open.

5

"What I'd like you to do," said Barrington, "is to give me your absolutely frank opinion as to how you think we can improve the hospital."

It was almost the exact scene that Adams had visualized on his first arrival at the hospital. The conference after dinner in the sitting room of Barrington's house; Barrington smoking one of the cigarettes that he rolled from native tobacco, while he himself puffed at the pipe he had so recently, and not very confidently, taken up. But in the event, Barrington had staved off any attempts to discuss general matters for the first month of Adams's stay. "It's all too new," he had explained. "You'll have to work here for several weeks at least before you can even begin to understand the problems we face. Just get yourself dug in. Keep an open mind. Then, when you've sorted your ideas out, we can start talking."

During the past weeks Adams had often felt impatient at Barrington's restriction on comment, but now that the time had come, he was a little nervous about expressing himself. The fact was that his experiences since the day of his arrival had consisted almost entirely of disillusion. He had expected poor facilities and a very basic standard of medicine. He was actually looking forward to improvisation. What he had not anticipated for a moment was a standard of care which seemed to him unnecessarily crude and old-fashioned. It was hard to realize, from some of the things that went on, that only just over ten years ago Barrington had been one of the most promising first assistants in the Metropolitan Hospital.

At the beginning he learned most of the running of the hospital from Miss Nairn. Barrington expressed great willingness to show him things, but in the event he always seemed to be busy organizing some construction job or mending machinery or settling a tribal dispute for the local chief. It was the rule rather than the exception for him to be called away in the middle of his daily outpatient session, and to leave the rest of it to Adams or Sister. There was little time to think or to discuss individual problems of treatment. The queues of patients outside the clinic seemed endless. Examinations were cursory and treatment was highly standardized. Barrington had instituted a system of codes for the common diseases and their treatment. An S or a B stamped across a patient's card entitled him to a course of injections from Toffee for syphilis or bilharzia. If the condition failed to respond, he was referred back to the doctor; if the symptoms cleared up he was never seen again. Charges were made for treatment by means of a bus ticket machine at the entrance to the hospital, an arrangement of which Barrington was inordinately proud. A sixpenny ticket entitled a patient to a consultation and treatment. If Barrington decided he had had his sixpennyworth or was a man of means, he would make him buy another. It was all, Adams found, very arbitrary and casual, and not at all like the description of Kalundani in Barrington's book.

Each morning was spent in the outpatient department, a bare, whitewashed room with a veranda outside on which the patients squatted, waiting patiently for hours throughout the morning, feeding their children at the breast, laughing and gossiping. All over the walls were crude colored drawings designed as an attempt at health education. Sister Nairn and Carl had drawn pictures with simple captions to demonstrate the symptoms of smallpox and malnutrition, and the correct food to give to a child. Each time a new one was put up the patients looked at it in great excitement, pointed at it, giggled, and showed it to one another; then, once it had ceased to be a novelty, they never looked at it again.

The patients suffered from a bewildering variety of diseases; almost all of them had several things wrong with them, and it was not easy to decide on the exact origin of the symptoms. All of them, without exception, had enlarged spleens from chronic malaria, and the majority of the adults, male and female, had gonorrhea. Tuberculosis was common, and most of their legs were scarred from old tropical sores. Treatment frequently turned out to be ineffective, even in curable conditions. It was always a gamble as to whether they would follow the instructions given to them. Only too frequently they would drink the liniment, or sell the medicine, or throw the tablets away.

In the wards the crowding and the squalor were oppressive. Everywhere Adams smelled the sweet, nauseating odor of sickness and poverty. At first it disgusted him, then he grew used to it and after a while he was no longer conscious of it. There were a hundred beds in the hospital, but there were over double that number of patients—those who could not find beds lay like bundles of rags on filthy mattresses on the mud floor. In the area around the wards there were shelters for the relatives, no more than sheets of corrugated iron supported by poles, to keep out the rain. When it was wet the families of the patients huddled miserably under this inadequate shelter; when it was fine they spread themselves on the grass outside. They cooked their own food in cooking pots balanced on a tripod of three stones. They lived almost entirely on a thick maize porridge, with which they ate a relish of peppers and ground nuts, mixed sometimes with a little dried fish or meat.

In the afternoons the doctors visited the wards, after which there was an operating list in the hut that did duty as a theater. There was only one aged sterilizer, a gift from a manufacturer who had chosen Kalundani as a philanthropic alternative to the junkyard. There were a few patched sets of rubber gloves, which were restricted to septic cases and worn by the surgeons as a protection for their own hands rather than to keep infection from the wounds.

Barrington's own surgical technique was rapid and effective, but had grown a little slapdash over the years. Adams was shocked to find that he performed a Caesarean section in almost all cases of difficult labor, sooner than involve himself in the intricacies of a forceps delivery. He was also surprised to find that Sister Nairn herself was in the habit of performing emergency operations, with surprising confidence and skill. He was unable to conceal his astonishment. "Do you often do this?" he asked, when she suggested that she should take out an appendix while he finished the outpatient clinic. She smiled sardonically at his innocence. "Who do you think looks after this place when His Majesty's away gallivanting in America?"

In the evening they all had dinner together in the communal dining room, with Barrington sitting like the father of a family at the head of the table. Sister Nairn sat on his right, Adams on his left. Next to Sister was Nurse Macready, a willing, cheerful Irish girl, and next to Adams was Carl Bergstrom, the silent Swede who shared the house with him. He was a wispy man with a fair, pointed beard and an El Greco face, who spoke very little. When he did speak it was in a voice so soft that it was almost impossible to hear. He was a useful amateur handyman, who helped Barrington with the carpentry and constructional work. The rest of the time he spent in the chapel in solitary prayer.

It was after one of these evening meals that Barrington asked Adams to accompany him to his house. "You know something about us now," he said. "If you're going to stay here, it's time you said your piece."

Adams was reluctant to begin. He was just experienced enough to know that people who ask for frank opinions are not always best pleased when they receive them. He was aware that this conversation might well be a turning point in his relationship with Barrington. Yet, as Barrington had said, if he was going to stay at Kalundani for any length of time, it was impossible for him to carry on without giving his honest opinion about the way the hospital was run.

"Well," he said slowly, "there are a number of things that have struck me. In all cases limitation of resources is a factor—I see that. But accepting that we're always going to be short of money and facilities, it still occurs to me that certain things could be done to improve performance with the resources we have."

Was that diplomatic enough? he wondered. Barrington nodded his head, apparently accepting it. At least he was not ruffled yet.

"The first thing that bothers me," Adams went on, "is the question of hygiene. Obviously our patients have no idea of hygiene, and we have to accept that and do our best, but I think we could exercise more effective control. Take, for example, these relatives all cooking their own food and leaving their rubbish around. It's uneconomical in time and effort, and in food too. It breeds flies and spreads infection. Dysentery's endemic in the hospital and I think that's a contributory factor. We have communal cooking facilities for the patients—we cook rice and maize in bulk for them. If we set up another communal kitchen for the relatives, they would eat just as well as they do now—probably better—and there'd be less filth about the place."

With apparent placidity, Barrington rolled himself another cigarette. "That's interesting," he said. "Go on."

"And then there's the organization of outpatients. There's a lot of wasted time by the doctor. It seems to me that time could be saved by leaving the sorting of patients and the management of the payment in the hands of a native clerk, while we confined ourselves purely to the examination of the more serious patients. As far as the theater's concerned—" He went on, warming to his work. He explained how the theater equipment was beyond a joke, the standard of asepsis was lamentable. In the wards, too, the African orderlies were slovenly and had no idea of a proper ward routine. There was need for a special course of lectures and demonstrations to bring them up to standard.

He paused, hoping he had not gone too far. But Barrington showed little more than polite interest. "Anything else?" he asked.

"Well, there's one final point. I think we have to look to the future. It seems to me that an absolute priority for any future expenditure should be an electricity generating plant. Without that, we're just picking at the problem really. We shall never be able to get anywhere near modern standards without electricity."

"I see." Barrington breathed deeply. "So that's it. Well, let's take your points of complaint in order. Why don't we cook food for the patients' relatives? In the first place, because we can't afford it. You couldn't charge them for their meals because paying money for food is something they don't understand. And you couldn't make them bring their own food since you'd need a whole staff to check who had and who hadn't and how much. And within a week of it getting around that you were dishing out free food you'd have people coming from miles around, swearing they were relatives. And you couldn't prove they weren't. So that's out." He crushed out his cigarette. "Now for the out-patients. The doctor has to control the patients and the admittance because if you had a native clerk he'd cheat the hospital and take bribes to let people see you. The operating theater's primitive because we haven't got the money to get better equipment. We don't run a course for the ward orderlies because we're working twenty-four hours a day as it is, and as for electricity, that's so bloody silly that I don't know how to answer you politely. Where the hell do you think we are—Clapham?"

"We could buy an oil-driven generator. It wouldn't cost more than a few hundred pounds."

"And where do you suppose we're going to get that kind of money from?"

"I don't know what money you have. I told you it was a question of priority. After all, you're planning to spend a good deal of money on that leper village down on the other side of the hill."

Barrington, who had been sitting back in his chair up to this point, suddenly sat bolt upright. His jaw jutted out. "Are you suggesting I abandon that—in favor of a generator?"

Adams had been expecting a violent reaction. He was determined not to be intimidated. "I went to a discussion on leprosy at the

School of Tropical Medicine before I came out here. The general opinion was that leper villages were a mistake."

"Oh it was, was it?" Barrington was scathing. "I suppose there were a lot of comfortable professors from Gower Street—"

"No. Some were from the East, some were from Africa. They said that leper colonies were out of date. They simply encouraged the natives to treat the lepers as outcasts. It should be treated as an ordinary infectious disease—"

"I know all that," said Barrington contemptuously. "I heard it first ten years ago when you were still learning about isosceles triangles. Maybe it's all right in Accra or Kuala Lumpur. I don't know. But we're dealing with some of the most uneducated and backward people in the world. You may have been filled with all the latest London theory about tropical diseases, but you must allow me to know something about the Luako. What these people need isn't diesel-generated electricity, it's intelligent understanding." He glared angrily at Adams. "Until you can grasp that—I might as well tell you you'll be no use to me."

Adams strove to keep his temper. "You asked for my opinion. What did you expect me to say?"

"I don't know what I expected," said Barrington wearily. "Common sense, I suppose. Humanity. Perception. Not all the priggish textbook stuff. You've been frank with me, I'll be frank with you. I'm disappointed in you. You've been here a month and it seems you've learned nothing." He looked at Adams with gloomy disgust. "I really don't know what to say about this. I think it would be best for you to go off to bed now. We both need a little time to think over where we stand."

6

In the weeks that followed their conversation, Barrington withdrew into a mood of gloomy contemplation. The episode had precipitated one of those depressive phases which were the counterbalance to his periods of almost unnatural energy and elation. He only spoke to Adams with the greatest reluctance, on occasions when it was absolutely necessary to the running of the hospital. Whenever possible he passed messages to him through Sister or one of the ward orderlies.

His mood cast a blight over the tiny community. Often now he would fail to join the others for meals. On the occasions when he did, he would sit glumly at the end of the table, saying nothing and eating little, and effectively killing all general conversation. Adams felt guiltily responsible for the misery he had brought upon everybody. He wondered fruitlessly what he could do to break this appalling atmosphere. It was obviously impossible for people living in such close contact to remain under this kind of tension for very long.

He pondered over Barrington's final remarks to him, trying to extract some specific meaning from them. Did Barrington want him to leave? Did he himself, if it came to that, still want to stay? There was surely no object in burying himself in this God-forsaken place if he was not welcome and his views were not to be considered. He made several efforts to speak to Barrington again to clarify the situation, but Barrington always evaded him. He was left in a state of miserable indecision.

Finally he resolved to speak to Sister Nairn. She at least had a greater experience of Barrington's moods than he had. One day when they were alone in the outpatient department at the end of a clinic, he said to her, "Tell me, Sister, do you think I ought to go?"

She was startled and, it seemed, alarmed. "Go? Go where?"

"Back to England. I'm not doing much good here."

"I don't know how you can say that," she said indignantly. "It's difficult to work here without doing some good."

"You know what I mean."

"You mean him?" She gave the word the particular emphasis she always used when speaking of Barrington. "Oh, don't fash yourself about that. He comes over like this from time to time."

"It's more than just a mood, don't you think?"

"In a way, I suppose," she admitted. She went over to the sink and began to dry some instruments. She had a tiresome habit of always feeling the necessity to some trivial job while carrying on a conversation. She claimed she was too busy to waste time just talking. She always had to be polishing or dusting, knitting or sewing. It was a habit that infuriated Adams. "Oh, do put that down, just for a moment," he said irritably. "This is important."

"It's all very well for you, my lad," she said, "but some of us don't have time to waste." Just the same she put the forceps away in the instrument cabinet and sat down. "Of course, he's annoyed because you spoke your mind," she said. "It was the same with me when I came here. I didn't like the way the orderlies did the dressings, and I told him so. Well, you'd be amazed at the fuss he made. He went right off the deep end. Told me I didn't know what I was talking about, and said who was the doctor here, him or me—all that, you know. I said to him 'Dr. Barrington, you may be a doctor but I can tell you that until you've run a ward as I have you can't know what's going on the moment the doctor's back is turned.' Well, of course, he got on his high horse—"

Adams listened impatiently. He wasn't really very interested in Sister Nairn's early conflicts with authority. He began to regret having confided in her; the trouble with asking advice was that you laid yourself open to all kinds of irrelevant reminiscence. Finally she said, "Anyway, to cut a long story short, he dug his toes in completely. But I didn't give up. I waited till he went to London about that book of his and I changed the system while he was away. And do you know, when he came back he never noticed it was any different."

She looked at Adams triumphantly. Noting a lack of response in his face she said, "You may say, what's that got to do with your difficulty. But the point is that there's no use trying to meet him head on. With a little patience you can get your way in the end. Now, for instance, with that chapel of mine—"

"Yes, you told me about that," said Adams hastily.

"There you are, then. What I'm saying to you is don't give up too easily. Bide your time. And don't talk to me again about leaving," she said earnestly. "You're needed here, believe me. Goodness knows, we're thin enough on the ground as it is. That boy Carl does his best, but he's no real use at anything medical. Mary Macready's willing, but she's a daft young thing, and a papist to boot. Toffee's good in his way, but he's not the same as a white man, is he?" She paused and added, "I really can't think how we'd manage here without you now."

"You managed before."

"Ah, but that was before we knew what a difference it would make to have you here. We've all come to rely on you, even in this short time."

Adams smiled awkwardly. There was a softer note in her voice than he had ever heard before. It was affectionate, almost maternal. She said, "I agree with you that there's a lot here needs changing. But we can get most of what we want in due time. It's just a question of managing him. There's nothing you and I couldn't do if we worked together."

Adams hesitated before replying. He was touched by her approach. She sympathized with him in his troubles with Barrington, and in her clumsy, inhibited way she was offering him her friendship and support. He was tempted to accept it on the terms on which it was given, but his natural caution prevailed. Whatever his feelings about Barrington at the moment, he would not be a party to an intrigue with Sister Nairn to impose their views on him. "I'm sorry," he said, "I know you mean well, but I couldn't agree to anything of that kind. I can only work here on a basis of absolute frankness with Dr. Barrington. If that won't do for him, I shall have to leave."

The light of expectation faded from her eyes. She gave a tiny shrug and went back to the instrument cabinent. Silently she began polishing a pair of forceps that she had already cleaned before their conversation began. He knew that so long as he stayed at Kalundani, she would never speak to him in the same way again.

*

Two days after Adams's conversation with Sister Nairn, Barrington failed to appear at breakfast. That was no great surprise, since nowadays he only joined the others for meals at irregular intervals. What was more surprising was that Sister herself was also missing. Adams was just finishing his breakfast and preparing to go along to the outpatient clinic when she came into the room. She looked busy and a little harassed. "Ah, you're still here," she said to Adams. "I'd like a word with you."

She beckoned to him to go outside. During the days since their conversation she had avoided Adams and seemed obviously embarrassed in his presence. Now her awkwardness was completely gone. "I'm afraid the doctor's ill," she said. "He sent me to ask you if you'd carry on for him."

"Yes, of course," said Adams. "What's wrong with him?"

"It's malaria. He gets bad bouts from time to time. He just has to see them through. They last about five or six days."

He turned to go up to Barrington's house. "I'll go up and see him."

"No." She spoke definitely, like someone under instructions. "He doesn't want you to do that. He knows how to treat himself. I'll do the nursing. He just wants to be left alone."

"Oh, but surely—"

"He really means it," she said urgently. "He can't bear anyone to see him when he's ill. It's a thing of his. I've nursed him through these attacks before. He looks terrible. He's all yellow and sweaty and shivering, and he's disgusted with himself. He just lies there in a darkened room and won't let anyone near him." As she saw that Adams was still not fully convinced, she explained, in a softer, almost tender voice, "He's got to be perfect, you see. He's God here, you know. You're not supposed to see God weak and miserable and helpless." She added with an ironic smile, "Not unless he's a real one."

"But that's absurd," said Adams.

"Yes, of course it is." She was gentler and more tolerant than he had ever seen her before. "But then we're all a little odd about something. Especially here. Perhaps if we were right in the head we wouldn't have come to Kalundani in the first place."

She appeared to him suddenly in a new light. He realized for the first time that behind her prim Edinburgh manner lay a sensitive understanding and a degree of tolerance he had not recognized. He smiled at her. They were quite at ease with each other now. It was as if the previous conversation between them had never happened. "And what about you? Doesn't he mind you seeing him?" he said.

"Ah well," she said comfortably. "I'm different, you see. He's known me a long time."

*

From that moment he took over the running of the hospital. At first the prospect did not seem too alarming. He had taken a good deal of responsibility in his hospital in England, and he had had over a month to get used to the special conditions in Kalundani. It had in any case been his impression that he had been doing most of the important medical work at Kalundani for the last week or two. He had been secretly nourishing a suspicion for some time that behind Barrington's façade of bustle and self-importance, he was like a great many medical chiefs and preferred to leave most of the real work to his assistants.

Soon Adams discovered, to his consternation, that the medical tasks he had been shouldering so self-righteously constituted only a fraction of the real work of the hospital, and by far the easier fraction at that. Each new day confronted him with new problems which bore no relation to anything in his previous experience. For the first time he was totally exposed to the maddening unreliability of the Luako. This applied not only to the patients but to all the staff, with the single exception of Toffee. Equipment was constantly disappearing. Sometimes this was valuable; sometimes, though vital for medical treatment, it was utterly valueless for any other purpose and it was impossible to understand why anyone should want to steal it. At one time or another he was infuriated to discover the loss of a spanner to open an oxygen cylinder, or the rubber tubing out of a transfusion set. When the ward orderly was questioned, he seemed utterly indifferent. He did not know. It was gone, and that was all he could say. When Adams lost his temper and shouted at him, he became sulky. The next day the orderly himself was missing.

In a dozen small ways the Africans contrived to frustrate any attempts at effective and organized administration. The weather turned cold and he ordered the issue of blankets. The next day he found that all the male patients had two each and the women had none. He insisted that the blankets should be shared out equally. With obvious reluctance, the orderlies, under supervision, restored half of the blankets to the women. But next day the situation was back as before. When he held an inquiry he was informed that it was the women who had objected. They would not accept the blankets so long as their lords complained of the cold.

The food was a source of incessant dispute. However it was arranged, the food which went into the vast communal cooking pots was never quite what he ordered. If he ordered a diet supplement of rice for the children suffering from undernourishment, he found that nearly ten times the amount had been cooked, and mostly distributed to the men's ward. Vegetables and fruit, obtained at great expense from the coast to treat patients with scurvy, were later discovered rotting in a storeroom instead of being handed out in accordance with instructions.

Bribery and privilege were everywhere, built into the fabric of tribal existence. Adams discovered to his horror that orderlies accepted tiny presents even for such routine tasks as dressing wounds or bringing bedpans. The chiefs and their families demanded and received special attention. On one occasion he picked out a young man who had pushed his way to the front of the outpatient queue and sent him to the back. Sister Nairn said, "If you don't mind my saying so, that was a mistake."

"He was out of turn," said Adams indignantly.

"I know that. But he's the son of the chief. They expect it."

"I don't give a damn—"

"It's not you that will suffer. It's the people who get in before him. He'll take it out on them later. Is there anything you can do to protect them?"

He was trembling with rage and frustration. "Really, this is impossible. These people—" He glared out of the window at the assembled Africans, squatting on their hunkers on the veranda. "Why do they accept it? Haven't they any spirit?"

She regarded him thoughtfully. "That's one of the daftest remarks I've heard made by anybody since I came here."

He glared at her, tight-lipped. "If that's all the contribution you can make—"

"And it's no use getting on your high horse with me, young man," she went on placidly. "I know just what you're going through, and I can sympathize. I went through it all myself, when Doctor went off to London and left me here alone. Be-

lieve me, you have to show great patience. It's the only way.
I've tried losing my temper and sometimes it's a great help. But
at other times it's a disaster. They just go away and you never
see them again. And then you remember what we're here for.
We're here to help them—whatever we think of the way they
behave."

"They're lazy and dishonest," said Adams furiously. "They think
of nobody but themselves."

"That's right. And it does you good to say it out loud once in a
while. I could see you at the beginning, thinking we were all a
bit brusque and impatient with them. Well, I think we are
sometimes. But as you see, it isn't easy." She said sympathetically,
"Maybe you'd like to stop for a while and have a cup of coffee."

"No, I'm all right." He pulled himself together. "Let's get on
and finish it." He opened the door for the next patient. The
chief's son had come back to the front of the queue. He stepped
in and waited expressionlessly for his treatment.

*

Adams found himself counting the days until Barrington would
be fit to return to work. He was tormented, not only by the
maddening problems by which he was confronted, but by the
revelation of his own inadequacy in dealing with them. He did
the best he could, but he was well aware that his best fell
wretchedly short of what Barrington did every day as a matter
of routine. He was utterly exhausted at the end of each day. As
he sat in his bed-sitting room he thought miserably that Barrington
had done all this alone, for ten years, and had built up the hospital
as he did it. He was bitterly ashamed.

Though he was exhausted when he went to bed at night, the
anxieties of the day preoccupied his mind and he slept badly.
One night, lying awake long after midnight, he heard steps moving
past his window. He hastily put on a dressing gown and went
outside. Over to the left of the houses there was a small knoll
from which it was possible to get an uninterrupted view of the
great rock behind them and the valley that stretched away to
the north. It was a clear night with a full moon. He could see a
tall figure silhouetted against the sky, looking out toward the valley.
He hesitated for a moment and then walked up to the knoll.

Barrington heard him approach and turned round to greet
him. He was fully dressed. "I'm sorry if I disturbed you," he
said.

"I wasn't asleep."

Barrington nodded his understanding. "Too much hard work."
His hostility toward Adams had apparently left him, as if his
illness had washed it away. He was gaunt and wasted, with new
lines cut deeply into his face. Yet he seemed more at peace with
himself than he had been for a long time. "That's how it is
here sometimes. It weighs on you. It tires you, but it won't let
you rest. Sometimes, at the beginning, I used to come out here
at night and I'd think it was time to make an end of the whole
thing. But I never did. There always seemed to be some good
reason to keep going."

High clouds passed across the moon, casting shadows which
raced over the valley. Barrington said, "You don't understand
the importance of the moon until you come to Africa. When
there's no moon, these people live in darkness twelve hours out
of the twenty-four. You don't wonder they act strangely sometimes. But when it's like this, it's the most beautiful sight in the
world. You swear you'll never leave it again."

He turned to look at the vast range of mountains which lay
to the west. Some of them, even in these equatorial latitudes,
were capped with snow and gleamed silver in the moonlight.
"I'd like to go across those mountains one day."

"What is there on the other side?"

"Rain forest. A thousand miles of it, east to west. Another
thousand north to south. Huge rivers. Swamps. Crocodiles. Insects. People even more primitive than we have here."

"It doesn't sound too inviting."

"It depends how you feel about these things. You can't think
about it logically." Barrington was silent for a moment. "That's
the thing about this whole project, really. From the very beginning I've had opposition from people who look at it and
say—why do it? Wouldn't it be more sensible to improve the
drains or teach them birth control or give them lantern lectures
on nutrition? I don't know how to answer such people. A man
like Crane, for instance. You know Crane?"

"You mean Sir Alan Crane?"

"Yes. He's a progressive. Not just a progressive—the progressive of all bloody progressives. He wants to take these poor devils down in the villages and give them a university education—train them as lawyers and architects and social scientists. He wants to do that before they know one end of a pitchfork from another. I don't know," he said in a baffled way. "When I go to London I get depressed. I have to leave after a while. Everybody's so polite and liberal and they want to help, but there's no heart in it, somehow." His provincial accent grew more pronounced as emotion rose within him. "God knows I'm no sentimentalist. But I was brought up rough and I know what it means. These people here exasperate the hell out of me and I'm pretty short with them sometimes, as you've seen. But I love them. I have compassion for them. I think they know that."

It was a question rather than a statement. Like lesser men, in moments of doubt Barrington craved for reassurance. "I'm sure they do," said Adams.

"Sometimes I wonder," said Barrington. He seemed to push his anxieties aside with a deliberate effort. "Well, that's my belly-ache. You always end up a bit fed up after the malaria." He crushed out his cigarette. "I shall be back on duty tomorrow morning."

"That's a relief." Adams searched for some way of making it clear to Barrington what he had learned during the past week. "I'll never know how you managed to run this place on your own for ten years."

Barrington laughed. "It has its problems. However, Sister Nairn tells me you made a pretty fair show of it. Coming from a cantankerous old bag like her, that's real praise."

Adams felt constrained to defend Sister Nairn. "I don't really suppose she's much older than you are."

"Or more cantankerous, if it comes to that." He guffawed cheerfully. "Well, there it is. I'm not going to apologize for any-thing I've said to you in the last week or two. We don't apolo-gize here. This is like a family—either you understand or you don't. Either you fit in or you drift away. But you ought to make up your mind fairly soon."

There was a question in his voice, but Adams did not reply straight away. In his present mood Barrington was difficult to resist, but it was not quite so simple to erase the effect of the past fortnight. Barrington said, "I shan't hold it against you if you leave. It's different for me. After all, this is my place. I can't visualize life anywhere else. I shall end my days here. But for anyone else—"

"I'll stay," said Adams.

"You're sure?"

"Yes. I'm sure."

"Good. I'm very glad. I can say it now—while I was lying there in bed I was wondering what the hell we'd do without you." As they turned to go back to the doctor's quarters, he said, "But I still don't agree with you about the leper village."

7

"So he got what he wanted in the end," said Adams. "He usually did, one way or another. Not everything, of course—nobody ever gets everything. Sister Nairn had her hymn singing in spite of him, and some days Carl would go into a sulk and flatly refuse to work for no obvious reason. It was as if they had to defy him on small matters to persuade themselves they were people at all. But in the main, it was his way that governed all our lives.

"He had this essential power, you see, of making an exception out of himself. It never occurred to him for a moment that he was bound by ordinary rules or ordinary standards of conduct. He was very puritanical in some ways. He believed in punctuality, reliability, and industry—for other people. He detested grumbles or complaints. If we fell short in any of these respects, or even showed any ordinary human weaknesses, he was shocked. He made it clear to us that he thought we were lacking in dedication and letting the project down. But personally he detested routine and couldn't cope with it all. His method was to work unbelievably hard for relatively short periods of time. During these phases he would like to pretend that this was his normal way of life and one which anybody could follow with sufficient determination.

But in fact he would soon exhaust himself. He would fall ill and have to rest. I don't say that he was exactly a neurotic, but there was certainly a psychological element in some of his illnesses.

"Also, of course, he had those world tours to stimulate him and break up the monotony. They seemed to become more and more necessary as the years went by. He had volunteers working for him in Europe and America, and they used to fix up lecture tours and fund-raising meetings for him. They also persuaded him to write a second book.

"It wasn't nearly so good as *Sunrise at Kalundani* in my opinion. He was never primarily an author—that wasn't where his true interests and ambitions lay. He had written the first book out of a very deep emotional experience, and once he had finished it, he had really completed what he wanted to say. It had fulfilled his purpose. It had made him into a person of consequence, which was very important both to him and to the project. But the book itself never meant very much to him. What he really cared about was Kalundani.

"It's hard to convey to somebody who's never been there what Kalundani meant to him. It was his life, his dream fulfilled. He could do everything exactly in the way he wanted it. There was no restriction on him. He had no organization to control him as the missionaries had. So long as he didn't ask them for money, the native administration didn't care what he did. They were naturally delighted to have this enormous celebrity operating in their country.

"Out there, he was a sort of a king. It was only a small kingdom, but it was made immeasurably bigger by the fact that the whole world knew about it and admired it. It had a significance for him far greater than the routine medical work that went on there. In any case, as time went by he left that more and more to me. It was the building he cared about. It never stopped, the whole time I was there. Sometimes it went slowly, sometimes quickly. Almost all the time we were short of money and short of staff to man the place. But still the building went on."

*

At first Adams worried constantly. His careful, economical soul was shocked by Barrington's casual and improvident handling of affairs. Grandiose plans were made on impulse and without any reference to their possible cost. The financial accounts of the settlement were hopelessly confused. When taxed with this, Barrington adopted the irritable, domineering manner of a man who cannot be bothered with trifles. His method of handling money matters, Adams discovered, was simple. He raised as much money as he could and spent it as quickly as possible. Then he demanded more. If the donors protested, he replied that if it were not forthcoming the project would have to be abandoned and all the previous donations wasted. He had no inhibitions about making demands which Adams privately considered to be outrageous. "You don't understand," he said. "There's no shortage of money. The world is full of it. Most of it gets spent on rubbish. Airplanes, motorcars, office blocks for businessmen to sit in while they peddle shares in worthless companies. I may not be a good accountant, but everything I spend goes to people who need it, one way or another."

As the years went by, Adams grew to believe that perhaps Barrington was right, and that God would somehow always provide whatever was needed. Like most of the others who worked at Kalundani, he gradually accepted that Barrington was exempt from the laws that governed the conduct of ordinary people. He was only too well aware that if he himself had been left to run the settlement, it would have remained forever an ordinary conventional mission hospital, lost in the vastness of Africa. If it had become a legend throughout the world, it was entirely due to Barrington's methods and Barrington's personality.

The initial isolation of Kalundani was gradually eroded by a stream of visitors. Some of these were genuine enthusiasts; others were lost, eccentric people who came there with vague aspirations to a life of service and inner contentment. Barrington was tolerant with them all. He enjoyed his celebrity and was prepared to put himself to some degree of inconvenience to please his benefactors. He had a natural sympathy with people who for one reason or another could not fit into the normal patterns of society. However, he was only prepared to give them a very modest amount of his time and attention. As a matter of practice, he held himself aloof. He greeted them politely and then, if they proposed to stay any length of time, he adopted various devices to keep them out of his way.

One of these was to instruct Adams or Sister Nairn to put them to work. Mostly they were incapable of making any useful contribution to the life of Kalundani and were a constant worry and responsibility. They got bitten by insects, cut themselves with axes or knives, or fell victims to tropical diseases. Few of them lasted more than a month or two. Only now and then, somebody like Carl would settle down and make his life at the hospital.

It was during these years that Barrington established the traditional image of himself which became imprinted upon the retina of the world. His figure grew heavier and more dignified in middle-age, his face became lined and he acquired that look of grave, saintly understanding which was recorded in countless photographs by the worshipers who visited the hospital. The boyish spontaneity which had still been present when Adams met him in London was gradually overlaid by a consciousness of position. He still laughed and talked and poured out his infectious enthusiasm, but he seemed now to be able to produce his vitality rather self-consciously to order, and to turn it off with disconcerting ease when it was no longer appropriate.

What remained always totally genuine and spontaneous was his love for the country, for the Africans, and for the various wild animals which he collected as pets. At Kalundani there were always fawns and leopard cubs, which he fed and protected and then let free when they were old enough to fend for themselves in the forest. A tame impala that had rejected its freedom followed him everywhere around the settlement. With the animals, as with the Africans, his manner never changed. It was without pose or affectation. It seemed sometimes to Adams that it was only with primitive minds that Barrington ever felt totally at ease.

With the continual increase in size of the hospital, the old atmosphere of casual intimacy gradually changed. The number of beds rose from a hundred to two hundred, then to three hundred. More nurses came from Europe and America, and more African assistants were trained. Guest houses were set up. The leper village grew continually in size. An area of bush around the hospital was cleared and houses were erected for the relatives of patients who had come from great distances. Many of them stayed on and proved impossible to evict. More bush was cleared, more houses were built. Children grew up and a school became necessary. Imperceptibly, a small rural township grew up around them. "It's a sort of African equivalent to the Mayo Clinic," Barrington used to say on his American lecture tour. "Only perhaps just a little less expensive."

Because it happened gradually, the change seemed inevitable to them all. Sister Nairn became a matron, Adams a medical superintendent. Only Toffee seemed a little bewildered by the mushroom growth of the settlement. Attempts to invest him with more authority were politely declined. He insisted on staying in his dispensary, checking the drugs, organizing the outpatient clinic, and patiently questioning the shyer patients for information which they were reluctant to give to the white doctors. A courteous, slow-speaking ghost of a man, he lived out his mysterious life in their midst, as much a silent part of the hospital as the walls of the building and the corrugated iron roof over their heads.

And then, as quietly and self-effacingly as he had lived, he died, bitten by a snake as he lifted a bundle of sticks to stoke the fire outside his hut. Barrington sat beside him throughout the last hours, and when everything was over he knelt down by the bedside and cried silently. Then the Luako took the body. They carried it to their own village, wrapped it in the skin of an ox, and laid it out in the hut of their chief. They built a pyre of dry faggots in the beaten mud outside the hut while the women busied themselves brewing enormous quantities of maize beer. All that evening they sat around the pyre, chanting and wailing and drinking. At midnight the chief's sons brought out the body and laid it on the pyre and set fire to it. Then they chanted and drank themselves insensible until the early hours of the morning.

Barrington and Adams watched from a knoll above the hospital. "It's a great honor," explained Barrington. "Toffee came of an important family among the Luako. He had the blood of the kings in his veins. But even so, it's a great honor." He turned his head away. The flames from the pyre lit up the tropical sky. "There goes all that was left of the old days at Manusha."

"Were they really so good as that?" asked Adams.

Barrington thought for a moment and shook his head. "No, I don't suppose they were. If the truth be known they were sheer hell most of the time. Yet it breaks my heart to think of them, just the same." He looked down at the large, rambling hospital, contemplating the magnitude of his own work. He said sadly, "There was a kind of wonderful simplicity about everything we did in those days."

The endless flood of work, of treatment and feeding and administration and settling quarrels, washed over Toffee's memory like sea water over rock, until in six months' time it was as if he had never existed. Then the war came, and brought with it a deep disagreement between Adams and Barrington. When Adams suggested that it might be his duty to join the Army, Barrington flew into one of his rages. He spoke bitterly of treachery and disloyalty. It became plain that as far as he was concerned the war was an irrelevance, the principal significance of which was that it would almost certainly interfere with the running of Kalundani.

Adams was a conventional patriot with a deep hatred of fascism. He pointed out to Barrington that the war was being fought to preserve precisely those principles to which they had both dedicated their lives: personal freedom and human compassion. Anybody more opposed to the fascist ideal than Barrington it would have been hard to imagine, with his wild individualism and his passionate attachment to people of a foreign race. Yet perversely, he insisted on taking up an attitude of vague, detached pacifism. He declared that European civilization was rotten and decayed, and that the war was the consequence of this. It was only among the so-called primitive races of Africa that there was any real civilization left. It was the duty of them all to preserve this island of sanity which they had taken so much trouble to create.

The two men quarreled. Adams defied Barrington and made the journey to Nairobi to enlist, only to find that he had a duodenal ulcer which in any case excluded him from service. When he returned to Kalundani he was received with delight by Barrington, who appeared to have completely forgotten the harsh words which had passed between them. After that, by tacit agreement, they refrained from discussing the war at all.

8

After the war ended, Barrington became restless. He felt it was time to make one of his world trips. He had not been to Europe or America since 1939 and his lines of communication with his supporters had suffered badly. His books were out of print, and people in those days were too preoccupied with their own survival to have much time or money to spare for Africa. All the missions had suffered, but Kalundani, because it had no religious organization behind it and depended very much on the magnetic power of Barrington himself, had suffered more than most. For the first time since the project had started, new building was almost at a halt. Indeed, if he had not had one or two faithful supporters in the United States, the mission might well have foundered altogether.

But when the time came to go, anxiety overtook him. He showed a nervousness that Adams had never seen before. In the old days, Barrington had always been in a state of elation before setting off. He had looked forward to the excitement and the sensation caused by his personal appearances. He enjoyed travel and was at his best when meeting new people. But now he seemed depressed by the possibility that during his long absence the world might have forgotten him. Twice he delayed the tour for no obvious reason, and it became plain to Adams that for the first time he was frightened of failure. He was nearly fifty years of age and his vitality was diminishing a little. He was no longer so completely sure of himself as he had been in the past.

Eventually he plucked up his courage and left. It became apparent almost immediately that his fears were unfounded. The world he discovered was vastly different from that of 1939. It was a world disgusted by the wretchedness of the war and the ugly complexities of the peace. It longed for a symbol of decency and heroism untarnished by self-seeking. Barrington, with his unerring instinct for the deeper emotional needs of his audience,

immediately presented himself as such a symbol. In addition to
his traditional pleas for Kalundani, he now developed some new,
rather cloudy philosophical concepts which had been fermenting
gradually during his years of enforced seclusion. To Adams, as
he read the press cuttings, they seemed well-meaning, but madden-
ingly hazy and non-specific. On a more mundane level Barrington
called for world government and abandonment of atomic weapons,
a repentance of Europe for its own materialism and a new surge
of generosity toward the underdeveloped world. They were all
excellent sentiments, and very much in tune with the mood of
frustrated idealism which had followed the war. What they meant
in practical terms was never exactly defined.

Fortunately few of the newspapers and magazines which followed his progress were in a mood to ask tiresome questions
about the significance of his message. After two months of energetic barnstorming, Barrington was as great a world figure as he
had ever been in the 1930s. He moved from America to Britain
and Western Europe, and finally ended up with a visit to the
Middle East.

Here he flavored his celebrity with a spice of controversy. In
his emotional, imprecise way, Barrington had always been attracted
to Zionism. It was hard to know exactly what it was about it
that fascinated him so much. Perhaps it was the grandiosity of
the conception and the deliberate abandonment of bourgeois
comfort for a life of dedication. Or perhaps it was just that the
Zionists were, like him, compulsive builders. He arrived in Palestine
at the height of the troubles and instantly declared sympathy for
the Zionist cause. He was feted by the Jewish community and
spent a week on a kibbutz, where he gave a press interview
criticizing the policy of the British Government. He flew back to
Africa amid a storm of abuse from the right-wing British press.

On the night of his return he invited Adams up to his house
after dinner to tell him about the trip. It was a Sunday and the
rest of the community were singing hymns in the chapel. Adams
said, "So it was a success?"

"A great success, I'm pleased to say." The strains of "The
Church's One Foundation" rolled up the hill from the chapel.
Barrington winced. "It seems that God's still on our side, in spite

of that bloody harmonium. Who says there's no Divine forgiveness?"

"You made quite a stir in Palestine."

"I suppose so. Of course, I knew I'd be criticized in England,
but I felt I had to say it. Fortunately the Americans were very
sympathetic. So perhaps it won't harm us very much in the end."

He spoke with the curious blend of idealism and hardheaded
calculation which Adams had always found disconcerting. At first
he had been shocked into wondering whether Barrington's spontaneous outbursts of emotion were no more than a cynical pose,
but experience had taught him that no such simple explanation
was possible. Barrington was a man of many sides, each of which
held total reality for him for as long as it was uppermost in his
mind. When he had inveighed against the British, he had certainly meant it with complete sincerity. Only afterward had he
consoled himself for the possible consequences by assessing the
compensations in other parts of the world.

Barrington went on to describe the week on the kibbutz. "It's
something quite unique," he said. "In a different way, they're
trying for the same kind of thing that we're working for here.
It's one of the few places I've been to in the last fifteen years
that I really felt I learned something." He paused and then said
casually, "Oh, by the way, I met a very interesting woman there.
She was very keen to hear what we're doing and wants to visit
us."

Adams nodded with resignation. It was the usual thing for
Barrington to pick up disciples on these tours, and invite them
to come to Kalundani for a visit. By the time they arrived, he
had usually lost interest in them and left Adams to look after
them. "Who is she?"

"An Englishwoman called Sylvia Forrest. She's a journalist.
She went to the kibbutz to write a story about them and was so
fascinated that she stayed and worked with them. Not being
Jewish, she can't really stay there for good. But she can't bear
the thought of going back to England as it is now." He paused
again. "She's a very energetic, intelligent woman. We might even
be able to make some use of her." He grinned at Adams, reading
his thoughts. "That will be a change from most of them."

*

Adams made the usual arrangements for women visitors. Sister Nairn allotted her a room in the women's guest house and Carl was deputed to pick her up at the railhead. Adams was busy and thought little about the matter. When he went along to the common room at five o'clock one afternoon he was surprised to find it occupied by a tall, dark-haired woman, sitting in an armchair. She was reading a magazine and had a cup of tea at her side. She looked up from the magazine and said, in a cool, self-possessed voice, "Dr. Adams?"

"Yes."

"I'm Sylvia Forrest." She stood up and stretched out her hand in greeting. She was slightly taller than he was, and he was startled to find that she was extremely beautiful in a dark, severe way. Her cheekbones were high and her black hair was bound behind her head in a chignon, giving her a faintly Slavonic appearance, yet her voice was unmistakably upper-class English. Her hands were without rings, yet they were soft and well kept; her simple blouse and skirt managed to convey a surprising impression of elegance. She looked at Adams in a way which made him immediately conscious of his dusty shoes and crumpled cotton trousers. Automatically he ran his hands through his hair to push it into some semblance of order. "I hope they're looking after you," he said.

"Very well. Sister Nairn fixed me up in my room and then I came here and helped myself to tea. I hope that was all right?"

"Yes, of course." He went to the side table where there was an urn and a number of thick cups and saucers. He poured himself a cup. He noticed, for the first time in years, how thick and black the tea was. "I'm afraid you'll find it pretty rough here," he said.

"You forget where I've come from. On the kibbutz, hard living isn't just essential—it's a kind of religion."

"So I hear."

He was a little at a loss. Her cool self-confidence threw him slightly off balance. Usually when visitors came to Kalundani they were different at first, oppressed by the magnitude of their pilgrimage and the experience of being exposed to this legendary place for the first time. They were also often put off by the primitive living conditions. Plainly Miss Forrest was not impressed by either of these two aspects of their life.

He said, "Was your journey all right?"

"Oh yes. The train was filthy, of course, not to mention hours late, but I gather that's pretty standard. It was good of you to send the car to meet me."

"I'm afraid there's no alternative."

"There's no other transport?"

"No."

"Why doesn't the government provide a bus service?"

"They tried it once. The driver killed three people in the first fortnight. Then he forgot to fill the radiator with water and the engine burned out. After that, nobody bothered."

She nodded. "Sounds a bit like the Arabs."

There was a trace of contempt in her voice. He said coldly, "I don't know the Arabs."

"You haven't missed much." She thought for a moment. "Would you mind if I asked you a question?"

"Of course not."

"That chap with a beard who drove me. Is he quite right in the head?"

"Why?"

"Well, he seemed to talk to himself rather a lot. Not that I mind. I just wondered—"

Adams frowned. He had a feeling he was not going to like Miss Forrest. There was something subtly offensive about her manner. In its own way, everything she said was true. The trains were indeed filthy, and there was no excuse for the lack of a bus service. No doubt the Arabs were everything she said, and as for Carl . . . One could hardly deny that he was odd by any ordinary standards. The fact was that they had grown used to him; nowadays they hardly noticed his silences and his way of talking beneath his breath to himself. Usually visitors were too tactful to mention such matters.

"I suppose we all have our peculiarities."

"I don't know," she said cheerfully. She looked Adams over. "You seem pretty normal to me."

"Thank you. I'm flattered."

Irony was wasted on her. She did not even seem to notice what he said. "As for Edward, he's something better than normal." For the first time there was reverence in her voice. "I've met a lot of remarkable people in my time, but nobody quite like him. He's without exception the greatest man I ever met."

Adams was reduced to silence. It was not her description of Barrington which so took him aback. This was the conventional view held by most of their visitors. What shocked him deeply, and afflicted him with a kind of alarm which he found hard to define, was her use of Barrington's Christian name. It occurred to him that in all the years he had been at Kalundani, none of them had ever dared to speak of Barrington with this casual intimacy. They had quarreled with him, railed against him between themselves, and criticized him endlessly, but always they had accepted without question the barrier that lay between him and all other people concerned with the project. But plainly this barrier did not exist for Miss Forrest. It was almost as if she considered herself his equal.

*

Dinner at Kalundani was a ceremonial meal. It was the only time during the day when all the members of the little community came together, and Barrington liked everybody to be present in the dining room punctually at seven o'clock. At exactly on the hour he himself would enter and go to the top of the table.

The food was very simple. Vegetable broth, followed by meat or boiled river fish, with rice or potatoes, then stewed fruit; sometimes, when a parcel had arrived from England, there were delicacies such as cheese or fruitcake. If Barrington was feeling like conversation, the talk revolved around him; if not, the others talked between themselves while he ate in silence.

On her first evening, Miss Forrest, as a guest of distinction, was placed in the seat on Barrington's right. As soon as they were seated, she began to talk to Barrington. She spoke rapidly and fluently, with an easy assumption of equality which caused Barrington himself to frown a little now and then. She told them stories of her experiences in the Middle East, and at one point delivered a short lecture on the importance of irrigation.

When the meat course came up, she poked curiously with her fork at the vegetable which was served with it.

"What on earth's this?" she asked.

"Boiled plantains," said Barrington. "It tastes not unlike potato."

She took a mouthful and then pushed it unenthusiastically to the side of her plate. "Is this the only sort of fruit you have?"

"Up here, yes. They have pineapples down at the coast."

"Have you ever tried citrus or melons?"

"They don't grow here," said Barrington curtly.

"That's what everyone always says in Africa," she replied. "But when you come down to it, the climate's not so different from Galilee. It's amazing what you can do if you really try. Why, I met a man in Ethiopia who was growing a commercial crop of strawberries on the high plateau, in a climate not very different from what you have here—"

"This is a hospital," said Barrington, "not a fruit farm. Our time is already fully occupied treating the sick."

He made it quite plain that she had overstepped the bounds of familiarity. The voice he used was one which had cowed every one of them at some time or another. Yet Miss Forrest simply raised her eyebrows. She had obviously registered the fact that he was annoyed, but it did not appear to disturb her very much. "I can understand that," she said equably. "Still, you could do with the Vitamin C, couldn't you? I mean, you've told me one of your principal troubles is malnutrition."

Barrington put down his knife and fork. "We have a useful rule here," he said with exaggerated politeness. "I hope you won't object to it. We always ask our visitors to spend at least a month in Africa before telling us how to manage our affairs."

The snub was so deliberate that Adams for a moment felt sorry for Miss Forrest. But he need not have concerned himself. She thought over what Barrington had said and then replied, "You know, I think you make a mistake. It's often first impressions that lead you to the real truth of a situation."

Barrington regarded her with an almost comical astonishment. He had become so used to domination that he had forgotten what it was like to be seriously challenged. He retired into thunderstruck silence for the rest of the meal.

His silence intimidated her no more than the rebuff she had received. She talked cheerfully to the others, ignoring Barrington completely. The next morning she greeted him at breakfast as if nothing had happened. Perhaps if she had looked suitably chastened, Barrington would have forgiven her. But plainly the experience had had no effect on her at all.

Barrington was maddened by his failure to make her realize the enormity of her blunder. Indeed, it seemed to Adams that he became quite obsessive about it. Throughout the following week, the small community watched with something approaching awe as he tried to impose on Miss Forrest the pattern of respect and subordination that had been accepted by everyone else at Kalundani for so long. He used all the means at his command in his determination to subdue her. At first he was reasonably polite. But when delicacy proved ineffective, he resorted to cruder and more violent methods. He snubbed her, he talked her down, he talked across her to the others. He was brutally assertive, as only he could be.

It was embarrassing to them all. Even, it seemed at times, to Barrington himself. He would fall into moods where he would be deliberately attentive to her, and flatter her in a way he never bothered to flatter any of the rest of them—as if to indicate that he thought well of her, in spite of everything, and that all might still be well if she would only accept his ascendancy in the same way as the others. It was as if he were repelled and fascinated by her at the same time. His determination to dominate her created a curious intimacy between them.

As for Miss Forrest (or Sylvia, as she insisted they should call her), she remained cheerfully enigmatic. Unlike anyone else who had ever visited Kalundani, she seemed to be able to stand up to the full pressure of Barrington's personality without flinching. Unattractive as Adams found her in many ways, he was shocked into admiration by her toughness and strength of will.

One evening, toward the end of dinner, when they were plowing their way through a particularly tasteless sultana pudding, the final explosion came. Barrington was in a gloomy mood that evening. The few remarks he had made had been curt and punctuated by heavy silences. As if completely unaware of anything ominous in the atmosphere, Miss Forrest turned her placid, handsome face toward him and engaged him in conversation.

"I'll tell you what you really need here," she said. "That's an airstrip."

"Indeed?" said Barrington.

"Yes. An awful lot of your difficulties are due simply to remoteness. You could buy a small single-engine plane. Fly in drugs, essential foods, and so on. Ship any very difficult cases down to the coast for special treatment. You could bypass this whole ludicrous transport system—"

Barrington put down his spoon and fork with a clatter on his plate. He seemed to be near breaking point. "Really, this is too absurd—"

"But why? What's absurd about it?"

He spoke as if to an idiot child. "The expense, for one thing. We haven't enough money for our ordinary purposes, never mind absurd extravagances like aircraft."

She regarded him shrewdly. "You know, I think you just say that because the idea's new to you. Stuck out here, it's difficult to see how quickly things are changing. Kalundani's a wonderful concept. It's been an inspiration to the whole world. But as it stands today, it's something rooted in an idea which you had twenty years ago. If your work's going to stay relevant, you have to bring it up to date—"

"You're talking nonsense," said Barrington. "I don't wish to be offensive, but the fact is you know nothing about Africa. In this continent, twenty years is nothing at all. It's a mere tick of the clock."

She shook her head. "Not any more. You'd be astonished what's happening. You can feel it all over the Middle East, and it's going to come here very shortly. The old days are gone. Nothing will ever be the same as it was before the war—not even Kalundani." She said urgently, "The modern world's going to come to you whether you want it or not. You can't hide from it in this valley."

She had provoked Barrington beyond endurance. "Damn you —who asked your opinion!" he said. "You know nothing. Nothing."

She said reasonably, "Don't you remember when we were in

Palestine? You were prepared to listen then. But now you've come back here, you seem quite different. You sit there in that seat like God Almighty. You give orders. You listen to nobody—"

Barrington was speechless with rage. He stood up abruptly, almost knocking the servant off his feet as he pushed back his chair. He glared around the table, his pale blue eyes flashing at them all, as if somehow he blamed them for not having saved him from this outrage. Then he stormed out of the dining room. A moment later they heard the outer door slam and saw him march up toward his own house.

There was silence round the dining table. Miss Forrest sat with her hands in her lap, frowning slightly and biting her lower lip. She seemed to be not so much shattered by Barrington's action as momentarily puzzled and uncertain what to do next. Then she made up her mind. She dropped her napkin on the table and followed him.

9

"Well," said Sister Nairn afterward, "what do you think of that one?"

"I don't know," said Adams. "I really don't know."

"He'll send her off with a flea in her ear."

"I imagine so."

"And good riddance. A real mischief-maker." Her mind, as so often these days, floated off into reminiscence. "She reminds me of a sister tutor I used to know in Dundee—"

Adams said thoughtfully, "She could be right, you know."

"Och, what nonsense!" She looked at him with disgust. "Go on with you now. There's such a thing as carrying Christian tolerance too far."

But as Adams sat alone in his room, puffing his pipe and running his eye through a two-month-old Lancet, the thought came back to him that Miss Forrest's battle with Barrington was not so very different in essence from the one that he himself had fought, and lost, just over a decade ago. He had no opinion on the subject of an airstrip or the possibilities of growing fruit at Kalundani. Details of that kind were not, he recognized, the real point of the argument. What had cut Barrington to the quick was the suggestion that the hospital was cast in a mold that appeared each year a little less relevant to contemporary reality.

It was a mold into which he himself had been reluctantly forced, after his initial rebellion. He had operated the system as conscientiously as he could, in the way of a loyal officer who trains his troops in a form of drill which he knows in his heart to be obsolete. After the first year, he had not chafed against the routine very much. He told himself that they were doing good, after all. Perhaps they could do more if they worked in a different way. But this was Barrington's way—and without Barrington, Kalundani would never have existed.

Barrington's way was warm, it was sympathetic and compassionate, and it rested as a theory on respecting the traditional patterns of behavior of the Luako. If these patterns were unhygienic, anti-social, and not infrequently cruel, they must be accepted nevertheless. Any tendency to disgust or censure on the part of the Europeans stirred Barrington to immediate anger. They were there, he never tired of reminding them, to serve, not to change.

Education at Kalundani was ruthlessly confined to simple matters of health and hygiene. The Africans were encouraged to use their traditional food more sensibly and to be more provident in the use of their land. They were taught simple facts about the spread of infection. But Barrington had no belief in higher education for Africans. He considered even secondary education to be a waste of time and money. "You train them to be clerks," he said scornfully. "You give them a pen when they haven't even mastered a plow. They need to be taught how to look after their land and their animals, not to mention their children. Africa needs farmers, not civil servants."

There was a good deal in what he said, and yet sometimes Adams wondered how much of Barrington's theory, like so many theories, was mainly an expression of deep emotions within himself.

His disgust for European civilization and his desire to save the Africans from it were genuine enough. But they took root less in logic than in a deeply conservative nature and a reverence for primitive traditions. He loved the simplicity and the quiet dignity of the Africans, he shared their sense of fun and respected the archetypal pattern of their tribal life. The laziness, the unreliability, the unexpected outbursts of rage and violence, aroused in him a momentary irritation but no permanent hostility. He was not outraged, as Adams still could not help being outraged, by the squalor and brutality and the humiliating subjection of the women.

It was partly because of this that the atmosphere in Kalundani was unique. Unlike almost every other mission hospital, it was not a European hospital implanted in Africa; it was part of Africa itself. But now Adams could feel the change in his bones. The vast, silent continent was stirring after its millennial sleep. Far over in the west, across the mountains and the forests and the swamp, there could be heard the faint rumblings of revolt. The grip of the European was weakening. The old, ordered days were coming to an end. Kalundani had held on to the ancient ways of Africa. Would it come to be destroyed with them?

*

They had all expected some dramatic sequel to the confrontation between Barrington and Miss Forrest. Strangely, nothing happened. She showed no signs of preparing to leave the settlement. She and Barrington spoke to each other quite normally at meals, though it was noticeable that she was less argumentative and tended to keep off subjects which might be regarded as sensitive. Barrington was abstracted in his manner. He moved into one of those phases of withdrawal, in which it was impossible to interest him in any aspect of the details of administration of the hospital. As always during these phases, Adams automatically took over the management himself, just as he did when Barrington was away on a trip. He knew that in time Barrington's interest would return as suddenly as it had been lost. From being indifferent about everything that happened, he would one day become violently concerned, insisting on taking even the smallest decisions himself and complaining that nobody ever told him what was going on.

Meanwhile Miss Forrest did her best to make herself useful. She volunteered for unpleasant tasks and helped in the wards and the dispensary. Adams had the feeling that she was trying to make up to him. She learned quickly and the questions she asked were always intelligent. She was consistently cheerful and her energy seemed boundless. Even Sister Nairn began to develop a reluctant respect for her.

"I'll say this for her—she's not afraid of hard work," she said. "I'll not say she's my favorite type of person, but since Doctor gave her the rough edge of his tongue that night she's been a great deal easier to live with."

Adams agreed. But there was something about Miss Forrest in her present mood which made him feel vaguely uneasy. She was more accommodating, it was true. But somehow she did not give the impression of a woman who had been put in her place.

"Have you any idea how long she's planning to stay here?" he asked.

"No." He could see that his unease had communicated itself to Sister Nairn. "But I'm thinking she's in no hurry to leave. She had a great box of clothes and things delivered from England only the other day."

*

One evening at dinner Barrington was particularly silent. At the end of the meal he took Adams aside.

"Have you time for a chat? I want to discuss something with you."

"Of course."

They walked up to the house. Adams wondered how many times in the last twelve years he had been invited to these after-dinner conferences. Or so-called conferences—usually they were no more than extended announcements by Barrington of what he intended to do.

When they were settled in the living room of the house, Barrington said, "I want to talk to you about Miss Forrest."

"Yes?"

"I don't think you like her very much. She's opinionated, I

know. She talks a lot of rubbish sometimes. Yet I have the feeling that she's got something we need. Youth, vitality, a fresh outlook. There's something very valuable in that."

"I agree," said Adams. It was impossible to deny it.

"Sometimes I think," said Barrington, "that we've all been a little too prepared to carry on just doing the same old thing, without questioning whether it was right or not. We have some wonderful people here, of course. But we've got into a rut. We shall never advance that way."

Adams clenched his teeth firmly around the stem of his pipe. He remembered his own attempt at rebellion and how ruthlessly it had been crushed. It was a little hard now, to be accused of excessive docility. But he knew it was useless to point this out. Barrington had a conveniently selective memory; he would assert, and implicitly believe his assertion, that nothing of the kind had taken place. It would only lead to an acrimonious argument and achieve nothing.

"In a place like this," Barrington went on, "there's just too much for everybody to do. That's part of the trouble. The sheer grind of keeping it going from day to day. Fighting against constant difficulties. Poverty and ignorance. Lack of resources. The climate." He sounded tired and discouraged. "What someone called the terrible prose of African life. It can take the heart out of you, Brian." He paused. "I'm getting on for fifty now, you know."

Adams waited. He knew the feeling Barrington was trying to describe. They all had it at times. Often he himself would lie awake and wonder miserably if he had made a completely pointless sacrifice of his life and career.

Barrington spoke as if carrying on an age-old argument with himself. "I've been so proud of my work here sometimes. And then at others I look at it and I see it as it really is—a tiny speck in a continent swamped in misery. We prolong a few lives, it's true. But what does that mean, in all the millions? When you look at the size of the problem, we're ridiculous. We're a joke."

"I don't think we should look at it like that," said Adams. "We're dealing with people. These are our friends. They trust us. You've given them a hope they never had before." He wanted to say that in the sight of God no work of charity was too small or too apparently futile, but he was afraid that Barrington would think him sanctimonious.

"Perhaps. Perhaps. But how long will it last?" Barrington sighed. "I'm sorry to burden you with this. But one gets very discouraged sometimes. Kalundani's like a picture I spent my life painting, and every now and then I look at it and I think perhaps it was the wrong picture or I painted it the wrong way. Perhaps I should paint it out and start again. And then I think— well, I'm getting old. I don't have the energy I had once."

"It's just a bad phase," said Adams reassuringly. He knew these moods of Barrington's. They were always accompanied by a feeling of lassitude and loss of drive which he feared might be permanent. But always in the past his vitality had returned unimpaired within a matter of days.

"No," said Barrington. "This time it's different." He paused. Then he said, "To come back to Miss Forrest. I don't know that we've been quite fair to her—any of us. I've been talking to her a good deal recently. That brashness of hers is just a façade. When you get to know her she's quite a sensitive girl." He saw the astonished expression on Adams's face and went on abruptly. "I'd like you to accept her more readily than you have done up to the present."

Adams could hardly restrain his indignation as he thought of the snubs and insults that Barrington had heaped upon her during the first week. Only a lifetime of self-control saved him from losing his temper. "I seem to remember you found her a little hard to take at the beginning," he pointed out.

"If I can change my views with experience, I don't see why you shouldn't," said Barrington rather priggishly.

Adams was near to saying that if Barrington found Miss Forrest sensitive, he must have seen a side of her which was denied to the rest of them. Instead he asked, "What exactly are you suggesting?"

"She wants to stay on here and I think we need her. If she does stay, she needs some specific job—something that will make use of her energy and capacity for organization. I thought of putting her in charge of the administration. The stores, the buying, the money—all that kind of thing."

Adams considered the proposal. It was sensible enough, in theory. The weakest part of Kalundani had always been its creaking administration. He himself was too busy with the medical work, and Sister Nairn too occupied with the nursing, to give it the attention it deserved. Barrington, who was supposedly in charge of it, had always been impatient and contemptuous in his attitude to paperwork. The hospital had grown so much that the methods they used to manage it were clumsy and out of date. Adams strongly suspected that they were being cheated by their suppliers and wasting money on a large scale. For years he had longed to turn over all this tedious detail to a professional administrator. And yet . . .

"It would give her a good deal of power, wouldn't it?" he said.

"I don't know what you mean by that." Barrington, as always, was made irritable by argument. "We all hate doing that kind of work ourselves. We're doctors. We don't like administration and we're not trained for it. You said often enough we need a really first-rate clerk." He looked at Adams, demanding compliance, and was annoyed not to receive it immediately. "I can't understand you. I thought you'd be pleased."

It was clear to Adams that there was nothing more to be said. Barrington's mind was made up, and there was never any possibility of moving him in these circumstances. He shrugged his shoulders. "Well," he said, "I shall be interested to see how it works out."

Now that he had secured agreement, the aggressive note left Barrington's voice. "It will make a great difference to us all," he said. "We shall be able to give our minds to our real work. You're going to thank me for this." Adams nodded stolidly and stood up. As he turned to leave, Barrington added, "About Sister Nairn—" His eyes wavered a little. "Will you tell her, or had I better speak to her?"

"I think," said Adams impassively, "it would be better if you had a word with her yourself."

10

From the moment that Miss Forrest took over her job it was evident to all of them that a new force had arisen in Kalundani. Her ruthless, exploding energy, which had before been dissipated in general criticism, was now completely concentrated on the task that had been given to her. She had a capacity, reminiscent of Barrington himself, of being able to regard any enterprise in which she was personally involved as the only one which was of supreme importance: anything else she brushed aside as being of minor significance.

After she had been in charge of the administration for a few days, it became hard to believe that for years this aspect of things had been managed on a casual part-time basis by one or other of them in between operations and clinics. She attacked their rickety, happy-go-lucky arrangements like a hurricane. She cleared out a store room and made it into offices, she set up a filing system, she went through accounts, she hired an African clerk to assist her, assuring Barrington that the very low wages he demanded would be amply paid for by the savings that would be made by proper bookkeeping.

She called in the contractors one by one and bargained with them ruthlessly. The Indian who kept the general store in the village ran up the hill to the house to complain, fruitlessly, that he had been insulted and slandered. A system of checks and measurements were instituted for the food and dressings that went into the wards. Requisitions were insisted upon and stocks counted. In her second week of office, she uncovered, to her huge satisfaction, a long-standing conspiracy by means of which the dispenser was pocketing a large proportion of the standard charge for prescriptions. While she did not actually succeed in the impossible task of controlling dishonesty among the Luako, she at least reduced it to manageable proportions.

In the course of her activities she contrived, in some degree or another, to upset everybody within the hospital. The African members of the staff had for so long been making a modest subsidiary income by selling hospital supplies that they had come to regard it as a legitimate part of their income. They were outraged by the breach of an ancient, and to their mind perfectly legitimate custom, and had eventually to be pacified by a payrise. The nurses resented the extra paperwork and the constant instructions to which they were subjected. Sister Nairn and Adams were maddened by the upset of their routine and the barrage of complaints about Miss Forrest which arrived daily from their subordinates.

Sister Nairn said to Adams when they were alone at the end of an operating list, "It's no use, I can stand it no longer. After all these years I've been here, it's not good enough. Only this morning she came around complaining that I hadn't signed for some X-ray films. Me!" she cried indignantly. "Me that begged the X-ray machine itself from my old hospital in Dumfries—"

"Yes, I know." Automatically, Adams tried to soothe her down. "She's a new broom, of course. She's very officious, I agree. She annoys me too sometimes."

"She's more than officious. She's an out and out pest and you may as well admit it."

"I think she'll settle down a bit in time," said Adams, without too much conviction.

"She'll drive us out of minds in the meantime. I tell you, Dr. Adams, it's simply not tolerable. For fifteen years I've worked my fingers to the bone for this hospital. We've had our differences here in the past, but we've made a pretty fair shot at working together one way and another. But this—" She threw some instruments in the sterilizer with a deliberate clatter. "It simply can't go on."

Adams had felt the same way himself, if not quite so violently. The close proximity in which they lived, the lack of leave, the tension of the incessant hard work, put heavy strains on them all. Even in the best of circumstances it was inevitable that they should get on each other's nerves. So far they had worked very hard at keeping their irritations within bounds. If anyone gave way to a spasm of ill-temper it was customary not to respond. If one of them went into a mood of silent gloom for a period of time, the others studiously ignored it. It was the only way to keep going. Adams had made one or two attempts to explain this to Miss Forrest, but he had found it impossible to make her understand. She simply could not comprehend that her manner might be annoying to anybody. She was not easily upset herself and had little understanding of the susceptibilities of others. She rejected his criticisms with indignation. Could anybody deny that the work she was doing was for the benefit of the hospital? Then what on earth were they complaining about?

Adams had also tried dropping hints to Barrington, but without success. Perhaps, he thought, it was his duty to try again. He said to Sister Nairn, "I'll have a word with Dr. Barrington about it, if you like."

"No." She shook her gray head decisively. "I'm going to talk to him myself. I'm going to tell him it's her or me. He can take his choice. I'm not going to stay here to be treated like this."

When she had finished her work she stormed up to Barrington's house. Adams did not see her again until dinnertime. When she came into the dining room he was alarmed at her appearance. Her face was gray and drawn, and when she made an attempt to smile at him, the smile crumpled on her face. He took her to one side and asked her what had happened. A large tear appeared in the corner of her eye. "He doesn't care," she said. "All these years of work, and it meant nothing to him. He just said, that if I wanted to go—" She stopped, unable to go on.

Adams could not think of anything to say. When she had threatened to leave the hospital, he had not really taken it seriously. It had been her life for fifteen years and she was an aging, lonely woman with nowhere else to go. But perhaps for a little while she had believed it herself. She had visualized Barrington so intimidated by the prospect of losing her that he would accede to any demand she made. It had been a pathetic, futile little threat, and Adams could have told her that Barrington was the last man in the world to respond to it. He was an impossible man to bluff since he never really calculated the advantages and disadvantages of a decision. Once he became committed to a course of action, he was prepared to go to any lengths and take any risks to get his own way.

Plainly Miss Nairn had encountered him in this inflexible mood. She had lost, not only a battle, but also an illusion about her own value to Barrington and to Kalundani itself. It was an illusion which had maintained her for the last fifteen years. Now she had been forced to see herself, no longer as one of the pillars on which the settlement had been built, but as an old hospital sister, doing a job for which somebody else could always be found if the need arose.

With an effort she controlled herself. She dabbed angrily at the tear on her cheek with her coarse linen handkerchief. After the bitterness and resentment, old loyalties reasserted themselves. "It's not him, really," she said. "It's that woman. He's never been the same since she came. Goodness knows what kind of a hold she's managed to get over him."

*

It was the beginning of a situation which was unprecedented in Kalundani, in which the greater part of the staff lived in a state of subdued resentment and rebellion. Though Barrington was plainly aware of the fact, he made no efforts at appeasement; indeed, he was more aloof than Adams had ever seen him. Apart from matters of work he spoke little to other members of the staff. He never joked or smiled as he ordinarily did. He spent his small amount of free time in his own house.

Adams thought at first that he was simply angry at their refusal to accept Miss Forrest. It was, after all, the first time that there had ever been any concerted resistance to his will; it was not surprising that he should resent it. But after a while, as he observed Barrington closely, he began to suspect that there was something more. Barrington looked unwell. He was beginning to lose weight. His face was drawn and his clothes hung loosely on him. He ate practically nothing. He tired more easily than usual. He developed a septic infection of the finger of his left hand, which seemed to take an unusually long time to clear up.

On one occasion he stumbled on rising from his chair, and would have fallen if Adams had not gone to his help.

"Are you all right?" asked Adams.

"Yes, thank you." He released himself from Adam's arm. "I just felt dizzy for a moment. I'm perfectly all right now."

"You're quite sure?" said Adams anxiously."

"Yes."

"Because I don't think you've been looking too well lately. Don't you think I ought to have a look at you?""

"No." Barrington's tone was abrupt. "There's no need for that. I'm perfectly well, I assure you." As if conscious of his own churlishness, he added, "Thank you very much, Brian, just the same. I appreciate your consideration."

Afterward Sister Nairn said, "Do you think he's really ill?""

"I don't know. He certainly doesn't look quite his best."

"It may be just one of his moods."

"I suppose that's possible," Adams said dubiously. Certainly Barrington had suffered from some very odd symptoms at one time or another when he was in his depressive phases. At these times he had sometimes lost his appetite, or had attacks of nausea or headache, for which no organic cause could be found. If he was suffering from any of the ordinary tropical diseases he would have recognized them himself. Adams turned the problem over repeatedly in his mind, and eventually he came to the conclusion that Sister Nairn was probably right. The likely explanation was that Barrington, in his present state of exasperation, was suffering from some form of psychological illness.

One day Adams had just finished his morning outpatient clinic. It was nearly lunchtime and he was tired and hungry. In an abstracted way, he went through the cards of the patients he had seen. It was an old habit of his to do this before leaving the clinic—every now and then you picked up a clue from the written history which had escaped notice at the time, submerged in the distractions and general turmoil of the clinic. His eye was caught by a list of symptoms on one of the cards. He read it through again. He looked at the diagnosis and the treatment. Then he closed the clinic and walked rapidly up to Barrington's house.

Barrington was sitting in his office discussing some item of administration with Miss Forrest. She was saying, "And it seems to me that if we could make an estimate of the likely rate of complicated pregnancies—" Adams walked in and said, "I'm sorry to interrupt, but this is important."

Barrington frowned. "What is it?"

"I'd like to speak to you alone."

"But surely—" Something in Adams's expression stopped him. "Oh, all right. Would you mind, Miss Forrest?"

She looked curiously at Adams, then gathered up her papers and left. "Well," said Barrington, "what's the crisis?"

Adams hesitated for a moment. "That septic finger of yours," he said. "I notice you've still got it."

A transient look of unease passed over Barrington's face. He shrugged his shoulders. "Infections are always slow to heal in this climate."

"Does it hurt?" asked Adams.

Barrington paused for a second. "No."

Up to this moment Adams had not been entirely sure of himself. But the evasiveness in Barrington's manner made him suddenly certain. "Did it *ever* hurt?" he demanded.

Barrington did not reply. His eyelids drooped a little, and the folds in the skin of his face seemed to deepen. Adams asked, "Do you mind if I have a look at your hand?"

Without a word, Barrington held out his left hand. Adams did not touch the small piece of sticking plaster protecting the end of the little finger. Instead, he picked up Barrington's hand and laid it on the palm of his own. The last two fingers were slightly bent. He straightened them out and let them go again. They sprang back into their previous position.

Adams felt in his lapel for the pin that he always carried there. "Don't bother," said Barrington. "I can save you the trouble. There's no sensation in either finger." He bared his teeth in something which approximated to a smile. "I have an ulnar nerve paralysis, sensory and motor." He sounded in a curious way relieved, as if a great strain had been lifted from him. They both knew that there was only one possible cause. "It's a fairly localized lesion, I'm glad to say."

"How long have you known?"

"For the last couple of months."

"How do you think it happened?"

Barrington shrugged. "Impossible to say. I suppose I must have been careless. After all, I've been going down to the colony every day ever since the beginning. One touches them all the time, one gets to feel it can't happen. Perhaps one day I forgot to wash my hands afterwards?"

"You've been treating yourself?"

"Yes. I've been using this new stuff, dapsone. Pretty rough it is, too. Far worse than the disease, believe me. You feel like death. No appetite, dizzy half the time—" He stopped. "I suppose that was what put you on to it."

"I just happened to be looking at the case record of a patient on dapsone. He had everything you had."

Adams looked at Barrington with pity. He tried to visualize what it had been like for him to acknowledge the fact that he had leprosy. It was a thing they all worried about secretly. Barrington had always made a great parade of discounting the risks of dealing with lepers. He pointed out to all the new arrivals that the infectivity was very low, and only people who lived in intimate contact were in any danger of catching it. Doctors and nurses were perfectly safe so long as they took the standard precautions. He would take people down to the leper village and demonstrate his own lack of fear by greeting his friends there with handshakes and slaps on the back. "In Africa," he was fond of saying, "men live by the sense of touch. From their earliest childhood their whole lives are built up on the basis of physical contact. To deprive an African of that is to turn him into a living corpse. That's the terrible thing about leprosy. If we want these people to have love for us and confidence in us, we must never be afraid to touch them."

He had believed in this and he had lived by his belief. And he had paid for it. Knowing him so well, Adams could see that what he suffered from most was not so much the disease but the damage to one of his most cherished beliefs. No longer would he be able to make that reassuring speech. The nurses and orderlies who had over the years lost their fear of the lepers would never have the same confidence again.

It was no surprise to Adams that Barrington had felt reluctance to speak of the catastrophe that had come upon him. But now that he had, he accepted his fate with dignity and without self-pity. "The question is," he said, "what do we do now?"

"I'd like to see the lesion, if you don't mind."

Barrington stripped off his jacket and shirt. Adams ran his hand up the inside of his upper arm. Under the skin he felt a well-defined painless lump about two inches above the elbow joint, almost the size of a hazel nut. "Not much doubt about that," he said. "Anything anywhere else?"

"No."

"I'd better make sure." Adams made a painstaking examination. There were no other nodules or signs of the disease. When Barrington had dressed again, he said, "I take it that you're on the top dosage of dapsone?"

"Yes."

"I should reduce it if I were you." Now that he was the doctor and Barrington the patient, he took up, without being conscious of it, a position of command. Barrington accepted it without comment. Adams could see that he was relieved to be able to pass on the responsibility of treatment to somebody else.

"Naturally I was anxious to get it under control," said Barrington defensively. "So I thought I'd give it as much as possible."

"Yes, I know. But it's obviously upsetting you. You ought to cut it down for a while anyway. And there's another thing—"

"What?"

"This is a very localized lesion, pressing on the nerve. Ideal for surgery. I think we ought to cut down and relieve the pressure."

Barrington nodded. It came to Adams that he had suspected this from the beginning. In a strange way he had wanted Adams to discover his secret and help him, yet he had found himself unable to speak about it. Perhaps from pride, perhaps from a deep feeling, common to all patients suffering from chronic and frightening diseases, that in some way disclosure to another person turns a nightmare into an unavoidable reality. In his fear and uncertainty he had forgotten that he was a great man, forgotten even that he was a doctor. He had acted like one of the most foolish and illogical of his patients.

He must be far gone indeed in illness and fear, thought Adams— so far gone that he had not even the strength to resent his own dependence. Adams had never seen him before in such a sub-

missive mood. He spread out his hands as if offering himself as
a victim. "When do you want to do this operation?"

"There's no point in delay. I'll get the theater ready for this afternoon."

I I

It was a very simple operation. Adams used a local anesthetic
and made an incision along the inside of the arm to expose the
ulnar nerve. The nerve sheath was infiltrated by the hard fibrous
tissue which was typical of a leprous lesion. He split the sheath
and released the compressed nerve fibers beneath. Sister Nairn
assisted him and prepared the instruments. The three of them
chatted companionably throughout the operation. Barrington
seemed more at ease now than he had been for some months.

"I don't suppose you'll get much relief straight away," said
Adams. "The most we can really hope for is to arrest the progress of the nerve damage. You ought to be prepared for some
permanent degree of claw hand."

"There are worse things than that," said Sister Nairn sententiously. "I'll knit you a wee glove to protect your finger end."

"So long as you don't sing any of those bloody hymns for my
recovery—"

"Dr. Barrington, I'm always prepared to make allowances for
a sick person, but when it comes to blasphemy and foul language—"

"Oh go on with you, you old witch."

It was quite like old times.

*

Barrington stayed in his house for the following week. Adams
went up each night to see him. After a few days on the lower
dosage of the drug, he began to improve physically, but the
buoyancy which had come over him at the time of the operation

turned out to be only a temporary phenomenon. He became
gradually more thoughtful and reserved as time went on. At the
end of the week Adams brought in a dressing tray and took out
his stitches. The wound had healed well. After a new dressing
had been put on, Barrington sat in his armchair and lit a cigarette. "There's something we ought to decide," he said.

He hesitated. To Adams's eyes he seemed unusually diffident
and ill at ease. He said, "We have to agree on what line to take
up about this."

He spoke as if he hoped that Adams might grasp from this
what he was talking about. But Adams was completely baffled.
"I'm sorry," he said. "I don't quite follow you."

Barrington went on reluctantly. "We have to think of Kalundani and the whole future of the project. That has to come
before anything, I think you'll agree?"

"Well yes, I suppose so. But—"

"The point I'm really trying to make is this. We can't afford
to let any news of this—illness of mine get to the ears of the
general public. It might do us a lot of harm."

"Might it?" The possibility had not occurred to Adams. "I
can't really see why. After all, we spend our lives preaching that
there's nothing shameful about leprosy. It's just a disease like any
other—not very infectious and completely curable."

"Yes, yes, I know all that," said Barrington impatiently. "But
I know the outside world better than you do. They don't think
sensibly. Their minds are full of vague emotional images. They
support me because I represent something to them. They have a
certain picture of me. I'm afraid this would damage it."

"I should have thought it would do you good, if anything. To
realize that you'd actually taken the risk of getting infected—"

Barrington shook his head. "You're being logical again. In
their heads there's still something repellent about the disease.
They'd recoil. They'd be afraid to touch me. I should be something they preferred not to think about, to turn their minds away
from—"

He spoke with the confidence of an expert. From the first
time when they had met in London, Adams had been impressed
by Barrington's instinctive genius for interpreting mass reaction,
and he was only too aware that he himself had no such gift.

He was prepared to accept Barrington's judgment on the matter, especially when delivered with such certainty. Yet he still did not understand exactly what Barrington was getting at.

"Anyway," he said, "why should they know? Your health is your own business. I hope you don't think Sister Nairn or I are capable of any breach of confidence—"

"No, of course not," said Barrington, dismissing the possibility with a wave of his hand. "But that's not the point. You don't understand what it's like when I travel about. I'm on display. I'm constantly photographed. I'm going to have a permanent claw hand of some degree or another. It's bound to be noticed. And people will start guessing. After all," he pointed out, "you guessed, didn't you?"

"That was different. There were special circumstances—"

Barrington shook his head. "Believe me, I know what I'm talking about. It's bound to be noticed. We have to have an explanation." He leaned forward earnestly. "Brian, you don't know journalists like I do. Once they think you have a secret, it puts them on their mettle. They never leave you alone till they find out what it is. The only way to keep them quiet is to give them some plausible explanation."

"But what kind of an explanation—"

"An injury." He spoke definitely, as if he had given the matter a lot of thought. "I don't know what—we could easily find something. I could have been clawed by some animal. God knows it happens often enough. We just feed the story to them in an oblique sort of way, and that's the end of it."

Adams was at a loss to know what to say. The whole idea disgusted him. "You're talking of something I don't know anything about. How do you 'feed' a story like that? What does it mean in actual fact?"

"Oh, don't worry about that," said Barrington. "It's easy enough. Miss Forrest could arrange it. She's a journalist. She understands how it's done."

Adams looked very carefully at the bowl of his pipe. "She knows about this?" he said eventually.

"Yes." Barrington's tone was too casual to be absolutely natural. "I thought it was better to tell her."

"And this idea—about feeding the story and everything. Was it hers?"

"No, of course not. It was mine." He met Adams's eye for a moment and then looked away. "Well, perhaps we worked it out between us."

Adams's pipe was now definitely out, he decided. He put it down very gently in an ashtray. He noticed, as if from a distance, that his hand when he held it was not very steady. He had a curious feeling of unreality, similar to that which he had had once before when he had first read about Barrington in a Sunday newspaper twelve years ago. It was a feeling that he had reached a point of decision on which his whole future life might depend. But he was a slow, cautious man. "If that's what you want to do," he said carefully, "it's your own business. I can't stop you."

"You mean you don't agree with it?"

"Does it matter?"

"Damn it, Brian, of course it matters," Barrington exploded. "You know that. We've had our disagreements in the past, but we've always been together in everything that counted." He looked at Adams like a man unjustly betrayed. "I was hoping you'd support me," he said, almost plaintively.

Adams shook his head. "I can't do that," he said. "It would be a lie and I won't be a party to it. I'll keep my mouth shut, of course. I wouldn't contradict it."

"That's not enough."

"Of course it isn't," agreed Adams. "We couldn't live and work together with that between us. It would make nonsense of everything I admired you for and everything I came here to do." He took a deep breath and forced himself to look Barrington straight in the eye. "I think you have to make up your mind about the future. Whether you want to do things the way we've always done them in the past or—" He hesitated. "Well, I won't say any more."

Barrington looked at him angrily. "Why don't you say it? It's Miss Forrest you object to, isn't it? The fact is, you're jealous of her. Like an old woman. It's Sister Nairn all over again—"

Adams was determined not to be provoked. "I'm not Sister Nairn," he said evenly. "I can do without Kalundani if I have to.

I can do without you too. If I say I'll go, I mean it. You know that."

It was the first real trial of strength between them since their conflict in the first months after Adams had come to Kalundani. Barrington glared at him as if wondering whether it might be possible to crush him by sheer force of personality. Then, with a sudden change of mind, he dropped his eyes and made a gesture of despair. "I don't know," he said. "I try hard to do what's for the best, but I don't know." His voice trailed away on this inconclusive note. He ran a hand across his brow. "I'm still not feeling my best, I'm afraid," he said pathetically. "Perhaps we could talk about it another time."

*

Adams was not surprised to hear next day that Barrington was feeling unwell and wanted to be left alone. It was a familiar pattern of behavior when he was crossed or was at a loss to come to a decision. Consciously or unconsciously, he retired from all human contact in the hope that by some magical means a solution to his problem would appear.

As Adams thought the matter over during the next few days, he found it hard to see how even Barrington, obstinate and willful as he undoubtedly was, would be foolhardy enough to sacrifice both his chief assistant and his matron on an issue like this. Things were much changed from the early days at Kalundani, when Barrington had been capable of running the entire enterprise on his own. The hospital had more than doubled in size since those days. Barrington himself was no longer young, and had for some years been in the habit of passing most of the routine work on to others. Surely he would not be able to face the prospect of starting again with an entirely new staff?

The more Adams thought of it, the more determined he was, on this subject at least, and in Barrington's own interest, to have his way. Barrington would no doubt try to bluff him, but he assured himself that he would not give way. As Barrington still failed to appear, he watched Miss Forrest for any signs of how the struggle might be going. She was noticeably quieter and less assertive than usual. She was agreeable to them all, but in a slightly remote way, as if they only existed in the background of her interests. It was hard to read anything of great significance into her manner.

One evening he was sitting in the small whitewashed office which served him as a consulting room, looking through some case records, when there was a knock on his door.

"Come in."

It was Miss Forrest. She had discarded the white coat which she wore during the day and was dressed in a silk blouse and skirt. She looked, as always, rather more crisp and elegant than was reasonable for a woman living on a mission station.

She sat down in a chair opposite to him and said, "I'm sorry to burst in on you, but we can't go on like this."

"Like what?"

"Oh, please don't pretend you don't know." It seemed to him that her manner was less cold and confident than usual. She spoke like a person pleading for understanding. "Edward's very worried. He knows you were upset by that conversation you had. He feels it was probably his fault and that he didn't handle it properly. After all, he's still a sick man, you know." She paused for a moment, waiting for a reaction. Adams remained silent. "Believe me, the last thing he wants is a break with you."

Adams took off his reading glasses and rubbed them carefully with a handkerchief. He was trying to hide his sense of relief. It was clear now that she had come to negotiate. It was good to know that he would never have to take his threat to the limit, and to risk breaking up his life. Now that he saw the prospect of her capitulation, he felt almost friendly to her. It must be hard for her to come to him with a peace offering. But he was still slightly resentful about Barrington. He might at least have delivered his apology in person.

She shook her head, as if marveling at his obtuseness. "Sometimes I wonder if you really understand him."

It was strange, the talent she had for saying the very thing which made his hackles rise. "I understand him," he said coldly. "I've known him for a very long time, you know."

She made a rueful grimace. "Oh dear, I can see I've offended you again. I didn't mean to, believe me. But everyone here seems to be so sensitive—"

"You have to see our point of view," said Adams. "We've all

been here for many years. Living together on a mission station is like a marriage. One gets to know every facial expression, every slight change in the tone of voice, every minor annoying habit. I can tell you when Sister Nairn is homesick for Scotland by a change in the way she speaks; I know when Carl is due for an attack of minor epilepsy when he sits on the edge of his chair at the breakfast table. We all understand each other so well that we don't need to talk about it. In fact it's better not, because if we did, there would be no privacy left at all. So you see," he added more gently, "it's a little annoying when you come to me after a month or two, and suggest that I don't understand."

She sat in silence for a moment, tight-lipped. He could see that her first impulse was to come back and defend herself. With an effort, she conquered it. She nodded agreement. "Fair enough. You're right about that and I'm sorry." She smiled at him tentatively. "Am I forgiven?"

"Yes, of course." He was sympathetic toward her in her defeat. "You know, when I came here I was like you in many ways. I wanted to turn everything upside down in ten minutes."

"He wouldn't let you?"

Adams smiled reminiscently. "We had our differences. In the end we had to settle down together. I got some of what I wanted. He got most of what he wanted. That's how it always works out in the end. In a place like this, you can't carry everything to its logical conclusion. You have to bend a little."

She smiled back at him. "You know," she said, looking him over indulgently, "you're really much more reasonable than I ever thought at the beginning. I'm sure we're going to be able to work together."

Her tone was not quite what he had expected, and he was not clear what she meant by working together. "I'm sorry," he said. "I don't follow you."

"When I came in tonight," she said, "I thought you were going to be stuffy and stiff-necked. Edward gave the impression that you just wouldn't budge at all but were determined to leave. I told him I thought that would be absolutely dreadful. After all," she said earnestly, "you're a part of this place. It wouldn't be the same without you—"

Adams sat bolt upright in his chair. "What are you saying? I don't understand you."

She did not appear to notice his sudden change in manner. "Well, it's a very small thing when you come down to it, this business of the newspaper story. The obvious thing is to pretend the conversation never took place. After all, if you hadn't known—"

Adams was almost speechless with rage and mortification. "You mean he's still hoping to go ahead with this absurd—this squalid plan of yours? Are you trying to tell me—"

She looked at him in surprise. "It's already done," she said. "I wrote to my contact in London a couple of days ago." She was genuinely puzzled by his reaction to the news. "But I thought you were being so reasonable. Talking about the need for compromise, and all that. I came here to beg you to change your mind and stay on. Didn't you understand?"

Adams did not answer. The situation was too ludicrous and humiliating. He could not bring himself to tell her that he had assumed she had come to him to capitulate. "I don't want to discuss this with you," he said. "I shall go and see Dr. Barrington myself."

"Well certainly, if you wish." She was obviously not in the least intimidated by the prospect. "As you know, he's not feeling very well at the moment, but by all means go to him if you want to. You'll find he simply confirms what I say."

She spoke with an assurance that alarmed Adams. Either she was a remarkable actress or she was in Barrington's confidence to a degree that none of them had ever approached in all the long history of Kalundani. He hesitated. Then fear made him angry. "Listen, Miss Forrest," he said. "I have to tell you something you may not know. For practical purposes I run Kalundani. When Barrington's ill, or when he's away, I run it alone. I've done so for years. Barrington's a great man, we all know that. He built this place and that was a colossal achievement. But he needs people like myself and Sister Nairn to keep it going. We've been loyal to him all these years. He owes us something. I just don't believe he'll throw us over to satisfy you."

"You're saying you're indispensable?"

He did not reply. "I'm going to see him."

"Please yourself. You'll find he's already made up his mind."

Her complacency infuriated him. "What do you know about him?" he said. "He and I have worked here together for twelve years. We've built this place between us. You only met him a few months ago. You know nothing about him."

She was quite unmoved by his outburst. "Dr. Adams," she said. "I understand how you feel about Kalundani—and about Edward. But as regards myself there's something I ought to tell you before you go any further." There was something in the expression on her face—a look of triumph, and at the same time of softness and self-fulfillment—which gave him a sick realization of what the news would be. "Edward and I are going to get married."

12

Adams paused in his narrative. There was a sound of clattering plates in the corridor outside and the servant came in to lay the table for dinner. He proceeded with maddening slowness, shuffling clumsily around the room on his mutilated leg. Adams waited patiently until he had finished and closed the door behind him. Then he went on, as if no interruption had occurred.

"I suppose I ought to have anticipated something of the kind," he said. "Looking back, there were plenty of clues. The change in his attitude toward her, the increasing amount of time they spent together. I just never thought of Barrington in those terms— none of us did. We'd got out of the way of regarding him as an ordinary man, with ordinary human weaknesses."

"It's hardly a sign of weakness to get married," I said.

"It depends on the marriage. In this case it was never right. I never believed in it. He was lonely, I think. As Kalundani got bigger, he became more isolated. He often talked about his first wife—he used to miss her a great deal. I think he had a number of"—Adams hesitated—"relationships of one kind or another during his world tours. One heard rumors. He was a vigorous man and very attractive to women. But there's nothing permanently

satisfying in that. And then, of course, those last few months he
was a sick man."

I could feel the depth of his detestation for Miss Forrest in
the excuses he made for Barrington. He spoke as if the marriage
could only be explained as a form of mental aberration. All his
religion, and over twenty years' lapse of time, had not been able
to relieve him of his resentment against her. I wondered how many
hours he had spent on his knees, begging God to bring him into a
state of forgiveness. I asked, "Was he ill for long?"

"No. Within a matter of months he was quite fit. But I was
gone by then." He paused and said reminiscently, "I think he
was genuinely sad to see me go. But he couldn't see any other
way. If it was a question of sacrificing one or other of us—" He
shrugged. "As for her, she was naturally very relieved to see the
back of me. After I left I used to hear from Sister Nairn and
the others from time to time. After they got married the real
changes began. All the things that she had suggested when she
first came—and that he had ridiculed. What she wanted, of
course, wasn't a hospital at all; it was a kind of model rural
settlement built around the hospital. They cleared land and planted
crops. They set up a school and a small flour mill. Even the airstrip,
in due course—"

"It must have cost a lot of money."

"A fortune, I imagine." He sighed enviously. "When I think
what we could have done for the hospital itself, with all that—
But then, of course," he added, with admirable generosity, "I
don't suppose we could ever have raised it for the hospital. It
was an idea, you see. And one of Barrington's great gifts was
for giving life to ideas and creating enthusiasm for them in other
people. It was a quality which made him quite different from the
rest of us. It brought him great opportunities. But there were
dangers in it too."

I was reminded of Father Valenti's letter to Rosamond, when
he had referred to the temptations to which men such as Barrington
were subjected. It seemed to me that there was an aspect of the
situation that Adams, for all his knowledge of Barrington, would
perhaps never be able to understand completely. For Adams not
only had a deep religious feeling to sustain him, but also an
innate submissiveness which made it possible to accept the in-

evitability of anything which he regarded as God's will. It was this that gave him the ability to accept the discouragements of his present life with such admirable resignation and dignity. But to a secular person such as myself, it made him a little remote.

It was conceivable that Barrington might have felt his remoteness too. I visualized his enormous surging vitality trapped for the duration of the war in the stultifying routine of a small bush hospital. I could see his moods and his neurotic symptoms as manifestations of frustration and boredom. He must have craved for fresh adventures, and the opportunity to use his pent-up energies in a new cause.

In a way, he was waiting for somebody like Sylvia. Somebody young and arrogant, who would break through the shell of habit which had begun to suffocate him. Once his first resentment was over she would have brought him the promise of liberation, a chance to relive the excitement of his lost youth.

He would need other new people, too, who could share this ambitious vision to which he was now committed. And support it financially. I asked, "Where did the money come from?"

"He still went on raising it in the old way, of course, but that wasn't nearly enough for what he planned to do. He needed a big benefactor—and in the end he found one. You've heard of the Mallory Foundation?"

"Lord Crane mentioned it to me just before he left."

"They put in a vast amount of cash, I believe. You really ought to talk to them." He paused. "I don't know a lot about them myself. The Foundation was set up by Mrs. Mallory, the widow of an American industrialist. But the person you ought to see is Horace Werner, the Secretary of the Foundation. He's the man who can tell you what really went on."

PART FOUR

Werner

"He was a nut," said Werner cheerfully. "But then, of course, in this business almost everybody's a nut. I'm not sure who are the nuttier, the great men or the phonies. It's my job to pick out which is which."

"And which did you decide Barrington was?"

"Well, we supported him, didn't we?" Werner hesitated. He was a middle-aged, rather podgy man, with owl-like spectacles and an air of cheerful irreverence which was slightly out of key with the oak-paneled offices of the Mallory Foundation in which he received me. "We went down the line for him. He was a stone in my shoe, but he appealed to me somehow. There was a kind of grandeur about the way he screwed up his own interests; he seemed to have no sense of self-preservation at all. I guess it made me feel protective.

"I don't think I've ever met anybody who could be so unreasonable with people who were trying to help him. Even abusive, too, on occasions. He just never seemed to try to understand anybody else's point of view . . ."

"Abusive?"

He opened a folder on his desk. "I think we could reasonably call it that. See what you think of these." He handed a file of letters over to me. "In 1952 we ran into a bit of budget trouble. The Foundation's income depends very largely on dividends from stock in Mallory Engineering. Well, that was a bad year for engineering. I forget why—they settled the Korean War or something. So the Board suggested we think about cutting back here and there. Barrington was our biggest running commitment, so I wrote and asked him what his plans were, and whether he could see his way to making some temporary reduction of expenditure. Knowing the cockeyed way he managed his financial affairs, I suggested very tactfully that we'd be prepared to send one of our boys out to help him try to sort things out. You'll see my letter there. I think you'll agree that I couldn't have been more tactful."

I read it. He was right. When an American sets himself out to write a conciliatory letter it is almost medieval in its courtliness.

"What did he reply?"

"He didn't. Weeks went by. The meeting of the Board was coming up and I didn't have any information to give them. So I cabled, asking him what had happened." He pointed to the next letter in the file. "Two weeks later I got that."

The letter was in longhand, in Barrington's unmistakable sprawling, childish hand. The ink was blotched from the damp and there was something in the quavering violence of the pen strokes which spoke of a man exasperated beyond all bearing.

Dear Horace,

I received this morning your arrogant, peremptory cable demanding an immediate reply to your letter. I suppose that, being financially dependent on you as I am, I have no choice but to jump to attention when you crack the whip. I have consequently had to abandon my clinic this morning and turn away a score of people, some of them seriously ill, so as to comply with your request.

I am, of course, consumed with sympathy for the plight of the ball-bearing manufacturers who are suffering from the cold economic winds caused by the unexpected outbreak of peace in the Far East. As a man of sensitivity and culture, you will no doubt appreciate the irony of the fact that our work for the well-being of the African turns out to be dependent for its finance on the continued slaughter of the Chinese. You ask me if I can suggest 'areas for a temporary cut-back in current expenditure.' If that is your businessman's way of asking whether I can manage with less money—

"When he wanted to insult me," said Werner sadly, "he always used to refer to me as a businessman."

—the answer, quite simply, is that I can't—or rather, that I can only do so by allowing a certain number of people to die.

I can cut down on drugs and let some of my patients be treated by the witch doctor. I can abandon the building of the extra wing, and leave the lepers out in the forest for another twelve months, or for as long as it takes for the engineering business to get on its feet again. Perhaps you would let me know which of these human sacrifices would be most likely to appease your Board of Governors.

The second part of your letter concerns accountancy, on which I have never presumed to be an expert. I can only assure you from the depths of my experience that every penny we receive from you is spent with great frugality on things which are vitally necessary for the good of the patients. Their needs, as you know from your visits here, are insatiable, and we would be betraying them as well as you if we were careless or extravagant. Speaking for myself, I have not bought so much as a new suit of clothes for four years. My assistants, as you know, work for practically nothing—the amount you spend on a meal at the Four Seasons would pay my hospital attendant for six months. The Land-Rover is falling to pieces. We already owe a bill for repairs which we are at a loss to know how to pay.

In these circumstances your offer to send out a financial investigator conveys an accusation not simply of incompetence but of downright dishonesty on our part. Of course Joe had not been to the Harvard Business School—

"Who was Joe?" I asked.

"Joe Makongo. He's a Nigerian who went through the London School of Economics. Mrs. Barrington used to run the administration, but when they began to expand the place she got interested in bigger things, so Edward handed the money side over to Joe. It wasn't one of his best decisions."

I turned back to the letter. *—but at heart he is conscientious and honest and works day and night for the good of the project. He would be bitterly affronted, and rightly so, if I acceded to your suggestion. The large sum of money which would be necessary to send your man out here would, I submit, be far better spent on medicines and dressings.*

I really do not know that there is any more I can usefully say. If you wish to withdraw your support from us, that is of course your privilege and there is nothing I can do about it.

If you wish to show this letter to your Board by all means do so. I at least have nothing to be ashamed of, and we might as well bring these matters out into the open.

Yours,
Edward

I handed the letter back to Werner. "Did you show it to the Board?"

"No, of course not. Anyway, I got another letter a week later. Take a look at it."

The next letter on the file was in the same eccentric handwriting, sloping up to the right-hand side of the page, but the penmanship was slightly more controlled.

Dear Horace,
I didn't keep a copy of the letter I wrote to you a few days ago. I cannot recall exactly what I said. But I think I may have been a little brusque with you. If so, I offer my sincere apologies. As you know, the climate here is very trying and I was suffering from one of my periodical attacks of dysentery, as well as having more work on my hands than I could see how to get through. Two of my nurses are down with malaria and that puts a great extra strain on the rest of us.

I think you know my real feelings for you. From the beginning I have relied more than I can say on your friendship, support, and understanding. What we should do out here if you ever lost patience with us and decided to wash your hands of the project, God only knows. But I have faith in your generosity. I know that you really believe in what we are doing, and are far too large in spirit to be put off by occasional explosions of ill-temper on my part.

Yours,
Edward

I could not help feeling a little touched at his anxiety to make amends. Werner saw my expression and smiled. "Pretty good, huh?"

"I think it was. It must have cost him quite an effort to write it."

"Yes, but something may have escaped your attention. He still hadn't answered my original letter. He never did, as a matter of fact." He grinned tolerantly. "It wasn't an uncommon device of his. He would evade a tricky situation by creating another situation. When he'd fought that one out and finally given in to you, either you'd forgotten the first one or felt too much of a heel to raise it again."

I found it difficult to accept this Machiavellian picture of Barrington. "Was he really as calculating as that?"

"Probably not," admitted Werner. "It was hard to know. It might just have been an instinctive device for getting himself out of trouble. Or it might even have been genuine. The only thing is that it seemed to happen rather often. And it worked pretty well, too. In the end I fought it out with the Board and got his money for him."

"And this fellow—Joe—what about him? Was he really cooking the books?"

"Oh sure. We all knew that. Even Edward knew, I think, though he'd never admit it. Mind you, that's not so awful as a European might think. When an African gets a big job, he's expected to look after his relatives—and Joe had a lot of those. It was partly Edward's fault for paying his people such miserable wages. It sounded very idealistic in theory, but in practice it didn't work. Joe would have lost face if he'd told his family how little he was getting, so of course he made it up by putting his hand in the till. I guess he was no more dishonest than custom demanded."

He took back the file from me and looked at his watch. "It's getting up to twelve-thirty. Mrs. Mallory has a luncheon party at one. How would you like to go along?"

"Is she expecting me?"

He replied evasively, "She'll certainly be delighted to see you."

*

Mrs. Mallory's house was only a short cab ride from the office. It was an imposing mansion in Sutton Place, of a kind rare nowadays in New York, though less uncommon in London. It was not unlike a town house in Belgravia or Kensington. The door was opened by a butler, who took our coats and told us that Mrs. Mallory was receiving in the drawing room upstairs. Most of the guests had already arrived.

The drawing room was a rather feminine room with a bow window facing out on to the East River. Mrs. Mallory held court at a seat placed carefully so as to frame her against the view. She must have been, according to my rapid calculations, over fifty now, but she looked about twenty years younger. Her clothes were simple but obviously very expensive, and her blond hair looked as if she had just that moment emerged from the beauty parlor. There were no discernible lines on the matt pale pink surface of her face and neck.

When Werner introduced me to her she smiled and held out a hand. "I was so pleased you could come," she said. She spoke as if I had braved innumerable perils to be at her side. Werner explained that I was interested in Barrington and would very much like to have a word with her after lunch. "Oh surely," she said, "I'll look forward to that." I was about to thank her when the smile faded and she turned her head to greet one of the other guests. Her secretary, a dark, silent woman who sat just behind her and to her left, whispered a name in her ear.

I almost walked backward out of her presence. This, I felt instinctively, was true royalty. Mrs. Mallory obviously had only the vaguest idea of the identity of the guests she entertained in her house. Werner took me by the arm and identified one or two of them. There was an ambassador from one of the Latin American republics, an official from the State Department, and a well-known newspaper columnist. The only person I had met before was Sir Frank Snelgrove, the current president of the Royal Society. He greeted me glumly and then stared in a bewildered way round the room. I had the impression that he was not very clear what he, or anybody else, was doing there.

We finished our martinis and went down to luncheon. The dining-room walls were covered with paintings, most of them post-Impressionist and so famous that they conveyed a feeling of banality rather than distinction. It is an unhappy fact that when one has seen several hundred reproductions of Van Gogh's sunflowers, even the original fails to excite any emotion but boredom. The conversation was worthy but unexciting. It concerned subjects such as the advancement of science and research, the promotion of peace, and the problems involved in aid to the underdeveloped countries. Most of the guests had the glassy, somnambulistic look which I had noted in Mrs. Mallory herself, as if in the course of their lives they met far too many people and took part in far too many portentous discussions on world problems, so that in the end both the people and the issues they discussed had become almost indistinguishable one from another.

After lunch, Mrs. Mallory saw her guests off and Werner and I accompanied her back to the drawing room. She sat in the same chair as before, her lady-in-waiting on her left.

"Horace tells me you're interested in Edward Barrington," she said. Without waiting for a reply, she went on, "I sincerely hope it's not with the object of writing something hostile about him. There was a person called Carlos Markham who came here—"

I explained to her the reason for my inquiries. She had never heard of Laidlaw but she knew Crane well. He had had a close relationship with the Foundation for a number of years. My connection with him seemed to reassure her.

"I knew Edward quite well at one time," she said. "He used to visit the United States every year and often he would stay here at the house when he was in New York. I always felt very privileged to know him and to be able to support him in his work. In later years, as you probably know, he retired completely to Kalundani and wouldn't leave it in any circumstances. So of course we didn't see him after that."

"Lord Crane tells me that you were his greatest benefactor."

"In terms of dollars and cents, maybe. But I don't want to claim too much credit for that. Writing a check's one thing, Mr. Perrin, and dedicating your life is quite another. When I think of some of the people we've been able to help, I feel very humble."

There was an intense, almost naïve sincerity in her voice. She obviously meant what she said. But unfortunately she was trapped in the conventional language of uplift. Her sentiments, like the pictures on her walls, were genuine enough, but they had been reproduced too easily and too often, and the magic had rubbed off them. As she went on speaking of Barrington, I became bored and a little restive. It was like reading one of those pains-taking journalistic biographies that tell you everything about a man's life except what he was really like.

And then, for a moment, she dropped her mask of propriety. It was as if she had temporarily forgotten that she was giving an interview. "Mind you, he had his other side, too," she said. "He could be mean when he liked. But somehow he was attractive even then. It made him more human. You could see where he got the guts to do what he did." She paused and then smiled. "I remember one particular incident. It was something quite small and unimportant, really. It was right at the beginning and I was trying to make up my mind how genuine he was. He impressed me a lot, but there was something a little studied about him. I didn't really feel I'd got through to the man underneath. Then one day we were traveling together in my plane to a conference in Los Angeles. There was nothing much to do so I offered to teach him gin rummy. He was rather patronizing, in that British way of his. When I tried to explain the tactics of the game, he said, 'There's nothing to it, really. It's just a primitive form of mathematics.' Well, I'm an old hand gin rummy player, Mr. Perrin, and that needled me. At the end of the third hand he threw his cards down on the table and accused me of cheating him." She chuckled reminiscently. "He was one hell of a sore loser. I liked that."

For a moment she was lost in the past. There was an affectionate softness about her expression, a feeling of regret, that made me remember Adams's hints about Barrington's adventures on his world tours. Was it conceivable that it had been something more than pure philanthropy that had bound them together? I looked at her again, but the mask had been replaced. She looked suddenly tired. "I did what I thought was the best for Edward," she said. "But I don't know." She was speaking almost to herself. Then she looked earnestly at me. "Believe me, Mr. Perrin, it isn't always easy to know."

Werner caught the sign of fatigue and stood up. It was time for us to leave, he said. She gave him a grateful glance. I realized for the first time how much she depended on him. He alone knew about the bewilderment and the vulnerability that lay beneath that regal façade. He was a protector as well as a servant.

As we walked back to Werner's office, he said, "She's interesting don't you think?"

"Remarkable."

"She gives these luncheons several times a week. That was
how she first met Barrington. I brought him along one day." He
smiled reminiscently. "It was just his kind of occasion. He put
on a terrific show. Lucy was impressed. Very impressed."

"And you?"

"Me too. I'll admit it. He had an act, I could see that, but I
thought there was a great man underneath it. I still think so.
Not that my views were too important at that stage. Lucy felt
she'd found what she was looking for. She was getting tired of
dribs and drabs—dishing out small sums all over the place with
nothing much to show for it. What she wanted to do was to
let herself go on one good project, where we could make some
impact. She decided Kalundani was it."

"When exactly was that?"

"In 1948. Just after Adams left. Barrington wanted to take
what you might call a great leap forward. Make it into something more than a hospital. A kind of model African settlement
with up-to-date irrigation and agriculture and so on. It was a
great prospectus, believe me. We found out later that his wife
had written most of it." He stopped and shook his head admir-
ingly. "Have you met Sylvia?"

"No. I've heard about her."

"She's quite a person. She hated my guts—still does, I guess.
Though we did them fairly well one way and another. For four
years we really pumped money into that outfit. Mind you, it
wasn't quite such an easy relationship as Mrs. Mallory implied
just now. It was a rocky road at times, as you saw from those
letters I showed you. But Edward usually got what he wanted.
Then he did something stupid."

"What was that?"

Werner hesitated. "Well, it was personal, really. Mrs. Mallory,
you've seen her, she's more than just the curator of a load
of inherited cabbage. She's a person—well hell, she has style, she
has distinction. Wouldn't you say that?"

"I would indeed."

"And beneath it all, she's a woman. She took a personal

interest in the whole thing. She used to exchange letters with Barrington on a fairly intimate level. Well, it was in 1954—Barrington sent in his annual financial summary. Months late and even messier than usual. The one clear fact that emerged was that he was fifty thousand dollars light. I discussed it with her. It was pretty bad. But she was prepared to help out. The only thing was that he'd have to start producing the kind of balance sheet that we could show to the trustees without giving them a heart attack. I asked if she wanted me to tell him but she said no. She'd write to him. She'd put it tactfully."

He said sadly, "I don't know what she wrote to him. And I don't know what he wrote back, though I can guess and I imagine you can. All I know is that she called me over to the house. I'd never seen her like that before. She was like someone who'd been kicked in the face by a favorite horse. But she kept a hold of herself. She just said, 'Get over there, Horace. Get over there and fix this for me. If he'll behave like a human being, I'm still prepared to support him. If not, I don't even want to think about him any more.'"

The next day Werner left for Africa.

2

The Cessna moved forward uncertainly to the gap between the two mountains. Werner sat beside the pilot, watching the instrument panel and listening compulsively to the laborious racket of the single engine. Every now and then he looked downward. The ground seemed a lot farther away than it did through the windows of the large commercial planes to which he was accustomed. The noise, combined with the feeling of instability, made him feel slightly sick.

The pilot was a cheerful young man who had become accustomed over the years to holding conversations in the close proximity of a two-hundred-horsepower engine. He had chatted to Werner

all the way from Nairobi, in the way of a dentist who feels
an obligation to keep his patient amused while performing a
difficult filling. He banked a little to avoid a cloud and then,
having cleared the mountain, began to lose height. The valley
stretched out below them, with a tributary of the great river zig-
zagging across it. Far across the plain a great rectangular mass
of rock jutted out from the foothills of the next range of mountains. "There we are," said the pilot. "That's what we're making
for. I'll have you down in ten minutes."

Soon Werner saw the white specks of the buildings of the
settlement. Separated from it by a strip of forest was a small
handkerchief of clear ground which represented the airstrip. The
pilot did a slow dummy run over it to drive off a herd of
wildebeest who were grazing quietly in the middle of the strip,
then circled back and came down. It was a very rough landing.

Werner climbed shakily from the cockpit. The heat struck him
as he reached the ground. The strip, which had seemed from the
air almost next door to the settlement, now appeared as a remote
island in a sea of trackless bush. The air was very still and quiet.
"We'll have to wait here for a little while," said the pilot. "They'll
have seen us from the hospital. They'll be over very shortly to pick
you up in the Land-Rover."

They waited beside the plane, sweating in the sultry heat.
Three small black children stood on the edge of the strip, star-
ing mutely and picking their noses. Werner tried waving at
them but they made no response. Eventually they heard the
sound of an engine. A Land-Rover emerged from the bush to
the right of them and bucked its way across to the aircraft. A
tall white woman got down from the driving seat and walked
toward them.

Werner had never met Sylvia before, but he had received
descriptions of her from visitors to the settlement. Even so, her
physical presence was impressive. Though unusually tall, she had
none of the angular clumsiness common among tall women. As
she jumped lightly down from the Land-Rover and walked over
and introduced herself, she assumed an instant command of the
situation. Her eyes rested on Werner for a moment, as if assessing
his quality as a possible adversary. Then she turned to the pilot.

"Have you got anything for us, Jim?"

"Some mail. And a couple of cases of dressings."

"I'll get the boys to unload them." Two African orderlies had climbed out of the back of the Land-Rover. She gave them a rapid series of orders in Luako. She said to the pilot, "Are you coming over to the hospital for lunch?"

"No. I think I'd sooner get back. There's some cloud over the mountain which could get worse. I'll be back for Mr. Werner on Friday morning."

She said to Werner, "Will three days be enough? We'll be happy for you to stay longer—"

"I'm afraid it's all the time I can spare."

She nodded acceptance. What he said was untrue, and they both knew it was untrue. He had timed it carefully, three days was long enough for him to get a picture of what was going on, and to give them time for reasonable discussions. But it was short enough to make it clear that he was here strictly on a business footing. He could see that Sylvia had grasped the point instantly. She made no attempt to persuade him to prolong his stay.

The mail was unloaded and replaced by some outgoing mail from the Land-Rover. Then she drove to the periphery of the strip and they watched the pilot turn the aircraft and take off. When the plane had disappeared into the heat haze they all got into the Land-Rover and drove back to the settlement.

She drove with considerable dash over a road that was little better than a rough track, forcing the sturdy little vehicle in low gear over potholes and stones and across dried-out water courses. Werner found himself holding on to the dashboard to prevent himself being shaken out of his seat. "It's a rough ride, I'm afraid," she said. "But that's Africa for you. Perhaps you can see why these vehicles don't last as long as they would in Europe." She gave him a sideways glance. One of the points in dispute between them was the size of Barrington's budget for transport. "This is nothing to what it's like in the rains."

She climbed a small bank and they were suddenly out of the bush. Before them stretched a straight dirt road with plantations on either side. "Maize," explained Sylvia, with a wave of her hand. "This is the beginning of the co-operative. I'll drive you round the whole area tomorrow. We also have millet and a certain amount of tobacco.

"Any cash crops?"

She hesitated. "Most of it goes to feed the people here. We mill it for them and make it into flour. The idea is to sell the surplus so as to cover the cost of seed and so on. But of course marketing isn't easy in this part of the world. I'll show you how it works tomorrow."

Her tone was easy and confident. Certainly, Werner thought, the plantation looked prosperous enough. He had seen enough of African agriculture to realize how much work and perseverance was represented by these neatly cultivated fields. "Did you have trouble getting them to join the co-operative?"

"At first," she admitted. "It's easier now, when they can see the advantages." She added after a pause, "Of course they're very backward culturally, you know. Not the easiest people in the world to deal with."

She was silent for the rest of the journey, musing presumably on the problem of cultural backwardness. As they emerged from the fields, the settlement appeared before them. It was no longer merely a hospital. Though the main block, with its wards and verandas, still dominated the site, a mass of ancillary buildings had grown up around it. Sylvia pointed out the flour mill, the storage warehouse, an office building and a small research laboratory. There was also the new guesthouse in which he would be staying. Through the settlement ran a main road covered in tar macadam.

She stopped the Land-Rover in front of the medical superintendent's house. This also, Werner noticed, had a new wing to it. In front of the new wing was a terrace on which Barrington was waiting for them. He stood erect and immobile, silhouetted against the enormous rock behind him. A small tame antelope stood at his side, its ears pricked up warily at the sight of a stranger. Barrington looked older than when Werner had last seen him in New York. His tanned face was deeply lined, and his hair was now almost completely white. He wore a long-sleeved cotton tunic which concealed the deformity of his left hand. He came down the terrace steps and put his arm around Werner's shoulders. "It's good to see you, Horace," he said warmly. "I thought you were never going to come and visit us. You must excuse me for not coming to see you at the airstrip. I haven't been too well lately. I hope the journey didn't shake you up too much."

"Not so bad."

There was a slightly awkward silence. In spite of the warmth of Barrington's welcome, Werner knew him well enough to recognize the cautious, watchful note that lay behind it. He knew that this was going to be a bad three days and he tried to think of something to say to soften the occasion and remind Barrington that whatever happened he was still his friend. But he could not find the right words. As he stood there indecisively, he felt something wet touch his left hand and he started. The antelope leaped away to the far end of the terrace and stood there with its ears back, its nose twitching nervously. "He's very young," said Barrington. "He still thinks everyone has sugar for him." A sardonic smile crossed his face. "He'll find out the truth one of these days."

He took Werner into the house and sent one of the boys over to the guesthouse with his suitcase. When Werner came back to the terrace Barrington poured him a drink from a jug of iced lime juice on the table. Werner relaxed in a cane chair and lit a cigarette. It was a luxury to be safely on the ground again.

They talked easily for a while, like old friends with no problems between them. Sylvia entered into the conversation, without intruding herself into the relationship between the two men. Werner was far too experienced not to realize that the whole scene from the moment of his arrival had been carefully planned and stage-managed. Yet it was possible to recognize the performance for what it was, and still be charmed by it.

The fact was, he thought, as the conversation proceeded through lunch, that he liked Barrington. It was true that Barrington had his affectations, his contrivances, his tricks for getting his own way. But then so, in Werner's experience, had most people that he dealt with. In the charity game, you had to recognize that you were stuck with prima donnas of one kind or another. The only difference was that some of them were difficult in a way you could take and some of them in a way you couldn't. Beneath his state of fairly constant exasperation, he had always had a great regard for Barrington. It had been, on the whole, a good relationship. He felt sad about it; he had a suspicion that after this present encounter, it was never going to be quite the same again.

As they sat over coffee after the meal, Barrington said, "And how's Mrs. Mallory?"

"Pretty good," said Werner. "She sends you her regards."

"You don't have to play the diplomat with me, Horace. What did she really say?" Werner smiled and said nothing. "You know she never replied to my last letter?"

"Yes."

"Why not?"

"I don't know. She didn't show it to me." Werner was impassive. "I gathered that she was a little miffed at something you wrote."

"It's nothing to what I've written to you at one time or another."

"Maybe. There's a difference, of course. I'm just old Horace, the major domo. I don't actually own the dough."

"Oh really, Horace!" Barrington made a gesture of disgust. "You Americans and your money—"

"Hold it," said Werner sharply. "Before you start shooting the works, just try and figure out who else would have felt inclined to back you in what you've done during the last four years. We're not the only country in the world with money. But we're sure as hell the only people who'll dish it out as easy as that."

"Oh, all right." Barrington withdrew cheerfully. "I agree. You're a generous, greathearted people." As Werner opened his mouth to speak, he went on, "No, I'm not pulling your leg, you really are." He added mischievously, "If I'm ungrateful sometimes, please try to bear with me. We're so used to doing without gratitude here that we forget how much other people need it."

"Yes, I know," said Werner. "You're the great white father, and the kiddies take you for granted. On the other hand, they don't exactly kick you in the teeth."

Barrington was suddenly serious. "They may one day. Quite soon perhaps." Then as if regretting his change of mood, he said lightly, "Perhaps I ought to write something nice to Mrs. Mallory."

"I'm afraid that won't be enough." It was unpleasant to have to destroy Barrington's illusions, but it was essential to make him face the situation. There was no possibility of charming his way out of this one.

"Oh, come along, Horace—"

"She means it, Edward. I know her. I've worked for her a long time. She doesn't want to hear from you until we've been through the books."

Werner could see Barrington speculating whether there was any chance of overriding him with one of his famous displays of temperament. He decided against it. "Very well," he said, shrugging his shoulders. "Take your time. Have a look at anything you like. We've got nothing to hide."

*

Werner spent the next two days making a detailed tour of the settlement. On the first day Barrington took him round the hospital buildings. He saw the wards and the operating theater, the outpatient department and the leper village. He was also introduced to the staff. They were mostly young and very enthusiastic. Barrington had recently introduced a scheme for taking on European and American doctors who were keen to do a few years in primitive conditions before settling down to practice at home. There were certain problems, Barrington admitted. "Of course, it takes them a while to get used to conditions out here. And they don't have time to learn the language. But they're extremely stimulating companions. They keep us up to the mark."

The nurses were of a similar kind. Barrington was affectionately paternal with them, but stumbled over one or two of their names. He showed Werner the old dining room, where they had all met together each evening in the old days. Now it was too small, unfortunately. The doctors and nurses ate separately, and the Barringtons dined in their own house. Werner asked if any of the old staff remained. Barrington shook his head. "People come and go at a place like this. Personal problems, illness, all kinds of things take them away." He smiled wryly. "I'm the only one who's condemned to life imprisonment." He led the way out of the doctor's house, locking it automatically behind him from long habit. "Carl was the last to go. I somehow thought he was here for good, but three months ago he decided he wanted to go back to Sweden."

*

The next day Sylvia took Werner in the Land-Rover round the newer part of the settlement. He saw the mill and the grain storage warehouse and the irrigation ditches by means of which they had reclaimed the land to the east of the hospital. There was a small but solid looking dam in a natural bowl on the hillside, and some neat terraced cultivation leading down from it. As they stood on the shoulder of the dam, enjoying the magnificent view over the valley, Werner's eye wandered to the farmland around the hospital. From here it was possible to see it as if laid out on a map. He picked out the track on which he had been brought from the airstrip. About half a mile to the north of it was another track, much wider and straighter, and also leading to the hospital. It looked very much as if it had been originally planned as a grand approach to the settlement. On either side of it were barren fields covered with sickly scrubby trees. "What happened there?" he asked.

"Oh," said Sylvia casually, "that was an experiment that didn't come off. We tried various kinds of fruit—limes and pineapples and so on. But the climate doesn't seem to suit them. On the other hand, we've had some success with bananas." She pointed to a banana plantation over to the right. "As for the basic crops—corn and millet and cassava—we've improved the yields beyond recognition. It's astonishing what you can do for these people with a little organization."

"Yes, I'm sure."

"I wish you'd seen it six years ago when I first came here. It was picturesque, I suppose, in its way. But really the whole thing was hopeless, if you looked at it from a logical point of view. You wore yourself out dressing their sores and dishing out pills, but it didn't make any real impact on the situation."

"Does this?" asked Werner. He thought of the vast areas he had flown over on his journey from the coast. He pictured the remote valleys, dotted here and there with collections of straw huts, and the occasional herds of emaciated cattle wandering across the parched and barren land. "It's no more than a tiny isolated speck, and after all—"

"It means something, though. It shows the way. It demonstrates what can be done. Surely that's worth a few million dollars?" She added with great intensity, "This country's rich, you know. It has everything, if it can only be used. When I think of what's been done in the Negev—"

"Africans aren't Jews," Werner pointed out. "Perhaps they don't even want to be. Had you thought of that?"

"They must be made to want it," she said. "We have to do it for them. If we don't, the Communists will." She waited for him to comment. When he did not reply, she went on, "Mr. Werner, I know you have problems with your Foundation, but I'm speaking to you personally. You're not just a stupid millionaire who thinks of nothing but money. You're an educated man. You have some vision—"

' He had been sympathetic with her obvious sincerity and dedication to her dream. But the clumsy attempt to drive a wedge between him and Mrs. Mallory annoyed him. Like so many enthusiasts, she was incapable of leaving well alone. He stepped off the parapet of the dam. "I'd like to go back now," he said. "I want to spend some time on the financial statements."

*

"Well," said Barrington, "have you seen everything you wanted to see?"

Werner nodded. It was the last night of his stay and they were sitting in the living room of Barrington's house after dinner. He had seen, not perhaps everything, but at least as much as he could reasonably expect to understand in a short visit of this kind. And he had no doubt as to his conclusions.

"I'd like to make one or two points clear before we begin," he said. "I hope you understand, Edward, that I'm probably one of the greatest living admirers of your work, and that I have the warmest feelings for you as a person. We've supported you for four years to the tune of about two million dollars, and in my view that money's been well spent. Our contribution to Kalundani is something we can be justly proud of. We don't want to back out of this. On the other hand—and I'm not criticizing you because God knows I understand your difficulties—it's plain that the situation's got right out of hand from an accountancy point of view. We have to straighten things out a little before we go any further."

"Horace," said Barrington, with exaggerated politeness, "will you do me a favor as an old friend?"

"Of course."

"Just stop being so bloody diplomatic. If you feel you have to tell me what a lovely person I am each time you dish out a piece of bad news, we shall be here all night."

Werner nodded placidly. He was not disconcerted. He knew that if he had omitted his preamble, Barrington would have accused him of being abrupt and discourteous. "If you want the plain facts, here they are. The first is that you've overspent your last year's grant by fifty thousand dollars. Right?"

"I've explained all that."

"Sure you have. Costs of building went up and so the new guesthouse was over budget. The roof blew off one of the wards. The weather was terrible—"

"It was."

"It couldn't have been more terrible than your bookkeeping. I went through the accounts with that fellow of yours—what's his name?"

"Joe Makongo."

"Well, Christ. I mean, we've got to have something different there."

"He got a First in Political Economy at the London School of Economics," said Barrington defensively.

"I don't doubt it. But what we need is someone who's done a night-school course in bookkeeping." The memory of Joe's ledgers brought him a pain which was almost physical. "Hell, Edward, we're not only short, we don't even know where we're short."

"I can't see that it matters too much."

"You can't?" Werner's voice rose an octave.

"No." Barrington swept an arm around the room in a dramatic gesture. "Are we living in luxury? Are we drinking champagne? Is Sylvia buying her clothes at Balmain? Do we own stocks and shares? My balance at the bank, which I'll happily show you, is sixty-four pounds and sixteen shillings. If the money has gone, it's gone on medicine or dressings or food for people who are by your standards so poor that they shouldn't be alive at all.

Could any of the other beneficiaries of your Foundation say as much?"

It was true in its way. Werner knew that Barrington himself was totally indifferent to money. No doubt Makongo was stealing in some way or another, but certainly not a scale which would seem significant by the standards of the Mallory Foundation. A great many of the grants the Foundation made went to projects which Werner privately considered far more extravagant and pointless than Kalundani could ever be. On the other hand, these other beneficiaries were robbing the Foundation within a context respectable in modern terms. They were producing accounts of some kind or another. Barrington could simply not be allowed to get away with this casual, perfunctory approach. It was worse than dishonest—it was by the standards of modern commercial bureaucracy, indecent.

"It's no use, Edward," he said. "It can't be done. We just don't know where we are. Frankly, I have my doubts about a lot of the agricultural aspects of this enterprise. When we come right down to it, you haven't been able to introduce any new crops here. It's just banana and millet and maize. Everything else failed."

"We get more out of the land," said Sylvia.

"Sure. But what happens to it? So far as I can see, you have a surplus but it isn't easy to sell, because of distribution problems. The flour mill's valuable, I can see that. But what's it all costing? We haven't an idea. For all we know, it might be cheaper to ship the goddamned stuff up from the coast and give it to them."

He could see the look of outraged disgust on Barrington's face and he pressed on quickly, "Yes, all right, I know that's not the object of the exercise, but we're dealing with people whose business it is to hand out money. They think that way. You have to accept it. They're terrified of open-ended commitments. They're scared that maybe you'll fall down dead and they'll be left holding the sack." He realized that he was doing what he had resolved not to do. He was referring to the Foundation as "they." He was apologizing for his own organization. Was it some quality of Barrington's or a defect in his own character, that led him after two days to begin identifying with Barrington and Barrington's point of view? He pulled himself back on to the rails. "What it adds up to is that the Foundation will find the fifty thousand, but on certain conditions. And the most important condition is that they're allowed to send their own representative out here to sort out the finance."

Barrington nodded thoughtfully. He had obviously been expecting this. "And tell me what I can do and can't do, I suppose?"

"It wouldn't be quite so hairy as that," said Werner. "But there may have to be some modifications. My guess is that some of the agricultural projects will have to be cut back."

Sylvia rose indignantly from her seat, but Barrington waved her into silence. He was at his most imperious. He spoke gently but with great dignity. "And supposing I don't agree?"

"We're hoping very much that you will. We want to go on helping you. We still have great confidence—"

"I said—supposing I didn't?" insisted Barrington.

"Then I can't promise to get you anything. Not even next year's running grant." Werner added with genuine unhappiness, "I'm sorry, Edward. This is a crisis of confidence."

"What you're saying is that you're prepared to break me. To throw away all my work, all the money you've already put in—"

Werner almost smiled. It was the escalation ploy, the oldest in the business. You milked more money out of the donor by threatening him with the loss of what he had already put in. It was surprisingly effective on all levels, from international politics downward. But it was no good this time. "You can't bluff us, I'm afraid. If we have to pull out, we will."

"Then damn you, pull out!" Barrington's façade of saintly detachment began to crack. "I can manage without you if I have to. I've done it before, you know."

"Not on this scale."

"It's no use trying to scare me. I've been in Africa now for twenty-five years. Whatever I've done, I was always told beforehand that it was impossible."

Sylvia burst into the discussion. "He can do it," she said fiercely. "He can manage without you. We don't need you. We can go out and beg. We've done it before. We have millions of supporters all over the world. Small people, not millionaires. People who know and care for Edward's work—" She halted, and then said, with the air of one playing a trump card, "You know he's been put up for a Nobel prize?"

"Yes," said Werner, rather wearily. "I know."

"If he gets that—"

"He won't get it."

"Why shouldn't he? Schweitzer got one."

"Schweitzer wasn't in hock for fifty thousand dollars." He turned to Barrington. "Edward, if you're counting on that, please don't. The Nobel's like a bank loan. They only give it to you when they're absolutely sure you don't need it."

"You're probably right," said Barrington indifferently. "I don't care. It doesn't matter to me. But I won't hand over control of Kalundani to you or anybody. It's mine. I dreamed of it for years. I built it. I sweated and suffered for it. I won't let it go. You can go back and tell that to Mrs. Mallory. It's my final decision."

Werner looked at Barrington's face and knew that he was telling the truth. In fact, he suspected that the issue had been predetermined before he had ever set foot at Kalundani. It seemed to him likely that Barrington had been chafing for some time at his dependence on the Mallory Foundation, and looked back nostalgically to the old barnstorming days when he had traveled around the world collecting money from wherever he could get it. Barrington was confident in himself, in the way a man is always confident who has succeeded against the continued warnings of experts. He believed in his own magic and could not really visualize a circumstance in which he might fail.

It was, thought Werner, one of the penalties of early success in the game of life, that one never recognized the day when the trick which had worked so often would be tried in new circumstances and fail. But he knew, with great sadness, that in this case it was bound to fail. He knew how much money Barrington needed, and how much there was in the world to be obtained. He knew all the sources and all the techniques. He knew the maximum that Barrington could pull in from a one-shot campaign, what his expenses would be, and what he could hope for in the follow through. Often he wished he did not know these things, but once known they could not be ignored or forgotten. Barrington had no chance—no chance at all.

3

As Werner sat at his desk in his Park Avenue office he heard
reports of Barrington's progress over the following months. The
campaign to raise money was similar to previous campaigns, but
it was now possible to detect a febrile, urgent note that had
never been present before. It was a campaign of a man calling
out his last reserves of support, straining his credit to the limit,
striving desperately for the magic that had brought him victory
out of defeat so often in the past. But now there was something
a little faded about the magic. The very urgency of the appeal
carried an undertone of desperation.

Even more damaging to Barrington was a subtle change in
the atmosphere of the times. Western interest in Africa was on
the wane. The great economic recovery of the 1950s had turned
the minds of Europeans to themselves and their own problems.
The colonial tide was running out. The British in particular,
surprised and hurt to find themselves no longer admired by their
subject peoples, listened without enthusiasm to appeals for money
on behalf of those who had rejected them. Barrington was still
revered, and his meetings in London were successful from a prestige
point of view. But financially the results were disappointing. The
money he so desperately needed was failing to come in.

Werner heard the news with regret, but there was nothing he
could do unless Barrington could bring himself to swallow his
pride and reopen negotiations. He waited without much hope.
One afternoon, when he returned from lunch, his secretary told
him that there was a call from London. When he went to
the telephone he was told that it was from Lord Crane. He had
met Crane socially on one or two occasions but did not know
him well. He had a vague memory of a prim, distinguished man
with a fondness for setting up committees.

"Mr. Werner? This is Alan Crane here. You remember me?"

"Yes, of course, we met last year in Geneva."

"I'm sorry to bother you like this, but I felt you'd want to know. It's about Edward Barrington. I take it you still have an interest in his work?"

"To some extent," said Werner cautiously. "We were extremely interested at one time, but during the last few months—"

"Yes, I know about that," said Crane. "Most regrettable. I believe he behaved very foolishly and I told him so. But I'm afraid something of a crisis has arisen. I can't tell you about it over the telephone, but it's really rather serious. If you *are* still interested—"

Werner knew Crane well enough to realize that the languid tone of voice held a very genuine concern. The fact of his being prepared to telephone across the Atlantic to a comparative stranger was an indication in itself that something serious had happened. "What do you want me to do?" he asked.

"If you could possibly find the time to come over here—"

Werner looked quickly at his engagement book. His annual visit to London was not due for a month or two. It would require a lot of reorganization. He said, "I'm pretty busy right now."

Even on the transatlantic line the disappointment in Crane's voice came through. He said, in the huffy tone of a man not used to asking favors, "Of course, it's entirely up to you—"

Werner drummed his fingers on the table and made a quick decision. "Okay, I'll fix it somehow. I'll try to get a flight tomorrow morning."

*

His flight brought him into Heathrow in the late afternoon. He checked into his hotel, had dinner, and then took a taxi to Crane's flat in Eaton Square. "I'm so sorry to drag you over like this," said Crane.

"I didn't think you'd have called me up unless it was important."

"As far as Edward's concerned," said Crane, weighing his words with his habitual care, "I'd say it was very important indeed. If he can't find a way out of the present situation, it may finish him for good." He made a gesture of impatience. "Of course, one has to admit that it's entirely his own doing. As you probably know, I've been connected with him in one way or another right from the beginning. I feel a certain obligation to help him, largely on account of his daughter, who has lived with my wife and myself ever since her mother died. But he's hardly the easiest man to advise."

Werner nodded noncommittally. He was familiar with Crane's reputation, not only as a public figure but as a man. He was prepared to recognize that he was a kindly and humane man, notable for his integrity and liberal principles; yet somehow, on close contact, he did not find him particularly likable. He was not quite sure why. Perhaps it was a rather petulant quality in his manner, common to men who had achieved such spectacular success in youth that later life is almost bound to come as something of a disappointment. Or perhaps it was his air of being so well organized in his own life that he found it difficult to understand the disorganization of others. He did not give the impression of a man who was tolerant of human frailty.

As Werner listened to Crane's well-bred voice, watching the occasional movements of his beautiful hands, and sipping his excellent whisky, he found himself comparing Crane with Barrington and not entirely to Crane's advantage. In every ordinary sense Crane must be regarded as a person of far greater distinction. He had a more subtle, logical mind. He had a record of brilliant research at a phenomenally early age and even now, when his creative genius had faded, he was distinguished as an administrator and a powerful supporter of far-seeing social measures. By contrast, Barrington appeared bigoted, aggressive, and unreasonable. His language was frequently vulgar and his actions inconsiderate. He could be egotistical to the point of brutality. And yet there was about him a quality of physical and mental energy which, when he cared to exert it, made both intelligence and charm seem trivial by comparison. When Barrington spoke of something he cared about, he seemed to blot out, both for himself and for his listeners, all other impressions. He managed to create on these occasions an event of supreme importance, which he was determined to share with you. In such moments Werner was certain, as he was never quite certain with Crane, that he was speaking to a great man.

"I can't tell you," said Crane, "what a disappointment it was to hear that he'd broken with the Mallory Foundation. He's always been hopelessly unrealistic about money and he would never listen to anyone who tried to advise him. When he went in with you, we thought at last there was somebody who could keep him straight."

Werner wondered who "we" were, who had been so relieved at being able to pass the Barrington headache over to the Americans. He could visualize them, Crane's people, men of substance, anxious that there should be an end to uncertainty and confusion. Barrington had never been their kind of man. They could recognize that he had important qualities and that what he did was good for British prestige, but they regarded him with apprehension. They could not be certain what he would do next.

Now, no doubt, it would suit them very well if once again the Mallory Foundation provided the means of salvaging a difficult situation. He said guardedly, "Perhaps you'd better tell me what's happened."

Crane paused to refill Werner's glass. "It's really rather ridiculous," he said, "considering how much there is at stake. Do you know of a man called Carl Bergstrom?"

Werner searched his memory. "No, I'm afraid not."

"There's no reason why you should. He lived at Kalundani for many years, but he kept very much to himself. He was one of those lame ducks that Edward tended to collect. But he stayed longer than the others. I met him once. He was a small remote kind of man with a fair beard. I believe he was very religious—" Crane shrugged. "And a little strange. He came of a wealthy Swedish family, but he'd never been able to fit in at home. Kalundani seemed to give him what he needed. He made himself useful there and it seemed as if he was happy to stay indefinitely. Then, six months ago, he left."

"Why?"

"Nobody's quite sure. I imagine the new regime didn't suit him so well. He may have got across Mrs. Barrington. Anyway, he just packed his bags without saying anything and went back to Stockholm. I gather Barrington didn't take much notice. After all, he had a lot of other things on his mind. But last week he got a letter from a London firm of solicitors who look after

the Bergstrom interests in this country. They're bringing a civil
action against him."

"For what?"

"They claim a sum of five thousand pounds which Carl lent
Barrington nearly ten years ago. Barrington says he took it as a
donation. But they say they have documents proving it was a
loan." Crane paused and then said rather primly, "From my
knowledge of the parties concerned, I shall be surprised if they
can't prove their case."

"You know the Bergstroms?"

"I've met Alex, the head of the family. They're extremely
reputable people. And I'm sure the money itself is of no significance
to them."

"Then why bring the action?"

"As a matter of principle, I gather. Edward's solicitors had
an informal chat with theirs. I gather the family are very sensitive
about Carl. They think he was taken advantage of. You can see
their point of view."

"I'm sure," said Werner, "that Edward wouldn't deliberately—"

"Oh no, no, of course not. But you know him. He's very vague
about such matters and he has a facility for believing what he
wants to believe." Crane shook his head gloomily. "It's really a
most frightful impasse."

"You couldn't talk to this guy Alex, or whatever his name is?"

"Out of the question, I'm afraid. I suggested it to the solicitors
and they were horrified. Evidently it would put us in a hopelessly false position. If the case ever came to court it would make
things very much worse for Edward."

"I suppose there's no question of him paying it?" It was a
question one had to ask, though Werner knew very well what the
answer would be.

"Impossible, I gather." Crane looked fixedly at Werner. "We've
got to find some way of helping him."

"Why?"

Crane looked startled. "Surely you wouldn't like to see him go
down?"

Werner was slightly amused at Crane's consternation. "Well,
you know," he said easily, "Edward's a big boy now. We all have
to face our own problems some time or another. You helped him

a lot in the past, I know. But I don't see why you should feel such an absolute obligation."

Crane pondered, almost as if it were a new concept to him.

"I have Rosamond to think of," he said. "It would hurt her a great deal to see her father disgraced. And then of course, there's the whole concept of Kalundani. It means so much to so many people—"

Werner could see that what appalled Crane was the thought of any kind of wanton destruction—of Barrington, of Kalundani, of indeed any institution that had somehow become part of British consciousness and national pride. It was a strange aspect of a man who had started as a socialist revolutionary, anxious to tear society up by the roots. Now those very roots had wound themselves around him to such an extent that he felt that anything long established had a right to preservation. To Werner, accustomed like most Americans to a world of destruction and construction, of scrapping and starting again, it was an odd and rather amusing attitude of mind. He said, "You don't really believe in Edward's work very much, do you?"

Crane paused. He seemed about to deny it, but the habitual accuracy of his mind would not allow him to do so. "You're quite right, I don't. I always thought it was misguided. But that's hardly the point, is it?"

"It would be for me," said Werner. "If I didn't admire what he was trying to do, I wouldn't give the matter another thought."

Crane accepted the observation and recorded it without emotion. There was neither approval nor criticism in his voice. "But the main thing is that even if we disagree about Edward's work, we still come to the same conclusion. We want to help, that's right, isn't it?"

"If he'll let us," said Werner. He added, "I've offered him help once. That offer still stands."

"Even with this present development?"

"I think so. Another fifteen thousand dollars isn't going to hurt us too much. We'd take care of that. But only on the same conditions. He'd have to submit to some kind of financial management." Werner paused. "You know, I had an idea as I was coming over on the plane. It may be that it was the concept of the Foundation being in charge that Edward didn't like. After all, I suppose we're foreigners to him. Perhaps if you could set up some controlling organization over here—you know, your kind of people—" He did not feel it necessary to enlarge on what he meant by Crane's kind of people. 'I think we'd be prepared to do business on that basis."

Crane's face lightened. "I'm awfully pleased you suggested that. As a matter of fact I was proposing to put something of the kind to you myself. It would be ideal, really. We could get together a strong committee with some good names—" His voice gathered confidence. Werner could see that when it came to getting together strong committees with good names, Crane felt himself on much firmer ground. "We could take all the fund-raising and accountancy away from Edward and leave him free to get on with the work he's really equipped to do." He was cheering up visibly as he contemplated the imposition of some kind of bureaucratic order on to Barrington's chaotic existence. "You know, this may very well turn out to be the luckiest thing that's ever happened to him."

4

The meeting with Barrington was arranged the following day in the office of Humbert and Cartwright, Barrington's solicitors. Crane picked Werner up at his hotel, and drove him to Lincoln's Inn. He said, "You'll find Humbert's a sensible fellow, on the whole. A bit limited, perhaps, and inclined to take a pessimistic view of situations, but sound. He understands what's needed here. In fact, it was he who persuaded Barrington to ask my advice." He added, in a confidential voice, "I arranged for us to get there a little early, so that you could talk to him before the Barringtons arrive."

They were shown straight into Humbert's office. He was a melancholy-looking man, with thin gray hair and rings under his eyes. His long sallow face was distinguished by a mole on the left side of his jaw which he stroked absently from time to time. "I'm afraid this is a very unhappy affair," he said. "For a man like Dr. Barrington to be in such a position—" He shook his head glumly. "I'm very glad to have your assistance in trying to extricate him from it."

It seemed, thought Werner, that they were all in a conspiracy to save Barrington despite himself. It was not a role that particularly attracted him, but he recognized the necessity for it. "I gather," he said, "that you think the Bergstroms have a good case."

"Watertight, I'm afraid. Frankly, Mr. Werner," Humbert said earnestly, "this is one of those cases where it would be absolutely disastrous for us to go to court. It isn't simply that we should lose. We should also have to submit to a detailed cross-examination on the state of our client's financial affairs."

"I can see that might be embarrassing."

"It could be more than embarrassing," said Humbert. "There's a possibility of being accused of"—he paused, searching for a delicate legal way of expressing it—"of actual irregularity."

"You mean fraud?" said Werner.

Humbert winced. "No, Mr. Werner, I do not mean fraud. Fraud implies an intention to misappropriate funds, and I'm sure that that was never in Dr. Barrington's mind for a moment. What I am referring to is a degree of carelessness in money matters which might possibly give that impression."

"Okay," said Werner tolerantly. The distinction seemed to him more apparent than real. "Either way the important thing seems to be the attitude of the Bergstroms. I suppose they can be bought off, can they? They're not out to gratify a personal grudge?"

"Good Heavens, no," said Humbert, visibly shocked. "This is a matter of principle with them. They think Carl is—to put it bluntly—a little simpleminded, and they're not going to have him exploited. They haven't even asked for interest, which I think they would have had every right to do. All they demand is the five thousand pounds of the original loan. And their costs, of course," he added as an afterthought.

"Very well, then," said Werner. "Now, as I understand it, we're all agreed on the best way out of this—"

They discussed Crane's plan for a while. It was obvious that
Humbert would present no problem. The main difficulty was
apparent to all of them. It was to get Barrington to agree. They
had begun to turn over various methods of persuasion when the
telephone rang.

Humbert answered it. "Yes, show them in right away." He
put down the telephone and said, "Dr. and Mrs. Barrington have
arrived."

As always when Barrington entered a room, he seemed somehow to diminish the size of everyone else in it. He looked
stronger and fitter than he had at Kalundani. He gave Werner
the impression of being stimulated rather than cast down by his
predicament. Sylvia was trim and elegant in a gray suit that
might well have been made in Paris, but had more probably
been picked up from a rack in a department store. They both
looked alert, wary and ready for battle.

Barrington's eyes ranged round the room. "All assembled, I
see," he said ironically.

Humbert shifted in his seat. "Lord Crane and Mr. Werner
arrived a little early. We were just discussing—"

"You don't need to tell me what you were discussing," interrupted Barrington. "I know both these gentlemen very well. Lord
Crane is a man of Roman virtue and a world-wide reputation
for progressive behavior. He doesn't really approve of me because
he thinks I'm a muddlehead who wastes his time on individuals
when he ought to be doing something more constructive in a
social way. Mr. Werner is a truly liberal and open-minded American, who has the unhappy task of acting as hatchet-man
to a hard-nosed lady in the machine-tool business. You've all been
shaking your heads over my improvidence and trying to think of
some way to save me from the fate I so richly deserve. Right?"

The melancholy on Humbert's face deepened. He felt the
mole on his cheek as if to make sure that at least one aspect of
life was in its accustomed place. "Dr. Barrington, I assure you—"

"Don't worry, Mr. Humbert," said Crane, with some impatience. "As Dr. Barrington says, we all know each other extremely
well. Neither Mr. Werner nor myself are going to take offense."
He turned to Barrington. "Edward, this is too serious for one of
your performances. This lawsuit could destroy you completely."

"I quite agree," said Barrington. "As you can perhaps imagine, I'm as keen to get rid of it as anybody. The trouble is," he added, with a baleful glance at Humbert, "that every time I suggest a way out, my solicitor says it's impossible."

"Dr. Barrington finds it hard to understand the legal difficulties—" said Humbert miserably.

"I can understand them perfectly well," said Barrington. "I just think they're bloody silly. Why shouldn't I use some of the money I've collected to pay him off?"

"Because it would be a violation of your own word," said Crane coldly. "I took the trouble to read your appeal. It states that donations will be used for current upkeep of the settlement. There's nothing whatever about paying off old debts."

"How many people do you suppose read that? Or care one way or the other, even if they do?"

"That's nothing to do with the matter. You've said it and you're committed. Morally and legally."

Barrington sat in silence for a moment. Then he said irritably, "All right then. But why the devil can't I get in touch with Carl?" He was overtaken by one of his sudden changes of mood. The bluster left his manner and he said sadly, "You know, I don't understand it. He lived with us for so long. We were friends. Kalundani was his home—it was a refuge for him. He was part of our family. I'd never have thought it possible for him to turn against me."

Sylvia spoke for the first time. "He was a weak man," she said. "I never trusted him."

"He couldn't help being weak."

"I didn't say he could. But men like that believe the last person who speaks to them. When he was at Kalundani he worshiped you. Almost beyond reason. Then, when his family got at him—"

"I don't know," said Barrington. "It's not as simple as that. I feel I must have failed him in some way."

She made an impatient gesture. Werner had the impression that this was an argument they had been through several times before. "Why do you continue to defend him? It absolutely defeats me."

"Because he was my friend," said Barrington obstinately. "You can't turn friendship off just like that. Perhaps he's ill, or perhaps they've told him something that isn't true. It just doesn't make sense to me as it is. Why didn't he write to me direct, instead of that filthy solicitor's letter?"

"That's not too uncommon," said Humbert. "Usually it's because people are timid. They can't bear a confrontation. They hide behind a lawyer."

Barrington seemed hardly to hear him. He was talking to himself. "After all we've been through together. There must be some misunderstanding. If only I could get him on the telephone—"

"I must ask you to put that possibility right out of your mind," said Humbert emphatically. "If the matter came to court their counsel would use it against us. We should be accused of trying to put pressure on him."

Barrington looked at him in disgust. "Yes, I know. You've told me before. So far as I can see, once you bring the lawyers in, it's the end of any form of civilized behavior."

Humbert stroked nervously at his cheek. There was an unhappy silence. It was broken eventually by Crane. "Edward," he said, in his most propitiating voice, "we all know how upsetting this is for you. What I think you must understand is that you can't beat it alone. I know you like to be totally independent, but in a difficulty of this kind, there's no disgrace in being willing to accept help. We're prepared to help you if you'll let us."

"In other words, you want to set up that Trust you've always gone on about?"

"I don't think there's any alternative."

Barrington turned mockingly to Werner. "Ever since I went to Africa, Alan's been shocked by the fact that I didn't have a committee of important individuals to give me respectability. It was like going round naked as far as he was concerned. It was even more embarrassing when I did so much better than the people who did have committees, but he felt sure his day would come. And here it is."

"I'm afraid he's right. There's no alternative," said Werner gently.

Sylvia burst out. "He's managed for twenty-five years on his own. He's done more than any man in Africa. And he's done

that because he relied on himself, not a gang of old peers and retired generals. Are you trying to say now that he's been a failure?"

"He's a very brilliant and wonderful man," said Werner wearily.
"Surely we don't have to keep on saying that. But we're confronted
with a crisis. It's a crisis that requires money. And you can't
get the money without sharing some degree of control." He was
suddenly tired of all this inconclusive argument. "Edward, I've
always been straight with you," he said. "There just isn't anything
to talk about any more. Either you accept the offer or you don't.
If you do, you'll be astonished at how generous and helpful Mrs.
Mallory will be, and how little we shall all interfere with you. If
you don't—well, that's it. You're on your own."

There was another silence. For a moment Werner thought
Barrington was going to give way. Then Sylvia spoke. "Surely
you're not going to let them beat you like this?" she said violently.
"After all you've said about standing on your own feet—"

"Be quiet for a moment." Werner was startled. He realized that
for all Barrington's aggressiveness in his dealings with others, he
had never before heard him speak brusquely to his wife. He
could see that Sylvia too was taken aback. Barrington rose from
his seat. His tall, erect figure commanded the room. "This is for me
to decide," he said. "I don't want to be cajoled or threatened or
persuaded. I make my own decisions. I'll let you know in the next
week what I decide to do."

5

Werner had friends on the South Coast who had invited him
to spend a few days with them before returning to America. If
Barrington did not get in touch with him during the next week,
he decided to wipe the whole matter from his mind and take a
plane back to New York. He spent the time walking and playing
golf and almost succeeded in forgetting Barrington altogether.

Then one day, as he was about to go into lunch, the telephone rang. It was Humbert.

"I'm sorry to interrupt your holiday, Mr. Werner—"

"That's all right. Has Edward made up his mind?"

"No, it's not that." Humbert's voice sounded even more lugubrious on the telephone than it did direct. "I've just had some very tragic news. Carl Bergstrom has been admitted to hospital. He tried to take his own life."

Appalled though he was at the news, Werner was not entirely surprised. Given the situation, and Carl's unstable personality, it was obviously on the cards that he might do something of the kind. "What happened exactly?"

"He slashed his wrists. They were able to get him to hospital in time and physically he's out of danger. It's his mental state that's giving rise to anxiety."

"Have you told Edward?"

"No. No, I haven't." He paused. "Frankly, Mr. Werner, I thought it would be better coming from one of his close friends. I tried Lord Crane but he's at a conference in Bonn and simply can't get away. I wondered if perhaps you—"

"You'd like me to come back to London and tell Edward?"

"If you would."

"All right. If you think it's better." He was slightly puzzled. It was a very sad business, of course, but Humbert seemed to be taking it more solemnly than he would have expected. "I was due to return to London tomorrow anyway."

He waited for Humbert to thank him and ring off, but instead the solicitor said, "I'm afraid there's something else I have to tell you. Something very disturbing. It seems that Carl received a letter from Dr. Barrington. Their lawyers won't tell me what was in it, but it was dated three days ago."

*

Werner telephoned Barrington's hotel in Knightsbridge. The campaign secretary told him that Dr. Barrington was out giving a lecture. He was expected back some time later in the day but there was a dinner engagement for the evening. Dr. Barrington had such a full program, he was very much in demand. Would Mr. Warrender care to leave a message . . . Werner had a voice in reserve for such people. "The name is Werner," he said. "Horace Werner. Put it down on your pad and get it right. And tell Dr. Barrington I'll be around at ten o'clock tomorrow morning. It's something very important."

"I'm not sure—"

"Tell him he'd better be there," said Werner, and rang off.

He took a train to London that afternoon. The next morning after breakfast he went round to Barrington's hotel. Barrington himself opened the door of the room. Sylvia was sitting at the writing table checking a pile of receipted bills. She gave a casual nod to Werner as he came in.

"Well, Horace, here I am," said Barrington cheerfully. "I don't know what you said to my girl, but you certainly frightened the daylights out of her. A rude American, she said, who shouted at her." He added humorously, "That's no way to treat the daughter of a bishop."

"I'm not concerned with your secretary," said Werner. "I've got news for you about Carl. He's tried to commit suicide."

All the gaiety left Barrington. He sat down in a chair and clasped his hands together as if making a physical attempt to keep himself under control. He did not look directly at Werner. Eventually he said heavily, "You say he tried?"

"Yes. He didn't succeed. It was evidently a fairly amateurish effort," said Werner with some bitterness. "They've fixed up the cuts on his wrists all right. But not his mind. That's going to take longer."

"His mind? What do you mean by that?"

"Frankly I don't know. I don't know how bad he is. I just got it from Humbert."

Barrington shook his head miserably. "Poor Carl. Poor, poor Carl. We'll never know what he went through." He thought for a moment. "That wicked family of his—driving him into this—"

Werner was suddenly outraged by the hypocrisy of it. He had been angry with Barrington ever since Humbert had told him about the letter. That was foolish and irresponsible, but it could just possibly be forgiven when one considered Barrington's impulsive nature and the desire to make some kind of personal contact with his friend. But to put the blame for its consequences on to somebody else was contemptible. Werner began to wonder if he had been totally deceived in Barrington all these years.

"Are you trying to say you don't know why he did it?" he said angrily.

Barrington frowned. "How should I know why he did it? I suppose he felt remorse or something. He realized what an awful thing he'd been talked into doing—"

"You didn't send him a letter?"

"A letter?" If his astonishment was feigned, it was done with amazing skill. "Of course I didn't. I wanted to, everybody knows that. But Humbert told me I mustn't. I gave him my word."

"Did you keep it?"

Barrington rose from his seat. In a tone of outrage he said, "I always keep my word."

Werner was shaken. It was really impossible to believe he was lying. "Humbert told me. He said there was no doubt at all. There was a letter. From you."

Barrington stood immobile for a moment. Then slowly, he turned and looked at Sylvia. She nodded her head. "Yes," she said, "I wrote to him." She added defensively, "Somebody had to. Somebody had to do something."

"But I gave my word," he repeated. It was as if he could still not fully comprehend what had happened to him.

"It was your word. Not mine."

He raised his voice angrily. "My word is binding on you."

"No." It seemed to Werner that she was more than a little afraid of Barrington. But she remained defiant. "I'd give my life for you, Edward, if I had to. But I'm not your property. I'll take my own responsibility for what I do."

Barrington looked at her as if she were a stranger whom he had just met for the first time. "What did you say to him?"

"What we both thought. That what he was doing was treacherous and disloyal. I asked him to remember what you'd done for him. I reminded him of what he was when he first came to Kalundani and how you'd been kind to him and given him refuge." She said, with an impatient shrug, "I said nothing that we hadn't said between us at one time or another."

He said nothing. His silence began to unnerve her. Her voice shook a little. "Naturally I'm terribly sorry that he's taken it into his head to do this, but I don't see that I can be blamed. We all know what sort of person he is."

Barrington turned to Werner. It was almost as if he had forgotten about her. "Where is Carl now?"

"At the City Hospital in Stockholm."

"I've got to see him."

"Would that be wise? We ought to ask Humbert—"

Barrington shook his head decisively. "We're beyond all that now. It's finished. It doesn't matter. All I know is that it's Carl and I have to see him."

"They might not let you."

"They'll let me." He spoke with a flash of his old arrogance. "Can you come? I'd like you to, if you can manage it." As Werner hesitated, Barrington said something Werner had never heard him say before. "I need you, Horace."

In a forced, unnatural voice, Sylvia said, "Do you want me to come too?"

Barrington regarded her for a moment. Werner could not interpret the expression on his face. There was no anger in it now, but there was no forgiveness there either. It was the expression of a man confronted with an entirely new situation that he could not for the moment bring himself to assess. When he spoke, it was in a calm, judicial voice. "Yes," he said. "I think you'd better."

*

Werner had arranged for a car and a driver to meet them at the airport. They drove straight to the hospital. Barrington went inside while Werner and Sylvia waited in the back of the limousine.

After half an hour Barrington came out again and got into the car. He told the driver to take them to the hotel. As he sank back into the seat of the car Werner saw that his face was ashen. With his right hand he grasped the strap on the door pillar to control the trembling of his body. "Did you see him?" asked Werner.

"Yes. There was a little difficulty, but they let me in."

"How was he?"

"It was terrible. Terrible." Barrington halted, as if the memory was almost too much for him. "He was speechless. He could only mumble to himself. His eyes wandered to and fro all the time, as if he were afraid, deeply afraid of something he couldn't describe. And his arms—" He put his hand in front of his eyes. "They were bound to a board on either side of him. It seems that if they leave them free he tears the bandages off and tries to open the wounds again."

"Did he recognize you?"

"I don't know. He saw me, but whether he knew me or whether I was just some part of his private terror—" He said helplessly, "I don't know. How can anybody know?"

He fell silent. They drove through the city to their hotel. Werner had booked a suite for Barrington and Sylvia and a room on the same floor for himself. When he had unpacked he went along to the Barrington's sitting room. Barrington was there on his own. He was sitting near the window, looking out into the street. It was late afternoon and the rush hour was just beginning. The streets were full of neat, smartly dressed people and traffic was building up around the square in front of the hotel.

Barrington hardly turned from the window as he came in. "Sylvia's gone out for a moment," he said. "Help yourself to a drink."

There was a bottle of whisky and some ice on the table. Werner prepared himself a drink. "Anything for you?"

"No thanks." Barrington spoke in a preoccupied voice, as if continuing the train of thought that had been dominating his mind. "You know, when I looked at Carl this afternoon he reminded me of something. It was when I was at the Metropolitan, a long time ago, and I was operating on a dog. It was only an animal, of course. One had to tell oneself that all the time. Yet it had loved me, in its way—it had trusted me to protect it." He swallowed, as if to remove a bitter taste from his mouth. "I remember the smell of it to this day. You know, the smell of an animal tells you a great deal. It speaks to you." He added bitterly, "It still makes me sick to think of it."

His voice had changed perceptibly from the one that Werner had grown used to over the years. Now it was rougher and deeper, and there was an unfamiliar broadness about the vowels.

It was, Werner suddenly realized, the voice of Barrington's youth, in the days before he had known success and fame and the reverence of the world.

Barrington went on, following his previous train of thought. "That was what told me what I had to do," he said. "I knew it then and I know it now. I've gone wrong. All this isn't for me." He made a gesture which took in the room with its elegant Scandinavian furniture, the smart bustling crowds in the street, the whole apparatus of European prosperity and civilization. "This —this *shit,*" he said violently. When Werner was about to speak, he went on, "I know what you're going to say. Some things have to be done. Suffering has to be accepted. I realize that. God knows, I've seen more than most in my time. I don't know the answer. I don't know the truth about the world. But at least I've learned what's right and wrong for myself." He stood up and said, "I'm going back to Africa, Horace."

"And the money?"

"I'll leave that to you. I'll do whatever you say. Send me the papers and I'll sign them. Just so long as I can keep my hospital. All the rest can go."

"It needn't be as bad as that—"

"Yes," he said decisively. "It has to go. I want it to go." He shook his head in disgust. "I know now that it was all wrong— this whole bloody ambitious thing. I suppose in my heart I've suspected it for some time. It was never really right. Not for me, anyway. Perhaps somebody else could have done it."

Werner protested. "Edward, I think you're taking this too hard. Just because things have got a little out of hand, that doesn't mean you have to give up completely. With a little extra financial control—"

Barrington did not seem to hear him. "I have to go back to where I started," he said. "Other people can attend to the big things you believe in. Education, agriculture, social progress. I'm going to stick to the work that only I can do."

"You're going to throw away five years hard work?"

"Five years isn't much in Africa." He gave Werner a thin smile. "I wasted your money, Horace—I'm sorry."

"Oh, the hell with that." Werner was genuinely distressed. It occurred to him that until this moment he had always had hopes

of salvaging the project, even when Barrington had been at his
most difficult. Now he knew from Barrington's tone that it was
hopeless. "Have you told Sylvia?"

"No. Not yet."

"Have you thought of the effect on her? I mean, the project
was her life. Are you going to ask her to go back and start over
again?"

Barrington did not reply immediately. There was a curiously
remote, self-absorbed expression on his face. It reminded Werner
of their last meeting at Kalundani when he had suspected that
Barrington was not only prepared for the break-down of negotiations, but was actually welcoming it as a break with a past that
was beginning to suffocate him. On such occasions he gave an
impression of total unapproachability, as if all outside impressions
were no more than shadows compared to the compulsions which
dominated him. At moments like this it was possible to feel the
power which enabled him to take any chance and to make any
sacrifice, either of himself or of others, to satisfy the demands of
his own will. Eventually he said slowly, "No, I'm not going to
ask her that." Before Werner could speak, he went on, "I want to
go back alone."

"Alone?" Werner looked at him in astonishment. "You mean
to leave her behind?"

Barrington nodded his head. "I'm afraid I must."

"But Edward, you can't do that." He was deeply shocked.
"For God's sake, she's your wife—she's in love with you—"

"I don't think so," said Barrington. He seemed to be trying to
persuade himself. "Not really. I think she was in love with
something she wanted to make of me. But it was a failure." He
frowned in the harassed way that was typical of him when
asked to explain his actions in logical terms. "It was never right."

A possibility occurred to Werner. "If it's to do with Carl—and
that letter—"

"No. It's not that." He walked restlessly up and down the
room as he tried to explain. In halting phrases he described how
his feelings of anxiety and doubt had grown throughout the
fund-raising campaign, finally coming to a climax in the dreadful events of the last few days. He seemed to see in it a parallel
to his early days at the Metropolitan and the last months of

disillusion at Manusha. Once again he felt the need to cut himself off, to make away with everything that reminded him of a discarded existence. He said, "I'm not blaming Sylvia for anything. It's just that something's ended. I hope she'll understand. But whether she does or not, there's nothing I can do about it."

There was finality in his voice. Werner realized now that nothing would shake him from his resolve. Barrington would follow his own way, pitiless in the pursuit of what he regarded as his destiny. Werner was not sure whether he admired such obsessive determination or was repelled by it. It occurred to him that Sylvia should be coming back any time now. He had had little sympathy for her in the past, but now it was difficult not to pity her. The least he could do for her was not to witness her humiliation. He said, "I think I ought to leave now."

"Yes, of course," Barrington walked with him to the door. He said, in an abstracted voice, "Is there anything more you want me to do about the money?"

"Not if you're absolutely decided—"

"Absolutely. I'm going back to Kalundani tomorrow. The rest is up to you." Noticing the faint trace of doubt remaining on Werner's face, he added, "Don't be afraid I shall change my mind. You have my word on it."

Werner closed the door behind him and made his way down the corridor. He was about to go back to his room and then remembered that he had to see the travel agency to confirm his flight back to London. As he stood at the travel desk in the lobby he saw Sylvia come through the swing doors from the street. She was carrying some parcels and looked cheerful and relaxed after her small shopping trip. She smiled at the porter who held the door open for her. Then she walked toward the lift which would take her up to the bedroom where her husband was waiting for her.

*

His flight took him back to London that evening. The next day he began to set up the mechanism for the Barrington Trust. Crane came home in a few days and began to round up some strong names for the executive committee. Werner was busy arranging with Humbert about the lawsuit, fixing registration with the Charity Commissioners, and explaining details of finance to a firm of accountants. It was hard work, but all a matter of well-charted routine. He felt the satisfaction of an efficient man at his capacity to bring order into confusion. Yet there was regret in it too, for the things that would inevitably be lost. Kalundani would never be quite the same when it had been turned into a routine, organized operation.

The papers and documents passed briskly to and fro between London and Kalundani. Barrington signed everything and contested nothing. Werner corresponded with him, regularly at first and then more intermittently as time went on, about the financial affairs of the Trust. But he never saw Barrington again.

PART FIVE

Sylvia

The house was not beautiful, but it had style. It had been built when the full and dignified proportions of the eighteenth-century country house had finally been overtaken by pretentiousness. The windows were mullioned and there were some unfortunate castellations around the edge of the roof. Yet the garden was magnificent and beautifully kept. The gravel drive was raked and weeded. It was the house of a competent, tidy, and well-organized person.

I drove up to the front of the house and rang the bell. Sylvia answered the door herself. It was strange to come face to face with her at last. She was in her middle fifties now, and the years had taken away the bold, flamboyant beauty that had startled both Adams and Werner when they had first encountered her. Her face was sallow and wrinkled from the years spent under a tropical sun. Yet the face was still full of life and dignity, and the figure was straight and trim. Her tweed suit was casual but elegant.

She took me into a drawing room with a view which seemed to extend over half of Wiltshire. A great Dane bitch came over and sniffed my trouser leg and then went back to sleep by the window. Sylvia said, "I'm grateful to you for coming to hear my side of the story."

"It seemed only reasonable."

"I won't ask you what those men have said because I know they all detested me. They wanted to own him, you see—each in his own way. They were afraid I was going to take him away from them."

She paused, as if trying to recreate the past in her mind. "Adams was the worst of them. A narrow, timid little man. He would never have had the courage to go to Africa at all if he hadn't met Edward. He was intelligent enough, and he knew in his heart what ought to be done, but he let Edward ride roughshod over him. He never forgave me for doing something that he hadn't the courage to do himself."

She paused. "It was a strange atmosphere there, difficult to describe unless you've actually lived in it. A real hothouse. They were all a little mad in their own way—Adams and Carl and that psalm-singing sister, not to mention all the other odd fish who used to come there. All of them working fourteen hours a day and reading their Bibles and sublimating all their wicked thoughts by worshiping Edward as a kind of saint. They'd got to the point where they hardly thought of him as a man at all. When they saw he had fallen in love with me, they were outraged. I'd stolen their hero from them."

I thought she was being unfair to Adams. But it was not my job to argue with her. I tried to move the conversation on to a less emotional subject. "What about Werner and Crane?" I asked. "I didn't get the impression that either of them regarded your husband as a hero."

"No," she admitted. "I suppose you're right there. Werner's trouble was that he wasn't his own master. He was all the time worrying about what they were going to say in New York. That made him fussy and irritable. He had the feeling that if he could only get Edward on his own, away from my influence, everything would be all right. He could satisfy his conscience and Mrs. Mallory at the same time. I sympathized with him really. I always felt I liked him more than he liked me. As for Crane—" She paused and then went on thoughtfully, "That was all rather strange. I used to feel that he was in some way obsessed by Edward—as if Edward had some secret about life that he desperately needed to understand. And yet, when you come down to it, they didn't really like each other at all."

"Crane was very good to him," I pointed out.

"Yes, enormously. All his life, he did everything he could to help Edward, according to his lights. Even to his own disadvantage. In the circles he moved in, it didn't do him a lot of good to be associated with Edward, especially in the later stages, when it got around that Edward was hostile to African independence. But I'll say this for Crane. He never ratted on Edward. He always stuck to his guns." She pondered for a moment. "The odd thing is that Crane came to agree with me after a while."

I was surprised. "About what?"

"About Kalundani. He admitted I was right. So do a lot of people now. Rural development's all the vogue. There are a number of projects linking improved agriculture and irrigation to a health center—the Scandinavians have a very successful one in Tanzania. What I failed to see was that Edward was quite unsuited for a project of that kind." She said regretfully, "I made a typical woman's mistake. I loved him for what he was and then tried to change him into something different."

I was diffident about mentioning it, but something had to be said, "How about Carl?" I asked her.

"I won't try to excuse that. I lost my head. Everybody seemed to be against us and I wrote that letter in a fit of desperation. But I paid for it. God knows I paid. Edward could be very ruthless, you know." There was melancholy in her voice. It was as near as I ever saw her to self-pity. It lasted only a second and was gone. "But he forgave me in the end."

*

Barrington's decision to go back to Africa alone was a shattering blow to her. At a stroke she had lost not only her husband but the cause to which she had devoted herself completely for the last five years. At first she was overcome by an almost suicidal depression. Then, as the months went by, the natural resilience of her nature began to reassert itself. She returned to her old occupation of free-lance journalism. Soon she had re-established her old contacts and was on the verge of regaining the position that she had abandoned when she had left England.

But gradually it was borne in on her that her heart was no longer in the work. Her life with Barrington had spoiled her for writing lively articles on murder trials or the sexual habits of young people. And she found herself ill at ease in London after the wild remoteness of Kalundani. When she received an unexpected legacy from a rich cousin she left London and the closed world of Fleet Street without regret. She settled down in the country and began to devote herself to charitable activities.

She used to get news of Barrington from friends of hers who visited Kalundani. She learned sadly that all the work she had done there was being allowed to fall into decay. There was no need for deliberate destruction—it had always been a struggle to keep the bush out of the plantations. Within a month the creepers had begun to strangle the banana plants and the weeds to block up the irrigation channels.

Now that there was no longer anyone to nag them, the Luako stopped bringing their children to school. The grass forced its way up through the tarmac road and the mud walls of the outbuildings began to crumble away. Kalundani was turning rapidly from a modern settlement into just another African village. The goats wandered up and down the paths and African families, relatives of patients under treatment, camped out on the verandas. The smell from a hundred cooking pots filled the still, humid air.

The Trust was functioning well. The Mallory Foundation had paid off Barrington's debts and had agreed to a running grant for an initial period of three years. A modest amount of money had been collected during Barrington's campaign, though it was found on investigation that much of it had been swallowed up by expenses of one kind or another. Detailed accounts and budgets were prepared and sent to Barrington for approval. He was told exactly how much he might spend in the year on capital projects, food drugs, and general overheads. He agreed to everything.

That was not to say that when it came to the point, he kept within the sums prescribed. He was always to some degree or another overspent, and the Trust gradually developed a system by which they kept money secretly in reserve to compensate for this. Barrington in time realized what they were doing and increased his expenditure accordingly; over the years a battle of wits developed between them. It was not a very efficient method of management, but it limped along somehow or other.

A number of the staff of the hospital left in disgust, outraged by Barrington's orders not to interfere with the traditional ways of the Luako, no matter how cruel or insanitary they might be. A few enthusiasts remained, and with them Barrington struck up the old atmosphere of casual intimacy that he had known with Adams and Sister Nairn. He went back to eating in the common dining room, sitting at the head of the table as he had in the old days.

In his loneliness, his tendency to eccentricity gradually increased. He developed a horror of taking life, which he extended even to the level of small insects. The only strict rule which he insisted upon in the hospital was his prohibition against the killing of animals—even the flying foxes were allowed to roost unmolested and pillage the grain and the bananas. Barrington would say, "Life is all we have. People talk of the quality of life. I'm not wise enough to assess that. But life itself is a wonderful and mysterious thing. I regard it with reverence. It's a terrible sin to destroy it."

He became a vegetarian, eating very little except fruits and nuts and bananas. His tall body was now thin almost to the point of emaciation. In conversation, his mind harked back constantly to the past and he talked often of Joan and Toffee and the old days at Manusha.

He had deliberately cut himself off, not only from the outer world but from all the events taking place in Africa itself. The struggle for political independence meant nothing to him. He would neither read about it nor discuss it. If any of his staff tried to draw his attention to the growing signs of a political upheaval within the country, he lapsed into a frozen, embittered silence.

It was in 1963 that the old king died. He had come to the throne as a boy, so long ago that few men, in a country where the expectation of life was always short, could remember a time when he had not ruled over them. To the Africans, who have great reverence for age, this fact alone had given him an almost mystical authority. But on his death it was as if the dam which had held back all the pent-up discontent of a generation had finally disintegrated. For all his personal qualities, the old man had never been more than a tribal chief. And the day of the tribal chiefs had come to an end.

There were new men now in search of power. Though not very many of them, they were young and educated and determined. And they were not men of the Luako. The Luako, like most of the great warrior tribes, were conservative and ill-adapted to the rapid changes taking place in the continent. They were astonished and bewildered to discover that they were hated within their own country and regarded as embarrassing reactionaries by the Europeans who had supported them for so long.

The civil war that followed took place mostly in the east, in the area of the capital. But as the battle went against the Luako, they retreated farther into their own hinterland in the mountains. Sylvia read the news in the papers with considerable anxiety. When she contacted the Barrington Trust headquarters she was told that all was quiet at Kalundani. It was far away from the front and there was hope that the war might be over before the fighting reached that part of the country. Then, one day, she was told that communication with the hospital had been lost. A week later she received an urgent summons to the Foreign Office.

2

Sir Frank Temple was a small man with a bald head and a high domed forehead creased by deep transverse wrinkles. He rose from his desk as she entered his office and greeted her fussily. "Mrs. Barrington—so good of you to come. I hope it wasn't too inconvenient for you." Without waiting for an answer, he said, "You know Lord Crane, of course."

It was nearly ten years since she had met Crane. He had aged considerably. At sixty he had still contrived to look like an athletic man of middle age. Now his hair was white, the skin of his face had lost its elasticity, and there was a rigidity about his gait that had not been present before. He smiled stiffly at her as she took the vacant seat in front of Temple's desk.

"You've probably guessed," said Temple, "that we want to speak to you about your husband."

"How is Edward?" she asked anxiously. "Is he safe?"

"At the moment, yes. So far as we know, that is," he added cautiously. "As you can imagine, communication out there isn't easy."

"When did you hear from him?"

"Indirectly, three days ago. He was in good health, they said, and the hospital was reasonably well off for food and supplies.

But the political situation's becoming increasingly difficult. The war has moved much nearer to Kalundani during the last few weeks. Naturally we're a little concerned about him." He scratched the bald patch on the top of his head. "There's a complicating factor in your husband's relationship with the Luako. Do you know a man called Bemba?"

"I met him once. He was an adviser to the king."

"Dr. Barrington was on fairly good terms with him, I believe."

"They'd known each other a long time. Bemba was the man who persuaded the king to give the land for the Kalundani hospital. He didn't appeal to me very much personally, but Edward was always very grateful to him."

Temple nodded. It seemed to her that he was asking questions to which he already knew the answers. "As we understand it, Bemba is now the commander of what's left of the royalist army. He's reported to be planning to make a stand in the hills around Kalundani. We're in touch with Guchiri, the President. He's anxious to finish Bemba off as quickly as possible. On the other hand he doesn't want any harm to come to your husband if he can possibly avoid it."

She regarded Temple with distaste. She had read enough in the newspapers to be aware of the source of his anxieties. "And you're anxious to keep on good terms with Guchiri, I gather?"

"Well, he won the elections, after all. Perhaps they weren't the most orderly elections in the world, but he won them. So he has some pretensions to be a democratic leader. We felt impelled to recognize him."

"Also, of course, you're very anxious to hang on to the copper concessions?"

Temple was not in the least disconcerted. He was obviously well accustomed to negotiating with people who impugned the motives of his employers. "Naturally, I wouldn't agree with such an interpretation of government policy. But in any case I don't think there's much value in discussing such matters. Our feeling is that it would be very much better for everyone if Dr. Barrington came home."

"You think it would be bad publicity if he got killed?" she said sardonically.

"Believe it or not," said Temple dryly, "we have his own

interests in mind. You must realize his position is one of considerable danger."

"That wouldn't worry him," she said with confidence.

"Perhaps not. But then he might worry about the future of the hospital. If we can get him out of there, it's much less likely to be destroyed."

He spoke intently, as if expecting some kind of positive reaction from her. She shrugged her shoulders. "You may be right. Whether you'll be able to persuade him is another matter altogether. He's a man who likes to make his own decisions."

"We understand that," said Temple. He scratched his bald patch again. "We were wondering if you would be prepared to help us."

"I doubt whether I could, even if I wanted to. I haven't seen Edward for ten years." She glanced at Crane, still standing glumly beside the window. "Lord Crane's on much closer terms with him nowadays than I am."

Crane spoke for the first time. He said in his thin, cultured voice, "I think this is one of those occasions when we all have to put personal feelings aside. As Sir Frank says, our communications with Edward are very poor. It's a question of messages through a rather inefficient bush radio. We've been trying to get him for some time to agree to talk to someone who can explain our views to him. We suggested either the ambassador or myself. Finally we got a message back from him. He said he wouldn't see anybody but you."

Try as he would, he could not keep the bitterness out of his voice. All those years of self-discipline and judicial impartiality were not proof against such a cruel blow to his pride. Barrington, she thought, did dreadful things to those who served him. She remembered the day at Stockholm airport when he had walked away from her across the tarmac. He had gone up the steps of the plane without even turning to wave good-bye, his mind already fixed on the work in front of him. She almost felt sorry for Crane.

Almost, but not quite. She looked from him to Temple and was suddenly struck by the comic aspects of the situation. Undoubtedly she was the last person in the world they wanted to ask a favor of at this moment. For months they had been playing their secret game of diplomacy and government, having confidential discussions in quiet offices, sending coded cables to the ambassador, putting pressures here and using persuasion there. And Barrington, with that genius he had for doing the unexpected, had in a few words punctured the whole absurd business. She felt a flood of affection for him, a tremor of excitement at the thought of meeting him again.

She smiled happily at the two grim-faced men. "Whatever you may think of Edward," she said. "You've got to admit there's nobody quite like him."

3

It had been decided that Crane should go with her. They took off the next morning on the regular flight to Nairobi and then waited for several hours at Nairobi airport until the Fokker Friendship that ran a daily service into the war zone was ready to take off. It was late evening before they landed.

She was taken aback at the sight of the airport. In the old king's time there had been two patched runways and several tin shacks for the reception of passengers. Now there was a large brick building of several floors in the conventional style of modern airport architecture. Inside, the reception hall was lavishly appointed and ablaze with light. But apart from a few policemen and two soldiers in battle dress carrying sub-machine guns, it was completely empty. The curio shops, the travel agencies, the banks, were all shuttered and bolted. The feet of the passengers echoed on the marble floor and they huddled instinctively in one corner of the lounge.

There was a long wait and then an interminable fuss over passports and visas. Their luggage was searched minutely by the Customs. Sullen-faced immigration officers examined each page of their passports and then questioned them suspiciously about currency and arms. As Sylvia and Crane waited for the formalities to be completed, Crane pointed to a tall, fair man who was pacing up and down with obvious impatience on the other side of the barrier.

"That's Hunter, the ambassador," said Crane. There was relief in his voice. He had been visibly upset by the lack of respect he had received from the immigration officer. Plainly he was unaccustomed to being treated in such a cavalier fashion. But the sight of a representative of the world of privilege obviously reassured him.

"You know him?"

"I met him last year when I came out to see Edward." He added gloomily, "Things were very different here then."

When they were finally allowed through the barrier, Hunter came up to them and introduced himself. "I'm sorry I couldn't do anything to speed things up," he said. "I tried, but it's impossible nowadays, I'm afraid. I imagine you've had a perfectly frightful journey."

"I suppose it's to be expected in the circumstances," said Crane. He was still a little ruffled.

"I hope you're not too exhausted, Mrs. Barrington."

"Not in the least," she said cheerfully. It was quite true. She had always been fairly indifferent to discomfort and had found the conditions of their arrival stimulating rather than alarming. She glanced ironically at Crane. "I'm used to taking the rough with the smooth."

"Yes, I suppose so." Hunter had not missed the barb in her voice. His eyes veered away from her. He was obviously not anxious to get involved in any sparring between the two of them. "Perhaps you'd like to come along to the car. The porters will take care of your luggage."

A large but somewhat aged limousine was waiting for them outside the airport building. Its Union Jack hung damp and despondent in the humid evening air. They all climbed into the back of the car, while the Embassy chauffeur superintended the stowage of the luggage. The car moved silently and sluggishly off toward the town.

"You're in for a long journey, I'm afraid," said Hunter to Sylvia. "We're nearly twenty miles from town here. Quite unnecessary, of course, since the capital's only about the size of

Budleigh Salterton, but it's the fashion nowadays. Like that enormous edifice you've just come through."

"It was rather handsome, I thought."

"I'm glad you're pleased with it," said Hunter acidly, "because
you paid for it. Several millions of British aid went into that.
And it's not exactly a hive of activity, as you see. Most of the
important traffic goes to Endu in the north, where the mines
are. Still, it's quite a sight when the President drives along here
to set off on one of his trips. Seventeen miles of double-carriage-
way lined with schoolchildren. Of course, they get a half-holi-
day—"

He seemed to remember something. He leaned forward and
made sure that the partition between them and the chauffeur
was tightly closed. Crane said, "Don't you trust him?"

"I like him," said Hunter. "He's obliging and efficient and he
drives very safely for an African. On the other hand I've seen
him in his off-duty driving about in a Mercedes 220. He couldn't
buy that out of what I pay him."

Crane made a grimace. "A little disturbing."

Hunter shrugged it off. "It's part of the job. By the way, I've
arranged an appointment with the President for tomorrow morning. I hope that's all right."

Crane nodded. "What can we expect?"

"Well—" Hunter paused. Then he delivered his professional
assessment. "Guchiri's an interesting man. He's the son of a
Sosima chief who had him educated by Jesuit missionaries and
then sent him to Oxford to study law. Afterward he came back
here and started up an opposition party to the regime. The old
king put him in prison a couple of times. It's a combination of
influences that has made him a little unpredictable. You'll find
him fluent and thoughtful, but not what the Americans would
call very outgoing. He has strong and, to my mind, very genuine
moral principles. Unfortunately, they're not our kind of moral
principles and so he sometimes seems hypocritical by Western
standards—just as we obviously seem hypocritical by his. He's a
very shrewd demagogue and party manager but an atrocious
administrator. He's one of those men who are fascinated by
large concepts—but he's easily bored by detail. The result is that
we have some of the most beautifully drawn plans in the whole

of Africa. We have advisers and consultants from every country in the world. But nothing really gets done. The trains are late and nobody answers letters and the policemen are drunk most of the time."

The cynicism of Hunter's assessment was visibly disturbing to Crane. "It is, after all, a young country," he reminded him primly.

"Of course," agreed Hunter. "Please don't think I'm attacking Guchiri. I'm just telling you the kind of situation you have to deal with. You'll probably be charmed by him at the first meeting —most people are. All I ask is that you wait a little while before you count up how much you've achieved."

"At least," said Crane, "he's had the humanity to hold up his offensive for the last fortnight."

"Yes, that's true. Mind you, he needed a bit of time to get things organized. The roads are terrible up there in the west. And then there's the question of his tanks. He's a bit put out about that, as a matter of fact."

"What tanks?"

"Didn't Temple tell you? We promised him some new Chieftains. I don't know why, really. By the time he gets them to the front, they won't be fit to use, but he attaches great importance to them. They've been delayed for some reason."

There was something in his tone that made Crane suspicious. "You mean delayed on purpose?" he said sharply.

"Well, it would be nice to get the Barrington business fixed up first, wouldn't it?"

Crane shook his head distastefully. "I don't like that kind of thing. How can we expect them to be honest with us if we don't set them an example?" Hunter said nothing. He was plainly not going to commit himself on the subject. After a short silence, Crane spoke again. "What about these atrocity stories the papers are full of? Are they true?"

"Some of them, I expect," said Hunter. "After all, the Luako have been kicking the others around for the last five hundred years, and there are a lot of old scores to be paid off. But I wouldn't go into that with Guchiri if I were you. He's very sensitive on the subject. He's liable to ask you what the British were doing when the old man clapped him in jail in 1958."

*

They spent the night at the Embassy and set off the next morning to see the President. Their appointment was for eleven o'clock at the Old Palace. The car climbed in its usual stately fashion up the winding hill to the plateau. At the top of the hill they were stopped by guards who examined their passports and made a telephone call before allowing them through. Most of the large houses on the plateau were now empty. The palace itself was surrounded by barbed wire. Instead of the two ornamental dragoons that stood before the gate in the old days, there was a platoon of militiamen armed with automatic pistols.

The officer scrutinized the chauffeur's pass and waved them through. They drove up the drive to the palace. The garden was overgrown, there were weeds in the path, and the white stucco was beginning to peel from the building. There were more guards at the door.

After a short delay a butler showed them into Guchiri's private apartments. The President was sitting at a huge boulle desk in one of the large drawing rooms of the palace. Standing on one side of him was a civilian, and on the other a man in the uniform of an army colonel. As they walked toward him Guchiri stood up and bowed formally. Then he came from behind the desk and shook hands with them. He was a handsome man of middle age with a round cheerful face and neat, quick movements. He was a typical man of the east, very different from the grave, slow-moving Luako. He said, after the introductions, "We'll go out and talk on the terrace."

It was the first time Sylvia had ever seen the famous view from the terrace. She stood for a moment in awe. Through the cypress and jacaranda trees that dotted the lawn, a huge plain was spread in front of her. "I must apologize for this place," said Guchiri, waving his hand at the Palladian façade of the palace. "It's ridiculous, I know, but unfortunately we haven't the money just yet to build a suitable modern house for the President. Also, of course," he added thoughtfully, "it's secure. There are still a few people about who can't accept that the old days are gone for ever. Tea or coffee, Mrs. Barrington?"

"Coffee, please."

The servants passed out cups of coffee and sweet biscuits and then retired. Guchiri said, "The Colonel will take you to Kalundani tomorrow. Do you think your husband will be reasonable?"

"I couldn't tell you. It's so long since I've seen him—"

"Yes, of course. Well, as I say, I hope he'll be sensible. We don't wish him to come to any harm. We're humane people in spite of what the British press says about us." He paused. "I'd like to make it clear to you that I wish no harm to your husband. I think he means well, in spite of the mischievous nature of his work."

She was momentarily taken aback. She could imagine Barrington's work being described in almost any terms except these. "Mischievous?"

"Yes. Yes, indeed." He brooded for a moment. "Your husband is a racialist, Mrs. Barrington. We can't permit that here."

She was outraged. "How can you say such a thing? He's given his life for your people."

He was unmoved by her indignation. "You can give your life for children or animals, without ever thinking of them as your equal. He loved the Luako, everybody tells me." Guchiri went on with some bitterness. "He loved them because they are cruel savages, which is the way he thinks black men ought to be."

"No, I assure you," she said. "After all, I was there. I lived with him. It wasn't like that."

He went on as if she had not spoken. "Even his idea of medicine was wrong," he said. "It was paternal. Patronizing. Missionary stuff. We are building a modern state here." He got up and pointed to a gleaming white edifice down on the valley floor. "Have you seen our new five-hundred-bed hospital?"

"No."

"I'll have you shown around it. It's not fully staffed yet, but soon it will be. It is as well equipped as anything you have in Europe."

She could no longer contain her indignation. She snapped back at him. "And what have you got out there in the bush?"

He returned her anger with an engaging smile. "As you know —nothing. Oh yes," he went on philosophically, "I can see how it looks to you. I lived in England for many years. You have been rich for so long that you have forgotten what real poverty is like. If there is enough butter for only half a pound per person per month, you ration it. That's right. But if you only had a tenth of that? Then your rationing would feed nobody. A few people get nourishment. All that there is for the rest is a promise that there will be butter for them tomorrow."

"And supposing there isn't any?"

"They will be disappointed perhaps. But not disillusioned. An African values a promise even when it is not fulfilled; somehow the hope it arouses gives him confidence and dignity. When I promise my people health services and education and better agriculture these are expressions of what I think they're entitled to as human beings. I'm not expected to deliver them tomorrow."

The subject suddenly seemed to bore him. He paused and then turned unexpectedly to the ambassador. He said acidly, "On the other hand, when I promise them tanks it is a somewhat different matter. What news have you for me this morning, Mr. Hunter?"

4

"There may be some risk," said the colonel. "We have taken every precaution, but nobody can guard against accidents."

He spoke in a sharp, admonishing tone, like a schoolmaster rebuking a willful child. He looked very young and slightly on edge. Sylvia felt a kind of maternal amusement—it must be an exciting, but at the same time alarming experience to be a colonel before the age of twenty-five.

"Don't worry," she said soothingly. "I understand."

"I can answer for our own men. They have orders not to shoot and they will obey. But the rebels have no discipline. They're nothing but a rabble."

He spoke with passionate contempt. It was strange, she thought, how quickly a myth could be destroyed. Fifteen years ago, when she first came to the country, this boy would have stepped fearfully into a doorway, his knuckles to his mouth, when a Luako soldier walked down the street. Since time out of mind, the Luako had been a race of military aristocrats and the other tribes had accepted their role without question. The Luako had stamped their feet and the earth trembled—the Luako had demanded the right to rule, and the Sosima and the Mongo and the Lilonde had bent their necks. Now there were American guns behind the rocks and British armored cars on the dusty roads; on the airfield farther back there was a squadron of Russian MIGs ready to take off when the order came. Guchiri had won the elections. And the massed forces of liberal democracy, greedy for copper, were anxious to help him toward his inheritance.

Now Bemba, who had been a prince for so long, cowered in the bush and waited for slaughter. She looked down from the hill on which they stood, wondering if she might see any sign of him or his men. But there was nothing but the haze over the valley and the faint trace of the river winding along its floor. Their position commanded the valley from the eastern side; with its rocky bluffs and deep crevasses it formed a natural stronghold. The Republican army had been halted there for the last fortnight, bringing up food and munitions. Tomorrow they were due to resume their advance across the valley.

The colonel repeated the arrangements for the fourth (or was it the fifth or sixth?) time.

"It is agreed that you are to be returned to our hands within six hours. After that time, if no signal is received, all agreements are to be null and void." He repeated it severely. "Null and void. You understand that?"

"Yes."

"After that we can take no responsibility for your safety. It is no use the British Government or the British press blaming us if you are kidnaped by these people."

"I signed the paper," she said wearily.

Crane, who was standing with them, intervened. "I really don't think you should worry about this, Colonel. Mrs. Barrington has made a statement saying that she is doing this entirely of her own free will and has been warned of all the possible dangers. I've witnessed it myself and so has our ambassador."

The colonel shrugged his shoulders. "So long as that is completely understood."

He walked away to talk to some fellow officers. Crane said, "You're feeling all right?"

She smiled. "You mean am I frightened? No, not really. I suppose it would be more feminine of me if I were. But I can't really believe anything will happen to me."

She had never liked Crane very much, and she knew that he had never liked her, but the sensation of sharing a vital experience bound them together in a kind of intimacy. She noticed with compassion the dark shadows under his eyes and the ugly red swelling of an insect bite on his left forearm; he was really getting too old for this kind of thing.

"I wish it were possible for me to come with you," he said fretfully.

"I'll do the best I can," she assured him.

"Oh, I didn't mean that." He did not explain what he did mean. Was it anxiety for her safety, desire to be a part of important events, or the feeling that only he could explain the issues adequately to Barrington? It was certain that he found the role of spectator deeply distasteful. She tried to visualize herself in his position and found herself consoling him. "It won't be long, you know," she said. "By this evening, Edward may be back with us."

"You think so?" There was doubt in Crane's voice. It was as if he finally lost confidence in his capacity to predict anything Edward might do. "We must all hope he'll be sensible."

The colonel detached himself from his friends and began to make his way toward them. "I think this is your signal to go," said Crane. Just before the colonel reached them, he pressed her hand and said, in his formal, slightly pedantic way, "We shall all be thinking of you. You're a very brave woman."

*

It was some kind of American Army vehicle, with red crosses on its sides and a flag of truce on the two masts arising from its mudguards. At the wheel was a Sosima driver; Sylvia shared the back seat with a taciturn Swede, who was attached to Guchiri's army as a United Nations observer. They descended the winding mountain path from the Republican headquarters. It was a slow and awkward journey until they reached the valley floor and picked up the dirt road to Kalundani. Then the driver put his foot down. He drove tensely, his head bent over the wheel. He was obviously intent on reaching the truce line as quickly as possible.

It was a road she knew as well as the lane that led to her own house in Wiltshire, and at first it seemed little changed from the last time she had passed along it ten years ago. But gradually she noticed an emptiness in the villages as they passed by, and a brooding stillness that had never been there before. There were no children playing around the straw huts, and no emaciated cattle grazing listlessly on the coarse grass by the roadside. The little village shops were closed and shuttered, and the plantations were empty of people. The valley was silent, holding its breath, waiting fearfully for the shadow of war to pass across it.

It was strange to think that the small vehicle in which they traveled was the only moving thing on the valley floor. From the hills to the east and the west, men were watching through field glasses as a tiny cloud of dust traced its way across the plain. The vehicle clattered across the bridge spanning the river. She realized with relief that they were not far away from the truce line now, and then was startled by the sudden clatter of machine-gun fire. The driver bent over the wheel and stepped on the accelerator. She saw splashes in the water behind them as the bullets hit the river. Then they were up the hill on the opposite bank and there was a long straight stretch of road. At the end of it they could just see the checkpoint.

The rebel soldiers wore uniforms similar to those of the Republicans, only distinguished from their enemies by the royalist flash on the breast pockets of their blouses. But they had the hard, lean look of men in adversity, and the aquiline, sullen features of the Luako. When she addressed them in their own tongue they replied curtly and without friendliness. There was delay while the Swede tried to establish his right to go to Kalundani with her, a request which was ultimately refused. Then she was shown to a rebel troop carrier, which bore a suspicious resemblance to one of the hospital Land-Rovers, and driven off with a military escort.

It was only a few miles from the checkpoint to Kalundani. Now the soldiers were everywhere. These were not the grinning, round-faced boys she had seen drilling sloppily behind the Republican lines, but rough, tattered, desperate men, digging trenches and gun emplacements, and guarding road junctions with their arms at the ready. To anyone accustomed to the sight of soldiers, a platoon of these men looked worth a regiment of Guchiri's, and for a moment she wondered whether perhaps the war might not be such a foregone conclusion after all. Then she heard the sound of jet engines overhead. A squadron of MIGs carved a pattern of vapor trails in the aquamarine sky, like performers at an air display. The soldiers looked sullenly up at them; one of them made the childish gesture of cocking his rifle and pointing it in the air as if to shoot at them. His noncommissioned officer yelled angrily at him and struck him, casually and brutally, Luako fashion, with the butt of his own rifle. There was a sickening sound as it connected with the side of the rifleman's skull. Sylvia turned her head away.

She had prepared herself for great changes at the hospital, yet the reality was worse than she had been able to bring herself to imagine. All the plantations were lost. Mostly they had gone back to bush; only here and there could she see small patches of cultivation where African families had built themselves huts and planted patches of ground with bananas or cassava. The high grass which grew like weeds in the wet season had encroached on the road to the settlement, so that the Land-Rover had to batter its way through a path that constantly strove to obliterate itself. The covering of tarmac had long since been torn away by the rains.

The mud and wattle outbuildings had mostly decayed from lack of attention, and even the more solid construction of the hospital was showing signs of dissolution. The wards, as always, overflowed on to the veranda, and relatives of patients squatted listlessly among their own refuse. Some had set up cooking pots in the path and had to be evicted by blasts of the horn of the Land-Rover. As they passed by, the Africans regarded her curiously but without obvious emotion. None of them seemed to recognize her. She felt oppressed by the indifference of it all, the total erasure of the years of effort and devotion she had lavished on it. Then, as they passed by the outpatient department, she saw the white coat of one of the medical orderlies. He did not recognize her at first, but when she waved to him his face broke open in a smile. He waved back and she felt a little better.

Barrington was waiting for her on the terrace of the house. He was very thin and his long-sleeved bush shirt hung loosely from his shoulders. His face was deeply lined and wrinkled and his graying hair was cut very short, giving him an austere, monkish look. There was an uncharacteristic shyness in his manner as he greeted her, as if he was not entirely sure of his reception. Evidently, even to a man as self-centered as he was, there was some embarrassment in greeting the wife he had cast irrevocably out of his life ten years before.

Face to face with him at last, all the resentment she had felt at his callous rejection of her fell away. She knew that the reproaches she had rehearsed in her mind during those long sleepless nights would never be delivered. The joy of being with him again was enough to obliterate all the bitterness she had felt. As they walked into the house, she said, "What on earth have you done to your hair?"

He put his hand up vaguely to the top of his head. "Does it look odd?"

"A little medieval perhaps."

"One of the new orderlies does it. I suppose he isn't very good." A touch of tenderness appeared in his voice. "Do you remember . . ."

She nodded. It had been one of the regular events that had punctuated their life at Kalundani. Every three weeks by the calendar they had gone into the kitchen after dinner and spread newspapers on the floor. He had placed himself in a chair and she had wrapped a sheet around him and had cut his hair. She had done it carefully and with skill, because she took his appearance very seriously. Begun almost as a joke, it had become over the years a ceremony they both looked forward to, an affectionate ritual. It was one of the small, unimportant things that had emphasized her loneliness when he had left her. But she sheered away from the emotion in his voice. "If you didn't need me as a wife," she said sardonically, "you certainly needed me as a barber."

He laughed and the tension was relieved. As they walked into the house, he said, "We have four hours. Let's have lunch before we talk about anything serious."

The house was much the same. Even when she had lived there it had never shown much of a woman's touch—neither she nor Barrington were very sensitive to the comforts of their environment. When she went into the bedroom to tidy her hair, she found the same old sagging double bed that they had slept in together, the dressing table with the mirror that would never stay in the right position. She felt a little nostalgia, a touch of regret, but that was all. To her active mind, always locked in the present, it was not easy to re-create the atmosphere of the past. It was all a little misty and unreal.

Even the lunch was the old Kalundani lunch. Perch from the river, indifferently cooked, with a thick white sauce; fried bananas and a limp vegetable that looked like seakale. It was served by Barrington's servant, now grown white-haired and even more forgetful than usual. Barrington ate only the vegetables. She asked him if it worried him to see her eat the fish. He shook his head. "It's a personal thing. I don't wish to impose my habits on anyone else. I know there's no way of avoiding the taking of life. Nevertheless—" He shrugged his shoulders. "I can't bear to eat it. It's as simple as that."

She took a mouthful of the tasteless fish. "Frankly you're not missing much," she said. "I could be a vegetarian myself on Mumba's cooking. No wonder you're so thin."

"I'm sorry," he said. "I'm afraid I've been letting things go a little. We have some cheese here if you like."

She pushed her plate away and finished the meal with bread and butter and processed cheese. Barrington ate very little. When she had finished he lit a cigarette. "Did Crane come with you?" he said.

"Yes. He's waiting for me back there with the army." She waved her hand toward the hills in the east. "He was really very kind to me."

"He always is," said Barrington. It was hard to know whether there was irony in his voice or not. "He's a good fellow. I've been indebted to him all my life."

"Yet you didn't want to see him?"

"No." He shook his head. "Not at this moment."

"He was very deeply hurt, you know."

"Was he? I'm sorry." He did not sound too concerned. It was as if nothing that existed outside Kalundani at the present moment held any great reality for him. "I wanted to talk to you alone." He smiled. "Surely one has a right to be a little self-indulgent at a time like this."

She saw an opportunity to raise the question of his returning with her. "He's hoping—we're all hoping—that you'll agree to come back with me."

He lifted his eyebrows. "You too?" She nodded. "You want me to leave the hospital?"

"Yes, I do," she said soberly. "I wasn't certain when I left this morning, but when I arrived here and saw it—I don't want to cause you distress, Edward, but it's finished. You must see that yourself." He said nothing. "It's been a great thing, but this is the end of it."

"Because the weeds are growing in your plantations?"

"No. I was prepared for that. But there's a dead feeling to it. You can tell from the look of the people. The soldiers even. They're just waiting. They know it's hopeless. You'd be sacrificing yourself for nothing." She was making no impression, she could see. She tried another tack. "Guchiri says that if you'll come out, he'll do his best to preserve the hospital."

"Do you believe him?"

"I don't know. Perhaps. It's the only chance, after all. Afterward, you could come back—"

"No. I couldn't do that." He was very positive. He got up from the table and moved restlessly around the room. "I can see that this is all very embarrassing for everybody. But perhaps that's my function—to be an embarrassment. And there are certain loyalties. Surely you understand that."

"Would Bemba care very much if you left?"

"Bemba?" He sounded surprised. "Oh no, I think he'd be quite pleased to see me go. I've served my purpose as far as he's concerned. You'd never have got here if he wanted to keep me."

"Who is it, then? Those people out there? They've only got another twenty-four hours anyway."

It was brutal, she knew, but it was the only way to bring him to his senses. He paused and then inclined his head. "Yes, you're quite right," he admitted sadly. "There's nothing more I can do for them."

"Well then, it's just pride, isn't it?" she said. "That's all. You just can't bear the thought of being beaten."

"Perhaps it is. But then, I'm not a true Christian. I've never understood why pride was something to be ashamed of."

He smiled. His brief moment of despair had passed. He was equal to her, as he had always been. She could tell by his manner and his tone of voice that he would not leave, that indeed he had never at any time intended to leave. Arguments meant little to him, because he had never in any of the important decisions of his life been governed by argument. He had a strong and subtle mind, but he had no trust in what it told him. Only in his emotions did he have any confidence.

Though she knew it was hopeless, she still could not prevent herself from taunting him. "Do you think it's going to make any difference to anybody at all if you stay here?" she said angrily.

"No," he said. "Only to me."

"Yet you're absolutely determined to stay?"

"Yes."

"Then why did you ask me to come here?"

"I wanted to see you," he said simply. It was typical, she realized, of both his arrogance and his humility. He did not want to get some final message to the world or to plead the cause of the Luako. He did not even consider what he was doing to be of any great significance except to himself. Yet when it came to the people he knew, his assurance was complete; he was utterly confident of his hold over her. He had never doubted that she would be happy to come halfway across the world for a short conversation with him.

The sound of the jets returned, growing and fading as they circled in the still air. They both watched them in silence from the window. They seemed so graceful and innocuous as they carved their vapor patterns in the sky. Tomorrow, within a matter of minutes, they would destroy the work of Barrington's life. She said, "It all seems such a terrible waste."

"I don't think of it like that," he said. "When we came here it wasn't to bring them bricks and mortar and corrugated iron roofs—not even medical knowledge. All those were important, of course. But the main thing was that we had compassion. We were kind to them. That's what matters."

"We didn't teach them that. Primitive people can be kind—kinder than we are."

"To their own people. Never to strangers." He said reflectively, "I was a stranger to them when I came here. I still am in many ways. I don't understand them completely and they don't understand me. Yet I helped them—and in their way they helped me. That's something, I suppose."

"And now, they want to get rid of you."

"They want rid of us all," he said, without resentment. "They have their own preoccupations now. They want to write their own tragedies in future. It's their privilege."

He turned away from the window. On the wall opposite to it there was a row of Luako ritual masks which he had collected over the years he had spent at Kalundani. They were his only valuable possession and they had always had a special, almost mystical significance for him. It was as if through them he had tried to make contact with the primitive, pagan world which had bewitched and baffled him throughout his life. He said, "There's one thing you could do for me."

"What?"

"The masks. I'd hate them to be destroyed. They go back over five hundred years. They're a part of the history of the Luako. All there is, almost. I'll bury them at the end of the kitchen garden when you've gone. Will you see they're looked after?"

"Of course."

His eye wandered down to the bureau, on which there was a faded photograph of himself with Joan and Toffee at Manusha. He was standing in the middle, a large, reassuring figure with one arm around each of them. Toffee was aglow with happiness. Joan was smiling, but tentatively, as if even in that moment she could not relax her vigilance against the perils around her.

Edward picked it up and held it for a moment. "Alan took

this, the first time he visited us." He sighed. "Poor Joan. How
hard she tried. I never knew until afterward."

There was a tender note in his voice that Sylvia had never
heard before. She said, without resentment, "You always loved
her best."

He did not deny it. "She was part of my youth," he said. He
added, "There was something very sweet and touching about
her. She needed so much protection." He looked at Sylvia, as if
remembering that perhaps he might have failed a little in protection toward her. "And you? Do you manage all right?"

She smiled. "Of course."

"Things like money and so on? I heard from Alan that you
came into some."

"Yes, I'm really quite well off." She was unable to resist teasing
him a little. "You mustn't spend too much time worrying about
me."

He smiled back, only a little embarrassed. "Well, you could
always look after yourself."

He moved nearer to her and put his arm affectionately round
her shoulders. She turned quickly away and looked out of the
window at the valley. "You made me cry once, Edward. But I'm
too old now. That's all finished for me." She saw a cloud of dust
moving up the road to the checkpoint. It was the Land-Rover
coming to take her back. She could not bring herself to turn
around and look at him. "All finished," she repeated.

*

She got back without incident to the Republican lines. The
next day the bombardment started. The fighter bombers began to
pick off the key position to the defense. Then the infantry went in.
There was some gunfire from the south side of the rock and
when the Republicans attempted to silence the battery a shell
went astray and hit a wing of the hospital. After that the firing
grew fiercer and the smoke obliterated the details of what was
happening in the valley.

Sylvia and Crane watched from the top of the cliffs like
spectators at an army exercise. It was difficult to realize that
only a few miles away men were being slaughtered, and that on
this fine, sunny day they were witnessing the final destruction

of a great race. The colonel brought them bulletins of progress every half hour. Each time he presented himself his smile was broader, his carriage a little more sharply military. Finally he announced that resistance had been broken. The Luako had held out until the position was almost encircled, and then fled into the mountains. Bemba himself had been found dead beside one of his few shattered pieces of artillery. About Barrington there was no definite news. According to one report, he had been killed when a shell had landed on his house.

*

The order came to move. The Republican staff were ready to go forward to inspect the conquered position. Crane and Sylvia and the UN officer were packed into the colonel's car. Once more they followed the familiar road across the valley. Every now and then they came across areas that the fighting had touched; they passed burned-out villages and collections of wounded huddled by the roadside waiting for transport. As they neared the hospital they saw two or three wrecked vehicles and the remains of a reconnaissance aircraft that had come down in the bush. On the Kalundani airstrip a large transport helicopter was unloading troops and medical supplies.

It was only when they breasted a small knoll on the road to the hospital that they saw the full extent of the damage. All the main buildings were completely wrecked. The wards, the out-patient buildings, the flour mill, had all been shattered by shell-fire and burned to the ground. Republican soldiers were picking about among the ruins, looking unsuccessfully for objects of value.

Barrington's house was a mass of smoking rubble. Standing guard over it was an agitated Republican lieutenant. He rushed up to the car as it drew up and engaged the colonel in excited conversation. The language he used was Sosima, which Sylvia did not understand, but it was clear that something had gone wrong. When he had finished, the colonel turned to her and said, "I regret to tell you this. Your husband is dead."

Through the pain of the knowledge she felt a sense of relief. At least he had been spared the humiliation of capture. He had gone out in his own way, with finality and dignity. He had controlled the situation to the end. She asked, "Where is the body?"

The cheerful, triumphant look had left the colonel's face. He said grimly, "It is not here. They have taken it into the mountains."

"Who have?"

"The Luako. Who else?" From the agitation of his manner it was plain that the news had upset him badly. It occurred to Sylvia that his own personal future probably hinged on the tidy disposal of Barrington in one way or another. A missing body was the last thing he wanted to report to the capital. "It was not soldiers. It was some villagers. They were making for Kumbo." He pointed to a tiny village high up on the eastern face of the massif. "If we hurry we can just catch them before dark."

He commandeered two army jeeps and a platoon of soldiers and they set off up the mountain track. It was a slow and hazardous journey. Once they were stopped by a puncture and once by a broken spring. The sun began to move rapidly down towards the crest of the mountain. Finally it disappeared, leaving them floundering on the cliffside, crawling slowly forward by the light of the headlights.

They moved on, largely because it seemed more dangerous to turn around than to press forward toward the village. They were still several miles away when they saw a great flame shoot up into the sky and the smell of burning wood was carried toward them by the wind. The colonel pushed the driver out of his seat and took the wheel himself. He covered the last few miles to the village with his foot on the floor, cursing and shouting in Sosima as he drove.

Even so, they were too late. By the time they arrived it was almost over. The remains of the funeral pyre were smoking in the center of the village and the Luako sat around it in a circle, moaning and chanting, their heads gray with the ashes they had heaped on them. When the Republican soldiers arrived, they did not even look up. The colonel touched one of them with his boot, to attract his attention. The man looked at him glassily for a moment, and then went back to his chanting. They were all of them, men and women, extremely drunk.

*

"And that's all," said Sylvia. "That was the end of the whole thing, whatever they try to pretend with their Trusts and Foundations. We went back to the capital and Guchiri was very charming and sympathetic, but it was obvious he couldn't wait to see the back of us. His idea was to wipe Kalundani out of everyone's memory as quickly as possible. As for Edward—" She smiled. "Well, he got one of the things he wanted, at least."

"What was that?"

"He often used to worry about the Luako and what they really thought of him. They're a very enigmatic people, you know. I suppose nobody can know exactly. But he's certainly the only foreigner they ever gave the funeral of a chief."

PART SIX

Laidlaw

There was a thin drizzle hanging in the air of Lincoln's Inn Fields. It was one of those March days when spring seems to have been indefinitely delayed. Outside, the trees were dripping and the tennis courts were dotted with puddles. Laidlaw's new Bentley swung round the corner from the College of Surgeons and stopped in front of our chambers. The chauffeur opened the car door for him and he hurried, with that distinctive bustling step of his, into the building.

A few minutes later my secretary showed him into the office. He seemed preoccupied, as if he had not yet been able to shake his mind free of some previous meeting. He said formally, "I'd like to thank you for your excellent report on Barrington. Most clear and helpful. I'm extremely grateful."

It was polite, but a little perfunctory. He might have been congratulating his accountant on a memo about taxation problems. I was disappointed. I suppose I had hoped that some of my own feelings about Barrington might have come through to him from the report. I said, "Have you decided what to do?"

He shook his head. "It's not easy, is it?" He looked me intently in the eye. "You know, I have a feeling that you yourself have considerable doubts about him."

"Doubts?" I was taken aback. This was not the impression I had thought to have given.

"Yes. Not in so many words, perhaps, but it runs between the lines. He wasn't quite the figure he was painted."

"Well, perhaps not, but—"

"I mean, if you take Markham's accusations—most of them had some substance, hadn't they?"

It is never pleasant to realize you have failed in a task you have set your heart on. I realized now that most of my report had been completely wasted. Either I had lacked skill in writing or Laidlaw had not had the time or the patience to understand what I was trying to tell him. Only the bare facts had came through—the bare facts that told nothing worth knowing.

I tried again. Perhaps I might succeed with speech where I had failed on paper. I tried to make Laidlaw see Barrington as I had seen him, as a man whose faults were very largely a function of his greatness. If nowadays the world saw the faults and forgot the rest, it was because the world itself had changed. What was heroism to one generation could seem absurd, possibly even wicked, to another.

I pointed out that Barrington had the particular vulnerability shared by men who actually do things in this world. I called attention not only to the work Barrington had done for the Africans, but to the way in which he enriched and inspired the lives of those who worked with him. I reminded Laidlaw that even those who might be expected to have the deepest grievances against him had all forgiven him in the end.

For a successful man, Laidlaw was a surprisingly good listener. He heard me out, then he said, "You're really involved in this, aren't you?"

It was not phrased as a criticism. He was simply interested. But his remark pulled me up short. It reminded me of my function and what I had been retained for. It was not my job to be a personal advocate for Barrington. I had been in danger of committing an unforgivable offense—of going beyond my brief. I said, "You're quite right. Perhaps I've said too much. It's entirely a matter for you, of course."

"Of course," agreed Laidlaw. He gave me a thin smile to show that he meant no offense. "And since you've taken so much trouble, I feel I must be honest with you. The fact is that we shan't be going ahead with the Barrington Trust. That's already been decided."

I suppose I had known it, really, since the beginning of our conversation. I nodded acceptance. "Just as you say."

"If it's any consolation to you, it was nothing to do with your report." I imagine I must have looked surprised. He went on to explain. "The Barrington Trust wasn't the only possibility we were considering. There were two other alternatives. One of them turned out so favorable for us that we decided to go ahead with it a month or two ago."

For a moment I was very angry with him. I felt he had made a fool of me. All the time I had been collecting information and laboriously preparing my report he had already made up his mind to reject it. He had probably never even looked at it. I could imagine him detailing one of his young men to make a synopsis of it so that he would not have to waste any of his precious time in unnecessary reading. But then I pulled myself together. After all, I reminded myself, much of a lawyer's life consists in giving advice which people are not prepared to take, and probably never really intended to take in the first place. So long as they are prepared to pay for it, one has no real grounds for complaint.

Apart from a minor blow to my vanity, what Laidlaw had done was not important to me. Nor, as I saw now, was it of any real importance to Barrington. As Sylvia had said, his story was finished now. The Trust was an irrelevance. His reputation in the future would be better resting on himself and his work than on a building in Portland Place and a yearly transfusion of money from Laidlaw's copper concessions.

Laidlaw began to tell me about the other project which had been chosen, and of his general ideas for doing good to Africa. He was very serious about it. He talked of rural development and infrastructure, and altogether it sounded a little like the draft of a speech he was planning to make some time or another.

I could see that I had almost disappeared from his consciousness. In a few minutes he would look at his watch and hurriedly take his leave. Then he would get into his car and be driven to some other meeting, an assistant would put a brief in front of him and he would have to say yes or no, or call for further information, in regard to another of the half-dozen decisions which made up the punctuation of his day. When he left my office the Barrington affair would be laid aside and forgotten, the money spent on it written off against tax in his balance sheet. I had a feeling that in a year's time, if somebody mentioned Barrington, Laidlaw would need a file handed to him before he could remember what it was about.

But then, in his way, he was not too dissimilar to Barrington himself, who had also lived in a busy egocentric world of his own devising. Barrington would have made use of Laidlaw if he could, just as Laidlaw would have made use of him—and would just as instantly have forgotten him if he had found it impossible.

As I had expected, Laidlaw stopped in the middle of his discourse and said that he was in a hurry, and he would have to go now. He would be getting in touch with me again about it later, when the matter had been officially passed by the Board. He made it clear that the Board discussion was a formality. There was no question of any change of mind.

On the way to the door he halted. "It's a pity," he said. "A great pity. I'm afraid the Trust will have to be wound up. They're badly in debt, you know."

I said I hoped they wouldn't actually go bankrupt.

"No. I think they're safe from that. They have some valuable stuff in that library. They were talking of putting it up for auction a year ago. When they thought there was a possibility that I might come in, they held it over. I imagine they'll go ahead now." He paused for a moment. "Have you had a look at the collection?" he asked.

"Just a cursory glance."

"Some of the letters and manuscripts should fetch a good price." He looked at me as if deciding that I was worth a piece of good advice. "But I wouldn't touch those masks. I had my art dealer look at them and he says they're fakes. They're not old at all."

There seemed no suitable comment for me to make. I waited for him to take his leave, but he stayed in the doorway, still pondering over a matter which obviously worried him.

"How can you ever understand those people?" he said. "He worked his fingers to the bone for the Luako for over thirty years and all he got from them in return was a handful of wooden carvings. And they even cheated him over that."

At least there was one point on which I could reassure Laidlaw. "He wouldn't have minded," I said.